Spies come in all sizes . . .

Grady looked around the cavern. "I wonder why they want a furnace from us?"

Susan said comfortingly, "At least they don't look like spies . . . Come on." She edged along the wall, headed for another hiding place.

Grady joined her as quickly as he could. "What are you doing? Let's get out of here."

"We can't. Not till we know for sure—"

He clutched at the rock in front of him, only partly for balance. The far wall had a tunnel through it, with a sign over it: GNOMENGESELLSCHAFT.

It was definitely and undeniably German.

Grady said nothing, then: "Oh, Jesus."

Ace Books by Nick O'Donohoe

THE MAGIC AND THE HEALING
UNDER THE HEALING SIGN
THE HEALING OF CROSSROADS
THE GNOMEWRENCH IN THE DWARFWORKS

THE GNOMEWRENCH IN THE DWARFWORKS

Nick O'Donohoe

ACE BOOKS, NEW YORK

THE GNOMEWRENCH IN THE DWARFWORKS

An Ace Book / published by arrangement with
the author

PRINTING HISTORY
Ace mass-market edition / July 1999

The Penguin Putnam Inc. World Wide Web site address is
http://www.penguinputnam.com

Check out the ACE Science Fiction & Fantasy newsletter
and much more on the internet at Club PPI!

ISBN: 0-441-00633-7

ACE®
Ace Books are published by The Berkley Publishing Group,
a division of Penguin Putnam Inc.,
375 Hudson Street, New York, New York 10014.
ACE and the "A" design are trademarks
belonging to Penguin Putnam Inc.

PRINTED IN THE UNITED STATES OF AMERICA

10 9 8 7 6 5 4 3 2 1

ACKNOWLEDGMENTS

WHEN YOU WRITE a historical novel, you can't thank everyone who shaped the setting. If the people who lived through the era touched your own life, it's hard even to thank enough of them to matter. There are many names below, and their contributions mattered a great deal to this book.

Thanks to Donald Maass, who can coax uranium out of pitchblende, and did so with my original proposal. Thanks also to Ginjer Buchanan, who has worked at turning my daydreams into my books. A final thanks to the indefatigable copyeditor of this book, Bill Drennan, who tirelessly searched out anachronisms and inaccuracies in my manuscript.

Plimstubb is not C. I. Hayes, where I worked for ten years, but I owe many people there my affectionate thanks: the inimitable Bob Martin, who could give me a restaurant menu from Bermuda when I needed it; Johnny O'Neil, who taught a chimp to do his job; Gert Sarli, for wise counsel and advice; Peter Parker, who still defines courage under fire; I owe Bernie Crane, Barry Palumbo, Steve Balme, Leo Carpenter and the late Russ Porter for many otherwise-lost stories; Mary Ann Emerson and Jacqueline Weintraub for helping arrange interviews for me with countless Hayes retirees; Bob Brodeur, Rodger Furey, and Syl Gookin, for their ability to build weapons out of spare parts; thanks especially to Bob for many hours talking about the book, as well as for listening to me fuss about it; thanks to Dan Herring, metallurgist, salesman, and fantasist for his encouragement and expertise, and Frank Knight for teaching me what heat treating furnaces are like and, more importantly, what selling them is like. I apologize to everyone I left out.

C. I. Hayes built furnaces for Mustang fighter engines and, without knowing what they were working on, for the Manhattan Project; the company has a memorable history. Despite the stresses of daily work in any factory, Hayes remains memorable for me as the kindest place I had ever worked in.

Thanks to Adeline Moretta, Anna Evans, and Bob Evans for reminiscences of dance hall days at Rhodes on the Pawtuxet.

Love and thanks to Lynn Anne Evans for her work on this book.

Thanks in general to Rhode Island: committed, colorful, and vital source of flyers, sailors, Seabees, and material for the war.

The accuracies of this book are from the contributions of these people. The inaccuracies are mine.

When I was young I was convinced that my parents had won the War. When I was older, I realized that millions of other people had worked and fought and sacrificed, and had also won the War. Now that I'm older still, I know that I was right: My parents won World War II, and I'd like to thank them for that.

I'm also grateful to the Klenske brothers, especially for the European Theater, Norb Stolz for his work in Alaska, John Ahrens for his service in Burma, Dano Donovan for fighting in North Africa, Loren Hintz who died in Italy, and his wife Gert who subsequently did so much for me and for so many other children, and especially also to my beloved grandfather, Erwin "Curly" Larson, who was recommissioned in World War II as a veteran of the Great War. The Army called such veterans "retreads." I called him my grandfather, and a decorated hero in two wars.

This book is dedicated with all my love to the memory of Captain James Edward O'Donohoe: father, friend, lifelong patriot.

—Nick O'Donohoe
nicholasod@aol.com

ONE

THE SUN FILTERED through the late summer foliage on the maples and elms, and a breeze off Narragansett Bay kept the air cool enough to make biking pleasant. Traffic was understandably reduced; the biggest noise in Washington Park at this hour was the morning racket of songbirds, and if you didn't look carefully at your surroundings, you could forget about the war.

Grady pedaled furiously for once, enjoying the speed and stopping only when a twinge of pain told him that the pressure on his ankle was too much. His cane was poked sideways through the basket on his handlebars, holding down the cloth flour sack that held his lunch, his tie, and a sales proposal he had actually bothered to take home. He bounced past a row of homes, noting as always the blue star symbol up in so many windows and throwing, as he did every morning, a quick salute. He looked more like he was twelve than twenty-two, his cheeks still round.

He pulled his hand down and slowed his bike considerably. In one of the windows was a gold star, as fresh and bright as the sunlight striking it. The gold star hadn't been there the Friday before.

So much for forgetting about the war. Grady rode on thoughtfully, wondering if he had ever seen the people who lived in that house and who had died, a father, son, mother, or daughter.

He pulled in at a white wood-frame house just like the others. He glanced more than casually at the blue star in the window, feeling marginally better as he pedaled up the drive. Mary greeted him at the back door before he could knock. "Julie fell back asleep. Don't you dare wake her up."

"Uncle Grady would never do that."

"Uncle Grady woke his niece up three times last week," she said grimly. "Breakfast?"

But she was already back at the stove, the eggs frying in the pan. There was toast in the oven, staying warm; Grady grabbed a piece and buttered it sparingly. "Someday I'll surprise you and ask for Johnnycake."

"Someday I'll surprise you and tell you to make your own breakfast."

"That reminds me," he said, munching. He reached into his pocket. "Dairy rations and gas rations."

Mary tucked them carefully in the front of her recipe box. "You don't have to do this. If you ever need to keep these . . ."

He ate, watching Mary clean up. Grady's dad always said you should clean up as you went when you cooked. Grady had never gotten the hang of it. Mary dried and put away dishes; as she moved in and out of the sunlight, Grady could see tired lines around her eyes. Running a family alone was starting to wear on her.

He sipped his coffee, wishing he could read the paper. He

had today's *Providence Journal* in the bag with his lunch and the sales proposal. He didn't pull the newspaper out and he didn't ask Mary to turn on the radio; the two of them were careful never to discuss the news at breakfast.

She poured him more coffee, adding milk without his asking. Grady loved this; he, his brother, and his father all took care of each other, or had, but somehow it felt different here.

As she finished pouring, she bent down beside him, and for one moment he thought she was going to kiss him on the cheek. Instead she whispered as though sharing a secret, "I got a letter from Kevin."

He was halfway out of his seat. She pulled the letter away, laughing. "First let me take out my page."

She extracted part of the letter, put it in her pocket, pulled it out again, glanced at it, smiled, and put it away hastily.

At the top of the first page was written, in block capitals:

MARY, BE VERY SURE *AND TAKE THE BACK PAGE OUT OF THIS LETTER BEFORE GRADY READS IT.*

Grady grinned. Once Mary had forgotten; she'd blushed so hard that he hadn't teased her—much—but he'd been ruthless when he wrote Kevin, care of ETO, European Theater of Operations. Now he read on:

Dear Mary (and Grady, except for the last page),

I'm safe and well. Things are going better than I could have guessed a month ago. I guess you know by now that the landing at Omaha Beach was pretty busy. They don't tell us what you know, but it would be kind of hard to hide.

I don't know if you got my last letter—

They had. Until it had come, they hadn't been sure Kevin was still alive.

—but we didn't come ashore till D-Day Plus 2. After that we kept moving forward, mostly to get away from the beach. Now it's a ways behind us. I can't say where we are, but Europe is like nothing I've ever seen. The houses are built different, and there are lots of red tile roofs where the buildings still have roofs, and old stone where the stones are still on top of each other. I saw a castle on the way here—I can say that because there are lots of castles in Europe. I hope we can all go see it again someday when the war is over and it all looks better.

It hasn't been too bad once I got over being scared. Landing on the beach was the worst part. Mary, remember when you and I and Grady went to Block Island? The beach was like that; sand and then these big cliffs. The Germans had been on top of the cliffs, but they were all gone. When I came ashore I remembered wading with you at the beach, and you tripping me in the surf. Then the guy next to me shoved on my back, hard, and I started moving again. We kept moving forward for the next two days, but I couldn't tell you where I was. Grady, I hope you don't mind my saying that I'm glad you're not here.

Grady winced. Of course Kevin was.

Mary's told me all you've been doing. I guess I'll have to quit calling you "Greedy." I can't tell you how much it means to me. I hear the guys talking here, some nights, and they're all nervous about things once in a while but what worries them most is the folks back home, are they safe, and how are they doing. That's one worry you've kept away from me.

For his own reasons, Grady winced again and checked his watch, thinking of work.

Anyway, we're all betting we'll be home by Christmas, so you'd better have a good present picked out for me. Give my love to Dad.

Grady, lost in thought, folded the letter and passed it to Mary, who was absently reading the final page to herself. Her bathrobe gapped over her nightgown; even though it was a modest cotton slipover, Grady discreetly looked away.

Mary shook herself and turned on the radio, automatically turning it to a sensible volume level. Without having looked at a clock, she had passed the news; WPRO was bouncing through a swing arrangement of "They're Either Too Young or Too Old." Breakfast was over; it was time to bike to work.

He made it to Promenade Street in no time at all; by now he had a route laid out that avoided most of the morning traffic. At eight o'clock and not a second earlier, Grady Cavanaugh pulled into the parking lot at Plimstubb Furnaces. He swung off his bike, whipped the cane out, knocked the kickstand down with a deft spin, and did a single ill-conceived lunge and flourish, grimacing as his foot twisted under him.

In his first semester of college, dreaming of Errol Flynn as Robin Hood and Tyrone Power as Zorro, he had taken fencing and loved it. By his junior year he was on the fencing team and was extremely good, perhaps not surprising, considering that he practiced with all the spare time he could break free. He had three trophies, but he didn't care about them as much as he did the fencing.

One Friday night, on a bet, he and two of his friends went to the gym and checked out foils. The two of them attacked him and he parried successfully, retreating until he was off the gym floor and backing up a flight of stairs. He fenced with them until he was even with the first landing, then turned and dashed up three steps. His lead opponent followed, leaving a gap, as Grady had hoped.

Grady leaped the banister and landed between the two of them, disarming the man below him and spinning to "stab" the upper one in the back. He brought the foil up in a quick salute before the pain hit and he rolled down the stairs, clutching his ankle.

That was Friday night, December 5, 1941. For one and a half days, Grady had received a great deal of attention about his ankle.

Before supper the following Sunday, Benny Parrish pounded on his door and opened it without waiting for an answer. Benny was curly-haired and big-eyed, like an extra Marx brother, and most of the time he looked funny.

He spoke in a slow, dazed voice. As he went on, Grady glanced numbly around the room at his slide rule, his mechanical pencils, and his case of drafting compasses and calipers, not yet knowing that he would remember exactly where they were at that moment for the rest of his life.

That spring, Grady watched his friends from the class ahead of him graduate and enlist. He shook their hands, promised to write, and leaned on his cane, watching them leave, realizing for the first time what a gulf there would now always be between most men's experience and his own.

•   •   •

Now he walked past the Plimstubb loading dock doors. The side door near them had a worn and faded sign on it: EMPLOYEES ONLY. ALL OTHERS USE THE FRONT DOOR. Grady walked through.

Just inside, next to a recently repaired quahog bull rake that had no business in a wartime factory, he stopped and said hello to the stocky, bushy-bearded swamp Yankee who stood at the door to the front offices. "Yo, Blaine. How's it going?"

Tom Blaine shook his head mournfully. "Some days I go into Sales, talk about a new project, and everybody looks at me like I have lobsters hanging off me."

Grady patted his shoulder. "Not for nothing, I hope they taste good."

"I'll probably mess that up, too." He picked up the rake, eyeing the fresh weld critically, and trudged dejectedly toward his office. "Gotta stay funny; gotta stay open. . . ."

Grady heard Blaine's officemate, Bill Riley, say confidently (and ambiguously), "We will." Riley, the design part of Research and Development, was eternally optimistic. He passed designs to Tom Blaine, who gloomily studied them, announced imminent failure, fire, and fatality, and patiently developed each design into a workable system. As always, they had a pot of coffee perking on a piece of tile, a bare red-hot electric heating element under it. Blaine admitted that it was dangerous, but Bill happily pointed out that in two years it had only caused one major fire.

Grady walked on past the rectangular and cylindrical forms on the floor of industrial furnaces undergoing assembly. There were still five out there, but they were all nearly complete. One of the last was a box-shaped oven on legs for the U.S. Navy; he looked at it a little resentfully and walked through a door to the front office, stopping at the receptionist's booth. "Morning, Talia. Are there any phone messages for Sales?" She looked at him vaguely. "Any telegrams? Does anyone want to buy a furnace?"

Talia shook her head, her shoe-polish black dyed hair barely moving. "Nobody wants to buy anything this early." She tottered away on absurdly high heels to the women's room.

Originally there had been a couch in the smoking area in the women's room; the company had taken the couch out because Talia tended to lie down on it and nap through large portions of the workday.

Grady choked as she wobbled by him. For every year that Talia got older, she wore higher heels and more perfume. By now, in her early fifties, she seemed to float above people in a cloud of musk. He grabbed a cup of coffee from the company pot, resolving to rinse his coffee cup sometime soon.

He ambled to his office. The same folder he had set out Friday was still on his desk. He opened it, but his work on the order was long done. He stared at the brick walls a while, smoking a Lucky Strike and sipping thoughtfully at his bad coffee while making a one-page list that said at the top, in urgent block capitals, TODAY.

Then he balanced his checkbook. He spent five more minutes checking the baseball scores in the *Providence Journal* and figuring out how his bets had come out. At eight-thirty he tore up and rewrote TODAY. He chewed his pencil and brushed the hair back from his forehead, writing immediately, "Noon: Get a haircut." He looked longingly at the stacks of *Astounding, Amazing* and *Thrilling Wonder Stories* on his bookshelf, but didn't pick one up.

At twenty-five to nine he walked back to the switchboard and woke up Talia to ask again if he'd missed any phone calls. He spent five minutes talking to her about her son Myron and which of the Rhode Island colleges would be best for him if he wanted to become an engineer after the war was over. "Geez, I don't know, Talia. Engineering school is a lot of work. . . . Do your kids take after you?" he asked, a little tactlessly.

At a quarter to nine, Tom Garneaux (half the place seemed to be named "Tom") leaned in. "Busy?" In spite of his silver hair, he looked excited, oddly like a fifty-year-old child.

"Nothing that can't wait," Grady said gratefully.

Garneaux plopped into Grady's chair without asking.

Grady sat on his desk, skidding slightly on the freshly waxed surface. "So how was the weekend?"

"Great, great. Say, what a restaurant I went to Sunday." His eyes went unfocused, remembering. "Had three Manhattans, Holy Christ, everything tasted great."

"I'll bet. Where was it?"

"Downtown Providence, just off the watch and jewelry district. Do you know, before the war we sold more furnaces in that twenty blocks than we did in the rest of the country? Speidel, Bulova—anyway, there's a new place, Canary's, a block from Mike's, it's a Portuguese restaurant. . . ." Predictably, he stood up and waved his arms, miming the walls and tables. "You know, with the checkered table cloths, the photos of the Canary Islands and the Azores, and street scenes of Lisbon—nothing fancy—oh, my God, the squid and the chareese—chorico—anyway, that spicy sausage they served . . ." His eyes shone.

Tom Garneaux had been to more restaurants than anyone Grady had ever known. Apparently Tom had never had a bad meal or a bad time.

Roy Burgess, the shop foreman, passed Grady's office and scowled in. "Canary's? Don't go. Went last week. Service stank, food was cold, sausages greasy, the drinks tasted like frog snot." Often Burgess had been to the same restaurants as Garneaux, and he returned complaining about the bad food, ill-mannered service, and sullen company. Once it turned out that he was sitting glumly three tables over from Garneaux, who had pushed three tables together and was having the time of his life.

Garneaux added a little too casually, "Anything selling?"

Grady gestured at the file on his desk. "A brokered job, maybe." He added defensively, " Something will."

"That's my boy." Tom punched Grady's arm lightly. "Optimism and confidence." He went back to his own desk. Grady watered his plants, taking cuttings and putting them in a water-filled coffee cup. He went to Shipping and got a box for trash.

He emptied the middle drawer of his battered pine desk and refilled it after throwing out all the old papers and putting extra lead in all the mechanical pencils. He waxed the scarred desktop. He cleaned the glass of his front office wall.

There was a letter from the government authorizing shipment of a batch furnace, a duplicate of the oven still in the shop, but this one was going to the Brazilian Navy for shipboard repairs. Grady frowned at the letter. Who had ever heard of the Brazilian Navy? It seemed as though everyone but he was fighting with the Allies.

The rest of the mail was nothing but advertisements. One of the envelopes said in red, white, and blue letters, WON THE WAR LATELY? Grady, embarrassed, threw it away quickly.

At ten o'clock, Grady smoked another Lucky, wrote one check, entered it in his checkbook, rebalanced his checkbook for the practice, and said out loud, "I am in serious trouble."

"Tell me about it," Susan Rocci said from the door.

He jumped. Susan walked in, smiling. "Ask Talia for a shot for your coffee."

"Shouldn't you ring some kind of bell? I'd feel better if I knew you were coming." But he was glad to see even her; casual conversation might fill up another ten minutes, and then the coffee wagon would be at the back of the plant.

"I'd feel better if I knew you were going." But she saw the nearly empty box on the floor, and her smile went out as though someone had thrown a switch. "Oh, God, I'm sorry. Are you—"

He followed her glance. "No, no. Just cleaning up."

He pulled out his chair for her.

"Thanks." She stayed standing. "I've just never seen your desk this clean."

Grady gestured to the folders on his desk. "There's still work on it."

"Don't lie till you get good at it. How many requests for quotation does it take to get one sale? How many requests have you had today?"

"Not many—"

"Not any. Talia's asleep out there." In spite of Susan's edge, she sounded fond of Talia.

"Let her sleep," Grady said bitterly. "It's not like there's business out there beating down the doors."

"It's a slump, that's all." But Susan didn't sound comforting or look reassuring. "Some firms ride it out, some don't."

On an impulse, Grady asked, "Do you think this place is going to make it?"

Susan looked at the doodles of baseball scores on his desk, at his checkbook, at the magazines. "Do you care?"

"Of course I do. I mean, look at it." He waved an arm at the glass door, at the people beyond it. "It's so nice here."

It was. At his interview, two years ago, Grady had asked

why the average age at Plimstubb seemed to be fifty. Instead of the traditional wartime answer, he was told, bluntly, "Once people get a job here, they don't leave." He had thought about that overnight and requested a second interview, which had netted him the job.

Susan surprised him by shrugging. "Nice? Depends."

"On what?"

"On who's trying to be nice."

Grady sadly watched her leave. Susan wasn't fitting in here. She was the only other young person at Plimstubb, and he'd miss her. He muttered, "If she'd just relax—"

Talia's voice came scratchily over the intercom speakers. "Grady Cave-gnaw, line five." She cleared her throat loudly, and the speaker whistled.

Grady listlessly punched up the call. "Sales," he said, wondering whether it would be his father again, or one of his friends.

It was Talia. "I guess I could have just rung you."

"No problem."

"I forgot to tell you," she said without apology. "You have a visitor. A customer, I think."

Grady stood up hastily, straightening his tie. "What's his name?"

"I wouldn't know," she said plaintively. "I've seen him before, though."

"Did you ask him?"

There was a long pause and she said, "Hold on." After muffled talk, she said, "Bob Renfrew. He says he's with the gov—"

Grady was out of his chair and headed for the lobby before she finished. He stopped in the men's room, brushed back what his father called his "Irish shock" of unruly hair that fell forward whenever his hair got long, and, as always lately, was startled by how slender he'd gotten. Between the biking and the cane, his upper body was nothing but muscle. He hitched his pants—he needed to buy a smaller size some day—and went out to meet Renfrew.

Renfrew was of average height, with a slightly pudgy baby face even though he was thirty-six. His light gray suit and the cut of the lapels said that he had tried, somewhere near the start of the war, to be a sharp dresser. By now the buttons were pulling tight against the belly of the coat. He checked his watch nervously.

Grady stuck his hand out. "St. Louis Browns came through again, four to one over the Tigers, even with Dizzy Trout pitching some for the Tigers. Pay up."

Renfrew shook hands. "You're up twenty-five. I'll pay you the next time Boston's in the Series."

"Braves or Red Sox?"

He considered. "Red Sox. The Braves look pretty good these days."

Grady sighed. "Yeah. They do. I'll stay with the Browns for another week."

"Maybe you'll stay lucky." He glanced surreptitiously at Talia. "Say, is she all right?"

Grady stared at her; she was nodding off while pretending to read the *Journal*. "She just gets confused. How long have you been waiting?"

"Ten or fifteen minutes." He shuffled back and forth. "Are you sure she's okay?" Talia's head was sagging now.

"She gets by. What are you doing here?" He almost added, "Fifteen minutes early?" Renfrew was chronically tardy.

"Waiting for a phone call. Have you got a room with two phones, a phone and an extension?"

"Sure," Grady said in surprise. "Conference room. It may take a few minutes to explain the setup to Talia, though. What's up?"

Renfrew took his elbow. "We'd better start now."

A few minutes later they were in the conference room, standing in front of one dial phone and one stand-up unit from the early thirties. They barely had time to sit down before both phones rang. Renfrew gestured to Grady, who answered, "Cavanaugh, Sales," in the falsely cheery tone his boss preferred.

"Cavanaugh?" the voice said sharply. "Stode. Subject: Solicitation number R-7352-N-57059." He paused, presumably to breathe. He didn't sound like he had ever needed to breathe in his entire life.

In the silence, Grady finally said, "I have the folder here." At present it was one of the few active ones on his desk. "We had it out in anticipation of your call."

"Yes." Grady was faintly irked that Stode hadn't said, "Good." "I gave you an extra five minutes, based on Mr. Renfrew's past behavior." The voice was crisp and clear. Grady looked at Renfrew sympathetically. Times were tough when your boss never forgave a mistake, even in front of an outsider. "Review: The solicitation involved molybdenum castings for high-temperature vacuum work. Molybdenum is in short supply, and the companies doing that sort of work are booked solid for the aircraft industry."

Grady nodded, forgetting that Stode couldn't see him. Plimstubb had built several furnaces for the National Committee on Avionics, totally unaware that the "Committee" was designing and building Mustang fighter planes. "I tried the companies we'd used before. Like you said—"

"Yes." Stode paused just long enough for the interruption to take hold, then went on. "You said you'd received a mailing from another job shop that could work with cast moly."

"That's right. They didn't give a phone number. They had a listing in *Thomas Register,* too—in the newest volume." Grady had found it in the Providence Public Library; Plimstubb's *Thomas Register* predated the war, and in fact the Depression. "There was no phone number there either. So I wrote them—pretty lucky, wasn't it, that letter crossing my desk just when we needed it?"

After the briefest of silences, Stode went on as though he hadn't heard, "Have you had any response to your letter?"

"Not yet."

"And you wrote them ten days ago?"

"Roughly." The letter had sat on his desk for three days while he reviewed it; Grady was hoping he wouldn't have to admit that.

"I see," Stode said icily, and Grady knew Stode wouldn't ask and wasn't fooled. "And you still can't call them?"

"The phone company's no help either." Grady was getting annoyed. The contract was thirty thousand dollars— but it wasn't that much compared to some of the air corps and navy contracts they'd filled.

"Call me as soon as you hear from them. I've left three phone numbers with Renfrew. Call them all, the Washington number first, until you reach me. Renfrew, give them to Cavanaugh now."

"Yes, sir." Renfrew fumbled in his pockets, pulling out a business card that said, DRAKE STODE and gave one printed and two hand-written phone numbers. The printed number said, "Washington, D.C." beside it. The other two gave only telephone numbers.

Stode added sharply, "And ask your contractor to confirm in writing that he has a source of materials supply. That was our primary initial problem with this contract."

"Sure." As he scribbled that on his notepad, Grady said, "Couldn't you just tell the government to divert some moly from a less essential contract?"

After a second he looked at the phone. "Hello?" He

tapped the cradle once or twice, listening for background noise on the line. There was no traffic noise, no typing or other telephones, nothing at all. "You still there?"

The receiver seemed to freeze as Stode said, "All the information you need is in the solicitation. Don't ever question my reasons again."

"No, sir," Grady said automatically. He remembered that he was supposed to end calls on a personal note, establishing a friendship with the customer. "So," he said feebly, "how's the weather in Washington?"

After another frozen pause, Stode said, "I don't engage in small talk." The receiver clicked. Grady stared at it before hanging up.

Grady turned to Renfrew, ready with a wisecrack about wartime bureaucrats. He didn't say it; Renfrew's forehead was dewy with sweat, but he looked as though he were about to shiver. "Wow. Did you ever work with him before?"

He shook his head. "He came out of nowhere with this contract, acting like it was the most important thing in the world."

Grady snorted. "If it were, he wouldn't be trying to scrounge materials; he'd bump somebody else's allocation. Did you meet him face-to-face?"

"Sort of. I took a train to New York, he took one up from Washington, we met at the Hayden Planetarium. He suggested it. I turned my head and there he was in the dark, like he'd been there all along." Now he did shiver. "He's got a sharp chin, a sharp nose, body's nothing but bones—Grady, it's like he's all made of angles. Nothing but edges and planes. Like there isn't a man in there at all."

It was hard to know what to say. "You're sure this guy is on our side?"

That was the wrong joke. Renfrew stared at him,

round-eyed. "Don't say that," he squeaked. "Please don't say that."

A thought struck Grady. "He said, 'based on your past behavior' he expected you to be late."

Renfrew tried to smile, but it was sickly. "And the once that I met him, I was on time. He knew some other things, too. Gotta go," he said, checking his watch; he smiled at it momentarily. Grady looked at him quizzically. "I know it doesn't look like a million bucks, but it's a radium watch. Glows in the dark." He cupped his hands over the face and Grady could see, faintly, the green glow of the hands and the dots by the numbers.

"Nice," Grady said politely, unimpressed. He'd seen a lot of them.

Renfrew walked out of the office, leaving Grady to wonder uneasily about Stode.

He was still wondering when the phone rang. "Sales, Cavanaugh," he said absently.

"I'd like to buy a furnace," the voice said. It sounded small and far away.

"Who is this?" Grady said. He was in no mood for jokes.

There was a pause, then, "Antony Miles van der Woeden." He sounded faintly hurt. "Of the Nieuw Amsterdam"—the briefest of pauses—"Metalworks."

Grady sat up. "Good morning, Mr. van der Woeden. How are you?"

"Fine." The voice went on cautiously, "Don't you want to know about the furnace?"

"Sure, yeah, one second. . . ." He scrambled in the wrong drawer, kicking himself for having straightened. He found a pad and a pencil, broke the pencil lead, pulled out a mechanical pencil, clicked the lead frantically until it fell out, gave up, and grabbed a pen. "First I want to talk about the letter I sent you—"

"Oh, the moly tray." Antony sounded relaxed. "Sure, we can do that. Hey, why do you want holes in the tray, anyway?"

Grady, startled, said, "So the heat will rise through it, of course. Just like the shelves in an oven."

"Yeah, but can't you let the tray heat up, just like a griddle?"

"If you did that, the top of the work would heat up faster than the bottom on the tray, and it wouldn't be uniform." Grady had learned more about heat treating at Plimstubb than at engineering school, but by now he thought all his customers knew things like that.

"Gotcha. Smart idea. Anyway, you can have the tray in three weeks."

Grady caught his breath. "Three weeks?" The lead time for most high-temperature metals was six or more.

"Is that a problem? I could try for two. Say, what's this being used for, anyway?"

"I really couldn't say," Grady said solemnly, as though he knew. "Where will you find the molybdenum?

Antony chuckled. "Gee, I really couldn't say, either. Anyway, send me a confirmation of the specs you sent us and we'll make it up. I'll start the work right away, while we dicker about the price."

This sounded pretty informal, but Stode needed the moly part badly, and anyway, there was nowhere else to go for it. Besides, Antony had said he'd like to buy a furnace. "The specs you have are accurate. I'll cut a purchase order and wait to fill in the price till I hear from you. Now," he said, trying not to sound too hungry, "about that furnace. What exactly did you have in mind?"

Antony became stiff and careful in his speech again. "I

was thinking of a Plimstubb Model CR-8-12-27 electric conveyor furnace with convenient integral control panel, and a freestanding Plimstubb DA-600 dissociated ammonia generator for creating a reducing atmosphere." He sounded as though he were reading aloud.

"Yeah, sure, we make those," Grady said idiotically. "Anything else?"

"And what you call a gas dryer, easily installed for our furnace needs." The voice, done reading, hesitated. "The dryer I can order right away, if you'll tell me the price."

"Jesus," Grady said quietly (and reverently) out of earshot of the phone. To the handset he said, "I'm afraid I'm not familiar with your process. What do you do?"

"Copper brazing mostly, right now." He paused again. "But we're"—Antony seemed to be having a lot of trouble with terms—"mostly a heat-treating job shop, for all kinds of metals processing. We quench and temper and anneal; we process silver, gold, and steel."

"Nice rhyme," Grady muttered. Aloud he said, "Where did you hear of us?"

The voice said noncommittally, "Oh, you've got a good name in the industry. And I saw a picture, from a trade show, of the CR—"

"Oh, that. Listen, the furnace is good. I should mention, we've updated the controls a little." Grady had been embarrassed by that ad for two years; these days the modern control instruments had large, hand-turned dials like a stove timer, instead of just a rheostat with a big knob and no readout.

"That's fine. Anyway, we want rheostat temperature controls, two zones of heat"—he was obviously reciting from a list—"plus overtemperature control, measured atmosphere flow, and an inert purge safety system."

"Sounds like a standard furnace." He added quickly,

realizing his mistake, "With the option package, which is extra. I'll run up a price for you. Is the gas dryer to be the size that goes with the furnace?" He whipped open a file drawer to see what size that would be, banging his own shin.

"Sure. I guess." The voice paused. "Say, if we get more than one furnace, we can always get another dryer, right?"

"Hey, of course." Grady found the table for dryer sizes. "Sure, that dryer's fine. It'll be an MDR-60, which dries six hundred cubic feet per hour of gas. It doesn't use much power, anyway."

"Power's not an issue," Antony said thoughtfully. "Space is. How big is this thing?"

"Bigger than a breadbox, smaller than an icebox." When Antony didn't chuckle, Grady said, "About four feet high, two feet deep, three feet wide."

"And the cost?"

Grady knocked wood quietly. "Five hundred dollars, without the option package. Terms net thirty days."

Antony said instantly, "Good. I'll"—he hesitated again—"cut a purchase order and mail it to you today."

"Fine." Grady thought, but would never have said, that the customer could have gotten everything in place before calling. "Looking forward to it." He waited impatiently for Antony to say more.

He wasn't ready when Antony said, "I'll send you the money up front. No sense in waiting, is there? Now," he said determinedly, "let me give you the changes I'll want on that furnace."

After five minutes, Antony took a breath. "That's it. Can you do all that?"

"We can do that. It's just a question of cost."

Antony chuckled. "Isn't it always? I'll call you back in a week. In an emergency, you can reach me through this number . . ."

After the number and polite good-byes, he hung up. Grady scribbled on a pad for fifteen minutes, estimating redesign costs and figuring in added costs. If he could have, he would have danced. He pocketed one of the issues of *Amazing* for later and took the pad to Talia to get it typed up.

At eleven-thirty, Talia Baghrati murmured, "Time to start winding down," put a cover on the huge L. C. Smith typewriter in the reception area, and put her head down. Grady had suggested several times that Talia be given a better typewriter, but the subject had always been dropped. Everyone seemed slightly afraid of what she might do with one.

Grady went past reception to Engineering, where design work was done. Susan's desk was nearest the far door. On the wall behind her hung three pictures: a framed recent photograph of Einstein, looking bushy and introspective; a much more sedate framed portrait photo of Marie Curie, hair pinned up and hands in lap; and, tucked in Einstein's frame, a snapshot of Vince Rocci, squinting and grinning into the camera from the deck of an aircraft carrier somewhere in the Pacific. His hair was tousled and growing out; his skin was dark, and he wore an undershirt over khaki trousers. He looked far too young to have a twenty-year-old daughter; Vince had been seventeen when Susan was born. Neither the name of the carrier nor any identifiable islands were in view, but the plane behind him, a Navy Mustang, had its name on the fuselage in cursive script: "*Sassy Suzie*."

Once Grady had made the mistake of suggesting she have the picture framed. "Why would I do that," she said, genuinely angry, "when by the time I got it back from the shop my father will be back?" Susan still looked like Betty Grable when angry; Grady reflected that Betty Grable looked a whole lot pleasanter.

She was angry now as Roy Burgess, passing through Engineering, said casually beside her desk, "Never let a day go by without a wop joke." He slid "day" and "go" into "Dago" so it was unmistakable. Susan bristled but said nothing.

"Nice one, Roy," Tom Garneaux said without looking up. "You learn that at the charm school you're paroled from?" Burgess grunted and brushed past Grady, who was wishing he could postpone speaking to Susan until she calmed down again.

To the right of her desk, near the door, her father's hat still hung on the coat rack; he had left it there on his final day at work before enlisting. According to Tom Garneaux, when Tom had called out, "Vinnie, you come back for your hat," Vince had shrugged and said, "Too far to walk. I'll pick it up when I'm working here again, after we've won the war."

"I got an RFQ," Grady said with forced casualness. "Here are the specs." He gave her the carbon of the notes.

Susan snatched them up.

"Aren't you going to wait until after lunch?"

"You'd be surprised what occurs to me over lunch."

At two minutes to twelve, a few dozen shop workers left for lunch, among them Benny "Benny Behind" Blaws, who leaped into his pickup truck, screeched out of the parking lot, floored the accelerator, and leaped up onto the driver's seat, simultaneously dropping his pants to his knees and hanging his hindquarters out the driver's side window while honking loudly. Most of Engineering stood to see him off. Susan refused, but her mouth quirked.

Grady glanced behind him. The girls from Accounting— "the girls" ranged from twenty to fifty—were eating at the Engineering conference table. "You could join them." They had invited her several times, and it was, after all, an invitation they never issued to Betty in Fabrication or to the other women on the floor.

Susan set a napkin out on her desk and unwrapped her sandwich beside her. "I have enough trouble convincing people I'm an engineer already." She looked wistfully aside at their laughter, and Grady thought she looked lonely. If he hadn't been headed for his haircut, he would have joined her for lunch.

But his barber was also his bookie, as often happened in Rhode Island, and Grady couldn't afford to break the appointment. He sat in the barber chair answering the backchat amiably while he read his back issue of *Amazing*. Murray Leinster had another story; it was great to enjoy it instead of missing all the writers who had gone to the war. At the end of the haircut he took his winnings from the Browns game, reinvested them in the next game, and came back clean-cut and no poorer.

Afternoons at Plimstubb were even quieter than mornings. Grady sat doodling caricatures of coworkers at Plimstubb. Sonny LeTour, cradling an archtop Gibson guitar, was a natural; Grady's boss, Warren Hastings, with a martini and a sailboat, was another. Grady was trying to figure out why he had drawn Susan Rocci with angel wings and with a crooked halo over her rich, curly blond hair, when the phone rang, an inside call. "How do," he said abstractedly. "Cavanaugh."

"Do good. Jane talk good, too, Tarzan. Rocci."

"Susan. Hi." Absurdly, he checked his zipper. "What did I do, I mean, what do you—"

"I've got problems with your RFQ. Come on down."

"Be right there."

He was there in forty seconds. Susan looked at him cynically. "What took you so long? Did I interrupt you?"

"What's the problem? What problem?" Grady, like all

sales engineers, was defensive and parental about potential sales.

"You gave me the specs on it—"

"Sure, and a reference job. Capital Order 11623."

"Similar to?"

"Well, yeah," Grady said defensively.

Nothing annoyed the entire factory more than the sales designation "similar to" on customized furnaces. Once Grady had found on Susan's desk the following sheet of paper from a Plimstubb Capital Order work summary:

ADDITIONAL BUILDING INSTRUCTIONS, EARTH:

STANDARD PLIMSTUBB EARTH-STYLE PLANET. SIMILAR TO C.O. 002, "VENUS," EXCEPT FOR:

1. LIVABLE TEMPERATURE
2. BREATHABLE ATMOSPHERE
3. INTELLIGENT LIFE.

ALL LIVING COMPONENTS ARE TO BE REPRO-DUCIBLE. SALES ORIGINALLY QUOTED THIS S.O. AS INCLUDING NO SIN OR DEATH.
SEVEN DAYS START-UP.

Grady had sneaked it off her desk and scribbled a copy for himself.

Now Susan tapped her pen against the specifications sheet, changing accents and syncopating while she thought. "Are you sure you got these dimensions right?"

He looked at the notes. "I don't see the problem. It's right there, written down; twenty-four inches."

"Did he mention legs or a support stand?"

"No. Isn't a quote for a furnace enough?"

"Is it going to sit on a worktable?"

"He didn't say." He was getting annoyed. "Look, if you don't feel you can do it—"

"Damn, I hate salesmen." She sighed loudly, grabbed a pad, and sketched for him. "This is an electric conveyor furnace with no legs and no stand."

He could draw it better himself, but he didn't say so.

It had the front loading table, the conveyor carrying work into a heating chamber, a cooling section so the work didn't burn anyone's hands, and an unloading table. "That looks normal."

Susan sketched in a stick figure at the front. "And this is a normal-size person." She drew it full height, then dotted it in doubled over. "Can you picture what she'd look like, bent over it?"

"Mind if I imagine it's you?" Garneaux called cheerfully from his desk. Susan flexed her fingers irritably, but ignored him and added pain stars and lightning lines to her drawing. "And this is what she'll look like by the end of the day if she unloads at that height."

Grady saw the point. "And the control panel's just above his knees—"

"Her knees."

"Either way, she can't read the switch labels and the instruments."

"Uh-huh. And the gas flow meters . . ." She sketched them in. "Just as bad. So it's a stupid design."

He said defensively, "But you can build it that way, right?"

"It's easy. In fact, it's cheaper. We just knock thirty inches off the legs and we're there. We'll have to move the transformers out from under it, but we can do that." She tapped her mechanical pencil against the desk, switching from duple to triple time every two measures. Susan had been a drummer in high school. "But why should we?"

Grady was deeply shocked. "Because the customer wants it."

"God, Grady, if a customer wanted a furnace with a phonograph and a fish tank, would you do that?"

Grady said plaintively, "I like music. And fish."

Susan's head snapped up. "What voice are you?"

"What? Singing?" He went on hastily before she could say something sarcastic, "Tenor. I haven't sung since high school. . . ."

Five minutes later he was a newly recruited member of the Providence Choral Society. He wished dazedly that he were as tough a salesman as Susan would have been. He said stubbornly, "I still say the quote for the furnace is normal."

"Nothing about this is normal." She tapped a pencil, thinking. "Why anyone would want something this strange is beyond me. Are they putting it in a tunnel, or belowdecks on a ship or something?"

"I don't know." Grady felt a chill. "The caller had a foreign accent."

Susan leaned forward and said with mock suspicion, "Maybe he's an Axis spy."

"No, he's just a customer." None of the salesmen at Plimstubb ever, ever thought a customer could do the slightest wrong.

"Okay. On the other hand, maybe Stode's an Axis spy, not really working for the government at all."

"Huh?"

"Why would a Washington supervisor check up so early on Renfrew's solicitation? I think he's not on the up-and-up."

Now Grady was lost. "They can't both be spies. Are you saying one of them is?"

"Maybe, but which one?" Susan was enjoying this. "It's

like Schrödinger's cat in the experiment. A subatomic event in a box triggers the death of a cat—or not, fifty-fifty chance. Is the cat alive or dead?"

Grady thought of making a bet. "Can't I just lift the lid and see?"

"Sure, but the observation changes the event." She handed him back the carbon copy of the RFQ. "Call this guy, or call Stode, and see which one's the spy."

He passed Tom Garneaux's desk on the way back; Garneaux was sketching a copy of a Betty Grable Royal Crown Cola ad, but the face on the pinup looked remarkably like Susan frowning. Since Grady had been at Plimstubb he had never caught Garneaux working, but Garneaux never fell behind. Grady glanced back at Susan's desk and muttered, "Why does talking to her make me nervous?"

Garneaux said cryptically, "Sounds normal to me. She didn't say yes, and she didn't say no, and she didn't tell you to go away."

"Terrific. I'm going away anyway."

Before calling Antony, Grady reviewed the advertisement. There was the CR-8-12-27, and it was definitely shown as more than thirty-six inches high at the load table. The ad copy he'd marked up said eighteen. Actually, Grady realized uneasily, Antony had been reading the ad copy aloud over the phone, except for the height changes.

Grady got an outside line from Talia, requested the number Antony had given him, and waited.

The phone rang ten or twelve times. Finally someone picked it up and said, "Howdy." The voice had a strange accent that Grady associated partly with the movies and partly with southern radio stations that showed up on frosty nights when there was a lot of skip in the airwaves.

He cleared his throat. "Is Antony Miles van der Woeden there?"

"I'm the only one here." Behind the voice came the sound of a passing car.

Grady's stomach hurt suddenly. "Is this the Nieuw Amsterdam Metalworks?"

"This," the voice said pleasantly enough, "is a pay phone in the parking lot of the Schuylkill Diner, which as near as I can tell is in the bunghole of central New York State. Are you sure you have the right number, son?"

Grady looked at the number he had scribbled down. "Absolutely," he said, suddenly unhappy. "Are you sure this is a pay phone in a parking lot?"

"If it isn't," the voice said, "I just did something godamighty foolish with a DeSoto."

Grady hung up and stared at the phone. "I am in so much trouble."

Antony was puffing as he dashed into the ditch, his marked-up copy of the Plimstubb ad rolled under his arm. He'd heard his fill of midget jokes for the day, he was behind on processing an order, and he'd be in trouble at work, again, if his absence were noticed. He didn't even think about what would happen to him if his errand were known.

The box culvert in front of him, apparently a dry drain into the right-of-way, was forty-eight inches high, possibly built to handle flood runoff.

He barely broke stride as he hopped onto it and dashed in, standing straight up.

He passed a sleepy raccoon, who cocked an eye and flicked her tail protectively over two restless pups. Antony patted her (a reckless move even for him) and sped by.

"Hello, Becca. I can't stop." He had named her after Calvin Coolidge's pet raccoon from a while back.

The pups chirped loudly. Becca sighed, rose to her feet, and waddled toward the culvert opening, looking over her shoulder to see that the pups were following.

Antony came to a grate made of rusty reinforcing rods and festooned with dried grass, as though a flood had run through it. He put his hand against the grass and smiled as the familiar warm air blew over his fingers.

He slid one reinforcing rod up and one sideways, and lifted the entire grate inward on its hinge.

Ahead of him lay a cave, lit by electric bulbs with circular reflectors behind them. The bulbs were strung together by wire pinned to the rock.

In the light beneath, figures moved to and fro calmly, nodding to each other with courteous familiarity as they worked. No one in the cave was more than four feet tall.

In a corner, by an open hearth with a vent over it, a dwarf with a dark, untrimmed beard in the old-fashioned style hammered at a red-hot metal bar on an iron hearth. He swung the hammer one-handed, holding the bar still with tongs. An assistant nearby squeezed a pig's bladder under his arm like a bagpipe, directing a small stream of air into the center of the hearth. When they were done, the dwarf with the hammer whistled and pointed, and the hearth shuffled farther into the fire.

Another dwarf, using tongs to pull a flat blade from a similar hearth, swung a horizontal pipe from the wall, opened a spigot, and ran water in a vat, all the while holding the glowing bar at arm's length in the tongs. She doused the red-hot metal in the vat beside her; seconds later, Antony heard the hiss of steam. A male dwarf as beardless as Antony stood idly holding a hand bellows, watching.

Leaving the area of a clay brick kiln, a woman effortlessly carried a pallet holding a tractor engine block across the plant. A red-haired dwarf said hello and she stopped to talk to him, not putting her load down. A carrying cart sidled under the load, waiting patiently. Above them, a single sheet of paper, probably a processing order, flapped purposefully across the plant.

At first glance the place looked busy, but Antony could see that the loading, the quenching, and the washing were going on at the forcibly leisurely pace workers use when they are desperate to stretch out a job. He sighed and swung down to the floor, padding quickly toward his work station at an open hearth. Another dwarf was waiting there, puttering with the tool rack. Over the low clatter of work he could hear the waterwheel at the far end of the factory, and the creak of the canvas drive belt off its axle. Someone was chanting softly in medieval Latin to a fireplace halfway across the cave; Antony could make out some of the words and predict what color the flames would assume. He shook his head unhappily and tiptoed onto the plant floor, grateful that he had come back unnoticed.

"Antony!"

He froze. A second male dwarf, fatter and much grayer, strode across the office platform and down the steps. A trade magazine in his hand was rolled like a baton, or a billy club.

"Antony, two hours ago I'm asking for the new disk blades for Mr. Leyden, and I'm not finding them. You think maybe I'd have them before he comes in this afternoon, when exactly I'm not sure?"

Antony winced. Pieter's English deteriorated when he was upset or angry. "I'll have them done."

"The forge is hot." Pieter gestured to a brick chimney with a coke fire in it. "The bellows boy Gunter, he has been nothing doing but sitting, this hour and half one." He pointed to an obviously harassed, beardless "boy" whom

Antony knew to be at least sixty. "These are not games, Antony. When business is slack, that is the time we work harder than ever. You know."

"I know. I'm sorry." He struggled for an explanation.

Pieter gave him no chance. "And Antony, what about the other orders? Deadlines are important to them; some of these people only walk the earth once a year."

"I know. Look . . ." He gave up. "I was outside." He stuffed the notes in his back pocket.

"Outside? During work?" Pieter was flabbergasted. "You thought to run home, maybe, and have a nice nap? Antony, what to hell were you doing?"

"I asked him to." They turned around. "He was doing me a favor," Kirsten said. "I was worried; thought I'd left my door unlocked, and he said he'd run and check. I didn't mean to take him away from work." She gazed with strong, clear blue eyes at Pieter but was careful not to look at Antony.

Pieter looked at her, then at Antony. He almost smiled. "You could say no to her when she asks for favors, boy."

"I could," Antony said grudgingly, "but I don't want to."

Pieter's laugh rang out and he squeezed Antony's arm hard enough to hurt. "I know you don't. Just ask next time." He added, as though Kirsten weren't there, "And be patient and let things happen, boy. It will all be right. I been once where you been now, many years ago." He smiled kindly at Antony, who suddenly felt ashamed at deceiving Pieter.

Antony looked hopefully at the copy of *Metal Heating* magazine in Pieter's hand. "Did you read it?"

"I looked at it," he said with a grunt. "Some of it's not bad. The article that says on process control and temperature uniformity, I can't even believe that anyone can be so exact—" He caught himself. "You're so anxious for change; go, you should get some orders off of your workbench."

He turned around and lumbered back up the stairs, limping slightly and turning to see if Antony were following. Antony was reminded forcibly of Becca, the mother raccoon.

Antony turned back toward Kirsten. "Thanks. That was kind—"

"I'd do the same for anyone," she said impassively.

Antony muttered, "Yah."

She looked from side to side to see if anyone were listening. "What did they say?" she whispered.

Antony tugged on her sleeve and jerked his head toward a quiet corner. He walked over; she followed, dubiously.

Before she could say anything, he said, "I ordered the gas dryer."

"Without Pieter's permission?"

"Yah." He grinned at her. "Change can be good for him, too. Of course, it's useless without the furnace. . . ."

"So he'll feel pressured to buy the furnace. What does it do?"

Antony regarded her earnestly and gestured as he talked, spreading his arms wide. He looked like a small child explaining something important to a sympathetic grown-up. "When we heat steel, you know how rotten it looks sometimes, all rough?"

"Of course. It's scale. Fire does that."

"Right, and it does something else, too, called decarb. It leaches the carbon out of the metal surface. . . ." He saw her expression and said hastily, "Anyway, the work looks terrible, and it can only be hardened a little, because of the decarb. But if we get rid of the contact with fire, we'd get rid of the problems."

She nodded. "So you use electric heat."

"Well, that's part of it." He sketched an imaginary box in the air with his hands. "This is the good part; I wonder how anybody thought of it. You heat the work in a box, and you pump a gas into the box to push the oxygen out. They call it a reducing atmosphere. No more scale, no more decarb. Not even any discoloration." He flipped his hands up at either end of the box. "Plus, if you run a conveyor belt through either end, you can heat work all the time, without leaving somebody standing there holding each piece."

She squinted at his hands, trying to visualize it. "Doesn't the gas leak out?"

"It burns out. You let it flow, and it burns away."

"Antony, does it work?"

"The magazine says it does." He was enjoying how round her eyes were, how impressed she was with him. Kirsten was never impressed with him. "So. You run the work in this end, and out this end. . . ."

"How do you cool it? Does somebody stand there with a bucket?"

"You line up U-shaped covered troughs full of water around the conveyor belt and cool the work gradually. Or if you want it to cool suddenly, you drop it straight into a tank of water or oil, and take it out in a wire basket afterward."

"So where does your dryer come in?"

"Well"—he pointed to the rear of the imaginary box— "so the bolts, brackets, whatever we're making, sometimes they come out discolored, right?"

"Always. But I thought you said the gas took care of that."

"Not if there's water in it. No oxygen, no oxidation. No water, no oxygen. Dry the gas until there's no water in it, and the last source of free oxygen goes away."

Kirsten shook her head dazedly. "This is chemistry, not metalwork; I feel like we're brewing beer." A thought struck her. "What if Pieter doesn't want the furnace?"

He shrugged. "I paid for the dryer with my savings. I've got enough."

Kirsten was definitely impressed. Antony's savings fund, like all their savings, was considered sacred. "He'll buy it, Antony. After all, it's the next logical step. We have the power." She gestured at the lights overhead, then at the plant piping. "We even have running water, thanks to you."

"I'm sorry I ever talked him into indoor plumbing," Antony said bitterly, "because now we can tell that this place is going down the toilet."

"And if it does?" Kirsten asked quietly.

As if drawn against their will, they looked downhill toward a tunnel, taller than dwarves needed and quite dark, over which a single word was chiseled in Futhark, runic writing. Below it, punched into the rock in Fraktur, was the German translation:

GNOMENGESELLSCHAFT.

From somewhere beyond the tunnel, they heard a long, high, sobbing wail. The wail ended in a scream. A few deep voices chuckled.

In the cavern beyond the Dwarfworks, the Gnomewerks was processing something. Antony and Kirsten shuddered and went hastily back to work.

TWO

IN 1904, WALLACE Ingalls Hiram of Providence, Rhode Island, received a letter from Ford Motor Company asking if, because of his expertise as a metalworker, he could solve a processing problem for them. The painted FORD lettering plates for the front grille did not dry rapidly enough for the rest of the assembly line, and heating them in a normal gas or coal oven left soot on them. Heating the plates with too much temperature variation left some of them dry, and some of the fronts crackled; heating them too fast in air discolored the backside of the metal plates (which didn't show but which bothered the company anyway). Could Hiram think of a way to dry the plates?

Hiram sat in his garage for the better part of a night smoking his pipe and rereading the letter, then took a ceramic liner from a gas kiln for pottery, sealed it tight except for two holes, where he piped in nitrogen and forced out air, and gave it a steel and asbestos door for an airtight fit. He wrapped the liner in baling wire strung over insulators and encased the entire thing in cement. Lastly he ran a current through the baling wire until it went red-hot.

It took six hours, but the whole box came up to heat and stayed there. After Hiram popped the plates in, he clamped the door tight and flushed out the air with nitrogen. After half an hour he cut the current, flushed the inside with cooler nitrogen and then air, unclamped the box, and took out dry plates. He mailed sample plates to Ford, along with two sketches of the furnace and one photo of himself standing beside the furnace.

His neighbor Harold Floyd Plimstubb took the photo. He also insisted on filing patents for the door seal and clamping, the nitrogen flushing, the heating elements, and the overall oven.

Wallace Hiram happily waited for Ford Motor Company to send him more plates. Instead they put in an order for fifty batch furnaces. Hiram sold his car—appropriately, it was an old Stanley Steamer—and Hiram, Inc., began building metal processing furnaces in his garage.

Assembly was slow, and Ford pressed for speed; Hiram didn't know what to do. Harold Plimstubb, on the other hand, had more vision than Hiram; he also had more money and a bigger garage. Plimstubb leased patents from Hiram and founded Plimstubb Furnaces.

Through the next thirty years, the two companies kept up a semiamiable rivalry. Whenever Hiram's business flagged, he slowly and patiently invented a new twist on heating metals. Whenever Plimstubb needed to catch up and Hiram needed development money, Plimstubb leased another of Hiram's patents. Neither of them was terribly concerned by the realization that he was keeping his own competition alive.

In April 1928 Wallace Hiram created the first efficient combustible atmosphere furnace, keeping oxygen and water away from the work and dramatically reducing scrap rates for production. By December 1929 he had invented a conveyor belt drive for an atmosphere furnace, open at either end, which never stopped processing work. It halved the scrap rate and doubled parts production.

The Depression was a bad time to double production. By the time Plimstubb had found buyers and Hiram leased the design to Plimstubb, Hiram's shoes had holes in them and he was worn out from dashing down alleyways off Broad Street to avoid anxious collectors for the Providence Old Stone Bank. Hiram took Plimstubb's check over the first hot meal Hiram had eaten in three days, and actually wept shaking hands.

And so they went, on into the early war years, like some odd vaudeville team. Hiram perfected a small tempering furnace for shipboard machine shops; Plimstubb mass-produced it. Hiram devised a return-conveyor system to semiautomate parts production at arms plants; Plimstubb set up the first furnace assembly line either of them had ever needed—and reversed historical trends by leasing the assembly-line plans back to Hiram. By now they both had side-by-side plants on the Moshassuck River, just below Federal Hill in Providence; they watched each other warily in the infrequent intervals when they had time.

In 1940 Plimstubb was approached by a spectacled, dark-suited gentleman named Stampe, from the War Department. Stampe wanted Plimstubb to come up with a gas-tight furnace for high-temperature alloy steel processing. The end product was to be a durable, heat-resistant, light weight propeller shaft. Plimstubb listened carefully to the proposal, asking as many questions about the war in Europe as he did about part size and cool-down rates. Stampe, cooling down some himself, assumed that Plimstubb was an isolationist.

At the end of the meeting Plimstubb thanked him and

promised to consider it, and, after Stampe had left for the train station, drove quickly to the bank.

Then Plimstubb walked unhesitatingly into Hiram's plant, threw a leather valise containing Stampe's request and thirty thousand dollars onto Hiram's battered drafting desk, and said quietly, "This one's on me."

Subsequently, Plimstubb became the chair of a committee overseeing metals processing for aircraft. The job was far more than full-time, and for the rest of the war he seldom visited his factory, which went its own way unsupervised, settling a little farther into neglect every day and dreaming its own creaky machine dreams.

One week after the initial visit from Renfrew, the Nieuw Amsterdam Metalworks government project arrived at Plimstubb. "Arrived" was the correct, unnerving word; one morning at seven, the molybdenum hearth grid was in a slatted open crate leaning against the shipping bay door. The front gate was still locked, and there were no signs of a break-in to make the delivery. A note tacked to the box said simply to notify Grady Cavanaugh in Sales that his order was in.

Maintenance, with stubborn glee, set it in the middle of his desk. Grady borrowed a hammer, pulled the note off the tack, knocked the crate open, and measured the hearth grid four times before calling Renfrew. He left a message with the secretary, grinning; of course Renfrew was late.

With some hesitation he called Stode at all the available numbers. It bothered Grady considerably that, at a government office, no one at all had answered the phone on a weekday at the first two numbers he called.

Stode answered at the final, unlabeled number. "Stode. Subject?"

"Cavanaugh." He cleared his throat. "Subject: molybdenum hearth grid purchased from the Nieuw Amsterdam

Metalworks." He glanced around for the note with his name on it, but it was nowhere in sight. Maybe it had slipped behind the desk. "It's here."

In the silence he said tentatively, "Do you have an address where we can ship it?"

"Is it complete?"

"Yes."

"Does the workmanship look good?"

"Very good." Grady had been impressed with the clean edges and smooth surfaces. Whoever worked on this was an expert machinist.

"Did you measure it?"

"Of course," Grady said curtly, glad that he had.

"Is the material good?"

"I haven't tested it." He added, trying not to sound plaintive, "I don't have any way to do a nondestructive test—"

"Call Renfrew. I'll visit your plant. Ten A.M. tomorrow." The line went dead.

Grady blinked. He had been fairly sure this was a long-distance call. He checked around his desk another time for the missing note before giving up; suddenly he had work to do.

After calling Renfrew back, Grady stepped out to check progress on the dryer. It was ridiculous, since some of the parts had a two-week lead time, and a dryer for private industry had a low priority unless the industry had a reason for rushing a wartime contract. Still, it was the first piece he had sold in three weeks, and he hoped that a speedy delivery would lead to a furnace contract.

He stepped through the doorway to the shop and was nearly blinded. He leaned on his cane, blinking back tears, and squinted into the east windows. Yesterday they had been so dust- and smoke-covered that the Fab Department, by the windows, had needed electric lights on all day.

Now two men on ladders, silhouetted against the windows, were polishing the glass with rags. Neither heard him coming, his cane taps hidden by the metallic slam-thud of the brake shear as it cut metal and the snarl of the grinding wheel as it smoothed the edges. He recognized one of the silhouettes. "Sonny!"

Sonny grunted, rather than answer with the usual amiable blues quote.

"How come you're not driving the truck?"

"'Cause it wouldn't fit on the ladder. Roy—Mr. Burgess—put me up here. I got nowhere else to drive."

"Not even to pick up parts, or . . ." He stopped as the implications hit him. Having no deliveries was bad enough, but a work crew with time to clean windows was scary.

The man on the other ladder, reaching too far, wobbled; Sonny stretched out a quick arm and steadied him. "You watch yourself, Mr. Franklin."

Jerry Franklin caught himself and said automatically, "Thanks, boy." He shook his head. "That sounds funny, me calling you 'boy.'" Jerry was fifteen, and had been at Plimstubb a week.

"Well, my name's Sonny. Just don't call me Sonny Boy."

Jerry gave a high laugh and sang in an overdone bad baritone, "Climb upon my knee, Sonny Boy. . . ." Sonny chuckled as politely as though it were the first time he had heard it, and steadied the ladder again.

Benny Behind passed him, headed for the drill press. Roy Burgess called out, "Hey, Benny! How's married life?"

Benny shook his head worriedly. "She don't blow me so good."

Grady's jaw dropped but Roy cackled; he'd been expecting the answer. Sonny frowned, looking beyond Grady. He turned and saw Susan, face a bright scarlet, looking in the shop door. She disappeared quickly; Grady waited until she was gone and went back to the front offices.

In midafternoon he went out again and stared, astonished, at the line of workers, time cards in hand.

Jerry said heavily, "No more overtime." It didn't appear to bother him much.

Billy Hancock, a stocky, bushy-browed electrician, added glumly, "And it wasn't replaced with double time, either." Billy never smiled at his own jokes or anyone else's.

Grady looked up and down the long line of slouching men. They already had jackets and hats on, and they looked uncomfortably like the bread lines in Providence when Grady was ten. "You're kidding me. Fellas, there's a war on."

A rich voice behind him boomed, "That's why we did almost nothing but navy furnaces for a year. That's how we lost half our civilian contracts when they had to go elsewhere." Warren Hastings moved forward, but not too close to the shop; his pinstripe suit was immaculate, and his patent-leather shoes shone. "We only kept the defense contractors. Shouldn't you be selling something?"

But for some reason he seemed almost genial, not his usual snappish self. He spun around and left, striding as always too fast for Grady to keep up.

Grady sighed. "What's with him? Usually he'd take my head off."

"Read the bulletin board," Billy said, and added hopefully, "Are you selling something?" Billy had eight children, and only the two oldest were in the service.

"Doing my damndest," Grady promised, and went inside to avoid more questions.

He checked the bulletin board in Sales. There was a

stained list of the year's paid holidays, an old and largely ignored notice banning playing cards for money during lunches and breaks, and . . .

Grady frowned, reading the announcement typed on letterhead.

> *Because of declining sales and the need to seek out new customers and new equipment, I am pleased to announce the promotion of Sales Manager Warren Hastings to vice president of operations. Mr. Hastings will focus on increasing customers through improved design and the manufacture of low-cost equipment.*
>
> *Sincerely,*
> HIRAM PLIMSTUBB

Below that, in an almost apologetic postscript,

> *I know that my War Board duties and some of my other work have kept me out of the plant more than I wished, and perhaps I should have watched our sales more closely. Please give Warren your utmost respect and cooperation in his new post; he has promised great things.*

Behind Grady, Susan said softly, "So the whole shop gets a pay cut and he gets more."

"We don't know that," Grady said. As her mouth quirked, he held up his hand quickly. "And you know what? I wouldn't say stuff like that around here anymore."

All she said was, "I thought you said this place was nice."

He sighed. "I'm going back to the shop. Want to come?"

He turned automatically for the shortcut through the

men's room, then spun back with a grimace for the long way, through the lobby. Susan, he noted, was careful to walk at his pace.

They entered the shop and stared. The afternoon sun gleamed through the west windows, shining on the deserted tool benches, one of them polished till it reflected the sunlight onto the ceiling in ripples. The shadows were sharp and clear on the bare floor where, just weeks before, half-built batch furnaces for the navy had stood row on row. The high, arched windows made the two-story brick factory seem like an abandoned cathedral, its stained glass broken and its congregation gone.

Grady opened his mouth but was afraid to speak in that silence, afraid of the inevitable echo in the emptiness. They turned quietly and left, Grady's cane, despite his best efforts, rapping on the worn concrete.

The next morning, a high wind whipped the American flag in front of the building to and fro; at the moment the wind was coming in from the bay, blowing at an angle toward the building and spattering the glass doors with huge drops, which banded together and ran down the glass in ripples. A hurricane had come up the coast, dumping heavy rain on Rhode Island. Grady's dad had been called out, along with the rest of the Seabees, to clean up damage and clear the streets.

Now Grady could barely see out, but there was little to see; the wartime auto traffic, light already, had reduced to nothing in the storm. Downtown was flooding; nobody sane would be out in this. Grady was haunting the reception area, waiting for Stode.

Grady had given up and was walking toward the door for Sales when Talia shrieked. He spun around. A bony hand, followed by a bony arm in a black cotton sleeve, had pushed the door open. The nearly empty sleeve flapped in the wind.

A dark coat, topped with a broad-brimmed dark hat, followed. The hat was tilted down until the brim met the turned-up coat collar; Grady thought for one jarring moment of The Shadow. Water ran in rivulets off the brim and down the coat, which seemed empty.

Then the brim snapped up and Talia cut herself off in a second shriek. Grady stared at a jaw as narrow and straight as the trench-coat collar. Just below the hat brim were a pair of sunken, dark eyes; below them, below the knife-edge nose but above the bone-sharp jaw, was a narrow, barely amused smile.

Talia let out a shaky breath. "You frightened me," she said reproachfully, and added in the same voice, "and you woke me up."

The man's head snapped to his left as he stared full-face at Grady. "Cavanaugh?"

Grady swallowed and said with more courage than he felt, "You're late."

An angle turned at the far corner of Stode's mouth; it might have been a bigger smile. "Your watch is fast."

And it was.

"Shall we wait for Renfrew?"

The angle—in fact, all angles—to Stode's mouth disappeared. "He'll be late. Show me the hearth grid."

They walked into Sales. Grady was disconcerted to find that Stode, striding ahead on legs like broomsticks, knew the way to Grady's office. Stode paused at the door to let Grady open it. Stode still had his coat and hat on.

He leaned over the desk, putting his palms beyond the moly grid, his face dropping nearly to the level of the desk. After a moment he said quietly, "It's remarkably smooth."

"I noticed that, too." The Nieuw Amsterdam Metalworks must have been polishing it around the clock for a week to get that finish. "It wasn't in the spec."

Stode nodded only slightly, his hat brim magnifying the gesture and nearly touching the immaculate grid. A drop fell on it; Stode rubbed it out with a single long index finger, tracing the moisture across the metal until it disappeared.

He turned. "Where is the off-site facility? What was their materials source?"

Grady said with barely a quaver, "The factory is near Wallkill, New York. I haven't asked where they got the molybdenum."

Stode nodded so briefly that no more moisture fell off his hat. "Find out."

"Yes, sir." Grady was frustrated; this was no normal relationship with a customer.

Stode left without shaking hands. Five minutes later, Renfrew dashed in, looked at his watch, and said miserably, "I missed him."

"Not only that," Grady pointed out, "but you owe me another ten bucks. It's gonna come down to an all–St. Louis series, Browns vs. Cardinals."

"Think so? That'll be a fight."

"You bet. Can you imagine an all-Boston series, Braves against the Red Sox?"

After a moment Renfrew said sadly, "No, I can't." He paid up. "Was everything all right?"

"Nearly perfect. Sorry you missed him."

"I'm not." He hesitated, then said frankly, "I've never met anyone like him in all the years I've worked for Uncle Sam. And you know what scares me? Nobody I know has ever met him. Nobody at all."

"It's a big government," Grady said, but he was shaken.

Within two weeks, the gas dryer was built. Dryers didn't cost much because they didn't involve much—two heated steel tanks about a yard high, filled with "catalyst" (knobs from rocker arms built for Ford Motor Company). Each tank had a heater, and the heaters, in alternation, dried the moisture out of the catalyst for the next flow of processing gas. A timer switched the gas flow from the tower that was soaking with moisture to the tower that was dry. That was all there was. Grady always felt faintly guilty about selling one.

It could have been done faster if it were built entirely of stock items and required next to no design time.

During that time, Grady called Antony's return number twice, getting no answer either time. Apparently nobody was near the phone booth. He sent the order acknowledgment to the post office box on Antony's original RFQ for the furnace. Two days later he sent another letter, with Susan's question about the height requirements on the original quote, and he was paged for a call.

Susan stopped him in the lobby just after he had taken the call. "Are you getting me the rest of the data for the Incredible Legless Furnace? Does your customer want to crawl in on his belly and check it out?"

Grady shook his head. "That call was about our letter."

"So, what did he say?"

"I didn't talk to him. I spoke to the postmaster in Wallkill, New York."

"Wallkill?"

"Yeah." Grady looked troubled. "Antony never picked up my first letter, acknowledging the dryer order."

"Wow." Susan considered. "You'd better hope he pays you for the dryer."

"Thanks." Grady stared out the front door at the slick street. "Come on. Is it raining?"

Susan said seriously, "No, and we're all really worried about that stuff falling from the sky. What do you think it is?"

She left for her desk. Grady stared at the rain, thinking dark thoughts.

For two weeks, he fretted that he had been victim of a practical joke; some of the people in the plant had a rough sense of humor. Susan pointed out, with some justice, that no one would pull a joke that was going to get them fired. "Can you see somebody blowing three grand, plus your time and mine? Not here."

"That's true," Grady said relievedly. "Nobody wants to leave."

"Nobody can. Their skills are dated. Once they get in here, they can't leave."

"Like a lobster pot," Grady said.

Susan frowned at a pin-up calendar hanging at Tom Garneaux's desk. "I hate to think what they'd bait it with."

The following Friday, Grady's phone rang twice, the signal for a switchboard call. He snatched at it and Talia murmured grumpily, "There's a package for you. That's two this month."

"Sorry."

Five minutes later Talia, with an exaggerated sigh, dropped a battered, bulky manila envelope into Grady's hands and sat back, probably to fall asleep again.

It was from Antony. A regular-size business envelope taped to the outside contained a cover note that said simply, "I have sent you payment in full for the gas dryer by overnight mail. I will be calling you today at eleven to confirm delivery." It was ten-forty now.

Grady rolled up the note one-handed, swung it like a baseball bat and made a clicking noise with his tongue. "Over the fence, sweetheart," he said happily. "Kiss it good-bye."

Talia already had; her head was lolled back on the chair

headrest and she was snoring lightly. Grady went back to his office.

Grady turned the heavy envelope over in his hands. The address was handwritten, which was common, but so was the return address—to the same post office box Antony had given as his address before. Most companies used a letterhead.

As he opened it, the phone rang. He answered, and Antony said cheerfully, "Good morning, Mr. Cavanaugh. Did you get the money?"

"Hey, Antony—sorry; good morning, Mr. van der Woeden. I'm opening an envelope from you now." A single sheet of paper fluttered to the floor. Grady stooped for it and, distracted, caught the flattened green bill that followed it down. He stared at it. "You paid cash?"

"Made sense to me. Why, is there a problem?"

"I—well . . ." Grady hit on an excuse. "Listen, we haven't invoiced you yet. I'm not that familiar with interstate commerce and sales tax; there may be some odd dollars added to this. What do you know about New York sales tax?"

"Not a whole lot." To Grady's ears, Antony sounded suddenly cautious. "Listen, I've looked over your quote for a furnace. It looks great, but that's a lot of money. Can I get back to you? I've got to think about anything this big."

"Sure. There are some other cost options on the quote; the big one is start-up and training. Is this your first furnace?"

There was a moment's silence, then: "Let's just say our other equipment isn't as modern."

Since the basic design of the furnace had been unchanged in the past ten years, that wasn't encouraging. "I'd recommend some training, then."

"I don't think so," Antony said quickly. "Our people here

are very good at picking up skills; we teach them all in-house."

"Okay. Would you like our help hooking it up?"

"No!" Antony added more quietly, "Our people can hook it up. All I need is for you to get it to the drop-off point."

"Drop-off point?" Grady winced; suddenly his sinuses were bothering him a lot. "We're willing to deliver to your loading dock."

"Oh, that won't be necessary. Listen, I enclosed a map with the money. It should make it easy to get to the drop-off—"

"You should have waited until we invoiced you," Grady said helplessly.

Antony was confused. "Why? You said you'd make the dryer for me if I bought it." He went back to the directions. "You take the Greenville Pike west and drive to Pough-keepsie, cross the Hudson, and turn south toward Wallkill."

His pronunciation of "Wallkill" sounded foreign to Grady. "What about highway numbers?"

"They're marked." Antony sounded uncertain. "Mostly. Go past Wallkill maybe five miles, turn uphill—I mean, left—and go another two miles. There's a diner on your right, the Schuylkill Diner. Pull in there."

"Just drop it off by the diner in the parking lot?" Grady said quietly. He was rubbing his temples.

There was a short silence at Antony's end. "Well, not right by the diner. Put it over by the trash bin, at the edge of the lot." He added, not too convincingly, "It's easier to load and unload there."

"By the trash bin."

"Sure. You can't miss it. Oh, and if you try the diner, have the apple pie with cheddar cheese. Nobody makes it better. Listen, I'd better go."

"Right. Call me again about the furnace quote anytime."

Grady hung up and tipped the envelope up to look inside.
Something round and heavy rolled out and tapped his nose;
he jerked his head back.

Four twenty-dollar gold pieces, still in near-mint condition, spilled across his desk.

At his end, Antony hung up the receiver and shakily hopped
off the rock by the phone. "He knows. Or he suspects." He
hugged himself, shivering. "Oh, God, I'm in so much
trouble." He ran back through the underbrush to the box
culvert.

At his end, Grady looked at the envelope as though it would
bite, and cautiously slid the remaining cash out. It was in
packets of different bills neatly tied with brown string; one
of the packets had come undone. Grady replaced the loose
bill on that packet and undid the other packets with his
Barlow knife. "Not for nothing," he muttered, "I feel like a
bookie."

He stopped and turned over a loose bill, staring. Grady
turned it over. He had no idea what it was, but knew that it
was unlike any U.S. bill he had ever seen.

After that he sorted through the packets carefully, checking the contents. The oldest one, a folded-up sheet of
foolscap, held a bank note from 1873, another twenty-dollar
gold coin with an eagle on it, and fourteen silver dollars
spanning five decades. Even the newest packet had strange
bills in it, of odd sizes and denominations, many with
elaborate engraving.

Grady took it to the company treasurer, Chester Traub.
Chester spent his entire nonworking life either reading or
going to the movies; Grady was confident that he knew
everything.

As Grady walked into the doorless office, Chester put

down his newspaper, folded back to Hedda Hopper's column. "Just killing a little time on a slow day," he said self-consciously. "What can I do for you, son?" Everyone under forty-five was either "son" or "kiddo" to Chester.

Grady handed him the bill. "What the hell is this?"

Chester barely needed to glance at it. "How soon they forget. A twenty-dollar silver certificate. Didn't you study history? William Jennings Bryan, the "Cross of Gold" speech, the gold standard?" Grady shook his head. "It's supposed to be redeemable in silver." He held it up to the light. "It's larger than a regular bill; now they're tens, and Hoover shrunk them." Chester added bitterly, "Just like he did Wall Street. You should see the early bills, all engraved like you wouldn't believe. Much prettier than real money."

Grady's stomach lurched, thinking of the stacks in his office. "They're not real money?"

"Oh, they're real, all right. The twenties just aren't issued anymore." He passed it back. "Find it in your dad's dresser drawers?"

"No . . ." He swallowed. "I got it in a cash payment recently."

"You ought to hang on to it; probably you can double your money, at least. You don't see many of these anymore."

"Terrific." Grady turned to leave, then spun around. "Chester, you know a lot about business."

He shrugged. "Somebody here should."

"Okay." He took a deep breath. "How can you tell when somebody's trying to smuggle something?"

"Look over your shoulder for pirates."

"No, I mean it. If I were quoting something, how would I know if the customer was planning to smuggle it out of the country?"

Chester pushed at his bifocals, thinking. "There're a

couple of ways. When an order is placed, the War Department may check on a customer." He grinned at Grady.
"Unless, of course, the government's doing the smuggling,
like they did for England at the start of the war."

Grady didn't think that likely. "What would the Feds
look for?"

Chester ticked them off. "Maybe the buyers are willing
to pay an outrageous price, or cash, or some informal
agreement. Maybe they're not telling you enough about
their use of the product so that you can be sure they're
telling the truth at all. Maybe they don't seem to know a lot
about the equipment, or about business. Maybe you can't
find them in *Thomas Register* or any other standard business
directory, or they're new and have no history. . . ."

Most of which was true about the Nieuw Amsterdam
Metalworks. "I thought you checked all that with every
purchase order." He swallowed. "Take that dryer customer I
have. When he pays—"

"Net thirty days," he said automatically.

"Okay." Grady realized with relief that he had thirty days
to turn the crumpled cash he'd been given into something
more sensible. "Will you try to check on him?"

"Why bother? Nobody'd buy one unless they had a
factory, and we know where the dryer went." He raised an
eyebrow. "If he asks for special delayed payment terms on
a furnace, I'll check his credit. But again, why bother? We
keep the furnace until all but the final payment." He
thumped his desk. "No mazuma, no machine."

"Makes sense. So you check the big purchase orders."

Chester looked guilty. "Not really. Not until they miss a
payment, usually." He waved an arm at his desk, which was
cluttered with overdue notices. "Look at this place; who has
the time?"

I do, Grady thought but did not say. Aloud he asked, "What else tells you that somebody's smuggling?"

"Well, if they ask for delivery to a warehouse or a middleman, or they seem cagey about telling you the final destination of the equipment. That's all I know." He beamed. "How's that?"

"Terrific," Grady said bleakly. "What's the penalty for smuggling atmosphere equipment?"

"You mean furnaces?"

"Let's say I meant dryers."

"Wouldn't make any difference. If it has a use for military application, prison and a fine for you, maybe, if you lie about it on a customs document. Are you selling something overseas?" He was too eager; Plimstubb had a number of bills ninety days overdue.

"Just curious." Grady fumbled for something to say. "Why would the government care about our stuff?"

"About the furnaces?" Chester tapped a pencil on the desk for emphasis. "Look at all the aircraft work we've done." He leaned forward. "Some of it top secret."

"Military secret?"

Chester looked at Grady's face and laughed. "Not really, not at our end. But anything that heats metal in a way you could use for aircraft they'd watch pretty closely. Has anybody ever told you how this place helped make the furnaces to build the Mustang P-51 prototypes?"

Grady nodded, but listened anyway. He had been proud of Plimstubb's role until just this minute.

"Well, I doubt that anyone else could duplicate that without the Mustang designs, but once they had them they'd need a Plimstubb furnace. And with that they could harden the alloy for the cowlings, the ailerons—"

"I get the idea. Thanks." Grady stumbled away to the water cooler. After a quick slurp, he stared at his ghostly reflection on the water bottle and said bleakly, "Oh, God, I'm in so much trouble."

He went back to his office and put the silver certificate back in Antony's envelope, wondering absently where Antony's cover letter had gone. Eventually, even though he hated it, he left his office, walked through Design Engineering, and stepped into Warren Hastings' office.

It was the only paneled and carpeted office in the plant. The desk was nearly as large as Grady's office. The meeting table, with its beautiful padded chairs, was larger. Warren Hastings was on the telephone in the corner, an idle finger close to playing with the dial. That telephone was the most modern piece of equipment in the plant.

Warren laughed at something and made a reply, brushing his sleek, dark hair back with one hand before he saw Grady. "Can I call you back?" he said easily. "Fine. Later." He put down the handset and said coldly, "I prefer that you knock when I'm on the phone."

"Sorry, Warren. I just wanted to ask permission; we're delivering that dryer this afternoon, and I wanted to go meet the customer face-to-face."

"It's not your territory, is it?"

"Oh, I know. I'll split any commission with Fleischer."

Ed Fleischer's office, Furnace Solutions, operated from a dilapidated Ford touring car. Ed was semiretired, but very defensive about his sales territory, with the result that little had sold in upstate New York in ten years. "I'll call Ed, or at least leave a message."

Warren nodded. "All right. Work the contact, get a feel for what they need." He smirked. "I'd offer you the company car, but—"

"Thanks anyway." The real company car, an unbelievably abused Model T, was up on blocks at the moment, waiting for money to replace four tires and a stripped engine. Warren, by contrast, had held out for a Cadillac (violating the company's Fords-only policy) as his own company-provided car when he took the job.

He picked up customers in it and drove it to and from work; he had never, to anyone's memory, let a Plimstubb employee drive it. "Enjoy your trip." His blue eyes bored coldly into Grady. "And try to sell something." He put more venom in it than the shop would have. "You haven't been terribly successful lately."

Grady struggled to say something less offensive than "Nobody here has" and less banal than "It's the war" and finally settled on, "Okay." He spun around.

Susan saw Grady leave Warren's office. "What's up?"

"I'm going along with the dryer."

"As an extra option, or as spare parts? I hope Warren got a good price for you." She looked at him narrowly. "Are you planning on getting my answers today?"

Grady shrugged. "Or at least a snack at the Schuylkill Diner."

Garneaux, while pretending to work, had been listening.

"The Schuylkill Diner? Say . . ." Garneaux dropped the blueprint he'd been halfheartedly correcting and rummaged in his right-hand file drawer. He doubled over as though he were diving into the back of it. A moment later, he straightened. "Here's the menu. Try the pork roast and the apple pie with cheddar." He winked. "And see if Nora is still there. What a woman."

"That's two votes for the apple with cheddar. Man, you've eaten everywhere."

"Pretty impressive, considering I've only worked here."

Susan said politely, "Oh, have you worked here?"

Garneaux frowned at her, winked again at Grady, and went back to the blueprint.

There was a loud honking; Grady barely looked up in

time to see Benny Behind, jeans to his knees, hanging his
backside out the driver's side window of his pickup truck.

Blaine, in from R&D, squinted. "Is he well? Seems to me
he's losing weight."

Garneaux commented, "Nah, but he's gaining time."

"It is early." Grady checked his watch. "Three-thirty?"

"Still no more overtime," Susan said, her mouth set in a
thin line. "There's not enough work."

Grady walked the hallway between Sales and Engineering and opened the glass door at the end. He walked all the
way out onto the factory floor.

The lights had been turned out; golden shafts of afternoon sun, flecked with dust motes, shone down from the
now-spotless windows near the ceiling and marked regular
squares on the nearly empty concrete floor below. It was
big, gray, and empty; now it felt like a long-abandoned
church. Grady shivered and went quickly back to his office.

The weather was beautiful the next day. The dryer was
spray-painted outdoors at eight-thirty, the paint was dry by
eleven, and it was loaded on the company flatbed by
eleven-ten.

The truck (a Ford; in spite of Warren Hastings, Hiram
Plimstubb had shown loyalty over the years) had more than
two hundred thousand miles on it; a shop worker with a
battered flivver of his own worked nearly full time keeping
it running. It had a rusted crane on the end; Grady looked at
it uneasily and shifted on the seat, listening to the springs
creak. Sonny LeTour, plant driver and handyman, was
assigned to drive the truck.

Roy Burgess stopped by to see them off. "You've got a
good day for it, anyway." He slapped the car door. "Drive
slow." Many Rhode Islanders said that, but Grady had never
met a Rhode Islander who drove "slow," wartime speed
limits or not.

Sonny tucked his head into a faded baseball cap that had once been blue, checked the mirrors, and called to Burgess, "I'm a natural-born easeman on the road again."

Burgess scowled. "Talk like a white man, goddammit."

Grady and Sonny both winced. Susan, by the water bubbler, stared coldly at Burgess.

Grady said as they pulled out, "Man, I wish he wouldn't talk like that."

"True as it can be." Sonny tugged hard on his side mirror, adjusting the angle. "Pull your mirror in some . . . Burgess is old, and hard to change. Just like everybody else will be, all my life." He caught himself. "Just like you and I, by and by." They rolled out the plant gate.

"So who said 'the natural-born easeman line,' Bill Broonzy?"

"Furry Lewis. 'Kassie Jones.'" He sang in a put-on croak, "'Lord, people said-a Kassie run over time, he got nothin' to lose but the one oh-nine . . .'" He went on, occasionally closing his eyes, all but ignoring the traffic as they switched lanes in U.S. 1 and sped up, headed south. Grady clung to his armrest; Sonny saw his face and slowed down.

At the end of the song, Sonny pulled over. "Can you shift one of these?"

"Not real well."

Sonny pulled out his battered six-string. "In that case, can you play slide guitar with a broken beer bottle?"

"I'll drive."

They pulled out again, jerkily. Ten miles later, Grady, cigarette dangling from his mouth, was singing along on "Rollin' and Tumblin'," his problems briefly forgotten.

The weather was crisp and clear; there had already been a frost, but southern New England was a few weeks shy of fall color. Grady didn't mind the drive, even when his ankle bothered him, and he truly enjoyed the singing.

Antony's directions were clear, the traffic nonexistent. Grady and Sonny stared out as the hills got higher; northern New Englanders call residents of Rhode Island "Flat-landers." The Appalachian Mountains in the afternoon sun made them both catch their breath at the foliage and the lush, tree-covered valleys.

The drive took four hours. On the way, Grady learned "Bulldog Blues," four new and unlikely verses to "Kind-hearted Woman Blues," and a song by someone who, Sonny insisted, recorded under the name "Little Hat Jones." He asked for that one three times, trying to memorize the words.

It was midafternoon when they drove down Main Street in Wallkill. Grady pointed out the factory at the end of the street. "Hudson Drill. They're one of our customers."

"You know 'em by heart?"

"That's not too hard these days." They swung out of town and up into the hills.

A half hour later they pulled into a parking lot of the Schuylkill Diner, halfway up Tuckamoose Mountain.

Grady looked around. "This is it." The Schuylkill Diner, a beautiful chrome and metal affair that looked vaguely like Car of the Future at the New York World's Fair, lay at the end of the gravel parking lot. The trash bin Antony had mentioned in his telephone call was at the other end.

The trash bin, a rust-red affair with splintered boards where it had been rammed at least twice, was flanked by thick brush on either side. It was, Grady realized uneasily, the least visible area of the parking lot. He drove over to it.

Grady stared out the driver's window at a fluttering note: IF I DON'T MEET YOU, LEAVE THE DRYER HERE. —ANTONY VAN DER WOEDEN.

Sonny put aside his guitar. "What now?"

"We wait."

They went into the diner. Grady had the pie, but he was too busy watching out the window to enjoy it. Nora the waitress remembered Garneaux and smiled. No one came in and asked about a gas dryer.

Three cups of coffee and nearly an hour later, no one had showed. They settled up and walked back to the truck.

"Now what?" Sonny didn't look much like he cared.

"Just a sec." Grady pulled a pen and a folded sheet of paper from his pocket and scribbled a quick note. He pulled some cloth tape off a patch on the truck seat and taped his note to the trash bin:

Mr. Van der Woeden:

I was afraid to drop the dryer off when you weren't here; it's small and easy to steal. Call me, and maybe we can make better delivery arrangements next time.

Regards,
Grady Cavanaugh

He frowned at it and added to the bottom, "I'm still very interested in quoting a furnace for you."

"Now what?" Sonny repeated.

"Now we leave."

Grady swung back into the cab and they took off for Rhode Island. Sonny stared into the gathering shadows and crooned mournfully, "Goin' down the road feelin' baaad. . . ." Grady felt like howling along.

Antony trudged back inside the factory dejectedly, the note clutched in his fist. He was so absorbed that he bumped into the raccoon, who made a low, resentful murmur. "Sorry, Becca." He patted her absently and opened the grating.

He had hoped they would simply drop it off and leave; this whole business was getting complicated. If he thought Grady would let it go now and keep the money, he would gladly have left his savings behind, but it was clearly too late.

Once in the cavern, he was still absorbed; he nearly walked between Dietrick and his forge. The older dwarf looked up resentfully, but didn't let go of the pallet he had shoved inside a brick kiln, and never stopped singing in his gravelly, almost tuneless voice. "Sorry," Antony said, and backed away before he distracted Dietrick and spoiled the work.

A hand on his back startled him, and he spun around.

"Kirsten." Normally he'd be happy to see her.

"Where is it?" She looked at the paper in his hands, as though the dryer might be wrapped in it.

Antony shook his head. They walked quietly over to the far wall, both of them glancing from side to side surreptitiously.

Antony noticed that Pieter was watching from the railing outside the main office door; Pieter smiled tolerantly and kindly and went back inside his office without saying anything. Antony felt even guiltier than he had sneaking out in midafternoon.

Not surprisingly, the area near the GNOMENGESELL-SCHAFT tunnel was deserted. Light flickered from one side onto the rock wall that blocked their view beyond the tunnel. Antony felt the hair on his neck prickle and move as they neared it; he couldn't tell whether that was something in the air, or his own nerves. Kirsten, after glancing into the tunnel, said, "What happened?"

Antony handed her the note. "They won't drop it off. They have to see me first."

Kirsten read the note quickly and folded her arms. "You can't consent to bringing them here."

"I know. Look, I wouldn't bring them in without your knowledge. I promise."

"All right." Her frown relaxed and she reread the note. "He doesn't say he needs to see the plant, at least."

"That's what I thought, too." He tried to sound eager. "So if I can just make arrangements to sneak out of here one more time—"

A soft, amused voice said, "Does this mean you are up to something?"

A huge shadow appeared on the rock wall beyond the tunnel entrance. Kirsten and Antony backed away.

The shadow was human but irregular, its outline changing constantly, as though the light that cast it were moving. "Of course I mean you, generic, not you, specific. Is your company making a business move of some kind?"

Tiny moths, attracted by the light, circled the outline of the shadowed figure. A bat detached from the entrance ceiling and flitted eagerly after the moths. "We have a deal, you know, your people and mine. It limits the scope of your independent dealings."

The shadow of an arm moved after the bat, and another arm, and another. The bat dodged and twisted, only its shadow staying in sight. "You wouldn't be trying to cheat us, would you?"

A final shadow-arm swept up and grabbed the shadow-bat in long, slender fingers. The bat squeaked, terrified; Kirsten made very nearly the same noise in sympathy. She stepped forward, then caught herself.

"Nobody's trying to cheat you," Antony said.

"And yet you're conducting secret business? My, my. If

you're violating the terms of our deal, your Pieter is in for a very harsh night."

Antony moved squarely into the doorway but could see no one. He looked up at the giant shadow and said, "Pieter hasn't done anything. My name is Antony; if you have a problem, you come to me."

"Oh, we might." The bat squeaked and struggled, and its shadow was suddenly unrecognizable. "Yes, we just might."

The voice added, muffled around crunching. "And my name is Klaus. Perhaps we'll meet again later."

The shadow shook one of its arms. A spot of blood flicked onto the archway near Antony; Kirsten and he ducked involuntarily. When they looked up again, the shadow was gone.

"Glad that's over," Antony muttered, and sat on a nearby rock.

"Thank you for protecting Pieter." Kirsten added, with a mild note of reproof, "That's my job, you know."

"Sorry. I just hate thinking something could happen to Pieter and it's my fault." He didn't add that he had known Kirsten would step in if he hadn't.

She looked at him dubiously but let his explanation stand. "Why are you sitting?"

"Because I'm shaking, and I don't want you to notice." He looked up at her. "You think I should just forget about modernizing?"

Kirsten glanced into the archway and said softly, "We lost another account today."

"You're kidding. Which one?"

"Elders of Chelm, in Poland. They had a standing order for—"

"Mirrors of wisdom, sure." In spite of his anxiety, he chuckled. "They reflect blank images for all but the wise. Every year they order more, saying last year's mirrors are broken because they can't see their reflections. It's steady work. . . . What, they finally figured it out?"

"I doubt it, and I don't think they're upset with us. We got a letter saying the village is gone. Something to do with relocation and the war."

"I hope nothing bad happened to them. Okay, so we need to replace the work, and we do need modern equipment." Antony stared ahead, not looking at anything. "Kirsten, what if I've put Pieter in danger?"

"Then I'll keep him out of it as best I can," she said firmly.

"If they think I'm doing contract business, you can't."

Kirsten said nothing.

Antony thought. "Can I have permission to leave the plant for a few days? You can tell Pieter it's personal business." He grimaced. "So far, it is."

"What are you going to do?"

"I'll go pick up the dryer."

"But they didn't leave it." Then she understood, and her eyes went wide. "All the way to Rhode Island? To a city?"

"Change is good for me," he said mechanically. He added, "And I'm not afraid."

He left to pack, wondering if he had just lied twice.

THREE

THE FRONT DOOR of Plimstubb was intentionally impressive. The oak panels were stained dark with factory smoke, but that only made them look older. The brass handle and knocker, constantly subject to salt tarnish, gleamed. Polishing that door was the first job of maintenance every sunny day. Wallace Plimstubb checked the condition of the door frequently, and said as often, "Remember, that door is the first anyone sees of us."

At a desk ten feet behind the door, Talia Baghrati dozed. Antony cleared his throat five times and finally knocked on the desk to get her attention.

She yelped, stared over him, then goggled down at him, hurt. "You frightened me out of several years of your growth."

"Sorry I scared you," Antony said politely. Actually, she scared him; he dealt with as small a number of humans as possible, and Talia didn't look like any of them. She had daubed on enough mascara that she looked like a well-dressed raccoon, and either she was wearing way too much perfume or she was in bloom. "I'm here to see a Mr. Grady Cavanaugh."

"You're in luck, then," she said, "because we have one of those. What a coincidence," she finished vaguely. "It never rains but it's wet."

Antony waited and finally said, "Would you call him for me?"

Grady was scribbling frantic reminders to himself: STAND UP STRAIGHT. LOOK CLIENT IN THE EYE. BE GLAD TO SEE HIM BUT NOT GRATEFUL; HE SHOULD FEEL LIKE THANKING YOU. He added, thinking of Tom Garneaux, OPTIMISM AND CONFIDENCE. He snatched up his cane and all but ran for the lobby at the first ring of the phone, spun back and answered it, thanked Talia, and barely remembered to straighten his tie before opening the lobby door. He took a deep breath and strode out.

He switched his cane to his left hand in time to shake hands. "Welcome to Plimstubb, Mr. van der Woeden."

Grady was smiling at Antony, noting that the customer's suit was new but seemed out of style; the lapels and the shoulder cut were too narrow, and something seemed strange about the breast pocket. Still, it fit perfectly and looked like it cost good money. Antony's hair seemed a little long, and his cheeks rosy, as though it were already cold. Before even noticing how short the customer was, Grady was staring at Antony's innocent-looking blue eyes and thinking before he even noticed he was looking down, "My God, he's young."

Antony was looking up at Grady's suit, which was short in the sleeves and tight in the shoulders; Grady was tanned and toughened from bicycling to and from work, but nothing else about him looked tough. His smile was open, his eyes genuinely friendly and innocent. Only the crinkling at the edges of the eyes and the bags under them said that he'd been taking on a little too much. Antony thought, stunned, *Hell, he's just a kid.*

Grady recovered first. "How was your drive?"

"Not bad. A couple of convoys—guess I shouldn't say where—but the drive was fine. I made as good time as the law will allow." He winked, though he wasn't feeling happy; he thought he'd been dealing with the head of sales.

Grady chuckled politely, wondering if Antony could possibly be authorized to buy a furnace. "Sorry for the mix-up earlier. Can I show you the dryer?"

"I'm hoping you can load it on my truck." Antony was anxious to get out and back as soon as possible.

Antony's evident nervousness bothered Grady. "Let's go look at it together and then the guys can load it up."

The shop was nearly empty; Antony looked at it shrewdly and decided to dicker on the furnace price. A few people glanced at them but kept working.

Roy Burgess, walking past, froze in midstride and said to Antony, "Say, how's the weather down there?"

Grady winced but Antony said easily, "Warm and continued sweaty since you came around. Aren't you about due for this month's bath?"

Roy blinked but tried again. "Guess I should call you Shorty."

"My friends call me Dutch." Antony smiled at him. "Hurry up and make a friend, so we can find out what they call you."

Roy considered this and turned to Grady. "I kinda like the little shit. Wait'll I saw the legs off a work bench and he's hired."

Grady said with a hiss, "He's a *customer.*"

"Oh, Jesus. I thought he was just some little rubbernecker. I meant . . ." Roy turned to Antony. "Mister, I'm sorry I was rude."

"Nah, you're sorry you were rude to a customer. But thanks." He stuck out his hand. Let's take a look at the dryer you built for me."

After shaking hands, Roy ducked back to his work. "Gotta check some tarps." As Grady and Antony stepped farther in, Grady quickly confirmed that, as he had requested, the Hudson Drill had a tarpaulin over it; the drill loading equipment, designed by Hudson, was proprietary.

Unfortunately, Roy was already in some kind of confrontation with Joe Cataldo, who was poking him in the chest. As Grady and Antony approached, Joe said with vicious triumph, "You remark on my words, one of us is a son of some bitches"—his voice rose—"and it AIN'T YOU!"

Roy rubbed his eyes. "Joey, you got it wrong again."

"What you mean?" Joe looked suddenly troubled. "I didn't say something nice about you, did I?"

"Forget it." He turned toward Grady and said hastily, "Get to work, Joey, we got a guest."

Joe ambled off, shaking his head and muttering, "Work on what? Nothing to do, nothing to do. . . ." It sounded like "Notha' ta da."

Antony barely noticed; the shop fascinated him. He flinched at the grinder sparks, jumped at the concussion from the brake shear, and delightedly traced the electrical cables back to their source. "This place has everything," he said enviously.

Grady looked at him uncertainly. "We've accumulated a lot of it over the years." The brake shear was rusty, the wire insulation frayed. He pointed to a band saw, the only new equipment (the old one had finally shaken itself apart). "We've started modernizing."

"Yah, sure," Antony said, catching himself and hoping he

hadn't looked naive. "Everybody's gotta keep up." He said to Roy Burgess, who was hovering nearby, "You run a great shop."

He stuck his hands in his hip pockets and puffed his chest out. "I do my best. Looks pretty good, doesn't it?"

"It's a fine operation. I was just telling Grady how much it has compared to shops I've seen."

Roy nodded proudly. "You bet your ass." He gestured to Grady. "Some college kid like this thinks everything has to be brand-spanking-new to work. He just sees how beat up the drill press is, or shit. Me"—he warmed to his topic—"I looked at all we got, hell, I feel like a Jew in a junkyard."

Grady froze. Antony sighed inwardly and said, as though confused, "You feel like Albert Einstein?"

"What?" Roy looked just as confused. Sonny LeTour, stacking boxes in shipping, stopped to listen.

"Maybe you feel like Sigmund Freud in a junkyard? I don't know what he'd be doing there.

"No." Roy's eyes darted from side to side, but nobody interrupted. "I mean, I don't know—"

"Or Jascha Heifetz. Maybe it's a music junkyard, you feel like Jascha Heifetz?"

Sonny, watching, was grinning.

Roy made a squeaking noise that could have meant anything.

Antony sighed out loud, apparently giving up. "I guess it's just one of those sayings that doesn't mean anything."

"That's it," Roy said with relief. "It doesn't."

"Doesn't matter, then." Antony pointed to the dryer. "Is this my dryer?" It looked like the picture in the advertising material.

"Well, sure," Roy said with surprise. "Hell, it's the only one in-house; if it ain't yours, we've both made a bad mistake."

"It looks beautiful." And it did, to Antony: two machined metal towers connected by neat-looking piping with right-angle bends and a motorized valve dead center. There was electrical wiring to some kind of timer, and power wiring to the tops of the heating elements.

But the paint job was scarred; Grady looked at it in horror. "Roy? I thought this was painted."

"This afternoon." He looked at Antony. "The cables rubbed some when we had it loaded before; we gotta touch it up. Hope you weren't planning on picking it up today."

Now Antony froze. "Actually, I was. Can't you load it on the truck?"

"Well, we gotta let the paint dry. It could dry on the truck, but it could smear, too."

"All right," Antony said unhappily. "I guess I can stay overnight." Though explaining where he'd been to Pieter when he got back would be interesting.

"Great, great." Roy walked away. "See you tomorrow."

Grady said quietly, "Roy is kind of free with his opinions—"

"Don't worry about it." Antony smiled, but his teeth were tight together. "I can handle him and anyone like him."

"Good for you." Grady was impressed; for someone as young as he looked, Antony had an awful lot of confidence. "Let's meet Engineering."

Susan, head down, was still working. Tom Garneaux, predictably, was looking fondly at a menu for Camillo's, on Federal Hill. He thumped it as they approached. "What a great place. Had four glasses of chianti and the veal parm; Jesus Christ, everything tasted terrific."

"Roy said he hated it there," Grady said cheerfully. "Tom, this is Antony van der Woeden, a customer of ours."

They shook hands. Antony, confused, glanced down at Tom's desk; there wasn't any work to be seen. There was a one-inch stack of restaurant menus, held down with a cross section from a thick metal rod.

Antony picked up the cross section and turned it over speculatively. Grady was silently impressed when Antony said thoughtfully, "Alloy steel—high hardness—light weight—you're doing work for the airplane factories, aren't you?"

"We did some aircraft work." Tom added apologetically, "That's kind of secret."

"It wasn't, back before the war. I'll bet you had companies doing their own tests at Hillsgrove."

"T. F. Green. Been a while since it was Hillsgrove. And actually, they tested at their own companies, in Ohio and California and wherever the hell they came from. It's changed since the old days, when the shops were at the airfields."

"Imagine that." Antony was far away, remembering. "Any fliers work here?"

"Some used to." Garneaux gestured at the picture behind Susan's desk. "Vince Rocci."

Susan stood. "My father." She extended a hand. "Good to meet you, Mr. van der Woeden. I did the prints for your furnace."

"They were good, too." Antony shook hands with her absently, then strolled behind the desk and stood on tiptoe. "Beautiful plane. Beats hell out of the old open-cockpit biplanes."

"I guess. At least it's made of metal."

Still admiring the Mustang in the picture, Antony said absently, "Piano wire and canvas did okay."

"Sounds pretty rickety to me."

"Rickety!" Antony laughed. "Say, they fell apart all the time, whether anyone shot at them or not. There was a pilot in the Signal Corps, Curly Larson, who crashed in France five times in one year. He was never shot down; he only crashed. He swore he was a great pilot but the planes were lousy. Once he stalled on takeoff and the field ambulance went tearing out, siren and all, to bring him back on a stretcher. They got there and he was sitting on the wreckage, ignoring the spilled gas, and smoking his pipe. They turned around and drove back, let him walk to the field. Curly was as mad as hell."

"You knew this pilot?" Grady stared again at Antony's smooth cheeks and youthful eyes.

Antony caught himself. "He told me the story himself. He said flying was crazy back in those days."

"It still is," Grady said with feeling. He had never flown and didn't intend to.

"It's not," Susan said firmly. "The old pilots were crazy. Now it's safe."

"You bet," Antony said hastily. "It's a desk job in midair now. I'll bet your dad is bored."

"Not as bored as I am," Susan said flatly.

Grady wished futilely that she had the knack of talking to customers. "By the way, Antony, where are you staying tonight? You didn't ask for hotel reservations." They weren't in Grady's sales budget. "Can I drive you to your hotel?" Grady was hoping frantically that the customer was picking up his own expenses. He couldn't hide the visit from Warren and turn in receipts at the same time.

Antony was wondering how to hide his absence from Pieter. "I hadn't figured on staying the night. Any chance I could stay at your house?"

Grady considered. "Well, sure. It's not the neatest just now—Dad's at Quonset, and Kevin's in Europe." He grinned. "Well, it's not the neatest when we're all home at once, either. But you're welcome to take Kevin's room for the night. Now," he said, and took a deep breath, "where do you want to go for dinner?"

Grady was praying that Antony didn't want to go to the Biltmore. It seemed to him every customer in the world had heard of the Bacchante Room and expected to be taken. Grady had no objections to a room full of tall, short-skirted waitresses with great legs, but he also had no desire to wear his good suit, which was four years out of date now, to anything but a funeral.

Plus he hadn't budgeted for dinner, either, and if Warren was in a bad mood when he got back, Grady would simply be out of pocket.

To his relief, Antony said easily, "Anyplace is fine."

Tom Garneaux interrupted, "You like fish?"

Antony said in surprise, "How do you know?" He was thinking uneasily of diviners and augurs, and the occasional Mirror of Truth. "I like catching them about as well as I do eating them, and I like catching them just fine."

"Fish and chips," Tom said firmly. "Or chowder. Maybe both." He scribbled an address on a pad. "Go to Ronnie's, at Hoxie Four Corners. Great chowder, the white and not the red, mind, I never liked his red. But I went there one Friday, took home a pint of chowder and an order of fish and chips, had four beers—"

Grady said, "I'll bet everything tasted fantastic."

"Fabulous."

Grady said thoughtfully, "I'll have to dine out with you someday."

"Any day you can afford the bail money. Say, Tony, do you have anything to do tomorrow?"

It took Antony a second to realize that Garneaux meant him. "Call me Dutch. I'm just driving home."

"Why doesn't Grady take you fishing? What do you usually go for?"

"Perch, trout—depends on where I am. I've caught a few sturgeon."

"Doesn't surprise me. You look patient enough." Tom looked away and said neutrally, "If you can deal with the noise you hear in the shop, you have the patience to fish."

Antony, relieved, grinned. "Hey, some of that noise is all right. They know their stuff out there."

"Some of that noise is pretty rude, Dutch." Tom grinned back. "I worked out there till I became an engineer. Then they threw me out for unnecessary roughness." He turned to Grady. "Hammer Houlihan has an old hulk he takes out on the bay. By the time you're done fishing, the shop boys'll have the dryer loaded."

That sounded good to Grady. A morning off work, a boat ride, no expenses. "What do you think, Antony?"

At first Antony didn't answer. He stared out the window, chewing his lip. Grady heard him murmur, "Change is good for me. And I am not afraid."

Aloud Antony said, "That would be fun. I've never done it."

"That's settled," Garneaux said with relief. "I'll talk to Hammer." He left his desk, walking quickly. Garneaux liked leaving his desk.

Antony watched him go. "Who's Hammer?"

"Hammer Houlihan. Works in the shop."

Antony nodded. "That's why the nickname."

Susan, catching Grady's eye, blushed. Actually, Hammer Houlihan also called himself the Hose of Tralee; if Antony thought the nickname came from a real hammer, that was fine with Grady.

His gratitude was short-lived. Susan looked up and said with real panic in her voice, "Ma!"

Mrs. Rocci bustled forward, bearing down on Susan's desk. She was carrying a purse the size of a bowling ball and wearing a threadbare cloth coat, and she was holding a second coat as though it were an accusation. "Hi, honey, you forgot this." She sniffed disapprovingly. "Has somebody been smoking at your desk?"

"Everybody." Grady tried not to grin as Susan casually shoved aside an ashtray full of cigarette butts with lipstick on them. "I don't need a coat; it's not that cold out."

She held it out unwaveringly. "You don't want to get a cold in your neck. Are you coming home for lunch?"

Susan resignedly took her coat. "Today. Tomorrow I'm having it with a customer."

Antony waved easily. "Antony van der Woeden. Good to meet you."

"Rose Rocci." She extended her hand but turned to Grady. "Where are you taking him for lunch? Someplace good?"

"Camillo's."

Rose looked horrified. "You know how much Camillo's costs, just for soup and a sandwich? Once I went there, I had a Coke and a nice plate of chicken parm, and you know how much that cost?" she demanded, as though Grady were personally responsible.

Susan said exasperatedly, "Ma, the company's paying." Grady quailed inwardly.

She waved an arm, her bracelet jingling. "You think this place is rich? Show me the tree out back, where they pick the money off. When the company's broke, who pays then?"

Grady blanched. It was an unwritten rule that a company trying to sell goods to another should not look desperate.

But Antony was enjoying the discussion hugely. "Your mom knows her what's what. I'll bet you ate good meals all through the Depression."

Mrs. Rocci beamed at him. "Doesn't she look like she ate good? Say, why don't you all come to my house?"

Susan closed her eyes. "Because then I'd have to shoot myself?"

But Antony was smiling back. "That sounds great. Grady, can you find me a place to buy bread and wine so I'm not a freeloader?" He was trying to be tight with his money, but there were limits.

"You've got it." Grady had no compunctions about pinching pennies.

"Till tomorrow then." He bowed without thinking. "It's been a pleasure."

"See you tomorrow," Mrs. Rocci all but cooed.

After she left, Antony said to Susan, "I think your mother's great."

"Good." She still had her eyes closed. "Marry her and take her out of state."

Dinner, a slow-cooking stew, was pleasantly drawn-out. At first Grady tried to chat about the Browns-Cardinals World Series, but Antony clearly knew little or nothing about baseball. After that, Antony asked questions, Grady answered, and somehow ended up telling the story of his life. At one point he realized he was standing, fencing with the butter knife, to show how he'd hurt his ankle. Antony responded with another story of the exploits of Curly Larson in the American Expeditionary Force. "He hadn't planned to box, but in Fort Snelling he slugged a military policeman."

"He slugged an MP?" Grady was impressed. "What did he do next?"

"About five days. It would have been more, but the MP couldn't find any witnesses."

Grady laughed. "Sounds like your friend Curly had a little too much beer."

Antony looked hurt. "Not a chance."

"No offense." Grady sipped at the wine, wishing he'd been more tactful.

Antony, sipping thoughtfully, slammed down his empty glass and said pensively, "Sloe gin. He never liked it again after that night."

"Where's Curly now?"

Antony looked out the window into the night, answering carefully. "I hear he reenlisted. He could be anywhere."

The rest of the meal was quiet. Antony looked around the house, at the pictures of Kevin and Grady and his father; the war was too much about absences. Antony insisted on doing the dishes and went to bed early with a stack of magazines under his arm, ready to read himself to sleep. Grady heard him moving around in Kevin's old room and slept better than he had since he'd begun sleeping in the house alone.

The next morning wasn't gray but white, one of those thick fogs that rolls in off the bay with no cloud cover above it and gradually turns brighter and brighter until it hurts the eyes. Grady dressed hastily and knocked on the guest room door.

"About time." Antony was seated on the edge of the made bed, fully dressed in khaki pants and a flannel shirt.

"How long have you been up?"

"Just a few minutes. I don't sleep late anyway." But he had his bag backed, and the stack of *Amazings* and *Astoundings* that Grady had lent him were nearly all upside down on the nightstand. Antony had his thumb on his place in the second-to-last magazine. "How's the weather?"

"Foggy." He saw Antony's face and added hastily, "But that means the bay will be mirror-smooth; you watch." He put on his own jacket and looked dubiously at Antony's shirt. "Are you gonna be warm enough? You could borrow a jacket from me—"

"Thanks, kid, but I'm funny-looking enough already. I'll be fine." But Antony's smile was strained.

Grady drove; Antony stared out the window in silence. They passed four other vehicles, one a milk wagon. Antony craned his neck to look at it. "Door-to-door delivery?"

"Well, sure." Grady wondered again where Antony lived. He rolled down the driver's-side window and smelled the tang of salt air. "Every other day. They were daily before the war."

The dirt road to the dock had deep ruts; Grady noted with relief that the only moisture on them was frost. They turned right, the trees gave way to marsh grass, and they had their first view of the water. It was barely stirring, but Grady felt the car seat shift as Antony stiffened.

He pulled to a stop. Antony said flatly, "We're not there yet."

"Almost." Grady hesitated, then said in a rush, "Look. Say the word and we turn around and go home. I'll tell everybody I overslept."

The dwarf bit his lip, staring at the water. "No. If I don't do it now, I'll never do it my whole life. But thanks. Thanks a lot."

Grady nodded and drove down to the harbor.

The dock was worn and slippery; the boards were bent. Houlihan, hearing them coming, said, "Step careful. That dock has seen some wear." He kept a patter up, talking Grady and Antony through the fog. "After dark through Prohibition, that dock was a goddamn parade. The first few years every boat that could make it three miles out to the supply ships brought back rum, whiskey, Scotch, you name it. Tommy and I used to get thirty-odd bucks on fifteen bucks' worth of booze. Later they moved international waters to twelve miles out. We did okay even then," he finished proudly.

Grady and Antony stopped at the dock end and stared down. Houlihan said, "Oh, not in this old hulk." He patted the side affectionately. "Tommy and I bought three Liberty motors off the navy, threw 'em in a hull, could outrun near everything in the bay that wasn't already hauling booze— and most that were. Coast guard never even saw me." He offered Antony a hand and all but swung him into the boat. Antony stood awkwardly, spread-legged and thinking that the worst moments of his life were just ahead.

Grady's worst moment was stepping onto the boat; he passed his cane in and stepped forward with his good leg, shifting his weight to that foot immediately. The boat rocked, his weight went to his bad ankle, and he would have fallen if Antony hadn't grabbed his elbow and lifted. "Here you go."

Grady sagged forward, afraid that he'd accidentally crush a Plimstubb customer. But Antony was startlingly strong; he held Grady's full weight up without as much as a grunt. "Here you go," he repeated. "Grab your cane."

Moments later they were moving away from the dock, so smoothly that it seemed as though it were the dock moving and they were standing still. In seconds the fog hid the land to either side.

Antony said nervously, "How can you tell where you're going?"

"Bells." Houlihan was ignoring them, concentrating. "And echoes from land." He added less reassuringly, "Plus I'll turn if I think we're gonna hit something."

"It's like flying into a cloud," Grady said casually.

"I never liked that either," Antony retorted, and said hastily, "from the sound of it. Do you fly?"

"Never have. I don't think I'd like it."

Antony chuckled. "I didn't think I'd like this, and you made me do it. You'll have to fly sometime."

"I don't think I'd like it."

Hammer Houlihan turned around, pointing to the rods. "We're out far enough. Start casting."

The rods were thicker, the reels larger than freshwater equipment. Antony hefted a six-inch yellow wooden plug. "Will anything bite on this?"

"See the tooth marks on it?" The lure was pitted and scored. "Cast out, reel in fast."

"How will we know when we get a bite?" Grady asked.

Houlihan snorted. "You'll know. One more thing: Remember, if you hit something big and silver, cut the line."

"Shark?" Grady asked more nonchalantly than he felt.

"Torpedo," Houlihan said matter-of-factly. "They test them down there off Goat Island. One or two get away. Mostly they sink to the bottom, but there've been some accidents the papers don't cover."

The boat swung to the east, toward Prudence and Patience Islands. "The channel here is shallow, and the bait fish come up here. The blues follow them." He gestured. "Start casting, dammit."

Antony cast out, reeling as the lure hit the water. Nothing happened.

Grady cast out. Nothing happened.

Nothing happened another six times.

On Antony's seventh cast, a plume of water exploded forty feet from the boat, and Antony's lure popped clear of the water. He stopped reeling and gaped. "Sacred Sun, what was that? Was that a torpedo?"

Houlihan, eyes wide, cut the motor. "Keep reeling! Keep reeling!"

Antony did so, pausing only to stare as the wooden lure leapt, as if by itself, three more times.

Grady cast in the same spot, reeling frantically, and lurched as his pole bent in an arc.

He stared out thirty feet from the boat. There was a silver streak rushing alongside the boat; for one frozen moment, he thought it was a torpedo,

Then the fish at the end of the line thrashed and bucked, a two-foot silver parabola of muscle, and Grady's jaw dropped as he started reeling again.

One final tug and the fish cleared the water, still thrashing. It fell into the boat and lay there, one glaring eye challenging the fishermen to remove the hook from a mouth that seemed all triangular teeth.

Grady stepped on it, holding it to the bottom of the suddenly sloshing hull as Antony knelt to remove the hook. Houlihan slapped his arm away. "Pliers! Pliers!"

Antony took the offered pliers and reached into the mouth of the bluefish, which snapped savagely at the pliers in a way that made Grady glad Antony was using a metal tool. He had never seen a fish this strong.

Antony felt a slap on his shoulder. Houlihan pointed to a flock of seagulls diving against the bay as though attacking it. "See that?" He gunned the motor, cutting it as they closed on the birds.

As they drifted in they heard a second noise, almost like rain, and it looked as though it were raining under the fish, with thousands of tiny splashes. Then the sunlight he hadn't noticed before caught tiny silver glints, and Grady saw the baitfish leaping desperately out of the water, trapped between the bluefish and the gulls.

Antony and Grady didn't need coaching; they were readying their poles before the boat pulled within twenty feet of the fish and the gulls. Houlihan, from the wheel, was watching tensely. "Any second now . . ."

And suddenly the water beside them was boiling, the

water itself rising above the surface of the bay as hundreds of snapping, thrashing fish broke water.

Antony cast the moment Houlihan cut the engine. Grady followed suit. The bluefish seemed to hit the plugs before they actually splashed in the water.

The next hour was a frenzy of casting, reeling, catching, and casting. All three of them were shouting, all three casting plugs into the boiling surface of the water. Amazingly, none of them hooked a gull. A breeze came up, and Grady didn't pay any attention except to brace himself on his good foot and against the rail.

By midmorning the last of the fog was gone, burned off by sun and torn by the increasing wind. The boat rocked constantly in waves two to three feet high. Houlihan shouted over the gull noise to Antony, "We have to go!"

He shouted back without pausing in reeling in his lure, "Just a little longer! We can make it!"

Grady said suddenly, his stomach knotting, "Why are my shoes so wet?"

They all looked down. There were four inches of water in the boat, rocking back and forth with the waves outside.

"The plug!" Houlihan was shouting, which frightened Grady more than the surrounding water did. "Where's the goddamn bilge plug?"

There was no plug floating in the bottom of the boat. One of the flopping fish, or one of the fishermen, had splashed it out.

Houlihan moved quickly toward the front of the boat. "I'm starting the motor," he said grimly, "And maybe—*maybe*—the water will flow out."

Grady stared, wide-eyed, at Antony, balancing precariously on a pile of flopping bluefish. "I had a good time," the dwarf said lamely.

A few seconds later the motor kicked in, coughing. The boat didn't move at all.

Houlihan threw a bucket at Antony. "Bail! Bail!"

Antony grabbed it one-handed and dropped into rhythm. Grady grabbed a second bucket and bailed.

At first nothing changed; the water level barely went down, the motor roared but the boat inched forward, and the three of them bobbed and tossed frantically, in danger of falling out as they bailed water. The wind had picked up, and the waves splashed at the bow. The gunwales were dangerously low; if the waves started coming in, it was all over.

Grady glanced over his shoulder between buckets. "You okay?"

"I went to Europe in a boat." Antony was white-faced. "I didn't get this wet." But he bent back down and tossed another bucketful of water. He was throwing two for every one of Grady's.

"Coast guard would come for us, right?"

"They would after somebody missed us. You got any-body's gonna miss you?"

"My dad," Grady said, and added, "next Sunday."

He turned back to the engine. "We'll be halfway to Block Island long before then."

Grady's back was starting to hurt, but he ignored it. After a few minutes he said hopefully, "Is this boat moving faster?"

Antony responded by bailing frantically, increasing a pace that was already impossibly fast. Grady joined him. Now the boat was definitely moving faster. Grady shouted, "Should we plug the hole if we can?"

"Are you kidding?"

He wasn't, but obviously they weren't going to plug the hole. Grady stuck his finger by it experimentally and was reassured to feel powerful suction; the boat was draining like a bathtub. "We'll make it," he said to Antony. "No question at all." He saw his spoken confidence reflected in Antony's relief, and was as glad as if he'd actually felt it.

By the time they passed Warwick Neck the boat was leaping forward and most of the water was out. Grady and Antony, no longer in danger of drowning, looked proudly at the pile of bluefish they had caught. When the boat docked, Antony leapt out, glad to be on something stable. "Thanks for a great morning. Keep the fish."

"Keep mine, too. And thanks, Hammer." Grady climbed up, taking Antony's hand. Antony pulled him onto the dock with one quick tug. Houlihan grunted and cast off again.

Grady hung onto Antony's hand, pumping it up and down. "Not for nothing, if you don't buy the furnace, request a quote on another one. You've got to come back up here."

"Call me again when the blues are running." Antony threw a muscled arm around Grady's waist. "But I bet we buy something; I'll call when I get home."

Grady was having such a wonderful time that it didn't occur to him until later what that suggested: that Antony, as Grady had suspected all along, wasn't authorized to buy a furnace.

The Roccis' kitchen was at the back of the house. The hallway had a whatnot with family pictures on it; the walls had portraits of the Rocci wedding party, one of Vince in his dress uniform and, inevitably, a picture of Susan at age five riding the photographer's pony at Rocky Point. There were pictures in the Cavanaugh household of Kevin and Grady each on the same pony.

Rose Rocci threw a pot of water on one burner and

simmered a tomato sauce on the other. "I made a gravy yesterday," she said over her shoulder, "just gotta warm it up."

"Take your time, Rose," Antony said, sitting down. "I just got here." He uncorked the wine with an expert twist Grady envied. "Susan, could you get me some glasses?"

An antipasto and a main course later, they were laughing. "The truth, Rose? I can't see you as mother and daughter. You're very different."

"She's got Vince in her," Rose said disapprovingly. "Thinks everything goes her way. That was why she decided to be an engineer—"

"I wanted to be a physicist."

"Fine, fine." She waved her hands. "But I kept saying, 'name a woman does this kind of work,' no matter what she did. And she could always name just one." She waved her arms. "And off she went."

Antony looked interestedly at Susan. "That's not easy."

"Oh, she's wicked confident. Always was. Let me tell you a story—"

"Which story?" Susan said apprehensively.

"It was when she had her second summer job, home from Columbia, did I tell you she went away to college? Anyway, she got up in the morning and was getting ready for work, taking a shower, and she was all naked—"

"Stop now, Ma." Susan was scarlet.

"And she remembered that it was day for the iceman, and she hadn't put the sign in the window—"

"Please, Ma."

"And she ran down with just the towel and put it in, but before she could get to the stairs she heard the back door opening—"

"Ma!"

Mrs. Rocci plowed ahead determinedly. "So she thinks,

where can I hide? and she goes to the basement stairs, and waits for the iceman to leave the kitchen."

She thumped the table, underscoring the surprise. "But the basement door opens, and it's the gas man, come to read the meter. So, you know Susan, always gotta have her dignity—"

"Not anymore," she murmured into her hands.

"—So she straightens up, looks the gasman right in the eye, and says, 'I beg your pardon. I was expecting the iceman.' She gets halfway upstairs before she realizes what he's thinking, you can just imagine."

They couldn't, but Grady was looking at Susan speculatively and, in spite of present company, just imagining a bit. He caught himself and looked guiltily at Antony, who was grinning at him.

Susan glowered at her mother. "Now that you've destroyed my life at work, can we talk about something else?"

"Relax, kid," Antony said. "It's an old story, told about a million women. Maybe—just maybe—it happened that way once," he ignored her blushes, "and it won't destroy your life as long as Grady and I keep our mouths shut."

"And we will," Grady said firmly.

"So the only question is, what's it gonna take to buy your mother off? Don't make it cheap, Rose." He smiled conspiratorially at Mrs. Rocci, who smiled back and brushed at her hair, suddenly self-conscious. Grady realized belatedly that Antony had immediately been much more comfortable with Susan's mother than he was yet with either Antony or Susan.

Once again, Antony insisted on helping with the dishes. To Rose Rocci, this was above and beyond. "Susan. Has your father, Vince, ever once done dishes in this house?"

Susan bristled. "Maybe not—"

"Did he ever change your diaper even once?"

"Ma!"

Antony put up his hands. "Rose, I have to draw the line somewhere." He glanced out the window and said with real regret, "Listen, I have to go if I want to get back near dark. I've had a wonderful time, and I want to thank you."

To Susan's astonishment, her mother bent down without being asked and Antony pecked her on the cheek. "I'll be back, and maybe I'll cook for you." He winked. Rose Rocci blushed and turned to the icebox.

Grady walked him to the truck. "What a great visit."

"I'll say. Kid, I had the time of my life. I wish I had another excuse to come to Rhode Island." He added hastily, "Other than buying a furnace."

"Then you'd better buy, right?" Grady added, "Anyway, we may have another contract to buy from you."

"Terrific." Antony beamed. "Who's your customer?"

Grady shrugged, smiling.

Antony nodded sagely. "I can accept that. Just as long as you keep as quiet about contracts with me—with the Nieuw Amsterdam—Metalworks." He hoped his wink looked patriotic and not sinister.

Grady nodded vigorously, wishing he felt as sincere as he looked. Antony shook hands with him and climbed into his truck.

Grady was standing and waving, but Susan grabbed his arm. "Walk to your car with me." Antony smiled at her, winked at Grady, and went on his way.

He did. "Is something wrong?" He'd hoped she wouldn't think anything was.

"Your customer isn't what he says he is."

"He didn't say anything except that he's a customer."

"He and your mother talked like they'd known each other for years."

"I know," Susan said. "Haven't you seen strangers talk like that before?"

"Maybe. Who?"

"People the same age."

The moment she said it, he realized it was true: Antony, when he talked, sounded much older than he looked.

"I know how old he looks. How old is he really?"

Grady licked his lips. "Tough to say. He's not old enough to be the boss, though." He said with difficulty, "He's not really authorized to buy a furnace."

"Do you think he's a grifter?"

"No," he said flatly. "He's honest."

"Get in the driver's seat. Do you think he's a spy?"

By now Antony was back in the truck, waving. He rolled slowly off.

Grady's answer was a long time coming. "I don't know."

"And he's buying our equipment, and he's got a government contract—"

"More than one."

"Shouldn't we be certain he's not a spy?"

Grady wanted to retort something about uncertainty principles and dead cats, but he also desperately wanted certainty. At least, he thought unhappily, she'd said "we."

Just before Antony was out of sight, Susan sighed. "Let's go."

He turned the ignition key while he made one final protest. "We're expected at work—"

"No, we're not; I told them you were seasick and I was helping my mother take care of you. *Move.*" She lit up a cigarette.

Grady hit the gas and settled into tailing Antony.

FOUR

TAILING ANTONY WAS surprisingly easy; Grady knew where they were headed and could hang back for much of the drive. A light rain began in Connecticut. Susan lit two cigarettes, inhaling, and passed him one. It was a Philip Morris and smelled of perfume, but he took it all the same.

They made good time all the way to New York and across the Hudson River. Grady looked wistfully at Hudson Drill as they passed; the building looked gray and old and extremely trustworthy. He wished that they were his new customer instead of Antony.

Susan tapped the windshield. "Eyes front. He's headed up the hill."

"Of course." But Grady sped up. It was nearly dark, and he could tail a little closer without Antony's seeing them as long as Grady didn't turn on the lights. A few minutes later, Antony turned on his. Grady sighed happily. "He'll be hard to miss now."

Seconds later, he blinked. Antony's truck was gone.

Susan pointed. "That driveway."

"It's just to a farm field." But he took it. The car dove between barbed-wire fences with traces of wool clinging to them (and if there were sheep on the hillside, why was the gate open?) and swerved as Grady followed the ruts around the hillside.

He drove carefully over alternate washouts and granite boulders. "This is not a normal plant driveway."

"This is not a normal customer." Susan said suddenly, "Pull over."

Grady did so, feeling vaguely as though he were parking in the country with a date. "Why?"

He looked ahead. There was nothing but a gate made of barbed wire and tree limbs.

To the left the hillside rose, broken only by moss-lined seepage where springs opened to the sky.

He leaped out of the car, looking around. Antony's truck was nowhere to be found.

To the right he heard the tick of a cooling engine; he leaned into the brush. Antony's truck was under a camouflaged lean-to.

He stepped forward carefully and peered in the driver's window. "No Antony."

"Where did he go?"

Grady snorted. "Look around you. He could be anywhere."

"No. There are no tracks in the mud, except"—She knelt, holding her lighter near the road—"down to this culvert." Susan stepped off the road and peered into the darkness. "He's not here now, but his tracks go in."

Grady clambered down carefully, using the cane. "There's no outlet. Where could he go?"

"Funny sort of culvert, with no outlet," she said thoughtfully. "And it's too high up to take in water."

"Maybe it flows out."

"Then why isn't it now?"

"Beats me."

He grinned in spite of everything as she swore and dropped the lighter. "What're we gonna do now?"

He was unprepared when Susan clambered in on her hands and knees, heedless of her skirt and stockings. "Are you crazy? Your lighter's too hot, and we don't have a flashlight."

Susan said reprovingly, "Many men would be grateful to be in the dark with me."

"Men who knew you?" he muttered. If she heard him, she gave no sign. He sighed and followed her.

On his hands and knees he was immediately comfortable, tucking the cane in his belt. The culvert floor was surprisingly clean; Grady suspected it had been swept. Perhaps Antony had made some kind of home out of it, and they were trespassing.

He was about to say so to Susan when he came up beside her. "A grating." She guided one of his hands to the bars.

"Then we're stopped."

"In that case, Antony's still in here. Do you see him?"

"Of course not." Their eyes were adjusting to the dim light from behind them—and from the other side of the grating, despite its covering of grasses and leaves.

"Then help me open this." She tugged on it futilely. Grady tugged with her, and the grating suddenly swung upward, catching both of them on their foreheads.

Ahead they could hear hammering, some sort of repetitive sigh, and the occasional hiss of steam. They stepped out cautiously, ducking behind a stalagmite before they even looked out at the cave ahead.

"This is like something from a serial," Susan whispered.

"Gene Autry," Grady whispered back. "*The Phantom Empire.*" In spite of the heat from the fires, he felt a sudden chill. He peered around the rock.

Dozens of people, all of them Antony's size, were stoking fires, beating anvils, quenching glowing metal in steaming buckets. Most of the men were bearded. The women were as stocky and muscular as the men.

Susan tugged at Grady's sleeve and pointed. One of the dwarves was speaking loudly to a steel grating and gesturing forward. The grating, parts loaded on it, walked carefully over the fire and squatted down. A bellows, pumping itself—that was the sighing they were hearing—picked up tempo on a command from the dwarf.

Something small and white flew by; Grady snatched at it. It was a memo, to someone named Gretchen, in Antony's careful printing. It tugged in his hand; he let go hastily and it fluttered off.

"What did it say?" Susan asked.

"I didn't have time to read it. Something about a deadline. But I think I know how all my notes from Antony disappeared." He looked around the cavern. "I wonder why they want a furnace from us."

Susan said comfortingly, "At least they don't look like spies—" She broke off suddenly. "Come on." She edged along the wall, headed for another hiding place.

Grady joined her as quickly as he could. "What are you doing? Let's get out of here."

"We can't. Not till we know for sure—"

"We know enough." He crouched down beside her, steadying himself with his cane.

She pointed toward the far wall. "We don't know about that."

"About what?" He looked, keeping his head low. There were process bins, a slung line that seemed to be a resting place for flying paper, a sign pointing to what had to be a foreman's office, the entry point for the electrical wiring.

He clutched at the rock in front of him, only partly for balance. The far wall had a tunnel through it, with a sign over it: GNOMENGESELLSCHAFT.

It was definitely and undeniably German.

For a moment he said nothing, then: "Oh, Jesus."

"Don't panic. I'll admit it looks bad—"

"The Depression looked better."

"For all you know, there's nothing back there." But she was standing again. "Let's go in cautiously."

"Cautiously," he said bitterly, but he followed her.

The tunnel was lit by torches in sconces. The stains on the walls were disturbing, and the lime-encrusted features, possibly former bodily organs and possibly not, were even more so. Grady was relieved when, before the last right-angle turn in the tunnel, Susan turned back and said firmly, "I've seen enough."

A gray, narrow hand with fingers as long as a human arm gripped Grady's shoulder. A second hand at the end of an arm that went on forever, gripped Susan. "We haven't met," a desiccated voice crackled, with a rustle like dead leaves.

Susan screamed, or Grady would have. Instead he spun his cane up and around in his wrist, bringing it down with an audible snap on the arm behind Susan. As the hand let go of her, he continued the circle of the cane as though it were a foil and turned on his good leg, slashing the cane up hard against the arm, still grasping the right shoulder despite his spin.

Grady stepped toward Susan awkwardly, still brandishing his cane.

Susan stepped even with him, holding a nail file from her

purse. "Come one step closer and I'll gut you like Friday's fish." Her voice never wavered.

Grady thought of moving in front of her, but that would put him too close to those arms writhing in frantic pain before him. He peered into the dark, but whatever was at the end of the arms was too far away in the shadows.

The crackling voice said in mild reproof, "Shame on you. Is that any way for guests to treat their host?" It was a cultured baritone with a suggestion of a hiss under it.

The file in Susan's hand wavered. "Then you're not going to—then you don't mean us any harm?"

The thing's laughter startled the bats on the cave roof, and skittered like them. "Of course I mean you harm." The figure moved into the light. Narrow but muscled shoulders between the arms supported a serpentine neck topped by a head the length of Grady's forearm. The eyes were dark with pupils that glowed more than they should in the torchlight.

Whispered chuckles echoed behind the creature, and the scraping of clawed feet on stone. The creature smiled, and the long, narrow fangs dwarfed Susan's pitiful nail file.

"Of course I mean you harm," he repeated in gentle reproof. There were whispered chuckles behind him, and the scraping of feet on stone as the creature moved into the light. "Those who torture and kill you generally mean you harm."

The creature moved forward, arms bent like some cross between a human and a praying mantis as it moved toward its prey.

Behind Susan and Grady, Antony said sharply, "Stop right there, Klaus."

Grady, relieved, fell back as well. He had no idea what waited for them with the dwarves, but knew it had to be better than what lay before him.

"Ah," the creature said, purring. "A short interruption." He peered over Grady and Susan in mock confusion. "Where could that huge voice be coming from? Should I be frightened?"

"You should. Stay back," a woman's voice said firmly. "If you won't honor your word, Klaus, fear me."

A woman who barely came up to his elbow stepped in front of him; she had golden curly hair and a very round, florid face, and her china-blue eyes stared ahead without compromise. At the moment her mouth was set in a frown. She put one hand on the hilt of a short sword that looked like silver.

She was three feet tall at the most, and her steel sword was barely a foot and a half long. Her shadow, flickering beneath the torches, came barely to Susan's knees. To Grady she looked like God's own avenging archangel.

The creature flinched back. "Why should I fear you?" he said, and Grady knew immediately that Klaus was afraid of her.

Antony, armed with a smith's hammer on a leather thong, moved in front of Susan.

"Thanks," Grady said to the female dwarf.

"You're welcome. Grady, is that right? And that would make you Susan." She turned her head to talk, glancing back at Klaus as though she were a pitcher eyeballing the lead runner. "I'm Kirsten Brijtkopf." She spelled it, smiling and looking them each in the eye in turn. "I'm in charge of plant security." She looked good at it.

Susan nodded. "As in, a guard?"

"It's much more than that; I make this place and its people secure." She turned back to Grady. "I saw you move the cane. You've used a sword."

He looked uncomfortably at the gnomes, who were

watching him appraisingly. "Only at college, in class and on a team."

She nodded, but seemed disappointed in his answer, or in the way he answered. "Trained but not tested. I'll bear that in mind."

A final figure, a red-faced dwarf with forge-tanned cheeks and a silver beard halfway down his chest, stepped forward. "Antony, what to hell are you doing this time?"

Antony said, "Pieter, these are Susan Rocci and Grady Cavanaugh, out of Plimstubb Furnaces. Folks, this," Antony said with his eyes closed and a strong sense of doom, "is my boss, Pieter Hein."

Pieter barely glanced at Susan and Grady. "You know this man, this woman? You brought them here?"

He shook his head. "I know them, but they came on their own."

The gnomes smiled at Pieter. "Oh, are these intruders yours?" Klaus purred confidently, and Grady knew immediately that negotiations had changed.

Pieter looked troubled for a moment and waved a hand angrily. "If Antony invited these people they are mine, at least for this visit. You stay away from them."

Kirsten, looking back at him, nodded and moved forward with the sword.

"But are they here in violation of our contract?" The skittering behind Klaus grew louder again. "Have you violated our contract? Or are you saying you never authorized their trespass, that they aren't truly under your protection? Or are you saying you authorized their trespass?" Klaus's speaking style was curiously formal.

"They talk in questions a lot, kid," Antony confided to Grady. "It's like dealing with supernatural underground lawyers."

Lawyers, however, didn't grow foot-long claws at the

ends of their wrists—at least, none of the lawyers Grady knew.

Pieter stared at Grady, then at Antony, uncertain what to answer.

Klaus asked more bluntly, "Are these humans here with your consent?"

"Yes," Antony said, and immediately, "No, but don't hurt them." He took a deep, shuddering breath. "They're my fault, not Pieter's. It's nothing to do with the plant, yet."

"'Yet'?" Klaus pulled back involuntarily, and one of his clawlike hands curled under his chin as he thought. "Tell me about 'yet.'"

Kirsten, with barely a glance backward at Pieter, moved by Antony's side.

Grady surprised himself by saying, "Antony and I had a small contract. Very small." He held a hand near the floor, hoping it wasn't insulting. "I'm here to negotiate the details of a larger one."

Klaus's face sagged, dropping his fangs a remarkable distance. "You haven't signed anything with Pieter?"

Antony opened his mouth, but stopped himself and turned hopefully as Grady said, "Of course I haven't." Pieter looked from one of them to the other; he didn't look happy.

He continued, "Plimstubb has a threshold; it's the difference between a net thirty days sale and a larger one with real terms and conditions. I visited unannounced to ask about the second sale."

"A sale." Klaus clasped his hands in front of him and shut his eyes. While he thought, his fingers darted and wove like snakes, and his eyes suddenly glowed yellow. The dwarves and the humans watched uneasily.

Finally he focused and said to Pieter, "I think it's time you invited me to your negotiations."

"There are no negotiations—"

"Yet," Antony said.

Pieter glared and repeated. "There are no negotiations. But if you maybe wish to come, we will be in my office. You will give us five, ten minutes first." He turned and strode into the Dwarfworks.

Klaus stared down at him disappointedly. "In that case, perhaps we'd all best negotiate together." He turned to Pieter. "Your office, five minutes?"

Pieter nodded curtly. "Give us the full five."

A large gnome behind Klaus spoke for the first time. "When we give specifics, we mean them." Klaus looked relieved, and Grady noted the change in the gnomes' postures. There was no question how much backing meant to Klaus.

"Alone," Kirsten said with emphasis. "Safe passage, so long as you're alone."

"I'll confirm that with my colleagues first." Klaus turned back and said abruptly, "Wilmer?" and more deferentially, "And Heinrich, if you would?" A rail-thin gnome and an enormous one moved to the back of the tunnel; Klaus joined them.

In Pieter's office, Kirsten dropped into a small wooden chair at the rough-hewn table and sighed. "You two have really thrown a gnomewrench in the Dwarfworks."

Susan said, "I don't know what that means."

Grady said, "I'm scared I do, or that I'll find out."

Kirsten smiled at them. Grady thought that for all her toughness, she was quite kind. "It means that you've thrown something orderly into chaos."

"SNAFU," Grady said. They looked blankly at him. "Situation Normal, All"—he hesitated—"Fouled Up."

Antony was grinning. Susan said, "Or TARFU. Things

Are Really"—she imitated Grady's hesitation mockingly—
"*Fouled* Up."

"Closer to TARFU," Kirsten said grimly. "This gnomewrench has a real gnome attached."

Pieter said heavily, "You should never have come." He
looked very tired.

She leaned forward. "Before he gets here: you've seen
the plant. Do you really think your equipment would do us
any good here?"

"Of course," Grady answered. Here, at least, he felt on
home ground. "You could lower costs and increase output.
You could reduce waste by controlling your process . . ."
He cut short as he realized how little he knew about their
market. "Do you think you'd have a larger market for your
work?"

Kirsten and Pieter exchanged glances. "For some of it
we would, yes." Pieter chuckled, and Grady and Susan
relaxed slightly; he sounded genuinely good-natured when
he wasn't angry. "Already, though, we have some very large
customers." He glanced out the door to where a three-legged
skillet fully the size of a small boat leaned against the wall.

Susan said, "By the way, why does a skillet like that have
a handle that long?"

"So the customer can pick it up one-handed when it gets
hot."

Susan looked from the skillet to Antony in disbelief.
Antony added, in all seriousness, "Fee, fi, fo, fum."

Grady realized that he knew absolutely nothing about
their market.

Before he or Susan could ask anything more, Pieter
stiffened, shaking off his tiredness.

Antony, looking toward the door, thought, *Sacred Sun, I
have completely done it now.*

Grady, looking toward the door, thought of every horror story he had ever read.

"Five minutes, exactly." Klaus stepped in. "As I believe you all know, I am Klaus." He added deferentially, "And this is our president and senior manager, Heinrich."

The other gnome was in a comparatively mild, rounded form, without claws, spines, or fangs. He didn't need them. He was larger than Klaus, but beyond that, something about Heinrich was impressive even when understated.

"So very pleased," he said in a quiet voice that was almost a hiss. "New associates are rare, and often enjoyable. Klaus, have you briefed them on our business practices?"

"Not yet." He turned his head and smiled at Susan, widening his grin and letting his fangs grow until they were the size of penny nails. "I'm hoping to brief the young lady soon."

Grady did a remarkably good job of laughing in the face of dripping fangs. "I'd love to see you tackle her on her home turf. I really would." He took a deep breath and stepped forward, rapping Klaus on the nose with his cane and said in his best W. C. Fields voice, "Now back away from her, boy, before you hurt yourself."

Klaus backed away involuntarily, and stiffened when Heinrich's rustling laughter was clearly meant for him. Kirsten looked quickly from the gnome to the human, and Grady was a little sorry that, in defending Susan, he'd made a nasty enemy.

"So," Klaus said easily, "will your equipment make more product, make better product, or both?"

"More and better," Grady said, adding hastily, "but for now I'd as soon sell to the Dwarfworks alone."

"I can well imagine." Klaus nodded, amused. "However, since the Dwarfworks is in our debt, by our rules we have a right to review any outside contracts." He extended a fingernail until it looked like a scimitar and swished it through the air, regarding it. "Penalties for violating that rule are extensive."

Pieter said, "We have not violated it."

After a long pause Pieter said, to Antony's delight and absolute astonishment, "Antony tells me I'm old-fashioned. This time maybe he is not right. We will buy this machine if Antony says it will help us. We will not buy it yet."

"Wise caution. Then for now"—Klaus tapped mobile and fluid fingers together—"we may assume we have an understanding, and a hope to conduct this purchase and possibly even others."

"We'll meet again and bargain over other equipment." Grady smiled, as though this were any other meeting with any other customers. "And I'll bet that Plimstubb and the Dwarfworks come to an agreement."

Pieter said in relief, "That's settled then."

"Not yet." Klaus pointed a finger like a ruler. "The contract laws are America's, but the final laws are the humans' or yours—and ours, as your creditors."

Grady looked inquiringly at Antony, who grimaced. Pieter glanced at them and said with a touch of bitter amusement, "Antony did not tell you? The dwarves owe a debt to the gnomes. Every contract, every purchase that is not too small, they have the right to sit with us when we make the deal." He added unwillingly, "And a little they can change the deal, if they choose."

Klaus folded his arms, retracting them to do it. For a moment he looked like a grotesque human, not a monster. "Your laws are not our laws. Do you need the Dwarfworks' business or don't you?"

"Why would I set up a contract on your laws?"

"Or I on yours? It's like the home field in baseball."

Grady thought wistfully of the St. Louis World Series, where there was no home field advantage. "It'll have to satisfy both our laws."

"I could challenge you to a contest, if you accept."

Grady, exasperated, said, "I can't agree to that. I have no idea what you can and can't do."

"Ah," Klaus said. "But I could restrict myself. That seems courteous. What if I restricted myself to things you've done already in your life?"

Kirsten took in her breath sharply as Grady said, "That sounds fair." He knew from the dwarves' faces that he'd made a mistake, but it was too late.

Klaus nodded slowly. "It does sound fair, doesn't it?" He grinned, fangs extended fully. "So be it."

Klaus's arm stretched out eight feet. Spindly fingers twitched left and right, a piece of chalk held like a cigarette butt as the gnome sketched across the cave floor.

He retracted his arm. Susan and the dwarves gasped to see a twenty-foot, numbered hopscotch layout.

Klaus tossed a fistful of pebbles negligently toward the squares and said over Heinrich's quiet, appreciative applause, "Go ahead, gimpy."

The cave fell silent. Grady passed his cane to Susan and took a deep breath before hopping forward.

Grady made it six squares on luck and five more on willpower. Three feet from the end, his right leg twisted out from under him and he sprawled on his belly, erasing the lines.

He gasped from the impact, and a puff of dust blew from his lips. Klaus said confidently, "This would explain why the armed services rejected you."

The dwarves and the humans were silent. Antony stepped forward and helped him up, saying heavily, "Remember from now on, kid: If a gnome says it and it sounds fair, you've forgotten something."

The rest of the paperwork was a brief formality. Grady, desperate to return to the car, signed his name on a letter of understanding.

In the middle of the Dwarfworks he paused to shake hands with Antony. "Not too bad," the dwarf commented. "You didn't get everything you wanted, but you showed you've got sand."

"In place of brains, maybe." Grady was still smarting physically and emotionally. "Antony, there's so much I don't know about this place if I'm going to sell to you. What is your special market? Who do you compete with?" He waved an arm at the forges, the anvils, the walking hearths. "What do you really do here?"

Antony sat on rock ledge to be eye-to-eye with Grady and Susan. "What we do? That's hard to explain . . . do you remember Aladdin and his ring and lamp? Arthur and Excalibur? Paul Bunyan and his ax?"

"Sure."

He swung his legs as he talked. "Did you ever wonder who would have made those things for them?"

Grady, sounding like a schoolchild, made a guess. "The dwarves?" Antony nodded.

Susan, encouraged, broke in. "And—okay, I get it; the Black Cauldron from Welsh folklore—the one that raised the dead to fight against Bran the Blessed, assuming that story was real"—she looked hesitantly at Antony and plunged ahead—"the dwarves would have made the cauldron?"

"Oh, no." Antony was genuinely shocked. "No, no. We would never." He glanced uneasily and involuntarily at the tunnel to the gnomes' factory. "That would be made by someone else."

"By someone more visionary, someone with a broader plan for production." All three of them jumped as Klaus rejoined them. "Earlier, you were curious about our facility. Please, let me show you."

Kirsten arrived from nowhere, looking stern. Klaus added, "And only you," and he waved a too-long hand airily at Kirsten. "I swear they will come to no physical or mystical harm, not by accident nor on purpose."

Her expression didn't change, but she nodded. Klaus bowed mockingly to her and, just as mockingly, offered an elbow to Susan.

His arm was bare; the skin was dark, encrusted, and pitted like a coal clinker. Susan said carefully and politely, "Thank you, but no." He grinned, showing too many teeth, and led the way. Susan and Grady followed.

The twisting corridor on the other side of the Gnomengesellschaft arch was darker than the Dwarfworks was; torches in intermittent sconces provided most of the light. Grady said, "What do you make here?"

"'Make?' Ah. What indeed." A bat hung nearby. Grady realized that for a cave there were surprisingly few bats. He understood why a second later as the bat flew off at their approach. Klaus reached for it—and kept reaching, his bones melting and stretching and his fingers spreading like a net. The bat evaded him, and he retracted his arm. "Speedy thing. What we make is hard to define. As do your short friends, we manufacture a great many products: swords, mirrors, rings, scissors, even the occasional toy. But what do we make?"

He turned the final corner in the hall and held open a large iron door. "I like to think we make unhappiness."

The cavern floor was an unbroken gray slab. There were

no electric lights here; knife-edge shadows crossed and recrossed in the light from fires and ovens. Periodically they heard laughter, but it sounded bitter and angry, like laughter at someone's expense.

The walk to the factory floor was like one of those dreams where you want to run but your legs won't let you. The hearths in the Dwarfworks had seemed like pets; the walking equipment in this plant cringed like beaten dogs. Where the electric lights shone in the Dwarfworks, here the torches flickered apologetically in the darkness.

They came around a corner and found themselves in the center of the production floor.

Susan said with revulsion and pity, "What's that?"

"That," Klaus said with relish, "is Mr. Garner Stanley Irving, formerly of Newcastle, England. When I say 'formerly,' I mean 'roughly a century formerly.' I do enjoy thinking that Pieter's people were having commerce with another Irving at nearly the same time."

When neither of them responded, he shook his head pityingly; it swiveled loosely on his long, thin neck. "Washington Irving, of course."

The eyes on the enormous head shifted toward them, regarding them incuriously. The head said nothing; Grady realized with a sick lurch in his stomach that an iron latch held the mouth closed. "What happened to him?"

"It's not so much what happened to him as what he did to us. We had a shop—one of our first true factories off the Continent—in a coal seam near Newcastle. We used candles and lamps. Explosions were frequent."

A dark figure stepped forward and levered Irving's mouth open with a pry bar. After extending the jaw to its fullest with an audible pop, he set the bar upright between Irving's upper and lower molars. He begin shoveling copper parts into the mouth with a short-handled spade.

"One day Mr. Irving's miners broke through into our shop. After some unfortunate confusion during which two men died and one was blinded, Mr. Irving negotiated a deal and agreed, in exchange for our mining help, to provide us with Davy lamps. That is a type of coal lamp that Sir Humphrey Davy had invented fairly recently, as we figure things. The lamps were sealed, and invaluable in an environment with coal gas."

The gnome below moved to one side of Irving and pumped vigorously on a large bellows. Grady stared, curious and repelled at once. Obviously the gnome was heating a large fire—probably coal, from the smell here—but where was the fire? The end of the bellows seemed to disappear under Irving's immense chest.

But the chest was heaving in rhythm with the bellows.

"I regret to say he tried to cheat us. One day we counted lamps, and realized he had been shorting our orders from the first. Our representatives spoke to him. Eventually he confessed. In restitution, we required his services." Klaus added judiciously, "In order to perform those services, it became necessary to modify him extensively. At any rate, that is what Mr. Irving did to us, so long ago by your standards."

The shadows disappeared from Irving's face; his cheeks were glowing a soft, faint red. A tear rolled out of his left eye and danced, sizzling, before disappearing into steam.

Klaus smiled, slowly and full-mouthed, exposing every fang. "As for what happened to him, it has barely begun."

They returned to the Dwarfworks in numb silence. At the archway Klaus stopped. "Please say good-bye to your hosts for me; I see no reason to trouble them just now." He said it with genuine regret; Grady shivered. "And I trust you understand why I showed you Mr. Irving."

●   ●   ●

Susan and Grady walked in silence from the Gnomengesellschaft all the way to the culvert and Grady's car. Antony and
Kirsten fell in behind them wordlessly.

At the car, Kirsten said to Susan, "You'll have to come
back."

Antony said, "And Grady, of course."

Kirsten was looking at him amusedly, and Grady realized
how anxious to be invited he must have looked. "Gotta
make that sale," he said awkwardly. He stuck out his hand.
"Thanks for everything. Call when you're ready to negotiate."

The two dwarves shook hands solemnly, then turned and
walked upright into the culvert.

On the drive home Susan said, "You were an idiot to claim
I could face down Klaus." She considered. "Hell, you were
an idiot to face him down yourself, even if you thought it
wasn't on his terms."

"Yeah, well, I was an idiot." Grady lit a cigarette, his
third since driving off. Normally Susan outsmoked him
three for one.

She rubbed her index finger across her lower lip and said
thoughtfully, "But I'll bet I could give him a run for his
money if I had time to think."

Grady said with a sigh, "That's all I said," knowing he
would never be heard. He would have given every dollar
he'd ever bet for time to think in front of Klaus.

Grady drove home while Susan slept. Somewhere in
Connecticut she woke up and insisted on driving. He
resisted as long as possible, then watched distrustfully while
she drove. Eventually his eyelids drooped, and it seemed to
him, when she shook his shoulder as she pulled up in front

of her house, that he had only just fallen asleep back in Hartford.

But once he was driving home, down deserted streets, it seemed to him that he had been asleep a long time, and had dreamed the strangest things he had ever known.

FIVE

THE FOLLOWING MONDAY was chilly but sunny; Grady dutifully pedaled to Plimstubb and saved on gas. He had breakfast with Mary and Julie, giving Mary his dairy ration cards. He was only mildly guilty about using his own gas ration card the Friday before; the trip to the Dwarfworks had been business, after all. He considered writing up an expense sheet and dismissed the idea; the less Warren Hastings knew about the dwarves, the better.

Grady slung his cane effortlessly onto the coat hook, then tossed a brand-new copy of *Astounding,* with the requisite spaceship and alien on the cover, onto his desk. Only then did he realize that there was a stack of blueprints on it as well. A note in Susan's handwriting said, "Check these over." It was Stode's furnace.

He unfolded the prints. Here was the secret of engineering, as fascinating as any science fiction story. Outlined on these schematics was an unbuilt piece of equipment, laid out so anyone with the skills and the materials could assemble it. He scanned down the wiring print, not checking the wire numbers but seeing in his mind the control panel that would have the switches and buttons connected here. One button was labeled START ATMOSPHERE; he turned automatically to the piping print to see the solenoid that would open and send gas flowing—he checked the overall print to see the shell of the furnace where the gas would flow. The door was heavily insulated, interlocked so it would not open once the heat went above three hundred degrees Fahrenheit. To the left of the furnace door was a simple control panel with switches and buttons, the complexities of the wiring print hidden behind it inside the cabinet.

The furnace had gone from proposal to design. Now it would go from design to purchasing, and the materials from thirty companies to the stockroom, and finally only a few months' work would see the completion of a new machine, something new to the planet. He sat looking from the design to the cover of *Astounding*; at moments like this he liked his job very much.

He filed the papers from Klaus and Pieter in a copy of *Amazing* and went to see Susan. She was on the floor, looking at projects.

Roy Burgess, behind her, complained, "I gotta get the blades on the exhaust fan straightened. They keep going, "Wopwopwopwopwop—"

Grady grimaced. Susan stiffened but otherwise didn't react. Roy frowned, then grinned as Benny Behind slouched past. "So Benny, is your marriage going any better?"

Benny gave him a worried frown. "She still don't blow me so good."

"Talk to her, Benny, talk to her." He was grinning. Susan once more was blushing furiously.

Hammer Houlihan stepped forward. "Learn some goddamn manners, Burgess. Jesus, you make me ashamed."

Roy frowned but, to Grady's surprise, flushed and strode off. Houlihan nodded to Susan. "He used to ride your dad pretty hard. It's his idea of fun."

Susan smiled faintly. "Thanks for calling him off."

Houlihan scratched his head. "Vince is a good guy. If he were here and he knew I wasn't looking out for you, he'd haul me up by the short and curlies pretty quick—" He caught himself and walked away.

Grady waited a decent interval before going to Susan's desk and saying, "I looked over the Stode furnace. Very nice."

"Thanks." But she didn't look happy. "I had a few questions."

He spread his hands. "I'll tell you everything I know."

"I'm sure you will," she said dryly. "So. What are the parts to be processed made of?"

"I don't know."

"What they shaped like? Do they have a lot of surface area, or just a little compared to their mass?"

"I don't know."

"How many of them will he be loading at once?"

When he said "I don't know" again, she tapped her pen on the desk thoughtfully. "For somebody who gets nervous around the uncertainty principle, you seem to run business by it."

"I understand about uncertainty," Grady said, nettled. "Just don't bring up that damn cat in the box again."

"Schrödinger's cat is a great example to explain it." But she was enjoying his discomfort. "Is the cat alive or dead? How can you tell, until you open the box?"

He grunted. "I can tell that the man who set up the box and stuffed the cat in it was no damn good." He added over his shoulder as he left, "And I'll bet someday we're all just as sorry we met physicists as that poor cat is."

"Or was," she called happily. She was right, and that just made Grady more irritable.

Grady put the prints in a manila envelope and dictated a letter to Talia:

Dear Mr. Stode:

The design work on your contract has been completed. Enclosed are wiring and piping prints. We are confident that the equipment as designed will perform to your specifications.

"What's that mean?" Talia asked.

Grady thought unhappily that if it didn't fool Talia it almost certainly wouldn't fool Stode. "It means that I don't know what he wants but that we're building it like he said."

"Then how can we be sure it works?"

"We can't. I didn't say it worked, I said it will do what he said he wanted." He had a sudden happy thought and went on:

I enclose several models of how quickly different parts, of different shapes and materials, will heat in this furnace. This should provide you with a better sense of how well it suits your purposes.

"And now the big finish." Grady concluded automatically, as so many of Plimstubb's letters did during the war:

Normally we ship our equipment south via the New York, New Haven, and Hartford Railroad. Please be advised that, although the furnace will be completed

*on schedule, due to troop train movements on the East
Coast we cannot guarantee delivery.*

Sincerely,
PLIMSTUBB, INC.

Grady Cavanaugh
Sales Engineer

*Encl.: Wiring, piping, overall prints, sample process-
ing times.*

"There, that ought to hold him. No, don't write that
down." Grady went back to his desk and tossed his cane at
the coat stand, hooking the bottom hook as always. He spent
the next two hours doing heat calculations; he felt like he
was back in college and felt, at the same time, as though he
was finally doing engineering work again. Mailing that
material to Stode was thoroughly satisfying; it was wonderful when his work felt worth something.

Grady spent the rest of the week sorting through RFQs and
gloating to whoever would listen; the Browns were still in
the Series. The Red Sox, sadly, were out; the Tigers, with
the amazing Dizzy Trout pitching, had wrapped them up,
8–2. Grady's bets were doing well.

That was better than his RFQs were doing. Most of the
quotations were for war contracts, and most of them Warren
refused to bid on when Grady brought them up. He typed
letters politely declining, eagerly requested more information for the few civilian orders, and spent the rest of his time
worrying about his desk still being straight and nearly
empty.

Nights off were barely more relaxing. Rehearsals of the
Providence Choral Society with Maestro Mandeville had

led Grady to conclude that the conductor was a kind of anti–Teddy Roosevelt, who spoke loudly and carried a little stick. The conductor faced the choir because, after the cutting things he said in rehearsal, he didn't dare turn his back on them. Apparently the maestro loved music but despised singers, Grady most of all. In the middle of rehearsing the "Gloria," Mandeville stopped the choir and bellowed, "Everyone turn toward Cavanaugh!"

They did. Maestro Mandeville said coldly, "I was unaware of your prowess as a composer. Please save your version of the Mass for your own concert, and for now turn to the vastly inferior, but unfairly popular, work by Franz Josef Haydn."

The choir chuckled. Grady turned beet red. Susan brought it up twice on the ride home, and Grady fell asleep dreaming that Mandeville conducted an underground choir for the gnomes.

Grady's own work slowed down. As the Hudson Drill furnace and the few other contracted pieces drew to a close, Grady felt more and more nervous and more and more helpless.

He also felt less and less part of the war effort. Warren may have had a vision of who the company ought to have for customers, but the new customers hadn't come along yet, and keeping out of the war was simply wrong. Grady thought of his father, and Kevin, and Vince Rocci, and all the people he knew who had interrupted their whole lives to enlist. He went for a walk in the plant, brooding.

He bumped into Joe Cataldo, who grabbed Grady's shoulders to keep him upright. "Careful there. You're going to knock your ass right on your hind end."

"Sorry. I wasn't thinking."

"Well, you think." He half-mockingly shook a finger at

Grady. "If you think hard enough, you'll sell something, and that would be good news, you bet your sweetcorns."

"I'll sell something." He shook his head to clear it. "Jeez, it's early and I'm nearly as sleepy as Talia gets."

"Talia?" He beamed at Grady and said earnestly, "Holy sacred cows, isn't she just as pretty as a picture of her photograph?"

"I guess she is," Grady said. She was too old for him to think of that way, but she was certainly the right age for Joe.

Intrigued, Grady thought he'd chat with her—not that he'd interfere with her life, of course, or stick his nose in—and bring up the subject of Joe Cataldo, just to gauge her reaction. She was asleep; he tapped on the glass to wake her.

Talia's head snapped up. "I forgot; you have a telegram."

Grady came as close to running as he had in years, dashing into his office and tossing the cane aside, this time hitting the coat hook mostly by luck.

The telegram was lying in the middle of his desk. He had a single frozen moment wondering if it would be about Kevin. Then he realized that that telegram, if, God forbid, it ever came, would go to Mary. He ripped the Western Union envelope open shakily, reading it with relief when he realized it was about work.

RECEIVED YOUR LETTER STOP PLEASE APPRISE RENFREW WHEN EQUIPMENT IS READY AND I WILL DIVERT TROOP TRAINS ON EAST COAST STOP CONFIRMATION WILL FOLLOW STOP

THANK YOU FOR INCLUDING SPECULATIVE PROCESSING INFORMATION STOP DO NOT DO THIS EVER AGAIN STOP

REGARDS STODE.

He read the telegram several times, feeling more confused each time. Finally he picked up his office phone dazedly.

"Rocci."

"Susan. Come to my office."

"You always come here." She added immediately, "Is your leg bothering you?"

"No. Come here."

She arrived, flushed and panting, twenty seconds after he hung up. "Is it family? Is it something about your job? Is it—"

He passed her the telegram.

She read it and then, to Grady's pleasure, reread it herself. She handed it back, and for once she looked even less secure than Grady did. "He can do that?"

"Or he wants us to think he can. Does Schrödinger's cat run the railroads?"

"Why did you call me here?"

"He didn't address it to the company. He sent it to me. I think he's telling me not to talk too much."

"Then you shouldn't tell me."

"You're already doing the design work on it." He grinned. "Plus, you're keeping a bigger secret with me already."

But to Grady's disquiet she shook her head slowly. "I'm not so sure." She took the telegram back and read it again. "Can he really do this?"

"How would I know?" But she kept looking at him, and he said finally, "If he really works for the government, I'd bet on it."

"'If . . .' Is there a way you can find out?"

"I have a tougher question: Is there a way I can find out without his finding out?"

"It doesn't matter."

"You wouldn't say that if you were the one—"

"It doesn't matter," she repeated. "We have to know he's legit before we build anything for him."

"We will," Grady said confidently, and promptly put off thinking about it for the rest of the week.

As Grady wheeled into the parking lot the next Monday, he saw Warren standing impatiently just inside the door. Susan, behind him, was signaling frantically and incomprehensibly. Grady dismounted, hit the kickstand with exaggerated care, and thought frantically of how to answer any number of difficult questions.

Warren's question was more than difficult. "I just heard about the Nieuw Amsterdam Metalworks proposal. Cavanaugh, what in hell are you thinking? You're supposed to keep me informed."

"I tried," Grady said with a bare ring of injured truth, "but you told me not to bother you with my proposals until they look solid."

"The customer visited. That makes it solid enough. I heard the design might be unusual."

"It's a normal design," Grady insisted feebly, "just a little short."

"Than charge them for shortening it, and put that in the price."

"Absolutely," Susan said, straight-faced. "Why not charge them more for less material?"

Warren spun around. "I wasn't speaking to you—but since you ask, charge them more for additional design time." Irritated as he was, he ran his eyes up and down her. "After all, let's assume that your time would be worth something." The tip of his tongue slid quickly across his lips.

"We can talk about it in my office," Grady said hastily,

hiding his disgust. "That's where the paperwork is." He
edged into the entryway, using his cane to cut between
Susan and Warren. "Excuse me." Susan walked off swiftly;
Grady used his slow pace to block Warren from following.
Warren sighed exasperatedly; this was not going to be a
good day.

At his office, Grady sorted quickly through his mail—
another stalling tactic before pulling the file out, though it
was still hidden inside the copy of *Amazing*. All the mail
appeared to be new RFQs, which ordinarily would have
made him happy. He did a double take at the last envelope,
buried under the mail—another telegram from Western
Union.

To Warren's obviously intense irritation, he picked up his
phone receiver and called the switchboard. "Talia, I have a
telegram here. When did that arrive?"

"When you weren't here."

Grady asked patiently, "When would that have been?"

"Friday. Noon."

Thanks." He hung up and opened the envelope hastily.
It was not from Stode but from the War Department:

*RE: RECENT LETTER REGARDING DELIVERY
DATE*

*WHEN EQUIPMENT IS READY INFORM CON-
TRACTING OFFICER AND WE WILL DIVERT
TROOP TRAINS ON THE EAST COAST TO AC-
COMMODATE SHIPMENT.*

There was no other listed source for the telegram.

Grady read it twice, blinking. Warren said impatiently,
"Are you going to tell me about the Metalworks proposal?"

"Not just now."

Warren narrowed his eyes.

"This might be more important." He passed Warren the telegram.

Warren read it once, looked up, read it hastily again. "This is the contract off that metals project?" Grady nodded. "Can we make the ship date?"

Grady turned to look at Susan, who had come in and was on tiptoes reading the telegram over Warren's shoulder. "If we expedite materials, sure." Warren turned sideways, his face nearly touching hers, and she stepped back hastily. "That costs extra, though. He's got to come to terms pretty quickly."

Warren had pulled the original proposal from Grady's desk drawer; Grady was irked and a little unsettled that Warren knew right where to look. "And you have a source for additional moly?"

"I confirmed that first." Antony hadn't even seemed surprised that Grady had asked.

Warren looked at him coldly, as though giving the right answer had been a mistake. "Did you confirm the price?"

"Same as last time," Grady said, hoping it would be and resolving to ask Antony soon.

"Ah." Warren scanned down the rest of the proposal and tossed it back to Grady. "Add ten percent to everything, tell him it's an expediting charge, and tell him you need a purchase order for the extra amount in three business days. No P.O., no met deadline."

Grady, stunned, ran his finger down the costs page. "If you don't mind my saying so, this guy Stode is nobody you'd want to play around with."

Warren leaned forward, and his smile was thin and cold. "I don't play with anybody, and I'd do this to any man alive. In this instance I'm telling you to do it."

"Yes, sir."

Susan looked at Grady disgustedly, and Grady hated that more than he hated working for Warren.

When they were alone again, Susan practically hissed, "War profiteering."

"At least it distracted him from asking about the Dwarfworks."

Susan was looking again at the paperwork for Stode's proposal. "I don't know if distracting him with this job was such a good idea. This looks pretty important."

Grady chuckled, finally relaxing. "Do you know, after meeting Antony once, we both trust him more than we trust Warren?"

"That's because we've met Warren Hastings more than once. How about Stode? Do you trust him?"

"Look at the telegram. It's from the War Department."

"It says it's from the War Department." She tapped it. "But it doesn't say who sent it. How would you check on this?"

"Call Renfrew."

"Do it," she said, flatly.

"Gotcha." He pulled the Dwarfworks folder from the stack of *Amazing* and other magazines. "I had this marked up for changes before Antony left. Drop it with Talia for retyping, would you?"

Susan, about to say something tart, glanced at his cane and took the folder without another word. Grady simmered; suddenly he would rather have taken it himself.

Miraculously, Renfrew was some help. At noon Grady pedaled his bike to the nearest Western Union office at the train station and dashed off the following telegram:

URGENT URGENT NEED MAILING-SHIPPING ADDRESS FOR WAR DEPARTMENT EMPLOYEE

*DRAKE STODE STOP PLEASE CHECK DIREC-
TORY AND SEND ADDRESS BACK TO ME BY WIRE
STOP
REGARDS AND THANKS GRADY CAVANAUGH.*

On the way back, he bought pastries at a bakery. He
dropped off a cannoli for Talia, who had a sweet tooth, and
asked her, "Did you retype that Nieuw Amsterdam proposal
for me?"

"I did it in two lamb shakes," she said happily and
indistinctly around the cream and pastry.

"Yeah, well, sorry to put you to the extra effort."

"I don't mind. You can't make an omelette without
breaking wind."

"Right," he said slowly. "Talia, where is the new copy?"

"Mr. Hastings took it for proofing."

Grady closed his eyes.

Grady walked to Warren's office as though he were walking
the last mile before being strapped into the electric chair.
When he arrived, Warren was reading the contract proposal,
squinting at it as though staring might reveal new details. He
looked up as Grady came in. "When were you going to talk
to me about this?"

"You told me not to," Grady said, surprising even
himself.

"Come again?"

Warren shrugged, accepting that. "You said take it to
engineering, don't bother you 'til it's firm."

"This proposal looks stronger than Rocci's furnace
design. That's a very good thing for your job."

Grady tried not to react visibly. It was the first time
Warren had directly threatened firing Grady. Aloud he said,
"It's a pretty good proposal."

"I only said it looked better than the furnace design." He leaned forward. "And now, some customer questions." He gestured to the chair in his office and barked, "Had you ever heard of the company before this year?"

"No."

"Do you know anyone else who has done business with them?"

"No."

"Did they give you a credit reference from a bank— preferably a bank you know?"

"No."

"Do they actually have a plant, and did you visit it?"

"Yes and yes." At least something about this deal sounded good.

"Did it look as though it had been in business for a long time?"

"I think so." At Warren's raised eyebrow, Grady went on hastily, "I didn't know much about their processing equipment."

"Did they pay for the dryer?"

"In advance."

Strangely, Warren frowned at that. "Maybe they just want to build up confidence. Was there anything unusual about processing the first payment?"

Grady was reminded uneasily of Klaus's questions. "Nothing much, unless you count paying in advance."

"Do they look as though they're doing enough business to pay for a furnace?"

"I couldn't tell."

"They have a major debt of some sort, don't they?"

"How did you—"

"Their terms, their terms. The clause about rules and terms of Gnomengesellschaft—now, there's a mouthful." The German didn't seem to bother Warren. "Plus they're trying not to move too much money at once. Which reminds me—does it look as though they could move their equipment in and out of their plant in one night? Think hard."

Grady, thoroughly startled, said, "Why would they want to do that?"

"Depending on how much we ask for up front, they might get the furnace and skip on their final net thirty days money."

"I don't get it. This is a small furnace; why would they do it?"

Warren tapped a pencil on the desk with each answer. "To get it, strip it down, and resell the design several times. To subcontract a big order by showing off the equipment, taking an advance, then skipping with the advance—and the unprocessed parts, if they're copper or silver or gold, and the equipment. To use as collateral for a loan they have no intention of paying back. To have it listed on insurance, move the piece, burn down the factory, and take the insurance money. That one's the sweetest: They don't pay us, they get paid for the furnace, and they still have the furnace somewhere else."

Grady said amazedly and with no tact at all, "You're good at thinking like that."

Warren scowled. "All it takes is common sense. That's why contracts aren't handshakes." He looked over the page again. "So, how do you feel about your little friend now?"

"He's honest," Grady said abruptly.

"Oho. You didn't like 'little friend,' did you?" But Warren's mood was mellowing as he reread the proposal. "Well, you've botched the first visit, that's certain, but the deal can be saved." He waved Grady out of the office. "Give me all the paperwork, and I mean all, and I'll be the contact from here."

• • •

Grady nodded and went to tell Susan, who exploded. "Who does he think he is?"

"Grady's boss," Tom Garneaux called from behind a racing form. "Also the guy you were accidentally screwing out of an in-house commission."

"What?" Grady was salary, and had assumed Warren was.

"Part of his pay. He gets a commission on every sale generated in-house. Cut him in on enough sales and he'll forgive you for hiding this one from him."

Susan's eyes narrowed. "I thought we were hiding it from you, too."

He went back to reading the racing form. "Not real well."

Susan snorted with disgust and turned back to Grady. "So what do we do?"

"What can we do? I'll write Antony and tell him that my boss wants to take over negotiations. He's a nice guy, and he'll understand; it happened to him with Pieter."

Susan said hesitantly, "Yes, but . . ."

"But Pieter seemed like a nice guy, too, and Warren isn't. I know." Grady sighed. "They're used to dealing with gnomes. They should be able to handle Warren."

"No doubt." But she didn't look reassured, and she chewed her lip thoughtfully. "Grady?"

"Yeah."

"I'm a little scared that Klaus will be able to handle Warren."

Grady remembered lying sprawled on the cavern floor. "Yeah. And you know he'll try."

He asked Talia four times that afternoon, but there was no reply from the War Department about Stode. Right now that seemed like the least of his troubles.

SIX

GRADY THANKED GOD that Warren spent so much time out of the building. Warren was a hard worker, but he much preferred expensive lunches with customers to paperwork with other employees. Today he had gone to New York City for a plant tour, dinner, and a show on a company expense account. He might even bring back an order, after enough trips.

Grady looked at his own meager budget, grateful that he'd won all his bets leading to the Browns-Cardinals Series, and wondering how he'd manage to hide this trip from Warren and still entertain Antony and Kirsten.

He had answered the phone two days ago; to his surprise, it was Kirsten. "I need to visit your plant before Antony comes again."

His stomach tightened. "Isn't that a little dangerous?"

"That's what I need to know. We'll come Thursday."

"All right."

There was a short pause, then: "All right. I'll be there." And she hung up. It took Grady a moment to realize that Kirsten, who had faced down a gnome without flinching, was terrified of coming to Rhode Island.

"Your friend's here," Talia said, "and he brought most of his wife." She added, "I saw her just a moment ago."

That took Grady a moment. When he met Antony in the lobby; Kirsten wasn't there. "She went on ahead."

"She said she was your wife?"

"It explains the height, doesn't it?" Antony said lazily. He didn't like it much. "We'd better catch up with her."

Grady remembered that Kirsten could face off with a gnome and not be afraid; suddenly he was more afraid for the workers of Plimstubb.

They caught up with her in front of the Hudson Drill furnace, talking to Sonny LeTour. "But isn't that dangerous?"

Sonny answered politely, "Well, ma'am, the bare wire is dangerous. Give you quite a shock, maybe even stop your heart. That's why we use covered wire, or we put guards on the places we can't cover—"

"You wanta cover something?" Roy Burgess barked. "Cover your lazy black ass in sweat, or find another job." He turned to Kirsten, who was standing with her hands on her hips, frowning at him. "What is this, the goddamn yellow brick road? Listen, sweetheart, shouldn't you be dancing under a toadstool somewhere?"

Kirsten said in a voice that crackled with reined-in anger, "Shouldn't you be treating employees better? Shouldn't you be trying to sell me a furnace?"

Roy did a double take, turned, and saw Grady and Antony. "Oh, no," he said in a small voice, then, trying feebly to save himself, "Hi, Dutch. Howya doing?"

"Fine, Roy." Antony, grinning, moved over by Kirsten. "You need to get a brake for that mouth, or maybe trade it in on next year's model."

Sonny chuckled. When Roy turned, he was sweeping seriously, as though it couldn't have been him.

Kirsten coughed before Roy could speak. He choked back what he wanted to say and said plaintively to Grady, "Jesus, can't a guy get some warning? You said 'customers,' not . . ." He left before he could get in more trouble.

Grady turned to Kirsten. "You're supposed to wait for an escort."

"I'm sorry." But she was unembarrassed. "I understand completely. I get nervous when anyone walks around our plant unescorted."

Antony chuckled. "You're never gonna win this one, Grady."

Grady silently agreed. "Why don't we go to Engineering?"

Susan was happy to see them both. Garneaux was out of his seat, shaking hands with Antony before Grady could introduce Kirsten. "Nice to see you again. You want to go fishing again on the bay?"

Kirsten raised an eyebrow. Antony said hastily, "No, no, not this trip. Tom, this is my, um, wife, Kirsten."

He took her hand, nodding. "Maybe we should find something to do that she'll enjoy more."

"We"? Grady groaned inwardly; this trip was already way too public. He was anxious to get them out of the plant before Warren returned. "I figured a quick dinner before they go back on the road—"

"No, no, no. Show them a real time. Have you ever been to Boston?"

Antony said, "Not in quite a while." Kirsten, eyes wide, shook her head.

He slapped his desk. "All right. We'll go first thing in the morning. Suzie, you come, too."

"Fine with me," Susan said. "Kirsten can stay with me. Grady, Antony can stay with you."

Garneaux raised an eyebrow; Susan had forgotten that the dwarves were supposed to be husband and wife.

Kirsten said coolly, "That sounds nice. Do you mind, dear?"

"Of course not—honey." Antony was having some trouble keeping a straight face; he turned to Grady. "This okay with you, kid?"

Grady said resignedly, "Sure." He pictured turning in the expense sheet.

At nine the next morning, the four of them stopped at Garneaux's front yard. It was a garden showcase; it had neatly trimmed shrubs, well-laid-out oval beds, a rose bush climbing a lamppost, and a gleaming fourteen-foot flagpole.

"How much do you guys pay him?" Antony said quietly. "This takes dough."

Grady looked around as they went up the walk. "Not as much as you'd think." The lamppost was painted iron piping of the kind used at Plimstubb. The brick lining the beds was insulating firebrick from the furnaces. And the flag-pole . . .

"Like it?" Garneaux stepped outside, dressed in wool pants, a dress shirt, and the loudest tie permitted by law.

Grady said, "Great flagpole. Alloy steel?"

He patted it. "The high-priced stuff. Nothing but the best for Old Glory. If somebody firebombed this house, the flagpole wouldn't even melt. Makes you proud."

"I'll say," Antony said admiringly. "It must have cost a fortune."

There was an awkward silence, after which Garneaux turned back to the front door. "Let me show you the rest of the place."

Susan peered at the furnace thermostat. Mounted on small metal frame, it was a Wheelco temperature controller very much like the ones Plimstubb used at work.

Actually, it was exactly like the ones Plimstubb used. Susan said, "Where did this come from?"

He looked at her innocently. "It says it's from Wheelco." She shut up.

Kirsten, standing on tiptoes to peer out the rear window, said, "What a lovely garden and footpath."

"I'm glad you like it. I've got a victory garden behind that, of course, but I didn't want to give up the flowers. I laid that path in myself."

"Nice job," Grady said. It was high-temperature furnace hearth tile.

"You should see it in June." Garneaux pointed out the different beds for flowers and sighed. "I had a stainless steel birdbath, too. Gee, it was beautiful. Somebody stole it, can you imagine?"

Kirsten clearly could.

"Say, Suzie, could you do me a favor?" Garneaux reached into a bureau drawer. "Would you carry this?" He handed her a fist-size roll with a rubber band around it.

Susan stared at it. Grady noted that the outside bill was a fifty. She said, "What are you taking this for?"

"Bail. Usually my wife carries it, but Helen's at her sister's."

Kirsten looked alarmed. Susan said, "Can't Grady carry it?"

Garneaux cocked an eye. "I figured he'd probably be in the can with me."

Susan sighed loudly and put the money in her purse.

The drive to Boston was surprisingly—almost distressingly—brief. Garneaux's Oldsmobile had power to spare; even Antony, who loved speed, gripped the door to his right. Garneaux shouted over the roar, "I always put a bigger motor in my car. Habit I've had since I was a kid. Gives it some pizzazz, though, doesn't it?"

As they gunned into downtown Boston, Garneaux turned his head toward the back. "What were your plans for lunch?"

Kirsten went white as they zoomed barely to one side of an oncoming bus. Grady said hastily after the screech of brakes, "You pick."

"Chinatown," he said firmly, and pulled in at the curb, pointing across the street. "Hop out and we'll try that restaurant."

"What's it called?" The red-and-gold wooden sign running the width of the restaurant across the top was in Chinese.

"Who cares? We're going to eat, not write the *Globe* about them."

The restaurant was the size of a storefront; scars and darker tiles on the floor showed the shelving layout from when, in its previous incarnation, it had been a store. The tables were close together, the kitchen was open to view, and everyone in the place was Oriental.

An old man approached them, arms folded, and pointed to one side. "Best table, Mr. Garneaux."

He patted the old man's arm. "Thanks, Lee. You don't have any bad tables. New menus, huh?"

They were in Chinese ideograms, with almost incomprehensible English next to them: "Soy thing. Hot spice meat surplus." That was probably meant to be "surprise." "The fish who caught the day over rice." Garneaux turned to the others. "I'll order." He did it by pointing at the menu.

The waiter bowed, then returned to the kitchen, shouting orders. He was the owner and also, as it developed when he seized a wicked-looking cleaver, the cook. Antony watched him uneasily. "What is he chopping up?"

Garneaux, pocketing a copy of the menu, squinted. "It should be chicken, pork, and fish. Why, what does it look like?"

"I don't want to know what it looks like; I want to know what it is. And what's that fourth thing?" It was too pale for meat, but it didn't look like any fish Antony knew.

Garneaux shrugged. "Food." The cook tossed aside the meat and chopped onions, celery, and something that looked like cabbage.

Grady muttered, "He's got a whole victory garden in there."

Susan said, "Yeah, but whose victory?"

Garneaux held up a warning finger. "Lee fled Manchuria and came here without a penny. Believe me, China's hated Japan a lot longer than we have."

Kirsten looked from one of them to the other dubiously but said nothing.

Along with the rice, six steaming bowls and four saucers came to the table. Garneaux pointed to each of the bowls. "Dip this stuff in ginger. Dip this in the mustard, but be careful, it's very hot. That stuff that looks like marmalade, that's a sweet and sour sauce; try the pork."

Kirsten and Antony looked at each other. Susan said to Kirsten, "Are you going to test his food for him, too?"

Antony moved first. "Change is good for me." He reached for the bowl of chicken.

Grady went for the pork. "And I am not afraid."

An hour later, the bowls were empty. Grady looked wonderingly at Garneaux. "How did you think to find this place?"

"I dashed inside one night and Lee thought I wanted dinner."

"Coming in out of the rain?"

"More out of the heat," he said vaguely. "Come on, I want to show our guests something."

A rapid drive through Boston and across the Charles brought them to the grounds of MIT. The classroom buildings were imposing and impressive. They drove beyond them, into the neighborhood of student housing.

Gesturing toward Antony, Garneaux said, "Our friend here asked about engineers. I thought I'd show him where engineers come from."

"Are you taking me to a classroom?"

Grady started to say "yes," but Garneaux answered, shocked, "What would you learn there?" He strode up the dormitory steps. "Nice-looking place. I wish I'd lived in one." He shouted, "Can we come on in if we bring a couple of cute girls?"

Susan bristled. Kirsten looked amused.

A man's voice, still young enough to crack a little, answered. "Are they really cute?"

"Absolutely. The tall one looks like Betty Grable when she quits frowning."

"Bring 'em on. Second floor. We hardly ever see girls."

Grady remembered that feeling from engineering classes. The first thing Grady noticed was that they all needed haircuts. He'd forgotten about living cheaply in college. The second thing he noticed, and it startled him badly, was how young they all looked to him. How long had it been since he'd graduated?

Finally he noticed the hall itself and the room doors, which looked odd.

One of the doors was bricked shut.

Another had an elaborate bolt, bar, and combination lock across the frame.

Still another had a steel door with massive hinges and a floor-to-ceiling bar pierced through with Yale locks running to U-bolts on a steel door frame.

Garneaux looked at it blankly. "What the hell is this, Fort Knox?"

"A challenge." A scrawny, earnest student with a tangle of uncombed red hair stared at him earnestly. "We're freshmen—"

"Imagine that," Susan murmured.

He shot her a look but went on. "We share the dorm with seniors. They're supposed to offer us guidance. What they do is ride us and make life rotten."

"So what's the challenge?" Grady asked, but he'd already guessed.

"They've taken two weeks to fortify their doors. If I can break into any of the rooms in one day, I can do anything I want to it."

"Anything?" Garneaux was impressed. "Shoot, I feel sorry for these guys already."

The scrawny student grimaced and pointed to the steel door. "Don't bother. I'll never get through all that."

"I wouldn't think so." Garneaux scratched his head. "Of course, if you're sure he said, 'break into the room' and not 'go through the door,' you're all set."

"You mean—oh, my God, the window. Someone could lower me on a rope, or I could use a ladder. . . ." His enthusiasm faded. "But I hate heights, and he did say that if I broke in, not a proxy, I could do it."

"My, oh, my." He shook his head. "I just don't know what they teach at these schools." He pulled a scrap of paper from his pocket—predictably, it was a menu—and sketched on it. "A dorm room is a rectangular solid. The door and the window are small planes on two of six faces."

He looked up. A small gaggle of freshmen watched him expectantly. He threw up his hands. "All right, all right. Get me more paper, cough up a sawbuck each, and I'll give you a design for each of your problems."

In short order Garneaux had a pocket full of tens. He had also designed a homemade wrecking ball out of rope and a footlocker full of bricks ("Anchor it in the ell of the dorm, swing from the roof, make sure you hit the right window"), a hose arrangement with a spray nozzle that punched through the keyhole ("Compressed air, cement and water; don't lay down more than six inches, or his room will be the next floor down"), and, Grady's particular favorite, a flume running from a bathroom sink on the fourth floor into the upper casement of a dorm room on the third ("Be sure to caulk the window and the door; you don't want to spoil the surprise").

The last room was the toughest: The windows were barred and shuttered on the inside, and the door was fronted with a door that apparently had come from a bank vault. Grady was enjoying all this but was quite glad he didn't own property anywhere near MIT.

Susan said suddenly, "The bottom side of the cube."

Garneaux beamed at her. "Good girl. What's the basement here like?"

They ran down. It was bare floor, and the ceiling below the room was unencumbered by plumbing or light fixtures.

Susan pointed up. "Two choices. The easy one is to saw away the floor and drop everything into the basement—"

"Perfect," one freshman said.

Another, who looked smarter, asked, "What's the other way?"

"Well, it takes a little lumber, and some, uh, borrowing of equipment." She stamped on the floor, listening. "It seems pretty solid. Do you know where you can get a hydraulic jack?"

There was the sound of heavy machinery from somewhere on campus. The smarter freshman smirked. "As it happens, I do."

She sketched a wood frame for the top of the press. "Build a solid framework below it, build a good cradle on top of it—watch for stress points here and here—and run it as high as you can." She handed over the sketch. "Then lower it, raise the platform under it, and run it all the way to the ceiling of the first-floor room."

The smart one said, "What about his desk and bed?" He corrected the sketch. "You assumed the stresses would be equal."

Garneaux said, "It sounds like you can handle it from here." He shook hands all around.

They left as the freshmen dashed out in a body to borrow—or find—a truck.

"You realize, of course," Kirsten said earnestly, "that everything you told those young men to do is wrong."

Garneaux sat up, startled. "You mean it won't work?"

"Of course it will work," she said exasperatedly, "but—"

"Oh. Well." He settled back down, contentedly counting his money. "For a minute there you made me think I'd been dishonest."

Susan said deadpan, "Well, now you know where engineers come from."

Antony said, "Let's get out of here before the cops come and we find out where engineers go."

Predictably, Garneaux said, "I know a place."

The bar, on the South Side, was named Gilhooley's; the sign was faded, the paint flaking. A NO DUMPING notice was barely visible above a pile of orange crates and cardboard.

Susan said dubiously, "From the outside this looks like a real dive."

"Doesn't it, though?" Garneaux rubbed his hands together. "Boy oh, boy, wait'll you see how bad it looks inside." He held the door open. Kirsten moved ahead of Susan, walking with her weight balanced and her hands ready. Antony snickered, but did the same in front of Grady, who bristled at being protected.

The place reeked of spilled beer; the floor was covered with damp sawdust. Grady and Susan stepped in gingerly. Garneaux glided past them like a dancer, bellowing to the barmaid, "Molly-oh! Beer and corned beef for four."

"Soda bread?" she screeched back. She was a plump, pleasant-looking woman with graying red hair that had probably been tucked up earlier in the day.

"You bet. Bring our second round right after you bring the first." As Molly reached for a pitcher, he added hastily, "No, no! The good stuff, the bottles."

"Both rounds? Big spender." She scooped five bottles into her apron.

Grady surreptitiously counted the remaining expense money. He could cover a round and part of another.

Molly set the drinks down looked quizzically at Susan and Grady. "Nervous, are you?" She pointed a stubby finger at Garneaux. "If that lot the next table over make trouble, you send these youngsters behind the bar."

"Will do."

She beamed at him and held out her palm. Grady sighed and moved to put the money on the table.

"Uh-uh." Garneaux waved the money from the MIT students at him. "My treat."

Grady pocketed his remaining expense money with relief. Now he could settle down to worrying about the five men at the next table, who looked harder than the floor under the sawdust and twice as scarred.

Twenty minutes later, the five of them were laughing at a convoluted and fairly coarse joke. The other five people around the table, including the one who told the joke, were laughing as well. Garneaux had his arm around two of them.

Kirsten said wonderingly, "I thought you'd all be grim and worried about the war."

Garneaux spread his arms out, relaxed and expansive. "Why worry? We'll win; you'll see. In the mean time, all work and no play makes Tommy a dull boy."

Antony raised his glass in a salute. "I'll bet you make work look like play."

Garneaux acknowledged the toast, not noticing that the group at the table had fallen silent. The five hard cases from the next table had disappeared completely, and Molly had her head ducked, polishing glasses.

A hand fell on Garneaux's shoulder and he looked up.

"I remember you," the cop said.

"That was somebody else."

"So you say."

The others watched nervously until Garneaux signaled for another beer. "This is Michael Doogan, one of Boston's finest. Formerly not."

"Ah, but those days are gone." He shook his head. "I can remember walking through these neighborhoods in the blistering summer, my fingers in my ears so I wouldn't hear the beer bottles explodin' in good folks' attics—"

Kirsten broke in, suddenly understanding, "Was this during Prohibition?"

"Now that," Doogan said solemnly, "I really couldn't say."

The beer came and Tom sat it at the edge of the table. "I'd ask you to sit, but clearly you're on your beat."

"Decent of you to understand."

"No drinking, I suppose." He slid the beer to the edge of the table.

"None." Doogan leaned on the edge beside it.

"Otherwise, it's not a bad beat."

"It's all right." He casually, with an almost unnoticeable scoop, picked up and set down the now half-empty beer. "Beats the far side of the Charles. All hell broke loose there today."

"No foolin'?" Garneaux said with interest.

"Bunch of MIT kids in a contest damn near destroyed their dorm. Crazy stuff, and then again pretty ingenious, you might say, but half of them lost everything and they're gonna have to live elsewhere. All for a bet."

Garneaux shook his head. "College kids."

Susan said with polite interest, "Was anyone else involved?" She had a hand in her purse; Grady was fairly sure she was checking the bail money.

Doogan's beer went up and down a second time, coming down empty. "Again, that I really couldn't say. Though they did tell a fascinatin' story. Thank you for your generosity, Tommy, and it was good to see you and, so to speak, not to see you."

He strolled away. Garneaux said with quiet emphasis but calmly, "Time to leave."

They walked through narrow streets back to the car. Shortly Garneaux stopped them. "You realize what this is?" He pointed down. "Cobblestone. The original street cover. Paul Revere walked this, and Sam Adams, and the men and boys who threw tea in Boston Harbor, and probably some of the men who died at Bunker Hill and in the Boston Massacre—"

He had tears in his eyes. "This is what we're all fighting for. This is the birthplace of American liberty. Can't you just feel freedom coming right from the buildings and stones?" He waved his arms. "Come here."

They moved toward him uneasily, Grady assuming they were all about to get a sentimental, drunken hug. Instead Garneaux dropped to his knees the moment they surrounded him and, shielded from view by their bodies, started digging a cobblestone out of the street.

Susan said blankly, "What are you doing?"

"This is an authentic symbol of American freedom," Garneaux said reverently, "and I'm going to steal it."

Shortly they were on their way back to Providence. Grady drove, savoring a cigarette and enjoying the power of the oversize engine. Garneaux, after expounding a little more on freedom and where the stone was going to go in his garden, fell asleep. Susan said to Kirsten, "Well, now you know a little more about the place than you expected." She added, with an edge, "Grady tells me it's a nice place."

"It is," Kirsten said. "I can see that; I'm comfortable with Antony visiting here. And I can see you don't recognize that it's nice, mostly because not all of it is. In time a lot of that may change."

Susan shook her head. "You take a longer view than I do."

"Of course I do," Kirsten said sadly.

Grady wondered why, but concentrated on keeping the engine from getting away from him. Lately it seemed that everything was getting away from him.

SEVEN

I T WAS INDIAN summer, and the Series was over. The Cards
had knocked off the Browns in six games, the last one a
3–1 victory. Grady, feeling flush and taking his car for
once, walked quietly in the rear door of the plant and
glanced either way. Warren Hastings was nowhere in sight.

Grady moved quickly and quietly to his office. Susan
would be waiting there.

Unfortunately, so was Warren. He was leaning negligently on the desk, thumbing disdainfully through a copy of
Astounding. He was also holding the Nieuw Amsterdam
Metalworks file. Susan, arms folded, was scowling furiously.

He held the file out toward Grady, but out of reach.
"When is your second round of negotiations with these
people?"

Grady tossed his cane onto the coatrack, mostly to stall
for time. "This afternoon," he said finally.

Warren nodded toward Susan with satisfaction. "You

see? If you're smart, next time you'll tell me the truth." He took her chin in his thumb and forefinger. She moved back, her eyes furious. He turned back to Grady. "I'll handle it from here, and without you."

Grady shook his head. "They won't let you in."

"They'll have to."

"Not if they don't want to buy. Believe me, everything about this customer isn't in the folder."

Warren raised an eyebrow. "Enlighten me on the road. Miss Rocci, stay home and do your own work, not ours."

"You need me," Susan insisted. "If there's a design change, you'll want it done on the spot."

Now it was Warren's turn to scowl. He considered, and finally grunted irritably. "All right—but you'd best both prove you were necessary." He added, brushing past Grady, "And I'll drive."

Five hours later, Grady was wishing he had let Warren come alone. Antony, swinging his heels under his chair, was wishing he'd never tried to modernize the Dwarfworks.

Antony had met them at the door to the plant, moving the vines and ushering them in. Warren, unflappable, had shaken hands with him, with Kirsten, and with Pieter, bending over too far and speaking too loudly. He had laughed too heartily at minor jokes, and he had spoken too admiringly of the plant, which Antony knew looked like a blacksmith's shop in a cave. Kirsten was immediately annoyed, Pieter disgusted but patient.

They sat down at the rough-hewn table in Pieter's office, and Warren opened his briefcase. Before he took anything out there was a knock at the door and an amused voice said, "I hope I haven't missed anything."

Pieter said resignedly, "Mr. Warren Hastings, please meet Klaus of the Gnomengesellschaft. We are under contract to him for some debt, so he has asked to be present."

Warren stood—Grady suspected that he always stood in the presence of money—and extended his hand. Klaus shook it without coming in, waited for Warren to react, then strode in, shortening his arm as he came. "Always a pleasure to meet a poised businessman."

Warren got a hard glint in his eye. "I enjoy it myself. Tell me, are you in the heat treating business?"

Grady looked at Susan's face and knew that she, too, was thinking of Garner Stanley Irving, the living furnace pinned to the floor in the other cavern.

"As a sideline. Still, I'm intrigued by what you propose here." Klaus curled a lengthy finger under his chin, resting on it thoughtfully. "Is it possible to make money with equipment this expensive?"

Warren smiled broadly, and this time it didn't look phony. "A great deal of it, if business is booming for manufacturers." He winked. "And if an industry is desperate, you can name your price. We deal a lot with aircraft companies. God bless the war."

Susan inhaled sharply; Grady caught her eye and shook his head slightly. Pieter, meanwhile, was doing the same thing to Antony.

"How nice for you. . . . I'm sorry to say that the Dwarfworks isn't exactly on a wartime footing. In fact, I'm at this meeting to express concern that a debtor of ours would spend so liberally." He smiled, and a second row of pointed teeth appeared behind the first, then subsided again. "I need to question the deal thoroughly."

Grady was almost proud of Warren for not flinching. "Ask anything."

"First you should ask me." They turned to Pieter, who was frowning. "I decide to buy. Or perhaps not."

Warren fell over himself apologizing. A frowning customer was a bad thing, particularly one who hadn't signed
anything. Pieter cut him off. "First is most important. We
wish to keep this place secret."

"We do not wish," Klaus said, and for a moment his eyes
glowed yellow. "We insist."

"Quite all right." Warren waved a hand airily. "We
always keep customers' names confidential."

Klaus nodded. "As do we."

Warren smiled at him slyly. "Reduces the competition,
doesn't it?"

It bothered Grady how well Klaus and Warren understood each other.

Antony interjected, "But you're also a customer of ours.
If we made something for your customer, can you keep from
telling him the source?"

Warren looked momentarily confused. Grady wrote
quickly, "The moly hearth," and passed the sheet of paper to
him.

"Oh, yes. That's no problem. The government's involved
in that one," he said. (Grady winced, thinking of "Loose
Lips Sink Ships" posters.) "It's easy to hide things from the
government. Prudent, too."

Grady wondered, a little wistfully, what Stode's response
would be if he heard that.

But Pieter nodded. "Then we can keep supplying the
work if they want more of it." Antony sighed, relieved.
Whatever trouble Warren would be, at least he wouldn't
expose the Dwarfworks to anyone else.

Pieter went on, "We have looked over your drawings,
and your catalog, and if it does what you say, it is very good.
But you have changed it for us, yes? The changes we should
review."

"They're on the prints," Warren began, but Pieter shook
his head.

"We have drawn our own. You will see. They are the same as yours, but easier to review." He set a roll of papers on the table and untied the binding ribbon, laying them in a flat stack.

"Actually," Klaus said smoothly, "we redrew them for the Dwarfworks. Professional courtesy, plus which we own the drafting process. We call it EGAD: Elf-Gnome Assisted Design."

"I wish to God I knew how they come up with these names," Antony muttered to Grady. "Sometimes I think they're just making fun of us."

"Unusual name," Warren commented, staring at the topmost print. It looked like a normal general assembly print, complete with bill of materials for steel. But the edges were lined with runes.

"Allow me to demonstrate." But Klaus caught himself. "Pieter? It is, after all, still your office."

Pieter nodded curtly. He stood before the pile of prints, made a fist, and smacked it dead center, shouting, *"RAUS!"*

Susan and Grady gasped. Even Warren stared wide-eyed.

Tiny arms appeared from the runes and man after man scrambled out of the flat page and strode around, scowling and hitching their trousers. The largest of them was no more than four inches tall.

The last man, fat and filthy, stamped his way to the center of the print, clapped his hands, and shouted at the others. From his tone and his expression, it was clear that he was swearing at them. From the gestures they made behind his back, it was clear that none of the little men much cared.

In twos and threes they scurried to the bill of materials in the corner of the top print. A skinny worker with missing teeth reached into the first item ("Steel channel two-inch, four six-foot sections") and pulled out, one at a time, four pieces of channel steel. Grady couldn't be sure, but he thought they matched the scale on the print.

When the others had pulled out all the items in that bill of materials, the foreman bent back a corner of the print and started on the electrical print below it. Then he did the piping, the asbestos brick insulation, and the conveyor belt drive.

At the center of the top print they quickly set up the frame and heating chamber, bricked it for insulation, ran a conveyor belt through it, piped it (the supply ends of the pipes were strangely out of focus and made Grady's eyes water), and hooked up small transformers and electrical controls. The entire time they spat, kicked each other, threw things, and laughed nastily at each other's misfortune.

They stepped back, the furnace complete. The foreman threw a switch, the furnace heated up, and they introduced nitrogen to take the oxygen out, then dissociated ammonia to run process materials in. A large blue flame appeared at the rear of the furnace, where the hydrogen burned off; the flame grew—

There was a table-shaking BANG, and flames shot out both ends of the little furnace. Several of the men fell down. When the others laughed, they leaped up and threw punches, and the print degenerated into a tabletop fistfight.

Pieter smashed his fist down in a clear area. *"HALTET!"* The little men dashed to the edge of the top print, sliding into the runes, and vanished.

Grady gestured at the print. "Is there any point to their being so unpleasant?"

Klaus smiled. "Aesthetics."

"That does not matter," Pieter rumbled. "We have the question, why did the furnace explode?"

"Air got in," Grady said immediately. "It came in the front, since there was still a flame at the back. But if they put enough gas in, there's no reason that should happen."

"Yes, there is." Susan pointed to the rear of furnace.

"Chimney effect. The back is higher than the front, hot gas rises—especially hot hydrogen—and as it goes, it's sucking the gas right out of the furnace like a chimney."

"Come on," Grady said, astonished. "We've built these for years. Is it possible—?"

"Yes, if you make a mistake," Susan said with loathing, and Grady recognized that the loathing was for herself. "I messed up a dimension on the rear legs when I cut it down. Use the figure from the front legs; I can't believe I did that—"

"People make mistakes," Kirsten said, and corrected herself, seeing Susan's expression, "All of us make mistakes."

Antony took an ordinary rubber eraser—perhaps it should have been turned in for the rubber drive, but it was darkened with overuse and probably had as much sentimental value as utility—and rubbed dutifully until by sheer erosion it wiped out the faulty rear-leg dimension; he then penciled in the one from the front. He raised a fist, but Grady surprised himself by saying, "May I?" It wasn't good to lose this much control of negotiations.

Antony looked startled, then grinned. "Sure, why not?"

Grady struck the print, shouting, *"RAUS!"*

The tiny workers scurried in from all sides, muttering and punching at each other. They assembled the furnace easily, installed the belt, heated it up, and began processing parts. The foreman gestured angrily and chattered at the others, who withdrew with a variety of obscene gestures. He stood beside the furnace alone, scowling and reaching inside his overalls to scratch his crotch.

"It works," Antony said, adding fervently, "God, I hate those guys."

Grady stared at the foreman a moment longer, looked up, and locked eyes with Susan, and they mouthed simultaneously, "Roy Burgess."

Warren gave a cursory glance at the pile of prints, as though this sort of thing were automatic in his life. "Yes, well, now that we've confirmed our product, don't you think we should confirm our price?"

Klaus said admiringly, "We can't do anything to frighten or impress you, can we?"

Warren looked him in the eye. "There isn't a thing in heaven or hell that can distract me from setting a price and signing a deal."

Klaus turned his misshapen head toward Grady. "Know this. You could learn a great deal at this table about negotiating a sale."

Grady smiled frozenly, thinking, *If I thought that was all selling was about, I'd quit now. War and all.* Then he said aloud, "Add one clause: We want Garner Stanley Irving shut down."

Klaus said, "Ridiculous."

Pieter said, "Yes, or we make no deal. I want it so, too. How much badly do you want this bargain?"

To Grady's discomfort, the gnome's eyes glowed golden. Klaus wanted this bargain badly indeed.

"Done," Klaus said finally. "Write in all copies that the furnace known as Garner Stanley Irving will be shut down and disassembled"—Heinrich looked disapproving—"for a period of one year after completion of contract, pending subsequent review for reassembly." Heinrich relaxed.

Pieter shrugged sadly and said to Grady, "It is what you will get, boy."

Grady opened his mouth. Warren kicked Grady's bad leg, hard, and Grady said unhappily, "Done."

"We will write it in." Pieter held up two papers. "Here is the contract for the furnace. The front we typed, but much of it is handwritten, one copy for each of us." He scribbled the new paragraph on both.

Warren waved a hand airily. "Just as long as both copies are the same."

"Of course." A thought seemed to strike Pieter. "Why don't you look at both copies. Antony and Kirsten and I, we will leave. Klaus, you leave, too."

The gnome stood obediently. Grady and Susan looked at each other doubtfully; something wasn't right.

In the office door, Pieter turned. "Do not make the workers come out of the print while we are not there. They are not to give information to others than to us."

Warren nodded without saying anything. The door closed and he said immediately, "You are about to learn what the term 'seller's advantage' means."

Susan began, "They told you not to—"

"They also said that the workers had information."

"Actually, they didn't," Grady pointed out. "They only said the workers weren't allowed to give information. You don't know what might happen if you strike that print."

"Salesmanship is risk."

Susan said with an edge in her voice, "You also at least implied that you wouldn't do this."

"Don't be weak." Warren poised his fist over the stack of prints and smashed it down, snapping *"RAUS!"* in a peremptory voice.

Grady jumped, pain or no, and Susan squeaked involuntarily as the little figures fled the print and dashed for every corner of the room.

Warren bent to look for them. Susan and Grady followed. Seconds later there was a thud as a final worker left the table and scampered to the homemade bookshelf in the corner.

Almost immediately, the dwarves and Klaus returned to the office. Antony said, "Is everything all right?"

Warren stood in front of the table, hiding the prints behind him. "Absolutely."

Pieter gestured toward the contract on the side table. "Then let's sign off."

Grady said uncertainly, "Why don't we reread it just one more time." The dwarves seemed way too anxious to close the deal, and were trying too hard to look casual.

Warren snorted. "Engineers. Cavanaugh, you've got to have confidence in yourself." This was true, but Grady thought that confidence without caution was bad, too.

Warren searched the table for his pen and gave up. "Cavanaugh. Pen." He took it without thanking Grady, moved to the back page of the contract, and signed with a flourish, handing the pen over to Pieter. Klaus watched, smiling entirely too much.

Pieter signed, handing the pen to Klaus. "You be a witness."

Susan said quietly to Kirsten, "You trust him?"

Klaus turned his head slightly, amused. Kirsten said even more quietly, "Gnomes honor every contract to the letter, and are bound by them much more than you are or than we are." She added more loudly, "And no, I don't trust them at all."

Pieter handed the pen to Klaus, who extended his arm slightly to reach it. The flourish from Klaus's signature rippled toward the ceiling, then pulled back without haste. "Perhaps before we leave this room we should read the document together."

Warren blinked. "What?"

"It's a tradition," Klaus said solemnly, as though it were the reading of a will. He passed it to Pieter, who cleared his throat and began.

The reading went on mechanically until the clause about delivery deadlines. After it was read, Warren stiffened and said, "Read that again."

Pieter dutifully read aloud, "If we fail in this delivery

date, we will provide free of any charge an ammonia dissociator, being a device that breaks ammonia into nitrogen and hydrogen under heat, the same device to be delivered within thirty days of the original delivery date. Failure of that date shall mean that the furnace is also free." He peered over his glasses at Warren. "Very generous terms, you men of Plimstubb give."

Warren snatched up his own copy and stared at it, moving his lips. On the bookshelf in the corner of the room, one of the little EGAD men stood on the bottom shelf, a pen nearly his height clasped by his side. He straddled the pen a moment, stroked it obscenely and meaningfully, stuck out his tongue, and vanished into the shelved paperwork.

Grady held his breath. It would be embarrassing, but Warren could dispute the contract and save the deal.

Instead Warren said with a snarl, "Too generous. Cavanaugh here clearly failed to negotiate with his own company or his own interests in mind." He stressed "his own interests." "We came into this session unprepared."

Grady had often wondered if this would happen under Warren, but had envisioned nothing like this. He numbly waited for the inevitable penalty, praying that it wouldn't be financial.

Warren said indifferently, "If he can sell furnaces with no concern for penalty clauses, he can get along on less money himself. Half time would be appropriate." He added as if to himself, "Maybe I'm too generous here as well."

The room was silent; Susan stared compassionately at Grady, who was numb. Pieter roused himself. "He could work here half time, if he is glad to work hard. I think maybe he could bring us business, if he worked hard maybe." He added, with a reassuring smile, "Welcome to the job, boy, if you think you can do it."

"I promise I will," Grady said earnestly.

Warren snorted with disgust. "Be careful what you promise. You'll be working for the people who just cheated you."

Antony thought that was pretty strong language from the man who had just outsmarted himself. "Nobody cheated you."

"Tricked, then."

"Not a trick," Pieter corrected. "A prank, it would be called. Sometimes we play a prank on someone."

"A prank?" Klaus wagged his distorted head, vastly amused. "What you did to Rip Van Winkle was a prank?"

Susan and Grady turned toward Pieter with interest.

"Rip Van Winkle was not hurt," Pieter said, unperturbed. "And that was maybe nearly two hundred years ago, before this was a country. We do better now."

"See that you do, especially on keeping your agreement with Gnomengesellschaft. And if for some reason one of the parties violates this arrangement—" Klaus chuckled. "Well, there's certainly a precedent for action, isn't there?" He reshaped his throat and sang in an incongruously high, fluting voice,

> *Look at all the feet!*
> *Little feet!*
> *Pretty feet!*

For some reason Kirsten and Antony bristled, but Pieter listened impassively. Klaus paused and shrugged. "I can't do the song justice." He left the office, followed by the humans.

Halfway to the tunnel, Klaus turned around. "Mr. Hastings, it would gratify me to speak with you in private, and it would be to your advantage."

Warren smiled for the first time since the reading of the altered contract. "I enjoy deals to my advantage."

Klaus looked quickly from side to side. "No one spoke of a deal." He gestured with a clawed arm into the darkness ahead. "Not here, at least. Please come with me."

Warren said abruptly, "Cavanaugh, Miss Rocci, meet me at the car," and disappeared into the tunnel. Susan and Grady walked quickly to the car, glancing over their shoulders nervously until they were safely out of the Dwarfworks and the gnomes' tunnel was far behind them.

Susan spoke first. "We wait half an hour, then we drive back."

Grady was shocked. "We have to go back for him."

"Do we?" She considered. "Dammit, you're right. He has the car keys." She lit a cigarette and puffed vigorously and irritably.

There was a tap at the car window. Grady peered out, then opened the door. Antony was standing there. "Listen kid, I'm sorry your boss blamed you for what happened back there."

"Sure." Grady struggled with his loyalties to Plimstubb and said, "He did it to himself."

"Didn't he, though?" Antony grinned. "He really must have rubbed Pieter the wrong way; he hasn't done that to anybody since—well, in a long time." His grin faded. "Your pay isn't going to be as much as it was."

"I'll take what I can get." But Grady thought unhappily about the money for gas, plus the bills for two households. Even with what the government paid for his father and Kevin, life wasn't going to be easy.

Antony liked Grady's answer. "On the bright side, we'll take care of your lodging and meals. Plus you get some other things." He pointed back at the hillside, where the main entrance was covered in vines and invisible. "You'll learn things you never dreamed of."

"Do you want me to sign an agreement never to reveal what I learned?"

"Of course not. If your word isn't good enough, neither is your signature. And with the gnomes backing our contract, you wouldn't dare do anything underhanded. Jeez, kid, don't think like Klaus." He shook his head. "Isn't he the scariest thing you've ever seen?"

"Pretty much," Grady said. Antony raised an eyebrow. On impulse Grady said, "Let me tell you about someone . . ."

He related as much of the story of Drake Stode as he could without revealing details about the contract. At the end, Antony nodded vigorously. "You're right. He's not Regular Army, and believe me, I know Regular Army." He brightened. "Did I ever tell you about the colonel who ordered a boxcar full of Scotch for an officers' club and was dumb enough to requisition it through Curly Larson?"

"Don't tell me yet," Grady said. "Now I'll have something to look forward to." He reached out and down to shake hands.

Antony grabbed his hand firmly, thinking what a hell of a nice kid Grady was.

As he left, Susan said to Grady, "What was that about?"

"I need some advice about Stode"—he grimaced—"and I can't go to Warren."

"You can't go to Antony, either."

"I can't tell him much. I can get advice." He added, "I know what I'm doing." He tried to sound confident.

Susan had nothing to say to that.

Twenty minutes later Warren, looking greatly satisfied, returned to the car. He hopped behind the wheel, tossing his briefcase in the back beside Susan. He also handed her a document written on parchment in a tall, spidery script.

Grady was annoyed that Warren didn't show them to him, knowing that Warren meant to keep him out of things as punishment for his supposed failure with the dwarves. "What are those?"

"Sample documents from Klaus. Nothing signed yet. He wants to dicker with me."

"He wants to cheat you," Susan said flatly.

"Of course." Warren shook his head, chuckling. "And he thinks he can. I know he could dupe you, Cavanaugh, but really—"

Susan squinted at the final paragraph of the contract. "What's this control warranty?"

Grady took the paper from her. Susan probably needed glasses and was too vain to wear them. Still, he had to squint to read the small print: " 'The company does not extend its warranty to theft, damage from inappropriate use, or malfunction due to malice.' "

Warren snorted. "Haven't either of you ever negotiated in a foreign language before? Probably it's just a bad translation for 'vandalism.' " He passed a second sheet to Susan, intentionally bypassing Grady. "If that worried you, you never would have had the guts to even read this."

It was a rider concerning proprietary processes, customer lists, and technology; Grady recognized much of the wording from his dealings with radio vacuum tube companies. The company listed at the bottom was simply, "Gnomengesellschaft."

"There," Warren said as he snapped the briefcase shut. "You two can thank God I stepped in to keep the two of you out of trouble."

A high-pitched snicker emanated from the glove compartment, and Susan opened it hastily. A final worker from the EGAD print made a predictably rude gesture and disappeared under a suspiciously large pile of gas-ration coupons.

EIGHT

FOR THE NEXT few weeks Grady was occupied with rehearsal, with writing and tracking his proposals and following up on his two jobs, and with cleaning off his desk before Christmas. Quite often he was so busy that he didn't have time to think about being laid off in late December.

Warren supervised his progress. "I'll need to know about these for myself. You'll be working in service."

There were already three shop workers who were part-time in service, going to customers' plants and repairing equipment. "Will there be enough service to go around?"

Warren's smile and reply were chilling. "By Christmas there won't be enough of anything to go around."

Grady had no reply; he simply ducked his head and worked harder. From time to time a memo would fly in from Antony. Grady would scribble an answer on it—the paper rippled as though it were being tickled—and send it out the window. Periodically Antony would call, seldom about anything important. Antony enjoyed talking to Grady as much as Grady did to him.

One chilly November morning Grady was trying to write a proposal for Remington Arms (a furnace for hardening rifle barrels) when his phone rang. He picked up the receiver, hoping it would be Antony.

It was Renfrew, breathing hard; either he'd been running or he was terrified. "He's coming back. He wants to talk to you alone again."

Grady didn't need to ask who. "Didn't he like the work?"

"He loved it. Well, he said it was satisfactory, which is the most he ever says. So it's got to be something else. Jesus, Grady, do you think he thinks I fouled up somehow? That's gotta be it. Maybe he thinks I led him to you, and something's wrong with you guys. Is something wrong with your order?"

Oh, hell, no, Grady thought. *Just that we're going broke, and our boss wants to be a war profiteer, and I'm secretly getting parts on war contracts from the Seven Dwarves.* Aloud he said, "Gosh, I can't think of anything."

"Well, think of something," Renfrew said vehemently. "Before he gets there. And fix it, too."

He hung up, leaving Grady to stare at the receiver.

Grady watched the lobby intermittently the rest of the day, and it was a good thing, too. Talia barely had time to blink before Stode whisked past her, his long stride taking him out of the lobby and onto the shop floor unannounced. Grady followed as fast as he could.

The plant floor was nearly empty; everyone but Hammer Houlihan, who was grinding rough edges off welds on the Hudson Drill furnace, had gone home for the day. Grady thanked God that the furnace for the Dwarfworks, sitting on a metal workbench, looked ordinary. Stode was looking this way and that, taking in everything as he walked from the employees' entrance to the loading dock at the far end of the plant.

At the dock Stode tested the outside door and frowned, saying to Houlihan, "Anyone could come in here."

"You did," Houlihan said. "Sorry, we're not hiring."

Stode looked him up and down and said flatly, "You have a record." It was not a question.

Houlihan never flinched. "Nelson Eddy, singing 'Indian Love Call.' You'll have to come over and hear it some night. Bring candy and flowers."

Stode turned his head sideways to scowl at Grady as he caught up. "And you let men like this work on classified projects?"

"Don't worry," Houlihan said as though he'd been addressed. "Your secrets are safe with me. Nobody in the front office ever tells us shit, even about what we're building."

Stode snorted, whether with laughter or disgust it was impossible to tell, and he walked briskly back to the front office.

Hammer Houlihan watched him go. "Jesus Christ, Cavanaugh, why'd you bring him in here? You couldn't get Boris Karloff?"

"Nope," Grady said tiredly. "Boris said you scared him. You don't seem very spooked, Hammer."

"You can't let people like him get under your skin." He hitched up his trousers. "All it takes—"

"I know. Optimism and confidence."

"I was going to say," Houlihan continued with injured dignity, "that it takes a set of clangers." He grabbed his crotch to make the point, then turned back to his work. Grady went after Stode.

Stode was already in Grady's office, pacing restlessly.

As Grady entered, Stode threw down a tattered copy of
Thrilling Wonder Stories. "Why do you read this stuff?"

"In case it's like the future. Don't you ever wonder about
the future?"

Stode's smile was unexpectedly bleak. "I don't have to.
I work for the future." He frowned. "Back to the present.
Talk to me about the oven you're building."

Grady thought wistfully of Tom Garneaux and the time
in Boston. "Why don't we discuss it over dinner?"

For the first time, Stode looked uncomfortable. "I'd
rather stay in your building." He stepped out, seemingly
unable to stay still.

Grady followed. "They lock it up at five-fifteen." Stode
looked unbelieving. "Look, we don't presently have any
overtime for the shop or the office, either one."

"'Presently.' But you will." Stode opened the door to
engineering, looking for signs of life. Warren Hastings was
out of the office yet again. Susan was reading an issue of
Nature, which contained far more physics than it did nature,
and doodling math as she read. Tom Garneaux was reading
numbers over the phone, which sounded technical unless
you listened closely and discovered they were horses, races,
win, place, and show. Stode turned back to Grady. "Arrange
to keep the building open."

"I can't." Stode opened his mouth and Grady said, "No
fooling, I can't. I wouldn't anyway; everybody here has a
family to go see. Wives, kids, grandkids—" He cut himself
off. "Warren could do it."

Stode nodded. "And he would."

"Sure he would. If you want to speak to him, I'll call him
at home. I guarantee he'll show up."

"If I wanted to speak to your boss, I already would have,"
he said levelly. "I want to talk to you. Now."

Grady looked at his watch automatically as Tom Garneaux threw on his coat and hat, walking out at exactly five o'clock. "Then you'll want to have dinner with me somewhere." He added as politely as possible, "Unless you're keeping a low profile for some reason."

Stode glared at him, looking as close to cornered as he ever would.

Grady had no intention of inviting Stode to his home. At Stode's request they drove out of Providence entirely and down U.S. 1, the old Post Road, all the way to South County in Rhode Island. Grady, already annoyed, was further irked that Stode was burning up valuable gasoline, Grady's gasoline, just to find a quiet place.

The bar wasn't crowded, but it wasn't quiet. There were a trio of navy pilots sitting at a table with a bourbon bottle in the center. Grady wasn't sure the whole setup was legal. The bourbon bottle was two-thirds empty; Grady thought the pilots looked close to full. At the bar, draped over stools, were four young women, talking to each other but watching the pilots from time to time. One of the women looked Grady up and down, then looked away.

Grady wondered if they were hookers, but somehow they were dressed more like bobby soxers slumming. He watched them interestedly, barely remembering to pay the bartender for the two beers.

Stode followed his gaze and shook his head disdainfully. "Don't even think about it. The ladies are here to marry a pilot. Think of it as an investment, like War Bonds."

"What's so great about marrying a pilot?"

"Nothing, for a long marriage. But they have the best odds in the service of being dead by next year, especially those men."

"Overseas?"

"No," he said shortly. "Night-flight combat teachers. Let's not discuss it."

One of the girls glided over to the table of pilots and said, pouting, "Say, what's going on? Frankie's not coming?"

"No," the dark-haired one said coldly. "Frankie's not coming." She took the hint and drifted back to the bar.

He refilled their shot glasses from the bottle of bourbon and raised his own. "To Charlietown, and to Frank. So long, pal." The others toasted and drank. He drained his and slammed the glass down.

"Drink up, fellas." He drummed on the table and said, slurring the words, "Tomorrow's a school day." The words slurred. He closed his eyes and sang loudly, "School days, school days, dear old golden rule days . . ." His voice cracked. "Through these portals pass the world's hottest pilots. Graduation day soon, and guess what happens then?"

What happened then was that the chair by Grady was suddenly empty. The pilot looked up in confusion as Stode said, "You're in public." For once his eyes were gentle. "Change the subject."

The pilot glared up at him, "It's the only goddamn subject I know." He stood up.

One of the other pilots said uneasily, "Eddie, sit down and knock it off."

The third pilot, obviously also drunk, snorted. "Maybe you're scared of him, Tony, but I ain't."

Eddie turned and grinned. "Atta boy, Billy." He faced off with Stode. Billy moved behind Stode; Tony stood reluctantly.

Without any warning, Eddie launched a haymaker, straight for Stode's angular jaw. The other two pilots moved in. Grady, not sure what he could do, stood up.

What happened next seemed to take no time at all. Stode stepped into the punch, moving his head slightly to one side as the punch sailed past his face. His left hand grabbed Eddie's arm at the elbow and tugged; Eddie fell forward.

Grady couldn't see Stode's right arm as it flashed into Eddie. There was a thud and Eddie continued to fall, right into the arms of Tony.

Stode turned around in what seemed a leisurely fashion, knocking Billy's uppercut aside easily. Stode stepped into and past Billy, who fell to the floor. Stode was holding him by the shirt; Billy whacked his head loudly and didn't move.

Tony, holding Eddie up, stared wide-eyed. "Listen, no black eyes. We have a job to do tomorrow."

"So do I." Stode took Eddie from Tony and propped him in a corner. "Your eyes should be at their best."

Tony raised his fists halfway and looked at Stode quizzically as the narrow man turned around. Stode faked a punch, Tony moved his hands in response, and he made a sudden coughing sound as Stode's hand flashed to his breastbone and back. He sat down, hard, in the chair behind him.

One of the girls was watching admiringly; the others were annoyed, as though Stode had damaged their property. Grady sat back down; he hadn't had time to go two steps.

Stode effortlessly pulled Billy off the floor and set him in a relaxed pose beside Eddie. He moved Tony's chair to the wall, propped him up almost tenderly, and turned to the bartender. "No M.P.s and no Shore Patrol."

"Nuts to you, Mac." The bartender had the phone receiver up already. "They work for Uncle Sam, not for you. And I don't work for you either."

"Tonight you do." Stode opened his coat slightly. Grady craned his neck but couldn't see what showed.

The bartender swallowed and said to the phone, "Forget it, honey; I'd only get a wrong number." He hung up.

Stode laid a bill on the bar. "Get them a ride back to the school."

"Yes, sir."

Stode returned to Grady but sat, one relaxed hand in his coat, facing the bartender. The girls at the bar had seen it all, but none of them understood what was happening.

Stode said, "Drink up." Grady did. The bartender brought another immediately.

Grady drank and said, "Why are you here? What do you want to know?"

"I want to know more about Plimstubb. Now I need to know about you."

"Know what?"

"Why you're working at a place that doesn't do much war work." He leaned forward, giving Grady a hard stare. "Where your loyalties are."

"You want to be sure I'm patriotic?" He slammed the beer glass down on the table, and the beer slopped over. It was only three-two beer, but Grady hadn't eaten yet, and who the hell cared? "After everything I've done, everything my friends have done, you want to be sure if I'm *loyal*?"

Grady heard the fury in his own voice. He knew this was a very bad thing to do to a customer, a worse thing to do to someone who had just beaten up three fighter pilots single-handed, but he didn't care. "You go back up there and take a good look at us, buddy. We're not what you're fighting for, we're your goddamn warriors. The Statue of Liberty says give us your tired, give us your poor—well, that's who's staying home working in Plimstubb, isn't it? You got your fifty-year-old men, you got your boys supporting their mothers while Poppa's off earning medals for dying, you got your immigrant riffraff who swallowed every line the papers told them about how it was their country, too, you got your women who weld because men are gone and can't, you got your genius physicist women who are engineers and take your shit every last day because you need them, you got your—your cripples"—he waved his cane, not caring as his beer spilled—"and all of them, every last one of them, won't matter a good goddamn to you when the war is over and everybody won. Well, they matter to me. All of them. The ones I love and the ones I hate. You don't like that, call Warren Hastings and fire me. Fire me, and bully someone else. Fire me and get it over with. Fire me now, while I still have a heart to break."

He stopped and saw like a man in a dream the heads turned toward him in a bar. One of the girls was grinning; he must look drunk. One was nodding; the bar wasn't far from Quonset and the civilian factories that supported the Seabees. Two of them looked pitying and turned away, and those were the worst of all.

Stode regarded him in silence and finally said, "You spilled your drink." He gestured; another beer appeared as if by magic. Grady sipped it as Stode said to the bartender, "Just keep working."

He handed money to the bartender; for a moment his right arm was directly in front of Grady, who said suddenly, "Let's talk turkey, Slim." He grabbed Stode's arm and, to both their surprise, held on to it even when Stode tried to spin it free. The cane had given Grady a strong grip. The bartender took the money and hurried away.

Stode raised an eyebrow. "Are you certain you want to do this?"

Grady ignored him. "You half killed a bunch of servicemen tonight; I'm not impressed. In fact, I'm even less impressed than if you let them beat you. How'd you do that, anyway? That wasn't boxing."

"Jujitsu."

"Some kind of Japanese fighting, right?" Grady looked at the unconscious pilots. "Where'd you learn that?"

"Around." Stode looked at him quizzically. "You have something on your mind. Spit it out."

Grady let go and folded his arms. "I'm saying that you won't get another contract through me until you prove that you're with the government."

"Renfrew's word should be enough."

"It isn't. I've asked him what he knows about you; he doesn't know enough."

Stode's mouth broadened until it was the widest smile his narrow face had ever shown Grady. "You're vetting me, like I'm your supplier?"

"Not yet. You're not even close to passing."

"Ah." Stode sipped, considering. "Well, that's difficult, isn't it?" He set his glass down with no noise at all. "Don't ask anyone about me. Don't tell them about me either."

"Are you The Shadow or The Joker?"

"This isn't radio or comics, either one. This is real."

Grady unfolded his arms and worked on his beer again. "Prove it."

"Tell you what. Who's the highest-ranking government official you've met?"

Grady said unhesitatingly, "Brigadier General Jessup. He came to review a contract for Thompson Aircraft."

Stode seemed to be enjoying this. "If you think I'm a spy, you shouldn't give details."

"How can you tell whether I'm lying or not? Anyway, the Germans have figured out what that one was about," he said with pride.

Stode's laugh sounded almost affectionate. "In that case, I'll mention Plimstubb to Andy Jessup if I'm allowed to speak to him. He'll call you and offer a reference. Be at your desk between nine and ten tomorrow morning."

"All right." Grady was dazed by how ready Stode's answer was. "What if I'd said I'd met General Patton?"

"He's a little busy right now." Stode glanced quickly around the bar and finished softly, "And anyway, George wouldn't give me a good reference. He always thought I was one scary son of a bitch."

Grady was silently impressed. From all reports, there couldn't be many people George Patton would find scary, or a bigger son of a bitch.

On the other hand, "Saying so means nothing. A letter means nothing." He looked Stode in the eye earnestly. "Can you get me that phone call?"

For once, Stode hesitated. "I need permission. I may not get it."

"Why not? Is it the same reason you don't want any M.P.s or Shore Patrol, and you don't want to talk to Warren Hastings, and you bounce from office to office? How did you know so much about pilots if you're not in the military?" He finished, "And till I know you're from the government, how can I tell you anything?"

Stode said immediately, "Are you keeping secrets from me?"

Grady scratched his head. "I try not to. You haven't asked about my materials source."

"I can't." He looked frankly at Grady. "You found the materials, and the parts were satisfactory. Your source is automatically acceptable." He blinked, looking as close to helpless as he ever could. "I have no choice. I have no time." He sighed and repeated, "Drink up. We're leaving."

Grady didn't bother reminding him that they'd planned on dinner together.

At the car Stode said, "You want me to drive?"

"As your friend in the bar said, nuts to you."

Stode ignored him. Grady drove slowly and carefully

back to Providence in silence, puffing on a Lucky without offering one to Stode.

As Stode got out beside his car, he turned to Grady. "Plimstubb is a heavy manufacturing concern. You have fabrication machinery, a capacity for fifty floor-shop workers, and more than ten thousand square feet of manufacturing space. You even earned an 'E' in '43."

"You should have seen how we did in the Munich Olympics."

Stode ignored him. "One of your customers, Imperial Knife, won an 'E' this year. They did it with your equipment."

Grady said woodenly, "To think they forgot to send me flowers." He reached for the shift.

Stode's arm shot in, grabbed Grady's wrist. "Get your company back in the war."

"How?"

"I have no idea. Do it."

"Okay."

Stode smiled his familiar narrow smile. "You have the confidence to be a salesman. I'd work on your manners."

He turned and was gone. Grady muttered, "Thank you, Emily Post" and drove home to throw together dinner.

But the following day at work, Grady didn't get any calls at all. At quarter to twelve he gave up and walked through the plant. He checked Stode's furnace first, then the Dwarf-works furnace, and then stopped by Susan's desk. She was still reading *Nature*; Grady looked at the article and blanched. He didn't read anything with math in it except for work, and he never, ever read anything with the word "quantum" in it.

She looked up. "How was dinner?"

"We never had it. "Remember you said that Stode might be the spy?"

"I didn't say that. I said, 'Is he or isn't he?'"

"Well, is he or isn't he? I can't tell." He spread his hands helplessly. "He doesn't operate like any government or military guy I ever met. None of his paperwork looks right if you look at it too long."

"Invisible ink? Secret code?"

"No, but it's too clear. All the red tape is missing. Plus when you boil it down, you can't tell who he works for."

Susan shrugged. "Take him on faith."

"No. What if I shouldn't have?"

"Then we're back where we used to be." She opened an imaginary box and peered in. "Is the cat alive? Is he dead?"

"He is if I get my hands on him."

Susan frowned. "Which?"

"That's your uncertainty, not mine." Grady walked away, happy to get the last word for once.

NINE

"THANKS FOR TAKING me," Mary said. "It was so nice of Susan's mother to volunteer to sit."

"Wasn't it?" Grady was fairly sure it was forced volunteering; he'd mentioned to Susan at the dress rehearsal that he'd love for Mary to come hear him sing, and Susan had set her jaw and gone home.

Mary settled back, sighing. "It's my first time out in months."

He smiled at her, thinking absently that when Kevin came back he'd miss her company. No more breakfasts, no more dinner twice a week.

Grady turned into the lot and saw row on row of automobiles, the tops of their headlights covered to keep the blackout. It made them sleepy-looking, as though they couldn't keep their eyes open any longer. "Wow."

"You're very popular."

"You bet." But the lot was only half full; Grady did a

quick estimate and compared it against the size of the cathedral, and his heart sank.

The choir was all huddled outside, having a last cigarette; Maestro Mandeville wouldn't let them smoke in the green room. Grady thought he was overly nervous about singers coughing during concerts. Why did he think the ad used to say, "I smoke Luckies and they don't hurt my wind"?

Grady had few hopes for this concert; people were busy, and the news from Europe—well, some of it was terrible. In November, Churchill had confirmed that the Germans were using a rocket, called the V-2, to bomb Britain; the rocket traveled faster than the speed of sound. As an American, Grady was horrified; as a science fiction reader, he felt a guilty fascination.

Far more serious news was that, in mid-December, the Germans launched a last offensive, trying to break the Allied line. The weather had helped them; there was little or no Allied air support on some stretches of the battlefront. Casualties on both sides were horrendous. By now, the brunt of German pressure was focused on a pocket, a dimple they had managed to push into the line, called Bastogne.

All of the Americans who had hoped to see the war over by Christmas were listening to the radio, reading the newspaper, waiting to see if the line would hold. Grady would sit at breakfast with Mary, both of them clinging to the rule never to talk about the war at breakfast, each of them half reaching for the newspaper through the meal.

In addition, concert preparation had, by the conductor's own admission, not gone well. In the second-to-last rehearsal, Maestro Mandeville had ranged from anger and sarcasm to bitterness and self-pity, all the way to depression and despair. Grady had the eerie feeling he was watching a Bette Davis screen test.

Grady's most embarrassing moment had come in dress

rehearsal. He'd had to skip dinner and stay at Plimstubb late, cleaning up the last of the sales proposals. He grabbed a couple of hot dogs at the Havens Diner, parked near City Hall downtown, and hotfooted it to the church, chewing frantically.

The choir was singing the "Gloria"; Grady checked his watch and hoped forlornly that Maestro Mandeville had done the movements out of order. Grady was impressed; he'd had no idea the group sounded this good.

As he hurried down the aisle, the conductor smacked his baton against the music stand and bellowed at the tenor section, "God*damn* it, Cavanaugh!"

Grady froze, the last hotdog jammed halfway in his mouth. Members of the choir pointed, laughing.

Mandeville turned around and said irritably and unapologetically, "Well, if you had been singing, it would have been you."

His mood wasn't Grady's fault; the dress rehearsal was pretty much a disaster. The soprano soloist was holding off to save her voice, the timpani player was late, and one of the trumpeters never showed at all. Maestro Mandeville compensated by singing along with the soloist in a strident falsetto and by whirling toward the percussion and shouting "BOOM!" but it wasn't the same. At least Grady hoped it wasn't the same. Grady worried that the soloists wouldn't be heard, and he wasn't sure that the choir or the orchestra or the maestro was doing such a great job, and frankly, he wasn't any too impressed with Haydn, either.

The smokers tamped out the butts and went down to the greenroom in the church basement. Grady said conversationally on the basement steps, "Too bad more people didn't come."

One of the other tenors, Michael, said startlingly, "More?"

"I'd have liked a full hall. The parking lot was half full when I came in."

"Well, it's full now. And it wasn't one person per car." Michael smiled, but the smile was nervous.

Just before the concert, Maestro Mandeville came into the greenroom. Off the podium he always looked remarkably short, and from this angle Grady could see the maestro's bald spot. "Sing clearly, sing carefully, sing well. Michael, sing softly." He paused. "The people who came to hear you want something special." He smiled; it looked distinctly alien on him. "They won't be disappointed." He disappeared. The choir lined up hastily and marched through the dimmed cathedral to the risers.

Grady had put a thick rubber tip on the end of his cane so it would make no noise on the marble. He walked onto the altar steps, moved into place, glanced beyond the area under the dome and the huge pillars, and smiled out automatically with the practiced sincerity of a performer.

Everyone in the cathedral looked tiny. Even the orchestra seemed the height of Kirsten and Antony. Everyone—

Grady gaped. Everyone he could imagine was here.

The nave was full to the back. The apses were full. The soft murmur of private conversations was loud enough to fill the cathedral, and the silence as it cut off was startling in itself. The audience, still in their coats in the chill of the cathedral, watched them expectantly, even hopefully. Every pew was full, even the balcony in the back. Grady looked back at the medallions in the ceiling, half expecting a row of women in cloth coats to be peering down in the company of all the saints and angels.

They came because the weather was good and the news was bad. They came because it was nice to be out somewhere and it wasn't nice to be alone. They came because a chorus, in the middle of the concert in the middle of a war, was singing a Mass in time of war.

After the concertmaster tuned the orchestra, Maestro Mandeville strode from the opposite side of the altar, the soloists with him. The applause was warm but not deafening; still, the sound filled the cathedral until, diminishing almost hand by hand, it stopped.

Maestro Mandeville bowed to the audience, took a deep breath, and unveiled a gentle speaking voice that went through Grady like an electric shock. It echoed under the dome and under the wood-beam ceiling of the nave. "Good evening. Welcome to our concert, and thank you for coming to hear us; I know we've all been a little busy lately."

The audience chuckled; one or two clapped. He stared the crowd into silence. "We all give so much time, and it's hard to set any at all aside for music."

Grady realized that he had never asked Maestro Mandeville what else he did for the war effort.

"Tonight's piece is Franz Josef Haydn's *Paukenmesse,* also called the *Missa in Tempore Belli,* the Mass in Time of War. Haydn was writing on behalf of a Hungarian count concerned about a war against France." He paused, struggling as though having trouble with his memory. "I would like to dedicate this performance to my son Paul, who cannot be with us tonight."

It was the first personal thing he had said in front of the choir.

He turned abruptly, raising the baton as briskly as though he were giving the signal to a firing squad. He raised his eyebrows as, sharply, every muscle in his face, neck, and arms tensed, and he brought the baton down.

The orchestra thundered in the cathedral, and Grady's jaw dropped open. This was music, but it was also cannon fire. Maestro Mandeville raised his head to the choir, and

Grady, with more fervor than he had shown in any rehearsal, thundered back, "KY-RIE . . ."

As he sang, Grady felt taken over: out of his body, responding only to the music and the baton. "God have mercy," he sang in Latin to the thunder of guns, "Christ have mercy." The sweet faith of the soprano solo comforted no one in the choir or the audience; the guns were still waiting in the darkness behind the kettledrums, and the cathedral was surrounded by casualties. The choir broke in again, and Grady heard the fear and need in their voices. *I didn't know this was the music,* he thought, and realized, *No. The music was waiting for us. This was in us, the singers and the audience.*

There followed an hour of heartfelt performance. All the weeks of being interrupted, insulted, bullied, even having the right to breathe taken away, had crystallized into technique. Tonight, caught up in the emotion of the night and the music's own history, the chorus pulled at the hearts of the audience, offering them shared doubt, shared resolution, shared joy.

The final note was still echoing as the last listener rose to his feet. The soprano soloist, out front near the first pew, was buffeted by shouts of "Bravo!" and Grady, exhausted by the concert's end, physically felt the applause and instantly had all the energy in the world.

Ten minutes later, downstairs in the greenroom, he pumped Mandeville's hand furiously. "What a wonderful concert!"

"Thank you." He seemed indifferent, unfocused. The concert had drained him physically and emotionally.

Grady said, "Maestro? I've had to take a part-time job out of town. I'll be gone every other week."

Mandeville stared at him silently. Grady rushed on, "But the people I'm working with are very musical, and they've

promised to coach me on my music. I'll get your notes to the
tenors from Joey whenever I come back, and if you want I'll
audition before the concert and not sing if I'm not ready."
He took a deep breath and launched into his final selling
point. "I know you need me, and I wouldn't dream of not
singing with you."

Still Mandeville said nothing, and the stare became a
glare. Finally he said with a hiss, "You are so very lucky
there's a war on."

The mood was festive in the car going home. Susan, the
inevitable cigarette lit, said, "We knocked them dead."

Grady, trying not to sound husky and exhausted, said, "I
knew we'd be that good."

Susan and Grady turned to Mary, hoping for confirmation that they were wonderful—

—And Mary broke *The Rule* and asked Grady, "The
radio's still full of stories about the German offensive. What
have you heard?"

Grady slowed down, trying to frame an answer. "The
usual stuff. The weather cleared and we bombed the
Germans. The ground forces are on the move . . ." He
added, seeing her face, "Except for that mess in Bastogne.
Mary, there's no reason to think Kevin's within a hundred
miles of that. . . ."

She shook her head quickly, trying to smile. "I know. I'm
being silly." She added, unable to stop herself, "But it's
going to be all right, isn't it? We'll still—the Germans
won't—"

He laughed as naturally as he could. "You watch. This
is a setup. The Germans all piled up over each other in
one place, and then"—he growled, even though his throat
was tired from singing—"we'll hit them like Dempsey hit
Tunney."

"Damn right." Susan growled in an echo from the back-seat.

He'd hoped Mary would laugh, and she did. "Kevin says that."

"Dad said it to us when we were kids." He pulled up at the house. "Back in a minute, Susan."

"Stall." she said, lighting up a cigarette on the butt of the last one. "Ask Ma how the baby behaved."

Susan's mother, sliding into the car, coughed and said annoyedly, "I don't know why young men's cars always smell like they're on fire. Bothers my sinuses wicked bad. Grady, you shouldn't smoke so much—and don't you ever give the habit to Susan."

Susan rolled her eyes and said nothing. Grady, face in the shadows, grinned.

At the house, Susan's mother strode in briskly like an older version of Susan. Grady, following in her wake, enjoyed the resemblance. Susan herself hesitated at the door. "You sounded pretty good back there when Mary asked about the war."

"Hey, thanks." Grady was tired, and the elation of the concert was fading. "You know, optimism and confidence."

"Sure." She looked involuntarily through the door for her mother. "Do you really think that's true, what you said?"

"Who knows?" He saw her face and added quickly, "But we'll win. We'll whip Hitler, and then we'll whip Tojo." He added lightly, "Like Dempsey hit Tunney."

"Sure." Grady had never seen Susan this uncertain as she stared down the hall toward the kitchen. Her mother was packing Susan's lunch for tomorrow. "Ma keeps saying Dad's too old to be a pilot."

"She wishes it were true, that's all." Grady thought fast.

"He's in his thirties, right?" He was younger than Grady's dad, who was stationed comfortably at Quonset.

"Late thirties, right."

"They're drafting guys in their thirties. They wouldn't keep him flying if they didn't think he was good." He patted her shoulder, letting his hand rest on it.

She looked at it but didn't move away. "Well, see you at work tomorrow. Good job tonight."

"You, too."

Grady drove away, his throat still sore but feeling unaccountably like singing again.

When he got home, Grady screeched the car to a stop. The house lights were on, and his father was standing in the living room, staring out the window.

Cane or no cane, Grady made it to the door as fast as he had run since his freshman year of college.

Before he could say a word, his father said, "Kevin's fine as far as I know." Grady sagged against the door frame. "Sorry I didn't get here in time to hear you sing. How did it go?"

"Fine, Dad. Great. Are you on leave?" Grady was confused; his father always called before leave.

"On leave?" His mouth twitched in a way Grady had seen on Kevin but never on his father. "Nope. AWOL." He added quickly, "I had to call in some markers to pull it off. I have to be back in an hour. Grady, I'm shipping out."

Only then did he see the duffel bag lying by the door and register what it meant. Grady stared at the curtains, trying to think what to say. He was looking right at the patch where, when he was eight, he and Kevin had a sword fight with the neighbor's tomato stakes and Kevin stabbed the curtain, claiming it was a bad guy. Their mother had always put a chair in front of that spot and always, always complained that doing so made the room lopsided.

Finally he said, "When?"

"Have to be on board tomorrow. I don't know when we sail."

Grady nodded. Of course he didn't know; the navy told as few people as possible when a convoy was leaving. Nobody wanted a U-boat waiting at the mouth of the Bay for them.

He shook his head. "At least I'm not supposed to—ah, what the hell. Ten tomorrow. Don't tell anyone."

"Of course not. Any guesses about where you're headed?"

His father grinned weakly. "We've started taking quinine for malaria. Plus we're learning to lay runways on sand and coral, so we're probably not going to the Aleutians." He faltered. "Grady, I'm sorry. I know this is the worst time for me to go. . . ."

In the silence he went on, "We don't know where we're going, and I couldn't tell anyway, but—well, let's say I'll see more of the beach than you ever do." He smiled, trying to get a smile back from Grady. "I always wanted to travel."

"Dad." His father was young enough for this, or at least had pretended to be so he could enlist, and the recruiting officer had pretended to believe him. "What's gonna happen to you?"

He put a hand on Grady's shoulder, and once again he reminded Grady of Kevin. "Relax, will you? I'm just a road builder. Nobody's going to shoot at me."

Grady had to say, "Sure."

His father relaxed. "Okay. I only came because I didn't want you to worry." But now he looked worried. "I know you start your new job pretty soon—"

"Day after tomorrow. Christmas Eve."

"What kind of place works on Christmas Eve, and on a Saturday no less?"

"A place I can't talk about." He tried to grin. "They want me completely trained by the New Year. Listen, I'll be fine."

"Will you be able to take care of this place?" For the first time he looked frightened. "It's winter. A lot of things can go wrong with a house."

"I'll be here every other week. I'll ask Frank Meara next door to keep an eye on the place when I'm not here."

"That drunk?" He shook his head "Ask someone you trust."

"Okay." The first person who occurred to him was Susan. That wouldn't work, he told himself; she had enough on her mind right now. "There's a lot of people."

"We just need one." He was smiling, but glancing toward the door. "I've got to get back."

"Sure. That's your car at the curb, isn't it?" He fell in beside his father.

"Well, it's the one I borrowed." They walked toward the door together, but his father slowed, as though a force in the doorway kept him back. "I don't like leaving." he said apologetically. "I know I haven't been living here, but I keep seeing the family all here, and I need to look after them. . . ."

Grady would never say so, but he had been looking after his father for years. "I'll be okay."

"I shouldn't have done this. I should've just been an air raid warden like other men my age."

"I'll be fine." Grady hated seeing his father like this. "Dad, I promise, I'll be fine. We'll all be here again." Grady said firmly. "You and me and Kevin."

He nodded but said, "And Julie, little Julie. Jesus, I've got a grandchild; what was I thinking when I enlisted?" He caught himself and looked back at the house, blinking. "All these years, and I keep seeing your mother in this house."

He grabbed Grady's shoulder, squeezing it hard. "You know, Grady, she'd be so proud of you."

Grady leaned on his cane and thought about tomorrow, when his father would leave for overseas and Grady lost half his sales job. "Sure she would." They went out into the dark, and for once they hugged each other and exchanged a kiss on the cheek.

Before going to bed, Grady methodically threw sheets over all the furniture except those in the kitchen and his own bedroom. He set all the faucets running at a trickle, in case of a cold snap, and finally he sat down and wrote three notes.

The first was to one of the neighbors, asking him to keep an eye on the house. The second was to the ice company, cutting delivery in half. The third, which took two drafts, was to Mary, explaining that neither he nor his father would be dropping the ration cards off as planned, and how she could pick up the extras on even weeks.

He finished, "I'm sorry for the inconvenience," rubbed at his eyes, and tottered off to bed.

Saturday was December 23. He gave Mary her present (a Sinatra record) at breakfast, and he left one (a rolling car, handmade in the shop) for Julie. It hurt to think that he wouldn't see her on Christmas. He left the note so she'd remember to pick up the ration cards. She was more upset about Grady's father than she was for herself or Grady. He kissed her good-bye, accepted a comforting hug, and fled to work.

Traditionally at Plimstubb Christmas Eve was a work-day; just as traditionally there was a noon party that drifted quietly into the afternoon. Usually, at three-thirty as the shop closed, Mr. Plimstubb walked around shaking hands and telling the office workers, "Merry Christmas. Go home early."

This time, Warren had told the whole plant to come in for Saturday and hold the party at eleven. He stressed that it was a half workday as well, the first overtime in a long time. Some people complained about losing a shopping day before Christmas, but they came.

By eight in the morning, Grady was frantically busy, cleaning his office and sorting his papers, filing all the letters he'd sworn he'd finally straighten out someday. "Someday" was finally here.

Only one ugly incident marred the party mood as eleven arrived. Roy Burgess once again waited until Susan was on the shop floor, this time to sample the lunch buffet in Wiring, to ask, "Hey, Benny! How's your marriage these days?"

Susan didn't even turn her head, but froze with her plate half full as Benny Behind said, "Know what? It's better."

"Better!" Roy was astonished. "I thought you said—"

"Sure, sure." He waved a hand. "So last night, Friday night, I brung in my girlfriend and said to my wife, "You watch how she blows me. She does good." He beamed. "Now it's all gonna be better."

Susan left quickly without eating anything more. Grady, halfway through a lengthy and confusing conversation with Joe Cataldo, looked after her sadly, wishing he could follow.

The first of the layoff notices came out at noon. Ricky Lewiston, who had worked in Wiring for ten years, came in and shook Grady's hand. "We had some good times." He had a shoe box of photographs and personal odds and ends under his arm, and his hands were cleaner than Grady had ever seen them before three-thirty. Grady watched him go, a patient, methodical man who had said frequently that he had worked all through the Depression.

One by one they trickled through the plant as they were called in and given pink slips. The front office went to see them go at twelve-thirty, witnesses to a disaster smaller than the *Titanic* or the *Lusitania* but no less devastating to people who thought they had taken jobs at the Unsinkable Plimstubb. Warren Hastings was nowhere in sight. A note signed by him on the board said succinctly, "WE WILL CLOSE AT TWELVE-THIRTY. MERRY CHRISTMAS." The bell for the end of lunch rang and the workers shuffled toward the door and a future they could not guess.

"Don't leave yet." Tom Garneaux, a wicked grin on his face, was waiting at the rear door of the plant. He had two burlap bags beside him, and he was grinning like he had just robbed Santa Claus. He was holding an immaculately wrapped, long, thin present. "Joe, you old Spaniard, c'mere."

Joe unwrapped it carefully, trying not to damage the paper, and stared reverently at the label on the bottle of wine. He turned in surprise to Tom. "How—"

"Spain's neutral, remember?" He winked. "I had a friend who used to import during Prohibition." He peered into his bags. "Next."

The entire plant fell into a line in front of the bags. No one doubted for a minute what was coming.

Benny Behind got a deck of playing cards. He peered wide-eyed at the naked girl on the ace of spades, licked his lips, and nodded his thanks to Garneaux.

Talia Baghrati got an aerator of eau de cologne. She squirted it at herself, and Grady, fifteen feet away, felt his eyes sting and water. She nodded happily. "Very subtle. Thank you so."

"You smell like a whole feather bed of roses." Joey assured her.

Grady opened his envelope in disbelief and spread a fan of gas ration cards. "How—"

Garneaux shrugged grandly. "'Thanks' beats 'how' any day."

"Right. Thanks. It's perfect." He resolved firmly that he'd find a gift for Garneaux at the dwarf factory.

Susan came up to Garneaux tentatively and suspiciously. Garneaux winked at her and pulled out a red-wrapped flat package; the green ribbon was crinkled from reuse.

She unwrapped it slowly and stared. *My Mother's Life,* the title said, and below that, "by Irene Curie." She opened the front and read the inscription, "To the Plimstubb Einstein."

"Oh." She leaned against the wall a moment. "Oh, my."

"What?" Garneaux was grinning. "You think we didn't notice?"

Susan leaped forward and hugged Garneaux tight enough to force air out, and Grady was surprised to find he was envious.

She muttered into Garneaux's suit, "Thank you so much. Oh, thank you."

He patted her hair. "Don't worry, kiddo. In six months your dad'll back, and you'll be back in school making us proud."

As she disengaged, Garneaux mouthed to Grady, "Optimism and confidence."

Grady nodded to them both. "I've gotta go." Sonny LeTour was already in the truck, the Hudson Drill furnace securely chained down and covered with a tarp.

Tom shook his hand. "See you in a week. Maybe you can come back for New Year's."

"Sure." He looked around the factory, at the faces that wouldn't be here next week. "I wish I'd be doing more for the war."

Susan said, "You wouldn't be doing much better here."

She stood back. "I'll see you in a week. I'll stop by and see Mary. My mother will invite her and Julie for Christmas."

"Your mother's already got your dad's relatives."

"My mother." Susan repeated firmly, "will invite her and Julie for Christmas." ·

"Glad that's settled." Grady said. "Thanks." He shuffled in place and said, "Well, good-bye." He tossed his cane up to the cab, hooking it on the side mirror, and climbed up, retrieving it through the door window. He waved, not trusting his voice, and was gone.

Sonny thumped the side of the truck. "We're rolling."

Grady stared out the window, thinking. Sonny looked at him. "You gonna like this job?"

"Maybe."

"Know much about it?"

"Some."

"The people friendly?"

"Very."

"That's what matters." He looked at the road ahead. "You still sing? I'm gonna teach you a new one."

Soon Grady forgot about everything but the next verse of "Chump Blues."

Sonny put the pedal down whenever he could, but it was quarter to five when they hit Wallkill. Sonny checked his watch six times. "Man, I wish I could make this earlier."

"We're nearly there."

"They're nearly closed." Sonny retorted. "They close before we get there, I got no place to go with this thing."

"What happens then?"

"I stay here in town over Christmas." He pushed the gas pedal down still farther.

Grady said, "Isn't Hudson Drill at the other end of Main Street?"

"You're right." Sonny said happily. "We took Main Street last time, right?"

"You bet." Grady hung on as Sonny turned sharply to the left onto Main Street.

There wasn't another car in sight; Sonny gunned ahead as storefronts, parking meters, and hanging fake evergreen ropes flashed past. Grady heard the evergreen flapping in the wind as the truck roared on.

They arrived at the loading dock of Hudson Drill with two minutes to spare. Three men were waiting at the raised plant door; they were pointing at the truck and laughing. Grady slid out of the cab, cane in hand. As he steadied himself, one of the dock crew said to another, "Ya know, Jim, these Plimstubb folks really know how to keep Christmas."

"That they do, Bobby."

Grady looked at them blankly, then back at the truck. His jaw dropped. The flapping sound on Main Street had been the furnace vent stack snagging every last bit of evergreen; the furnace and flatbed were festooned with wreaths, rope, fake candles, and ribbons.

Sonny looked at Grady, then into the side mirror, and leaped out of the truck in panic. "Shit! Shit! Oh, my dear Lord." The men on the dock never stopped laughing.

Grady walked to Sonny. "Listen. I'll talk to Roy when I get back. Maybe he'll only chew you out—"

"You think I'm worried about getting fired?" Sonny sounded angry but looked terrified. "I just stole a whole white town's Christmas decorations. You know what a town like this is gonna do to a colored man who ruined their Christmas?"

Grady glanced at the men on the dock, who were still

laughing in spite of Sonny's obvious anxiety. "Wait here."
Grady said quietly. He climbed the steps beside the dock,
leaned on his cane, and regarded the men with a smile of
charitable concern. "It's good you didn't panic."

Bobby was still chuckling. "Why should we?"

Grady nodded vigorously. "You're dead right, Bobby. It
is Bobby, right? And you're Jim." He turned to the third
man. "And you are—?"

The third man stopped chuckling and stared at Grady
suspiciously. "Who wants to know?"

Grady waited until the man said sullenly, "Fred."

"Are you in charge, Fred?" Grady had already guessed
that he wasn't.

Fred edged away involuntarily. "Ah, hell, no. It's Bobby."
Jim nodded vigorously. Bobby, sold out by his buddies,
looked unhappy.

Grady said quickly, "Bobby, I don't want you to worry at
all." Which wasn't strictly true. "Sonny and I will get you
out of this, and we'll keep our mouths shut."

Bobby said plaintively, "Why should we care? It's not
like we did anything—"

"That's true, but nobody needs to know that. If we're
asked, I'll say you warned us about the decorations before
we left." He glanced inside the door. "Can you find us a box
or two, quickly? The longer the truck looks like that, the
likelier that someone will see it and call the cops—or the
plant owner."

Bobby opened his mouth uncertainly. Grady went on
smoothly, "Sonny and I will hide the decorations, and you
can decide on the twenty-sixth whether you want to tell the
plant owner about it." He added, "Unless you want me to
call him now—"

"No!" Bobby glanced fearfully up the denuded Main
Street. "Cripes, he's head of the Chamber of Commerce."

He made a decision. "Freddy, Jim, get the boxes, then unload the goddamn truck and get these guys out of here. Move!"

Sonny leaped onto the flatbed and began tossing evergreen down.

In five minutes, Hudson Drill had unloaded the furnace. In an amazing fifteen minutes, Grady and Sonny had the decorations boxed up with help from the other three. Grady shook hands all around and said solemnly to Bobby, "Shall I wait for you to call me on the twenty-sixth, or do you want me to put in a call to the plant owner then?"

"No. Jesus, no." His eyes bulged as though someone were squeezing his throat. "I'll take care of this shit." He looked down at the boxes. "I got a pretty good idea how to handle it."

By the time Grady was in the truck, three of the boxes had disappeared.

Once they were out of town, Sonny let out a huge sigh. "Thanks."

"I'm just glad it worked." Grady, exhausted, slumped in his seat, the past twenty-four hours catching up with him.

Sonny shook him awake at the turnoff to the Schuylkill diner. Antony, coffee cup in hand, was waving out the diner window.

Grady said, "I guess this is it, then." He reached for his cane with one hand and his suitcase with the other, but Sonny was already passing the suitcase out the window to Antony.

Antony caught it easily. "Thanks, Sonny. Good to see you. Grady, come on in."

Kirsten arrived, out of breath from running. "Hi, Sonny. Grady, I'm sorry you had to start tomorrow; it's not a holiday for us—"

"That's okay." He turned back to Sonny. "Thanks for the ride—"

A scrap of artificial pine, with a red ribbon on it, drifted down from the cab onto Grady's shoulder.

"You looked like you could use some Christmas, man." Sonny's eyes looked large and gentle with concern. "You gonna be all right here? You not, you sneak out and call me. I'll come get you."

"I'll be okay. But thanks." Grady was moved. "Hey, I'll be fine. In three months, if you need anything, I'll come get you."

Sonny laughed. "You been listening too much to Garneaux." He patted Grady's shoulder fondly, and for a moment nothing mattered but friends needing each other. "Merry Christmas, Grady."

They watched him drive away. Antony said, "It's good to have friends."

Kirsten, watching Grady, said, "It's good to be one. Let's go see your new home."

Grady followed, realizing that he knew next to nothing about the place where he would be working and living.

She led him to a jumble of rock in the hillside, one of many places where, apparently, farmers had cleared boulders from the land and piled them. "Watch carefully." She grabbed the largest boulder and tugged.

It swung open easily, balanced on a pivot point. The rear side had a dead bolt.

Grady followed her in, stooping, and stood up in wonder.

He was inside a one-room cottage with plaster walls and wood molding. One end had an iron stove; a kerosene lamp sat on a table in the middle. A hastily extended wooden bedstead occupied most of the room.

He looked up into the high-peaked roof. It reminded him of a visit to Tarrytown, years ago, and the old Dutch homes.

There were two small windows. The rear of the cottage had a door as well, but it was a double door.

"That one goes into the factory." Kirsten said. "Normally we'd have a storage loft, but . . ." she dimpled. "I thought you'd be more comfortable with it out."

He looked in the pantry. The top shelf was level with his chin. It had a jar of raisins and some fresh bread, but no cooking utensils.

"You'll have breakfast with us." Kirsten said. She glanced at the inside door, and smiled when a scuffling sound came from it. "In the meantime—"

She flung open the door and six more dwarves marched in, holding lit candles. Antony and Kirsten fell in with them as they sang "Deck the halls with boughs of holly" and hung greenery around the molding in the cottage.

They paused for breath. Kirsten said, "This is Gretchen—"

A blond dwarf with laughing eyes and, Grady recognized, a flawless soprano.

"This is Bernhard—"

He nodded seriously. He seemed worried about something; Grady wondered if he always did.

Kirsten introduced the rest of them, then with a flourish produced a wrapped package from nowhere. "You know that it's your holiday and not ours, but presents and friends are always welcome."

Grady unwrapped it and grinned. It hadn't cost much: a stack of *Action, Detective,* and *Wonder Woman* comics, plus a few old pulp magazines featuring Captain Future. "Terrific. Thanks."

"Our pleasure. We weren't certain which ones you liked; I would have called Susan—"

"That's okay." he said hastily. "Really. You did a great job."

Kirsten looked relieved. "In that case . . ." She gestured, and they launched into the final verse:

> *Fast away the old year passes,*
> *Hail the new ye lads and lasses. . . .*

When it was over the other dwarves bowed and exited. Kirsten looked at them, then at Grady.

"'Fast away the old year passes,'" she murmured and leaped up. It seemed to Grady that her stocky body hung in the air a moment as she kissed his cheek, then dropped and walked out without a word.

Grady rubbed his cheek thoughtfully. Antony said, "Don't worry about it, kid. She just hates how transient you are."

"Transient?" But he knew.

Antony said uncomfortably, "You know. Short lives, sixty–seventy years." He tugged at his right earlobe and said defensively, "She's sweet that way."

"Sure." Grady, watching Antony's face, said, "You like her a lot, don't you?"

"She's all right." Antony said with studied indifference before giving up. "Okay, you caught me. I like her. A lot." But his smile didn't last. "Hell, I've been trying to date her for fifty years."

Grady managed to say, "That's rough."

Antony looked at him and grinned crookedly. "Oh, she's worth it."

Grady was having trouble focusing on the conversation. He'd had four hours of sleep in the past twenty-four, and had faced other people's crises for most of it. "Antony? How old are you?"

"I was born in 1874." He jerked his head toward the inside door. "To Pieter, that makes me the kid."

"You're seventy?"

"Good at numbers, aren't you? No wonder you went into engineering."

"So those things about World War I—"

"The Great War." he said wryly. "Sure, I was there. I was the shortest pilot in the Signal Corps." He considered. "Probably the shortest guy in the whole army. Fighting my way in was tougher than any fighting I did in Europe. I had to promise to provide my own uniform; thank God Pieter made me learn to sew."

"And Curly Larson—"

"Best friend I ever had. Life's tough without friends when you're in a strange place; I don't see how I'd have made it through Europe without him.

"Which reminds me"—he fished in his pocket—"I brought you a present of my own." He held up a ragged, dirty envelope. "It doesn't look like much, does it?"

It looked like trash. "Maybe it got a little beat up in your pocket."

"Maybe it got a little beat up on the way from Europe."

Grady snatched at it.

Antony grinned. "Gotta go. Enjoy your night." He turned in the doorway, almost as Kirsten had. "Merry Christmas."

He shut the door, and Grady was alone.

Grady set the kerosene lamp by the bed and turned the wick up for brightness. He lay down, tore the envelope, and unfolded it shakily.

The handwriting was shakier still, as though it were written hastily in the dark, but he knew it as well as he knew his own:

Grady—

These guys swear they can get a letter to you. I don't know how but I hope they're right. You wouldn't believe me if I told you what they look like.

I'm in Bastogne. It doesn't matter that I said that, even if the Krauts get this. In a couple of days they'll have us, or what's left. We won't surrender.

I'm sorry I won't be coming home. Tell Mary I loved her more than anything. And tell Julie the same thing when she grows up. I wish I'd held her just once.

I love you, big brother, and I'm proud of you. I'm proud of your great job, and the work you do for the war, and how you'll always be there to take care of my wife and my little girl. Tell Dad I loved him, too, but don't tell any of them at Christmas dinner.

Kevin

He threw the letter aside. Grady turned his face to the wall and wept as he hadn't since the night he realized his mother wasn't ever coming back.

TEN

THE FIRST THING in the morning there was a knock on Grady's outside door. Kirsten was there, holding—he blinked.

It was a sword, longer than his arm and gleaming as if freshly forged and honed to a razor sharpness. At her belt hung a shorter version.

She was also carrying two quilted jackets. "Merry Christmas Eve. Time to practice."

"What about breakfast?"

"Afterward, at work." She passed him the larger jacket, walked inside, and opened the inside door of the cottage.

Grady stepped through, stopping. He was in the far end of the Dwarfworks cavern, on the north wall. To his right was a dining table; to his left, an open space where Kirsten waited. He slipped into the jacket.

"Perfect fit," Kirsten said with satisfaction. "We had to guess at the measurements."

"It's great." He gripped the sword and swung it experimentally. "Listen, it's been years since I used one of these—"

Kirsten's blade lunged for his heart; he barely beat it aside in time. "Now it's been a few seconds." She stepped back and went *en garde*.

After a few bruising minutes, much of Grady's fencing came back. He found himself watching the point of Kirsten's sword, checking her wrist and eyes for signals, peripherally watching her knees bend and her weight shift from foot to foot. Soon whenever her sword came up, his own was there.

He nearly fell twice—once trying to sidestep a lunge of Kirsten's, once when he got excited and overextended on a lunge of his own. His ankle gave, then, and he toppled sideways.

Kirsten caught him, steadying him one-handed. "What happened?"

"My ankle quit on me. Honest to God, I shouldn't even try this."

"I know your ankle gave. Why?"

"I put all my weight on it. But I have to, if I want a long reach."

"Then fight with a short reach, or find another way." She looked at him severely. "And don't say you shouldn't do something you want to or need to. Never give up. It's not as though I can wave a wand and make your ankle better. I can only teach you to fight as you are." She gestured with her sword. "This time, fight from a triangle: left foot, cane, right foot. Shift the triangle by moving the cane as you lunge."

A half hour later Grady was sweaty, panting, and elated. Despite her own short reach, Kirsten won every match, but Grady was improving every minute. He had even scored a touch on her by parrying her knee-high low lunge even lower and tapping her chest before she could get back in position.

"Good!" If possible, she was more pleased than Grady was. "You drew my guard away. Remember, you can't draw mine up unless I do something foolish." She leaped in the air; Grady fell back but saw that, if he had been ready, he could have swung at her legs and knocked her sprawling before she landed.

He raised his sword, ready to try. Kirsten looked at his face and laughed, a happy, strong sound. "Let's go to breakfast, or you'll be too tired to work."

The other dwarves were already at the table. The few he had met smiled at him; the rest nodded shyly. Grady nodded back, but gaped at the breakfast table. The spread was practically obscene: butter, milk, eggs, pancakes and syrup, ham, sausages—for a moment, looking at the unrationed and unquestioned abundance, Grady felt as though he were eating with Rockefellers or Roosevelts.

"Here, kid." Antony took his plate and filled it, adding a mug of hot coffee that seemed to be just for him. "Would you like something to eat?"

Behind him a walking hearth, still smoking, tapped impatiently on the floor. Grady cautiously lifted a piece of toast from it and spread the toast with butter and strawberry jam. "I'd be crazy not to."

Kristen watched him eat and added with a knowing smile, "And your letter last night should have made you happy."

The breakfast suddenly tasted like ashes.

Kirsten cocked her head. "What's wrong?"

He took the letter from his wallet, unfolding it carefully. He'd save it until Kevin was officially dead, then give it to Mary.

Kirsten read it quickly, her face twisting and working. "Grady, I'm so sorry."

"Thanks."

"We meant to make you happy. . . ." She thrust the letter back at him. "Excuse me." She rose from the table quickly and left. The other dwarves looked at him but said nothing.

Grady was moved by how much his distress upset her.

At the end of breakfast, Antony said, "Let me show you the place and then show you your job."

"I figured I'd run the Plimstubb furnace."

"You figured wrong, till it gets here." Antony was grinning. "Grady, you're about to learn a thing or two."

Grady learned a few fairly modern things, a few very old things, and a few that, he suspected, were older than anything he had ever known.

Antony proudly showed off the electrical system. "Two hundred eight volts. Runs the lights with a step-down, plus any hardware we'd want—saws, grinders, anything. It'll run your furnace—"

"Plimstubb's furnace."

"When you send it to us." He grinned, but he was embarrassed. "It's not gonna make the deadline, is it?"

"Not a chance." Which the dwarves had known, or guessed. "Better have enough current to run a dissociator, too."

Antony, disconcerted, said, "You'll have to explain about current. I thought you just hooked up the wires and things ran."

"How I wish. Can't the gnomes tell you more about it? They'd like it; current can kill people."

"They know less than we do."

"I'll teach you what I know." He considered. "Let's hope Klaus doesn't want to know." He shook his head violently;

the combination of gnomes and electricity could be ugly. "Anyway, today you're teaching me."

"Right." Antony pointed. "That big area with the benches is the main forge. On cold days that's the most popular place here. On warm days it's deserted."

A sudden squeal of laughter announced that it wasn't deserted now. The first figure dashed around the forge, and Antony grabbed her.

"Guess you haven't met Katrina. Sooner or later everybody does."

With eyes and a face like a china doll's, Katrina looked up in awe at Grady. She came to his knee. Grady was charmed instantly.

"Those two behind her are the twins Hans and Torvald. Okay, they're behind Bernhard."

Bernhard had run forward in a futile attempt to stop Katrina. Now he stood regarding her solemnly. Two flaxen-haired boys, the size of human two-year-olds but clearly six or seven, each peered from behind one of his legs.

"Last of all is Thom. He's the shy one. Don't figure on seeing him anyway."

A curly-haired head barely the size of a softball ducked behind the forge chimney.

Grady offered his hand. Katrina shied away.

He offered it to the twins, who popped out of view. Grady sighed and scratched his head, wondering what to do.

On an impulse he popped off a shoe and a sock, leaning on his cane and offering his lame foot to shake. He wiggled the toes invitingly.

No one moved; then Katrina giggled and shook his big toe.

"Pleased to meet you," Grady said. He hopped forward and offered it to the twins, who shook it less eagerly. Finally he leaned dangerously far back on his cane, raised his leg, and waved his toes vigorously in the direction of the forge.

A tiny hand waved back.

As he put his sock and shoe back on, he glanced across the Dwarfworks and saw Kirsten looking at him, shaking her head and laughing. He shrugged and waved his foot at her as well.

Antony, watching, said lazily, "We'd better get on with the grand tour."

Grady went with him, but was watching the children. "You just let them run around here?"

"Got to, if we want to see them during the day."

"Isn't it dangerous for them here?"

Antony looked after the children, and his heart felt heavy and full of dread. "When you're their size, it's dangerous everywhere."

He shook himself. "I oughta show you some of the products."

"I'd like to see the customers."

"One thing at a time." They stopped at the first small forge; a wicker basket of dark metal cylinders lay beside them. "These are the casings for magic lanterns."

Grady said dubiously, "My grandmother had one of those. She put postcards in it, showed the image on the wall. It was okay, I guess."

"These lanterns do more than that," Antony said dryly. "You can't hide a thing from them." He pointed one at Grady in play. "Want to find out what your worst failings are?"

"Put that thing down."

Antony did; he didn't like them either. "And these are cornucopia."

"Horns of plenty?" Grady peered inside excitedly but saw nothing. "You mean they have incredible amounts of food stored in them?" He turned it upside down and shook it, looking in the opening.

A small amount of dust hit him in the face. Antony, amused, said, "Only after you fill them. We only make them."

"Who buys them?" Grady thought about the paintings he'd seen, of robed women feeding the world. "I'd like to be there when they come in."

Antony said feelingly, "Believe me, kid, we all love to be there when they come in."

The remaining forges were banked or cold. Grady was reminded of the open spaces on the shop floor at Plimstubb; this place wasn't in great shape either.

They moved past the last of the forges to a grand open causeway leading to the wall. "And this is the main entrance." He pulled a massive stone door open, exposing the vines draped over it. "When you leave, pull it shut and make sure the vines cover it. Wild grape. You can eat them in summer." He folded his arms. "That's most of it. Any questions?"

Grady pointed across to the dark mouth of the Gnomengesellschaft entrance. "You haven't showed me that." He said frankly, "I didn't want to see it. I feel like it's looking at me, waiting for me."

Antony frowned, regarding the tunnel. "It's waiting for us all the time." He hesitated, then decided. "I guess you have a right to know."

"Know what?" But Grady had guessed.

"The bad contract Pieter signed. The contract with Klaus's predecessor."

"Predecessor?"

"Oh, sure. Gnomes hit each other like Al Capone used to hit his pals. Klaus has lasted a long time, though; he's good at it." He sighed. "Guess you saw that."

Grady remembered sprawling on the floor, chalk on his clothes. "Oh, yes."

"Well, the earlier gnome, Johann, he wasn't as good, but he was close. It was during the Civil War. The gnomes showed up, and Pieter needed money to keep this place going, you can't guess how bad things were. So . . ." He shrugged. "He cut a deal. Sold them production space, borrowed money from them, signed a bad note."

"What did he use for collateral?"

"All of us." He let that sink in. "And gnome notes are for the long term; if you work here, you're automatically collateral until the day you quit. Maybe not even then, depending on the terms of the loan. That's why I'm telling you. If you work here, you're part of that."

Grady remembered Garner Stanley Irving and shuddered. At least the gnomes had agreed to dismantle him. "What is my work, exactly?"

"We're hoping you'll tell us."

He led Grady to a machine, at knee height on Grady like so much of the machinery here, which looked fairly new. On the other hand, it didn't look so much modern as crazy: an inch-thick tube connecting a metal cube and a hand crank, with a funnel dropping into the center of the tube. There was no trace of soot stain, though that could have been removed by polishing, and none of the metal parts was corroded. Antony said with obvious pride, "Can you guess what this is?"

This was going to be tough; it looked like something Rube Goldberg had made and thrown away. Grady knelt and put his hand near the unit, checking for warmth, then ran his hands around it while he looked at it. One of his professors used to say that engineers see best with their fingers. Around the base of the funnel, near the center of the tube, was a sharp edge where someone had cut through the precast tube. At the right end of a tube Grady found a nick where a gun sight had been removed, and the rounded weld where the framework for the crank and drill had been added. At the far end, what he had initially thought was a smooth metal block had a barely discernible seam.

He stood. "It's a shotgun barrel with a funnel stuck in it. It's not the old-style Damascus barrel, but a single piece, so it's pretty new—by dwarf terms. Somebody's sealed a hand-crank brace and bit on one end, with the drill bit stuck inside the shotgun barrel. There's a casting mold on the other end—wait." He knelt again. "And it clamps onto the end, so it's removable. I'll bet you have other molds here."

"Not bad." But Antony was admiring, not grudging. "Now the tough part: Can you guess what it's for?"

Grady knelt and peered down the funnel, tempted to light a match but sensibly cautious; flame sources around strange machinery were a serious mistake. The funnel was tin; nobody could have poured molten metal down it. Anyway, the whole apparatus showed no sign of being heated at all, even the mold at the end.

In the bottom of the funnel, passing along the shotgun barrel, was the drill bit, sized to match the hollow of the shotgun. The drill bit had tiny pellets of metal clinging to it; some of them shone even in this faint light.

"It's some kind of injector. You're pushing metal powder into the mold at the end."

"Wow," he said flatly. "How'd you guess?"

"I read about it in college. A spark plug company did something like this in the twenties, back before I was in school—"

"Back before you were in long pants, you mean," Antony said, grinning.

"Okay." Grady was nettled. "But they did the ceramic bodies of the plugs; they didn't do anything with metal."

"Gee, imagine that. How come?"

"You can't," he said simply. "Nobody knows how yet. Some things happen with powder metal now—parts for aircraft—"

"That's been around a while," Antony said lazily, in the way Grady already associated with Antony being irked. "The Greeks used powdered gold for jewelry. Back in the sixth century, the Indians cast an iron column of powdered iron, and it's still around today." He narrowed his eyes at Grady. "So why don't you do more of it yet?"

Grady thought.. "For one thing, you're limited to what shape you can make, because unless you heat the mold itself to melt the powder together, the whole thing falls apart when you open the mold. You can put a binder—a kind of gummy, waxy stuff—in with the powder, but you still can't do very fancy shapes or you can't get the mold apart."

"And that's such a problem?"

Grady's answer was heartfelt. "It's a big problem. Everybody would love easy-to-mold, strong metal, with less machining than on cast parts. You can even make some parts lighter by reducing the density of the powder. But so what? The powdered work is still really limited." He said with suspicion as much as hope, "Why, you know a way to do more?"

"Watch." Antony traced a quick design on the mold left-handed, then said softly, "Remember." He tilted the mold sideways. A stream of powder poured out, catching the sunlight as it dropped into a bowl on the floor. Grady looked at the shapeless heap in embarrassment for Antony.

"Doesn't look like much, does it?" Antony said glumly. "Ah, hell, let's heat it up anyway."

He set the bowl on the hearth and stroked the leather bellows, saying softly, *"Atque vita."* The bellows coughed once and breathed deeply and steadily, taking the coals to a bright red, then a light orange. The hearth followed.

The powder in the bowl steamed, losing the last of its moisture. Grady's nostrils caught the hot, dry scent of metal heated beyond normal temperatures; it had always seemed to him that he could taste the metal on his tongue. He watched, fascinated, as Antony bent low over the bowl.

Antony traced a figure over the powder, this time with his right hand, bent low—his cheeks turned ruddy with the heat immediately—and called coaxingly to the metal, "Remember?"

Like a sand castle dissolved on film and running backward, a ring materialized in the ceramic bowl. There was a grape leaf border, crossed with a rose and thorns, circumscribed by a dragon gnawing savagely at his own tail.

"How's that?" Antony said.

"Terrific." Grady added disappointedly, "But I can't sell that to General Motors."

"Keep at it, kid. If there's one way, there's usually another." A carafe of white wine and a pitcher of water stood by the forge. Grady had assumed they were left over from yesterday's lunch. Now Antony picked up the bowl with tongs and set it on a stone, then picked the wine carafe up. He looked this way and that and took a small sip. "Riesling," he said, smacking his lips. "When the war's over, I'm begging Kirsten to let me make a run over for some more."

Then he lifted the still-glowing ring from the bowl and suddenly poured wine over it. Steam rose and the ring quit glowing, but the dragon's eyes seemed to glow for some time.

"Now pass me the water."

Grady watched him pour the water over the ring, then bounce the ring on his palm, blowing on it to dry. Lastly he murmured to the bellows, *"Vita dispersam est."* The leather quit moving, and the fire settled back to a dark red.

Antony passed the ring casually to Grady. "I hope you like it."

"What?" Grady turned the ring this way and that in the light, focusing on the red highlights. The smith's fires seemed to find an answering warmth greater than reflection. "That's not all gold."

"It's gold, and silver, and dragon's blood." He frowned. "The blood has been tough to get since Japan took over China. We're mostly saving the rings for customers, till the war's over. Don't lose it."

"You—gee, thanks." He slid it on his finger, where it hung loose, and the dragon constricted until it fit snugly. "It's beautiful."

"It's also your project." Antony smiled ruefully. "We're hoping you can figure out a nonwasteful way to test these."

"The metal?"

Antony said with a slight edge, "Oh, hell no; don't you think we can do that? I've been assaying gold and silver since before your dad was born. I mean the wishes."

Grady stared at the ring as Antony went on, "I mean, you can't just waste them. This one's nothing but a pretty ornament after one wish, and with the other kind, well, who ever heard of a two-wish ring?"

"This ring has one wish?"

Antony shuffled and finally said apologetically, "There are strings attached to the three-wish kind, a sort of trial period. I hope you're okay about only getting one."

"Oh, sure! It's great, just great." He closed his hand for a moment, feeling the metal. "How, um, how big can the wishes—"

"You can't end the war, if that's what you're thinking. You can't win it, either." Antony stretched his arms out and back, as though enclosing something with his palms. "But it could help you win a fight, or an argument . . . look, it's hard to explain, but after a while, you'll feel it. Wishes are sized to the person." He changed the subject. "Anyway, you'll know all that by the time you've finished setting up a way to test the ring. Good luck with the wish."

"Thanks." Grady added, with more confidence than he felt, "I'll figure out something." He added hopefully, "Are you going to teach me to do magic?"

Antony chuckled. "I was hoping you'd teach us to mass-produce metal products."

"Well, sure. I mean, I'll try. But if I do, what'll we mass-produce? He waved his hand in the air, enjoying the golden shine. "Wishing rings?"

Antony blanched. "Sacred Sun. You thought that was what I wanted?"

"Makes sense to me."

"Makes sense to—kiddo, name one person you would never trust with three wishes."

Grady thought briefly of Benny Behind and shuddered.

"Right. Now think of two more. Now make a thousand of these one-wish rings, hop in the cockpit of a plane, and drop them in downtown Providence on a Saturday night." He shook his head, eyes shut to block out the carnage. "Can you imagine?"

Grady, who read a lot of science fiction, could. "So how do you know who should have the rings?"

"You knew who shouldn't. You also know who should, if you think about it. Magic is for heroes, not for everybody."

"But you gave me one."

"That's right." He put a hand on Grady's shoulder, a small, older man to a younger. "You may never need it, or you may need it to save your life. Don't ever forget what it's for."

Light as it was, the ring felt suddenly heavy to Grady.

Antony finished, "Back when heroes won wars and not just battles, we could change the world. Wars now involve millions of people. We don't dare make these things for millions of people, just for the few good ones."

Grady was thinking. "But if you could make a hundred thousand in a year—"

"And we shipped them straight to France for combat, so they'd go to heroes? Then the army would give them out at the officers' clubs, and the hell with the enlisted men. That's how it was when I was over there, and I'll bet that's how it is now." His smile was half cynical, half sad. "Grady, it's too damn big. Anything we can do matters a little, but nothing we do will matter a lot." He reached up and patted Grady's shoulder. "Magic is a pretty small skill, kiddo."

Grady looked at the ring thoughtfully. "Maybe you should mass-produce these."

"Weren't you listening? I said—"

"Batch-produce. Can you do two at once?"

"Sure."

"How about three? Can you do that handwriting in the air—"

"It's a rune."

"Okay, could you do it over a whole tray of these rings?"

"Sure. What difference does it make, though, if I heat a bunch of them at once?"

"Batch sampling. It's how they test mass-produced items, like car parts or rivets. You make sure the process is uniform all through the tray, and you make sure the quenching with the wine is uniform"—Grady was thinking out loud now—"you might have to pour wine through a sprinkler, like a watering can, and you test a ring from a different part of the tray every time till you've tested every position. Sound good?"

Antony looked at him for awhile in silence and suddenly laughed, slapping Grady's shoulder so hard Grady nearly toppled. "Kid, you're gonna earn your keep."

"And don't forget, you have a wish coming with each ring. Can't you just wish for two wishing rings?"

"If we could, do you think we'd make them by hand? But we could wish the ring would fall back into powder and reprocess it." Now Antony was thinking out loud. "We'd have to test that one separately the first time. . . . Let's set it up and then show Pieter."

"Show him what?" Pieter was standing behind them, polishing his spectacles on a handkerchief. "Antony, you're not working that poor boy to the death his first day, are you?"

Grady said quickly, "I'm learning a lot. This is a wonderful plant."

Pieter looked around it with pride. "It is. I have made— we have made a good place to work." He added, "I want you to be happy here."

Grady nodded. For reasons Pieter was unlikely to change, Grady wouldn't be happy soon.

Pieter watched, his face changing. He said gruffly, "Boy, Kirsten spoke to me this morning. I am sorry for your news."

Grady nodded. "Thanks."

"You have other brothers? Sisters?" Grady shook his head.

Pieter regarded him with concern. "But why do I ask? If you had dozens, this boy your brother would still be precious." He turned away quickly.

Antony said quietly, "Pieter thinks a lot about family."

Grady stared around the cavern. "So do I." He turned to Antony. "Give me something else to think about, will you?"

•   •   •

Christmas passed and the day the Canadians call Boxing Day. Late in the afternoon of the twenty-seventh, Grady and Antony had performed their tenth successful batch test of a wishing-ring tray. Antony slapped Grady's shoulder, nearly knocking him down. "It's great, kid. Perfect. Let's show Pieter—"

"Show him what?" Pieter didn't wait to find out. "Grady, we spoke to those who helped us get your letter before. The letter we thought would be a gift for you, for when you started here."

Grady began, "That's not your fault—"

Pieter held up a hand. "And those who helped us, when they heard of the first note, they sent word back overseas." He added, as though angry, "and this time they hurried."

He passed Grady an unmarked envelope and waited. Grady turned it over, afraid to open it.

Inside was a hastily scrawled note:

GRADY, PATTON MADE IT. I'M FINE. I LOVE EVERY SONOFABITCH IN THE THIRD ARMY. SORRY I WASN'T HOME FOR CHRISTMAS. NEXT YEAR FOR SURE. LOVE, KEVIN.

Grady's knees gave. A walking hearth, fortunately completely cool, edged behind him; he sat on it, patting it absently with one hand.

Pieter reached out and steadied him with one heat-weathered hand. "Easy, boy. Your brother, is he alive?"

Grady nodded, unable to speak. He passed the note to Pieter, who read it slowly and carefully, whispering a question to Antony, who grinned and whispered back. Pieter handed the note back. "I'm glad. This is good for you." He finished, a trace wistfully, "Family is always good."

He shook his head quickly. "So. You feel better now?"

Grady licked his lips, staring down at the note, then up only slightly into Antony's eyes. "I think I'll like it here."

Pieter gave a great booming laugh.

Grady spent the remainder of the afternoon watching Antony scrub hearths clean. "You want a hand with that?"

"Not tonight. Maybe after they know you better."

Grady watched and occupied his time by picking up a leather-bound volume that had "Materials Receipt" in gold-inlaid letters on the cover. The first pages were written in goose quill. "How far back does this thing go?"

"Hmm? Oh, that's Volume Two. Stops in the Civil War." He shook his head. "Bad time for business. We did some swords for Union officers—like I said, officers always get the good stuff—but we were cut off from a lot of our trade. Voodoo and gris-gris for New Orleans, mojo for Memphis, things like that." He gently shoved a hearth aside and beckoned to the next one. Antony liked this part of his work; it was like currying horses.

"What about before the Civil War?"

"You'd have to ask Pieter for details. Or Bernhard, if you can get him to talk about it. New York was full of abolitionists; you should hear the stories about this place and the Underground Railroad. Only time Pieter was the one who said we had to open it up to humans."

"He doesn't trust me, does he?"

Antony said carefully, "He tries. He has his reasons."

Grady thumbed through the book to the last few entries.

The book, filled out now with a steel nib pen, listed smaller amounts of raw materials. Business was less than it had been.

Grady expected to see and saw great quantities of copper, tin, iron, zinc, and aluminum. He was not surprised that they also bought steel, bronze, and brass, even though they clearly could have made their own. He raised his eyebrow at the listings under nickel, chromium, and titanium. "Somebody's been brushing up on steel alloys."

"I'd take a bow, but at this height who'd notice? I still read up on airplane manufacture."

"Maybe Plimstubb should hire you." He trailed his finger down the list, frowning. Charcoal, sure; talc for keeping gold from fusing to the tray you heated it on, maybe. Rhinoceros horn? Hanged man's teeth? Unicorn horn, for God's sake?

He smiled on reading an entry, but stopped as he read the date. He looked at it again, trying to remember—sure. He'd spoken to Antony during the pennant race. "Antony?"

"Mmm." He was wire-brushing a hearth, which was arching its grid against the strokes. "Sure, kid," he said absently.

"How'd you know to order the moly in advance?"

"What?" Antony swung around. "Oh. It wasn't much in advance—"

"It was before we spoke."

"Sure." Antony nodded. "Well, sometimes you guess and you get lucky. I think we got that for another project. It's like the time Curly Larson—this was after he'd crashed so many times they wouldn't let him fly—he was put in charge of feeding refugees. He looks around, he's in France, right?—outside Saint-Lô. First thing he does, even before the refugees arrive, is order as much wine as possible, figuring that they'll all drink lots of wine with their meals. The roads and the rails are all shot to hell with the war, but he uses the phone, he sends letters, he begs, and he gets the wine in plenty of time.

"Then the first of the refugees show up, and they're all children.

"Big problem, right? This is France, so the kids drink a little wine, but they'll never get through all that he ordered."

Antony chuckled. "So he used the wine as trade goods. Bribed officers, sent it to quartermasters—it was like he was the Army Signal Corps' personal vintner. In exchange he got candy, chocolate, fresh fruit, lemons and limes even, meat, poultry, everything he could ask for that would keep a kid healthy. At the end of the war he got more decorations for feeding people than he ever earned for shooting them.

"My point is, this is like that. Sometimes you get lucky." He turned back to the hearth, waiting.

"I guess so," Grady said slowly. But if so, Antony was damned lucky; it was the right amount of molybdenum to fill Plimstubb's order with hardly any waste.

He shook his head. Surely that was the smallest miracle he'd seen today.

Grady loaded another fixture of copper bracelets (for joint stiffness) into a crucible, clamped the lid on tight, dropped it on a walking hearth, and whistled for it to waddle over the fire. He sat on a rock, put a sheet of scrap steel on his lap, and made notes rapidly. Antony, beside him, sang quietly in a language that sounded like Dutch or German to Grady but was probably older.

After half an hour, Grady stood up as Pieter approached and said thoughtfully, "Mind if I sit and write for a while?" He looked at Pieter's face and added hastily, "It's work."

Pieter, still frowning, tugged at his beard. "We have jobs in house, Grady. When the work is there, then you work."

Appearing behind Pieter, Kirsten said quickly, "We hired him for what he knows. I'm sure he'll get the work done—"

Antony added, "And the kid has a plan to bring in more work."

Pieter swung toward Antony and regarded him dubiously. Finally he chuckled and threw up his hands. "You and Grady and your plans." He walked away, still chuckling. "Go ahead, boy. Do what Antony wants and make us all rich."

Grady, watching him go, said to Kirsten, "Thanks for helping me out."

Antony said reprovingly to her, "But that's my job."

She smiled. "I seem to remember saying that to you."

Antony sighed as she left. "She's tough."

"Sorry you don't like her," Grady said with a straight face.

"She likes you, though," Antony said lazily. "Let's empty this load, kid."

Grady said politely but stubbornly, "Is there a typewriter here?"

Antony shrugged. "Kirsten's office." He jerked a thumb over his shoulder. "I'll finish unloading."

Grady tossed his cane onto the coat hook, a tough shot since the hook was only three feet from the floor. The typewriter was a beat-up Royal that had yellowed keys and a battered black body. The platen was worn; from the stacks of carbons, Grady guessed that it was mostly used for invoicing. Grady stuck in two sheets of paper sandwiching carbon paper and hunched over the keys, kneeling on the floor in the absence of a human-size chair. He struck a key and jerked back hastily as the papers struggled frantically out of the typewriter and flapped around the room agitatedly. "Sorry." They settled on a high bookshelf, out of reach.

He got two more sheets, tested them by dropping them, and rolled them gingerly into the typewriter with a carbon. After typing the date cautiously, he relaxed and wrote, consulting his notes frequently.

Dennis Auto Parts Machining
3509 N. Washington
Cleveland, Ohio

   Attn.: Walter Byerlie, Materials Engineer

Dear Mr. Byerlie:

Recently Plimstubb was forced to refuse a sintering contract for your plant because our heat treating operation was overcommitted with projects of a higher wartime priority. At that time you were not interested in purchasing a furnace of your own.

He grinned to himself and wrote:

If at any time that changes, we will be happy to quote equipment to you.

   However, I have found a solution to your processing needs. A recent customer will be receiving a Plimstubb suitable for sintering and annealing. I confirmed with him that he would be able to take on your work and would give it priority on the equipment. I regret that, because of the nature of the plant and its work, I cannot give you a direct shipping address. I enclose a railroad shipping address for materials and an address for billing. . . .

Once done, Grady offered to borrow the Gnomeworks company truck and buy supplies. Pieter took him up immediately; errands in the outside world, even with trusted merchants, involved risk. Grady bought groceries, some hardened drill bits, and spare light bulbs. He also mailed his letter.

Before coming back he bought Katrina a yo-yo and, out

of guilt, rubber balls and jacks and more yo-yos for the other children. He wasn't sure what to get children who could play with magic toys, and hoped they wouldn't be disappointed.

Grady was the hit of the play hour before supper. Katrina had to stand on a chair to drop her yo-yo full length; while she was up there she gave him a hug. He looked back up to see Kirsten smiling at him fondly, and to his surprise he blushed.

Dinner was as rich as lunch, with the addition of ale and wine. Antony complained that the wine was from the Finger Lakes in New York, but he drank it. Grady had milk; he was tired enough that he was afraid he'd fall asleep.

To his surprise, Gretchen came to him and said seriously, "Only water or wine from here." She had a pleasant, clear voice. "Milk coats your throat. Meet me by the main forge."

Grady met her after dinner. She had a small stringed instrument, which she called a rebec. She played it with a bow and they vocalized, working on his range and tone. After half an hour she said, "That's enough for now. Bring your music tomorrow night."

"This is so nice of you," Grady burst out.

"Kirsten's orders."

"Well, it's still nice."

She smiled and left. Bernhard, listening and watching, regarded him solemnly but also winked before following her. Grady returned to his cottage—he was already thinking of it as home—and fell asleep instantly.

He woke up twice. Both times he read Kevin's second letter and fell back asleep.

ELEVEN

THE NEXT FEW weeks were busy, but were among the happiest in Grady's life. Every day he woke to something new.

Mornings at the Dwarfworks began with swordplay for him and then breakfast. The rest of the morning he trained on different kinds of processing. During the first week he had batch-processed wishing rings, learned a holy-water quench for a silver bracelet that forced the wearer to speak the truth ("As you can guess," Antony said wryly, "that's more of a gift item than something people buy for themselves"), and tempered arrowheads that would always hit their mark. Grady was relieved when he learned that the arrowheads were for hunting.

After a week of careful training, Antony pronounced him fit to work with customers; Grady waited for his first contract. Grady began corresponding with customers, including the buyer of the giant pans he had seen. Grady had to run back and forth to read that letter; he wrote the answer on a bedsheet, using a stick of charcoal taped to a bamboo fishing pole. He also met with a customer on January 6, when he returned to the Dwarfworks. It was a tall man who spoke with an aristocratic but archaic English accent and, aside from being extraordinarily lean and muscular, seemed normal in every way except for the rack of antlers on his head. He chatted amiably about hunting in winter, purchased a dozen silver choke chains for hunting dogs the size of draft horses, and paid in venison—at least he said it was, and Grady hoped fervently that it was. On leaving, the man suggested politely that Grady keep indoors until after midnight. Grady did.

Toward the end of that week, a pounding on his inside door awakened Grady. He opened it and blinked sleepily. "What time is it?"

"Middle of the goddamn night." Antony was nervous and testy. "Special customer."

"Who?"

Antony didn't answer. "He needs to talk to you, kid. He insists; you're the one doing the processing." Antony added, "And this one you have to see. Ripley's 'Believe It or Not.'"

Grady threw on a dress shirt and pants and automatically grabbed for a necktie. Antony shook his head slowly. "Uh-uh. This one we'll give you the neckwear. And it ain't Brooks Brothers."

The cumstomer stood calmly and patiently, waiting for Grady. "My name is Zoltán," he said politely, almost shyly. He was smooth-skinned, dark-haired, and extremely handsome. He wore work pants and suspenders, but the pants were nicely pressed and the shirt under the suspenders was blindingly bleached. He twisted a flat cap in his slender hands. He looked young, but Grady had learned to discount appearances.

After all, he looked alive, too.

"I would like"—he laughed embarrassedly, covering his face and turning away—"I would like something," he said slowly. If Zoltán had any blood of his own, he would have been blushing.

He reached out and, with an immaculately manicured nail, almost touched the strand of garlic around Grady's neck. "Where this is, I would rather wear cravat."

"I'd rather wear a tie, too," Grady said frankly. "My employer thought that wearing this was a good idea."

Zoltán nodded vigorously. "Is good idea. Excellent. I try to be polite, but sometimes I find my wish, my want, my . . ." He gestured with his hands, pulling something invisible toward his heart.

"Desires."

"Yes, desire. No, not desire." He looked serious and sad. "Craving. I have craving, and sometimes I cannot be good."

"I know how you feel." Grady grinned at him. "Some nights I can't be good either."

Zoltán laughed out loud, and with great presence of mind Grady didn't flinch back at the sight of the fangs. "But I want something you make." He held up a finger. "Let's think." After a short pause he said, "My mother, I wish her to come to this country. She could come the same way like me, and I think she would be glad, but I want much more for her. I want her to feel safe for the trip, and more I want her to feel that she comes to money. She is afraid to come, and the way she comes will make her feel more safe." He was struggling with words, but the words came out rapidly anyway.

Grady nodded. "So you want to show her—and maybe her friends—that you have the money to bring her here."

"Yes! Yes! But it isn't money, it is way to travel. Like in train, when you go first class." He hung his head. "Sadly, like me she must go by freight. But I want it to be good freight, you know what I am saying?"

Grady did. "You want it to be a nice"—he struggled for a better word. There wasn't one—"coffin."

"You know. Maybe you wish something nice for family when they travel."

"I wish something nice for my family now while they travel," Grady said frankly, thinking of Europe and the Pacific. "Can't you just buy it from an underta—— from a supplier of beautiful coffins?"

Zoltán looked at him disappointedly. "Of course not, no, because they are metal. Even when they are making the lid of mahogany, which is nice though cedar smells better inside, they are making metal hinges and handles. It is uncomfortable, but there is nothing else that looks good." He dropped his hands. "So I ask here."

"Wow. That is a problem." Grady stalled as Zoltán nodded vigorously. "And they make rope handles, but who wants that? And iron—don't get upset, I'm only thinking out loud. Like you said, 'Let's think.' Silver is—"

"Is the worst. Very bad."

"Okay, and copper—"

"Tarnishes. So does bronze. So does silver, really, but it hurts, too, so I do not care about the tarnishing, you know?"

"I see." Grady thought hard while Zoltán watched him earnestly. "So silver hurts the worst, and iron still hurts." He had an idea. "Would you like a glass of water while I think?"

"I do not need it, but water is always nice, yes."

Grady whispered to Antony, who raised an eyebrow but filled a battered beer stein with water and set it on the table near Zoltán, who lifted it, took a deep swig, and set it down. "Thank you."

Grady pointed to the lid of the stein. "That's pewter. It's

made from tin and lead. We could cast beautiful handles out
of it, and if it didn't hurt you, it won't hurt your mother."

Zoltán stared at it and with a sudden cry grabbed the stein
and held it tight to his palm. Grady rushed forward but there
was no need; he let go and stared at his hand delightedly. "It
does not hurt or burn. Grady, you have done a wonderful
thing."

Grady smiled back, pleased at solving the problem. "It
won't shine up as well as silver, but we can ornament it for
you. Is there anything else you'd like while you're here?"
Two sales were always better than one.

"No. Yes." Predictably he said, "Let's think." He thought.
"I do not think you can help me this time."

"You didn't think that last time. Let's try. What do you
need?"

"My mother does not see herself." He looked infinitely
sad. "She was great beauty when young and alive, even
visiting the court of the emperor in Vienna. She has shown
me pictures, an ivory painting. She is sad."

"And you want to help her see herself?" As Zoltán
nodded, Grady said carefully, "Zoltán, are you sure? If she
hasn't seen herself in a long time, maybe she'll be upset—"

"No, no, no. She is beautiful. Most beautiful woman her
age I have ever known. I swear, she will be pleased." He
added, "My friend, you are kind."

"And mirrors don't work, do they? How about water?"

"Very faint. Remember that this is at night."

"What about with a flashlight shining on the water?"
Zoltán looked confused. "You could try that, but there's got
to be something better. . . ." He turned to the dwarves. "Do
any of you have a camera?" He corrected himself. "A fairly
new camera, new in human terms?"

Predictably, it was Antony who leaped up. "A Kodak box

Brownie. You don't get more up to date than that." He scampered away to get it.

Kirsten, smiling as she watched him, shook her head. "He loves machines."

But Zoltán wasn't smiling. "My friend, you have thought well so far, but in this you are wrong. Camera does not show us. We are not on plate when it changes—makes from negative—develops."

"When was the last time any of you tried?" Grady was grinning, fairly sure he was right. "1860, 1890? Was it a daguerreotype, or silver-point?" Zoltán looked lost now. Grady went on with emphasis, "Zoltán, they used silver and other metals in the process. Now they don't, or they use less, I forget which. They don't use plates, but film, and it's chemical—metal in the compounds, but less of it. I'll bet you'll get an image."

He added, with a sudden thought, "If that doesn't work, there's a thing called a camera obscura—it gives an upside-down image, but you can reverse it with a lens. Maybe you could rig that some way—"

"That I have heard of." He frowned. "It has been around many years. Would not one of my people have tried it?"

"Maybe not. It works best with a strong light source, and electric lights have been around a shorter time than daylight has."

Zoltán mulled this over as Antony came back, panting, with the camera. "Film and all. Ready to be a star?" He pointed it at Zoltán.

Zoltán raised a hand quickly. "Wait." He took a comb from his coat and ran it through his hair carefully, by feel. "I will show this to my mother. It must be perfect."

"Hang on." Grady stood in front of him. "I'm your mirror. That's the other way." He mimed Zoltán's motions, helping the young man to smooth stray hairs. "I could do it for you, but I don't think you want that."

"Not the way I see your hair, no." Zoltán mussed Grady's hair, which had not been cut in a while. Grady laughed, unoffended.

Antony raised the camera. Grady backed off, but Zoltán said suddenly, "No." He gestured. "I want picture to mail my mother. Of me with my real American friend."

Grady stood beside him. Zoltán put a cold arm across his shoulders and hugged him affectionately, and they both smiled for the camera.

"If this works, I will pay you so much. We have accounts with interest since before our deaths; all of us are wealthy at home—"

Grady waved a hand. "No charge. You can buy the cameras anywhere. Leave us your address; we'll send the negatives and a copy of the pictures to you in New York."

He pumped Grady's hand vigorously. "So. When my mother arrives in America, I will write and you will come to dinner."

Kirsten nudged Grady, hard, as Zoltán added too casually, "Freely and of your own will."

"Or we could meet in a restaurant," Grady said lightly.

Zoltán tossed his head back and laughed. The bats in the cavern flew around madly. "Well said, my friend Grady. But I would never harm you."

Grady chuckled politely, noting that Zoltán had said nothing about what his mother might do.

Zoltán checked his watch. "It is soon dawn, and I have long ride." He dug into his pockets. "Here is money. You take what it costs, you say we have, what it is, you call, a deal." He pushed the bills at Grady. "If is not enough, then it is, you say, what you say, payment down."

Grady glanced at Kirsten and Antony, who looked back

impassively. "I'll check the price with my boss. I don't think this is a down payment; you may even get cash back. He added, "And if it works for you, tell your friends, the ones like you, and tell your mother to show the handles to her friends before she leaves. They should all have such good sons, right? I'll keep the molds for the handles, if you don't mind others having the ones you have."

He wobbled a pale hand in the air. "Maybe not quite so good handles for the others."

"All right. We'll change the mold."

Zoltán nodded and put on a dark, bulky overcoat. He probably didn't need it, but he would certainly blend in better with it this time of year.

"This is good country," he said seriously to Grady. "Wonderful. The air is full of dreams all the time, so thick you can see them." He took Grady's arm, his face so earnest that Grady could ignore the cold, dead fingers. "When I come here, I want those dreams, too.

"I found a place that needed night work. They ask me, can I do the work? I say, of course, even though I am not sure. Because what do I have to lose?" He laughed, and it bothered Grady that all the bats in the Dwarfworks squeaked with him.

"So I took the job, and it was hard but I learned it. And my first paycheck, it was like gold from heaven! But I walked into the streets with it, and on Canal Street a policeman, he grabbed my shoulder and said, "What are you so happy for?" And he threatened to jail me if I did not sign my money away to him. And he called me a dirty Bohonk."

Zoltán sighed heavily. "Of course I cut his throat with a fingernail and drained him upside down like a pig, but even so."

Grady said, "It's not all like that."

"Some of it is."

"Sure." He waved an arm at the factory. "And some of what we produce here is scrap." Pieter and Antony blanched simultaneously. "We do our best, we take every job like it's the only one that matters, but some of it still turns out wrong. People are like that, too. We do our best, we try to do right, but sometimes we don't." He was blushing and practically pleading. "We're good, but we're not all good."

Zoltán said amusedly, "You could have lied to me."

"I could have," Grady said honestly and immediately. "But you'd remember twenty years from now, and I wouldn't get your business."

Zoltán stared at him fixedly, then said to Kirsten and Pieter, "I am ready to leave. I will buy more of the handles, because I know and believe they will work." As he wrapped a muffler over his workingman's collar, he said determinedly, "And I wish to see that young man when I come back."

The dwarves drew back from him as he walked through the plant door without its being opened.

Kirsten said to Grady, "Do you know why you solved his problems?"

Grady was embarrassed. "Because they weren't that tough."

"No. Because you took them seriously." Her eyes were shining. "You're a genuinely nice guy, Grady."

He thought of Warren Hastings, with his immaculate suit and company-bought car. "I hear nice guys finish last."

"Never believe it." She grabbed him by the hipbones, which startled him until he realized it was the best height for her to reach. "Not for an instant. Nice guys finish loved and honored, recognized by those around them." She shot a look at Antony. "If no one gives medals for that, it's because medals aren't worth much." She patted Grady's side with sudden affection, then turned and left.

Grady said, "What did she mean?"

Antony said lazily, "She thinks you're pretty good."

"No, the part about the medals."

Antony stared at the rock wall before them, bitter and unhappy. "Oh, I might have thought a medal or two would impress her, and I might have been wrong."

Grady's job change in his own plant contrasted sharply. The first thing he did every week was mail a letter to his brother. It was the last thing, too; the gaps between letters hid that he was away from Plimstubb every other week.

Kevin wrote back intermittently (through normal mail now), hasty notes that had little detail and arrived almost intact. His father wrote back frequently, chatty, detailed letters that were heavily censored. Whatever his father was waiting to build, it was important.

To his father he wrote admitting that he had part-time work, that he hoped to be back in Plimstubb full-time someday, and that he was learning a great deal.

That last was eventually true at Plimstubb, but some of what he learned was unpleasant. Stode was pushing for a second furnace order; Hastings was stalling. His sole reasoning was that he didn't want to commit to wartime customers while he could build his civilian trade. Rumor had it Hastings was going overseas for civilian customers. Grady felt uneasy. He had helped with the paperwork when Plimstubb had sold a furnace to the Brazilian Navy; though Brazil was an ally, the paperwork and red tape had been unspeakably complicated. He suspected that Hastings wouldn't file all the paperwork for his sales.

As for Grady's new service job, his training had been remarkably brief. He approached Hammer Houlihan in the shop and said, "Roy Burgess says you used to work in the service department. He says you should show me how this afternoon."

Houlihan looked from side to side in apparent desperation and burst out, "They think they can teach a chimp to do this job."

Grady only said, "Shouldn't I have some training?"

Hammer Houlihan scratched his head, thinking. Finally he said, "The atmosphere furnaces are painted blue."

"What about the vacuum furnaces?" Grady asked.

"They're blue, too." He walked away.

Grady went on his first service call that afternoon. The plant, a small chain factory in Pawtucket, was filthy with soot and powder. Grady looked around the factory for a conveyor furnace or a top-loading vacuum bean pot and found neither. He didn't expect to find the bean pot; anyone that modern would clean the plant once in a while.

The plant owner and manager strode up and stuck out an oily, blackened hand. "Ralph Douglas." He had a slight Scots accent. "Ye're the Plimstubb service engineer?" He looked dubiously at Grady's cane.

"Sure am. Grady Cavanaugh." He leaned on a metal cabinet and said casually, "So, where's this furnace you need fixed?"

Douglas looked even more doubtful. "Ye're leanin' on it."

It was a batch oven from World War I, probably bought from army surplus. Grady had only seen them in pictures. He opened the door in two tries, peered in at twenty-odd years of muck, and shook his head. "Wow. When did it quit running?"

"When I called for repairs. Look, can ye really do it?"

"If I can't, Plimstubb will send someone else." He tossed his cane on a nearby rack and opened his knapsack of tools.

The Dwarfworks had already taught him patience. He stood for two hours, scraping carbon off connections and checking wiring links. The powdery asbestos insulation on the wiring tickled his nose, but otherwise it wasn't bad work.

Two-thirds of the way through he found melted metal, probably from processed work that had overheated, splashed across a connector, and shorted it out. He kept looking and found more. He checked the wiring a final time and found a loose connector he'd missed the first time.

At the afternoon's end he closed the oven door, lit a cigarette, and turned on the furnace. It had no control instrument, just a rheostat. Grady checked temperature by looking in a sight port and checking the color of the elements and the brick as it heated up.

Douglas peered over his shoulder. "When you started, I didna think—well." He clapped a filthy hand on Grady's shoulder. "Thanks, and good job."

"You're welcome." He packed up. "If your work picks up, one of our belt furnaces would give you four times the output."

Douglas shook his head. "Ye're no plant manager. Run the equipment till it will never run more, that's how to make money."

"Maybe." Now Grady looked as dubious and worried as Douglas had at the start of the afternoon. "But if you say you can do the extra work, other people will pay to have you do more work. And we sold a big belt furnace to Federal Chain last year."

He left, aware that, behind him, Douglas was chewing his bushy beard and thinking hard.

When he returned to Plimstubb, Roy Burgess pointed to the wall clock repeatedly and snarled about laziness, late-

ness, and deadlines. Since service calls were paid by the
hour, this was unfair. Grady endured it without comment
and left when it was over to wash up.

Watching Grady at the shop sink, Hammer Houlihan
said, "You know, Burgess is a son of a bitch." Grady said
nothing. "He told me once, 'If you chew out the servicemen
once a week whether they've done anything or not, so they
leave your office in a white-knuckle fury, you're a good
service manager.'"

Grady looked up from drying his face. "Thanks."

Houlihan nodded. "So, how bad did you bitch up your
first service call?"

"It went okay," Grady said easily as he walked away.
"Me, I think they could teach a chimp to do this job."

Behind him, Hammer Houlihan shouted terrible things
involving Grady, his sexual behavior, two deviants, their
mother, the Savior, His mother, and a goat. Joe Cataldo
looked up from his work bench interestedly, obviously not
taking in more than one word in three. Grady closed the
shop door with satisfaction and went home. At choir
rehearsal that night, Maestro Mandeville's repeated insults
didn't even faze him.

By the end of the week he had used lit sulfur sticks to find
leaks in dissociated ammonia piping, had installed a new
conveyor belt on a belt furnace, and had rebricked a furnace
with new insulation, having nothing more to go on than a
faded packing print and some childhood experience with
building blocks. He felt much more confident, and he knew
more about the machinery he had sold than he had ever
expected to learn.

His final call of the week took him to a jewelry plant,
Gold Chain. It was one of several new factories in Rhode

Island that took advantage of the new wave of immigrant labor to manufacture and assemble intricate necklaces and bracelets at low cost. Grady suspected that when the war was over there would be more and more of these plants.

The owner, Johnny DellaTorre, said there was a stuck solenoid in the nitrogen line. "It should open automatic," he said, showing the valve blade motion with his hand. "Flush the whole thing out so it don't burn. Not that I care, while it's running, but safety, you know?"

"Good for you." Grady had already realized that many customers considered safety an accessory. He shut off the gas and prepared to cut the electrical power.

DellaTorre shook his head vigorously. "I got it heating up already; I got product to run. Can't you, you know, work around it while it heats up?"

Grady eyed him narrowly. "Is there any hydrogen in that furnace?" Most furnaces for gold ran a lot of hydrogen; called a reducing atmosphere, it bonded with any oxygen and kept the gold from discoloring. Of course, if a lot of air got in—say, while someone had a pipeline disassembled and open—it would blow flames out of every opening.

"Oh, sure. Gotta keep going. Do me a favor, can't you?"

Grady nodded. "I'll just turn it off and go back to air while I do the wiring." He undid the pipe unions of the nitrogen line. It was easy—unscrew two little threaded rings, pop the old valve out, slide the new valve in, and screw the unions onto it. "This'll just take three minutes." He popped open the main power switch and, while it was off, carefully undid the wires to the electrical valve motor one at a time and screwed them onto the new solenoid. Just before connecting the last wire he opened the nitrogen valve again and let nitrogen flush the pipeline to the furnace. He was proud that he'd thought of that, getting the last air out of the safety system.

After connecting the last wire, he stood and showed the old solenoid to DellaTorre. "The mechanism got all this powder in it. It's jammed."

"Talcum. I put it under the chains on the belt, it keeps them bright and they don't pick up nothing from the belt." He patted Grady's shoulder. "Thanks for keeping me running, I mean that sincerely."

"Glad to." Grady looked at a decrepit and seemingly asleep old lady who was standing watching them. "The furnace needs to be purged of air again. Is that your operator?"

"Who? Mabel? Aw, she's all right. Anyway, she's what I can get. War and all."

She was peering at the furnace as though she had never seen it before. Grady said apprehensively, "Would you like me to give her some safety training?"

"Nah, nah. She does good," DellaTorre said earnestly. "You watch how good she does. Mabel, fire it up."

The woman tottered to the furnace, peered at the panel, and, with both arms straining, tugged the main power switch on. The panel lights went on; she peered at them nearsightedly for half a minute. Satisfied, she bent down stiffly, left hand pressed against her spine, and twisted a valve open with her right.

Grady was horrified. She had opened the hydrogen valve, and the furnace was still full of air.

He stepped forward, but DellaTorre grabbed the back of his shirt. "No, no, stay back; this is where it gets good."

He cupped his hands and called encouragingly, "Better get out of the starting gate, Mabel."

Mabel nodded, stood up straight, and stumbled with heartbreaking slowness toward the shop bathroom.

Grady watched with the helpless feeling of a witness at a train wreck while she fumbled with the sticking door, half fell back as it shivered free, and ducked in quickly, closing the door behind her—

Just as the furnace gave an ear-splitting BOOM that spat flame eight feet out both ends. Dust filtered off the rafters while Grady stood deafened and blinking. Mabel kicked the bathroom door open and peered out before leaving.

"You see?" DellaTorre said reasonably in his ear. "She hears the bang, she knows there ain't no air left in the furnace and it's safe to come out."

Grady said over the ringing in his ears, "What if she falls down before she gets to the bathroom?"

DellaTorre's forehead puckered with concern. "Ooo. She better not do that."

Grady nodded tiredly.

When he returned to the Dwarfworks that week, Sonny followed him in the truck, taking the Plimstubb furnace to the Dwarfworks. They both hunkered down over the steering wheel as they drove past Hudson Drill, but no one stopped the truck.

The furnace had been shipped on a single skid, with unpacked insulation and thermocouples in a separate box. With the help of the dwarves, Sonny unloaded the furnace and box onto the empty hillside. Antony shook his hand and said apologetically, "I hope you don't mind that we don't invite you in."

He looked around, not seeing anyplace to go in, and said emphatically, "I hope you don't mind if I'm glad about that." He shook hands with Grady to say good-bye and said to Kirsten, "This young man doing okay?"

Kirsten smiled. "He's doing very well."

"Then he can set the furnace up for you. I bet he knows how just fine." Sonny smiled at him, amused.

Grady said, "I bet I'll get it done, even if I don't know how." Sonny laughed and drove off.

In the end the bricking was easy, like playing with blocks. The thermocouples were a snap once he had lined up the holes in the brickwork with the holes in the metal outer shell of the furnace. Even sliding the metal heating elements in the brick slots was painless; it had all fit together in Plimstubb's shop, and it all fit back together now.

The wiring scared him. Susan had left him with a list of wiring sizes and had packed what he needed. To his astonishment, she had taken him into the shop and showed him how to splice wires, run ends through contacts and relays, put in junction boxes, connect power wiring to transformer taps. "How do you know all this?" he'd asked.

"My dad showed me. Also, it was how I made money at Columbia and Chicago; the labs always needed someone to help wire equipment." She added, unreassuringly, "Remember, you're dealing with a lot of amps here. The juice through this transformer would kill you."

Grady thanked her for the information, but he didn't feel grateful.

Now he wired it to the prints and to her sketches and notes. He made sure each connection was tight, so there wouldn't be any arcing and sparking. He traced all the connections, especially the main wire from the fused Dwarfworks line to the furnace transformers. Finally he set the L-pad switch, an L-shaped metal bar that rotated across a semicircle of connections, to the lowest tap.

Nothing happened, of course; the ON switch was still off. He reset the mechanical control instruments and, ready to jump back, turned the CONTROL POWER OFF-ON switch to ON.

A yellow light labeled CONTROL POWER ON turned

on. The needles on the temperature controller and the overtemperature controller climbed slowly. That was all.

Grady wiped his damp forehead and said to Antony and Kirsten, who were watching interestedly, "Piece of cake."

Kirsten smiled and moved away. Antony moved to Grady and said quietly, "The last time I heard someone say that, it was Curly Larson, pretending he made a pancake landing that smashed the undercarriage because he wanted to."

Grady said back, "Any landing you walk away from, right?" Every pilot he'd ever met was cocky, and by God it was Grady's turn.

That was the start of his fourth week in the Dwarfworks. By now he loved the people, the children, the magic, and even the cavern. Then there was the processing itself. Until the Plimstubb furnace was up and running, it was all being done with fires, kilns, hearths, and bellows. Once Grady got used to it, he fell into the rhythm of the work. He often found himself breathing in rhythm with the bellows.

Every day he learned more about the processes that went into gold, steel, all manner of metals. Between his work here and his new job with the Plimstubb service department, he found himself watching heated metal with that protective and slightly possessive fervor people reserved for their favorite baseball teams, their hobbies, or their victory gardens.

On this particular afternoon, the work in the crucible was a bracelet. At times like this Grady found himself thinking how metal had once been as much an essential part of clothing, and what civilization had done to make people think they were apart from stone or metal the way that urban people thought they were apart from animals. The bracelet, a chain of dancing figures, was a Navajo design to keep the

wearer from harm. It had been purchased by an old man in
Arizona for his son in the Pacific Theater; his son was
something called a "code talker," receiving military com-
mands in Navajo so the Japanese could not decode them.
Grady followed the directions in the recipe—including,
though he limped and felt foolish, the dancing during the
chants—and he added his own wishes for the man in the
Pacific, plus a quiet wish of his own: "Save my father." He
glanced frequently at the chart during the cool-down period,
when he was supposed to dance counterclockwise around
the fire. Maybe it was solely for timing; then again, given
the work around here, maybe not. He leaned on his cane and
pushed hard.

As he finished, a voice said, "Kid, you look like someone
coldcocked a chicken."

Grady answered, "Hey, Antony, learn to dance before
you criticize. What's up?"

Antony held out an envelope. "One hell of a lot. Who
knows you're here?"

The envelope had a Cleveland postmark. Grady snatched
at it and read the letter inside quickly.

"You're grinning."

"Read it." He passed it over. Antony read it quickly and
nearly dropped it.

Grady was still grinning. "Don't tell Pieter yet."

"You're kidding."

"Nope. I'll go to the railroad station, you'll help me
unload, we'll start it in the new furnace."

Antony's eyes glowed. "I'll get it up to temperature."

It was too late to go tonight. Grady made small talk at
dinner, sang badly for the ever-patient Gretchen, and said
goodnight to Kirsten as she walked through the plant
checking that all was well.

Kirsten said back, "Good-night, Grady. No work tomorrow, of course."

"Are things that slow?" Grady said nervously. Maybe this new job wasn't such a good idea after all.

"Of course they aren't. It's Hunt Day—that's right; you wouldn't know." She looked at him seriously. "It's a holiday of ours. We'll be here together all day, but we won't be working. No sword-fighting lesson, either. You can stay home if you wish."

After some hesitation she added, "Or you can join us."

"Are you sure? I can stay away if it's private—"

Kirsten, embarrassed at being caught, shook her head quickly. "No, that's all right. We've trusted you to come here, you're certainly welcome." She put a hand on his arm. "Please join us," she said, and Grady had no way to back out.

"Should I wear anything special?"

"You don't have to wear a suit, if that's what you mean. If you have dark clothes, that would be good."

The following morning Grady washed quickly, shaved, had a cup of coffee and a cigarette, and walked to the Dwarfworks at the usual time. His first surprise came inside the door; the electric lights were off. He checked the nearest torch sconce; it was still empty.

As his eyes adjusted, he saw a flickering light across the cave. At the same time, Antony said softly, "Come on down, kid. Watch your step."

Grady moved slowly and carefully across the work floor, using his cane as much for guidance as for support. Gradually he saw more and more as he moved closer to the candle.

Soon he saw other candles, half shielded in dwarves'

hands. A pretty silhouette blocked the light; Kirsten came forward soundlessly and led him to the others. The dwarves were at a makeshift table of boards and barrels; an upended barrel at the end in front of a raised plank table was clearly for Grady's comfort. He nodded his thanks rather than speaking; they all seemed awfully quiet.

"Glad you could come," Antony said. Even he seemed subdued.

"Wouldn't miss it," Grady answered, taking care not to raise his voice. "Can you tell me what I should be doing, though? I'd hate to be rude by mistake."

The dwarf grinned at him. "There isn't much to it. You eat, you drink, you have a good time." He raised a warning finger. "But no bright lights, no loud speech except for some singing, and move without making noise." He added, grinning, "Later tonight we'll make as much noise as we want."

Someone passed him an apple, a chunk of cheese, and a hunk of bread. It tasted good. Gretchen handed him a goatskin; it turned out to be full of apple juice. Dessert was a handful of nuts. "Interesting menu," he commented.

"Nothing you can't carry in your hands," Kirsten said quietly. "That's the rule, until sunset."

"How will you know it's sunset?"

"We take turns keeping watch. That's part of Hunt Day, too. And games to keep children quiet, and hide-and-go-seek."

Kirsten nodded to Antony. "But now we're going to sing."

Grady looked from one to the other. None of them looked happy about it.

They tilted back their heads, and their perfectly tuned voices rang through the cavern:

Look at all the feet!
Pretty feet!
Little feet!
Over hedges, over stiles,
Dodging, running, many miles. . . .

The song went on for verse after verse, all about little feet running through the country. Pieter sang with his eyes closed. Kirsten kept her hand on his through the entire song.

At the final verse and the closing line, "So pretty to catch!" Kirsten clapped her hands together once. It was not applause. "And now the children hide."

Katrina and the others leaped up happily, tired of sitting and ready to play. Grady looked at Kirsten. "Does someone chase them?"

"Exactly. The monster chases them—"

"I could do that."

Kirsten faltered. "You?"

"I'm awfully big to them. And they like playing with me." He waved his cane. "It's not like I'll run too fast for them."

Kirsten looked dazedly from the hiding places to Grady and nodded. "All right. You're the monster."

"Fine." He glanced toward the stalagmites and whispered conspiratorially, "What do I do now? Do I close my eyes and count?"

"No, you start chasing them." Kirsten shouted at the children, "Here comes the monster. Run! Run and hide!"

The children scampered away, excited and happy. Grady good-naturedly hesitated a moment before chasing after them.

At first he couldn't find any of them; clearly this wasn't the first time they had played hide-and-seek in the factory. Finally Grady adopted a strategy. He shuffled over to an obvious hiding place, peering over his candle uncertainly; when he was close to a range of stalagmites, he pretended to stub his toe and yelped, hopping on his good foot and waving the cane wildly.

It worked; someone giggled. He pointed with the cane and called, "I see Katrina!"

He hadn't, of course, but she ran out laughing anyway. He grabbed her and hugged her.

"You're out," Kirsten said to the little girl.

Katrina pouted, "But I want to play again."

"Can't she go back and I'll catch her again?" Grady said.

"Of course not," Kirsten said, exasperated. "You already caught her. She's dead."

Katrina started to cry. Kirsten sighed. "Take her to the table and get her some food. I'll be the monster from here."

Grady fed Katrina nearly half a bowl of sugar plums. Antony sidled up. "Didn't work out?"

"I guess I'm too scary." Grady badly wanted a cigarette but assumed it wouldn't be appropriate. "Antony, what's going on? What is Hunt Day about?"

Antony looked around to see where Pieter was before beginning. He said quietly, "In the 1600s, Holland was a great place to live. It sold most of the salted herring Europe ate. It traded spices and gold and everything you could think of. It had hundreds of little shallow-draft ships that could sail into any harbor in the world. The Dutch said they ruled the seas. And the dwarves lived in Amsterdam and Rotterdam, making trade goods that went all over the world, and life was good for us, too."

Grady raised an eyebrow at that "us" but said nothing.

"But the English wanted to rule the seas, too. They built up a navy, and the Dutch built up a navy, and sooner or later there was gonna be a war."

The dates came to Antony as easily as Pearl Harbor

would always come to Grady. "It started in early summer of 1652. It didn't look like it'd be bad. The Dutch had an admiral named Maarten Tromp, he'd been at sea since he was nine, and everyone thought he was the greatest admiral who ever lived—hell, the English even knighted him for service to their queen, before the war. So if the Dutch had him, everything would be fine, right?"

Grady nodded. "So what went wrong?"

"There was a gnomewrench in the dwarfworks. A big one, this time. The war started, and Tromp was winning or fighting to draws nearly all the time. Nobody'd really invented naval tactics yet, and like I said, he was one smart sailor.

"Then in July of 1652 he took a fleet of ninety-two ships out to fight the English. Everything went wrong, mostly the weather. Tromp ended up blown away from the English while the British Navy shot up the Dutch herring fleet. That cost a lot of money later.

"In early August, while Tromp was still at sea, a freak storm blew up, a big one. Wind, rain, high waves, the works. When it cleared he had only thirty-four ships, and he fled home." Antony sighed, still watching Pieter. "The Dutch court-martialed him, but the navy mutinied. So the top brass put Tromp back in charge and looked for another excuse for the failure."

"Which was . . ."

"Officially, another batch of captains whom they court-martialed. Unofficially, witchcraft."

"You're kidding." But Grady hadn't grown up that far from Salem, Massachusetts; he knew what charges of witchcraft could do in the seventeenth century.

"They started a campaign against dwarves. It began as humor and some choice lies—that we were poisoning people with our metalwork, that we held a party every time a Dutch ship sank or that we took a job away from a guildsman, things like that."

Grady nodded sagely. "So people got a little hostile."

"A little." Antony was amused. "They stoned us in the streets. So we pulled back from people and hid. Some dwarves wanted to leave, but the others said that it would blow over. When the Dutch start winning, they'll like us again. And sure enough, a freak wind turned a naval battle against the English, and everyone said the dwarves had done it."

"And things got better—"

"Nope. People don't like witchcraft." He went on, "And then the Dutch started losing again.

"On August 10, in the middle of a big naval battle—a hundred and twenty ships on each side—Tromp was shot by a musketball and died. The Dutch captains fell apart; more than twenty of them just turned tail and ran. The English Navy lost two ships. The Dutch lost thirteen ships and thousands of men were killed or wounded. Holland still had a navy, but not much of a one for now. By midwinter of 1653, the English had Holland blockaded, every harbor.

"Know what that's like for a country that lives on trade? People were starving. There was grass growing in the streets; things fell apart that fast. There were more than a thousand empty homes in the cities."

"And they blamed you."

"You bet they did. And they saw us, and they started rumors that we had all kinds of food and money stored up, and we were just hiding it until the English won. But people still bought from us, mostly on credit. We sold, but you can't eat debt, can you. And nobody worried about not paying us.

"And one day, everybody decided that if they got rid of the dwarves, they'd get rid of the Dutch bad luck."

"How did they find you?" But it was obvious. "Your customers. The people who owed you money . . ."

"Now you get it. The people who bought from us turned us in and erased their debts. And one late winter morning there was a whole new sport: dwarf-hunting. With game nets and guns. On horseback."

A child far behind Grady giggled. The hide-and-go-seek game had started again, and Kirsten had nearly caught someone.

"What happened then? To you guys, I mean."

"What happened to us?" Antony's smile was tight and spectral, with too many teeth showing. "All kinds of things. Bone meal compost. Buttons. Real-hair wigs. Go to a Dutch museum with a clothing exhibit from the 1660s; you'll still see children's leather vests and not be able to tell what kind of leather it is."

Grady felt sick. "So you all left."

"Oh, no." Antony shook his head vigorously. "Hardly any of us left." He looked into the distance, remote and sad. "It's been two generations since then, the way we count. There are still hardly any of us."

"How did you get to America?"

"The survivors stowed away on a ship for New York. They found a small boat and sailed up the Hudson and into the country. There are lots of places to hide in the Catskills; eventually they settled on this cave, where we've worked ever since." He turned and stared at Grady meaningfully. "And we've hardly let any humans know about us since."

"I'm the monster," Grady said thoughtfully.

"Yep."

Something clicked in Grady's mind. "You said two generations. Was Pieter—"

"Pieter's mother got caught and shot because she couldn't

run fast carrying him. And Klaus knows it. That's why he sang the Hunt Song to Pieter."

"Jesus," Grady said feelingly. He'd hated Klaus before, but this . . . "How did Pieter get away?"

"At the last minute she stuffed him in a drain pipe and led the hunt away. Another dwarf found him and raised him."

Antony paused, then said in a rush, "Kid, did you follow the reports about Auschwitz and Birkenau this winter? About how many people got killed, mostly Jews?"

"I heard."

"I'll bet you were shocked. We weren't."

After a long time Grady said, "Did you ever find the rest of the dwarves?"

"It's been nearly three hundred years. We haven't met any."

After a silence, Grady punched his arm. "All the more reason for you and Kirsten to get married, start a family."

Antony sighed. "Well, I think so."

There was a cry from one of the twins at the far end of the cavern. The last of the dwarf children had been caught.

"What's next?" Grady asked.

Antony shrugged. "It's over. The kids are all killed."

"That's it? They're killed and it's over?"

"Of course. That way they'll remember. We hope. And now," Antony said happily, "we cook and we eat, to celebrate finding a new home. This is the best meal of the year. How good a cook are you, kid?"

"I'm not, today. I have to run an errand." He winked.

"I'll cover for you." Antony added, "But get back before dinner. Kirsten pushed to make sure you were invited; she'd feel rotten if you skipped it."

"Then I'd better hurry." He ran to the truck.

The rail station, predictably, was near Hudson Drill; it ran a spur line there. The freight manager, a tired old man with bifocals hanging halfway off his narrow nose, made Grady sign in three places for the work but never asked for any identification. Afterward, despite his tired and frail look, the freight manager loaded the pallets on the truck himself, with a chain and hooks on a swing crane. Grady was back at the Dwarfworks in forty-five minutes.

Antony had enlisted Bernhard; together they carried the pallets easily, even though each pallet held four hundred pounds of metal. Grady did his best one-handed to help; he was probably only in the way, but he was too excited not to try.

Grady peered in the front tunnel of the Plimstubb furnace; it was red-hot in the heat chamber. "Eighteen hundred degrees," he said confidently.

"You can't know that." But Antony checked the control settings; the temperature indicator matched the settings. "Let's start."

An hour later, Pieter looked up from his thoughts at dinner. "Antony, Grady, where to hell have you been? Come, eat."

Antony, grinning, said, "No, you come over here, boss. We have something to show you."

Pieter rose. The others, curious, followed. Bernhard was with them; for once his serious face had a broad smile.

Antony and Pieter stood in front of the stacked pallets as though they were small boys trying to hide a broken basement window. Antony nudged Grady. "You tell him, kid. You did most of it."

"You stuck your neck out for it."

Pieter sighed. "One of you tell me now."

Grady stepped forward slightly, holding an envelope in his cane hand. "I wanted to thank you for inviting me."

Pieter waved a hand. "That was Kirsten."

"Maybe, but you could have said 'no.' Thanks." He

handed Pieter the envelope. Pieter took out a one-page
letter, read it dazedly, and let it hang from his hand.

> *Dennis Auto Parts Machining*
> *3509 N. Washington*
> *Cleveland, Ohio*
> *To: Grady Cavanaugh*
> *P.O. Box 1705*
> *Walkill, NY*
>
> *Dear Grady,*
>
> *Thanks for thinking of us. I promise we'll buy a
> furnace from you if business ever picks up. I mean
> that, pal.*
>
> *I've shipped our first lot of ten thousand parts.
> Troop trains don't run big to the barrel on this line, so
> they should show up the day this letter did. We need
> these back by the middle of the month. If they work
> out—and I know they will—we'll send another set for
> next month. Attached is the check, in advance.*
>
> *I hope I see you the next time I'm at Plimstubb. In
> the meantime, thanks for getting us out of a jam.*
>
> *Sincerely,*
>
> *Walt Byerlie, Materials Engineer*
>
> *Encl.: Materials specifications; check for services*

Grady and Pieter moved aside. Pieter looked at the
check, which had three zeros, then at the stacked pallets of
unprocessed parts. "Grady, you mean well, this I know." He
waved an arm helplessly at the pallets. "How can we
possibly do so much work so fast?"

Antony jerked a thumb toward the Plimstubb furnace.

"Check the first load, boss." At the end of the conveyor was a cardboard box on a short stand. Brazed parts, cooled nearly to room temperature, were exiting the furnace slowly, dropping off the belt a few at a time. Pieter peered into it, unsure what he would see.

The box had more than a hundred parts in it already. Pieter picked one up, turning it over and over, checking the quality as much by feel as by eye.

Like a man in a dream, Pieter turned to Grady. "How much long, how many—I am sorry. For how long have you been brazing these parts?"

"About forty minutes."

"And it runs all night if you want, boss." Antony pointed to the front of the conveyor. "You can idle it at high heat, turn it back up before breakfast, and run product first thing in the morning."

Pieter watched the box slowly filling. He went to the front end of the furnace and loaded the belt for a few minutes while everyone watched in silence.

When he spoke, his voice was soft and shaky. "Equal this is to one-half our normal production. Grady, I cared for you and took this care for you because I knew you were young and you needed the help of all of us. I never knew how much we needed you. Thank you, from all of us, and thank you for your talent and your gifts." Pieter's eyes shone. "Thank you for helping my little plant, with all the other things you should be thinking about for yourself."

Grady had often pulled in purchase orders. He had frequently signed off on terms-of-condition sheets where the negotiations were flexible to Plimstubb but crucial to the customer.

He had never before helped set up a contract where, to the people signing, the agreement on the contract meant the difference between bankruptcy and survival.

Bucked by the good news, the party picked up considerably. Antony strapped on an accordion to go with the rebec, and Bernhard puffed out his cheeks on a J-shaped reed instrument that Antony said was a krummhorn, and they took turns on the drums and dancing. Even Grady played the drums, enthusiastically and badly, while they laughed. He hopped one-legged for some of the dancing, and at one point, to everybody's amusement (even Grady's), Gretchen picked him up by the legs and carried him through the figures of a reel. It was nearly midnight when, exhausted but unable to sleep, he arrived at his cottage; it was twelve-thirty when he heard a knock at the outside door.

He opened the door. "What can I do—" He froze.

College is not a cloister; Grady had seen any number of photos of naked women. He had seen burlesque, and he had even, in a bachelor party, seen a clumsy but mock-enthusiastic stripper bare all. On a few occasions, mostly in bad light, he had seen naked and excited women—though on those occasions he had been more than a little excited himself, and not a reliable witness.

But all those occasions had come with some kind of prelude, drinks or a lot of talk, or, in the case of the photos, a buildup by the college man who had brought them back from Tijuana.

This had no buildup at all. He stared down at Kirsten, who was smiling, shiny-eyed and completely nude. She stood, feet planted the width of her stocky shoulders, and said, "Aren't you going to invite me in?"

He looked frantically up and down the hillside. "Come in quickly. No. Wait." He was bright red, and getting redder. "Where'd you leave your, your clothes?"

"At my house. I'll run get them later." Her voice took on her tone of command. "Grady, it's cold out here."

"Right, sorry." He held the door open wide, pulling his

stomach in and arching back so they wouldn't accidentally touch. Kirsten looked suddenly uncertain but strode in briskly. She turned and smiled at Grady fondly, like an exasperated teacher. "Of course, we'll get cold if you don't close the door."

He shut it gingerly and moved to a chair at the opposite side of the room from her. He noticed how pink, almost rosy, her skin was; how she was solid muscle on a body shape that, on a human, would have been laden with fat; how red her nipples were. He blinked and looked away involuntarily.

Kirsten frowned now. "Is something wrong?"

"Huh? Nothing." He was floundering. "Does anyone know you're here?"

"Of course. You don't think I'd sneak behind their backs—oh. Is Antony what's bothering you?" She looked at him sharply. "Grady, it's my heart and my body, and I'll offer myself to whomever I choose."

"Offer yourself?"

"Yes, offer myself." She tapped her foot impatiently; incongruously, Grady thought of Susan. "Did you think I just wanted to go for a midnight naked stroll?"

"No, no." This was way too fast for Grady—and with Kirsten, whom he thought of as a hero, not as someone he'd . . . "Listen, this isn't a good idea."

She wrinkled her forehead. "What's not good about it? Grady, is this your first time? I know I'm older than you—"

"No, no, no." If possible, he blushed more. "It's not my first time—wouldn't have been my first time."

The wrinkle became a furrow. "Wouldn't have been? You're saying no?"

"Well—I—"

"In front of everybody?"

Grady glanced out the window, as though he expected

bleachers outside and faces pressed against the glass. "Do they have to know?"

She stood straight and, for her, tall, breasts jutting forward, a proud stance except for the hurt in her eyes. "You don't want me?"

"No," he blurted, relieved that it was over.

Except it wasn't.

Kirsten took her hand off the bed. "How can you say that? How can you do this?" She sounded stunned and awkward. "Do you know what everyone already thinks of me for offering? Do you know what they'll think when you turn me down?"

Grady said nothing. That annoyed her. "I can't believe you'd do this to me. After I helped hire you, made you at home, cared for you"—her face flushed more deeply, the red spilling gradually down her neck—"saw to it that you were trained, watched over you, invited you to Hunt Day—didn't anything I did for you matter?" Her voice rose. "Didn't it mean anything to you?"

"It meant a lot." He was frustrated himself, words falling out of control. "You were good to me. That was nice. I'm grateful. But now you want me, and I don't want you, that's all. At all."

That last "at all" hung in the air like a death sentence. Grady looked at the chairs, at the window, anywhere but at the bed.

She snapped, "If I'm so hideous, stop staring at my breasts."

Grady whipped his head sideways as though he'd been slapped.

"Everyone thought I was perverted to come to you." She slumped on the bed. "Now they'll know you refused."

Grady was hopelessly out of his depth. "If you want, you

can stay here long enough so they'll think—I mean, I'd
never tell them—"

Her eyes flashed fire. "I wasn't going to lie to my own
people before. Do you think I will now?" She stood straight
and proud. "Please get out of my way."

Grady moved hastily from in front of the door. "Listen,
it's cold out. Why don't you take the inside door, or take a
blanket?"

"I came naked, I'll leave naked." She tilted her head up
and looked him angrily and proudly in the eye. "And I will
never take a thing from you."

She strode out of the house, head high, looking more like
a stately queen than like an angry and humiliated woman.
Grady watched her go and closed the door, relieved. He
latched it, muttering, "Thank God that's over."

He spent a restless hour repeating, "Thank God that's
over." He fell asleep still thinking that it was.

The knock on his outside door the next morning astonished
him. He opened it sleepily. "What—"

His fencing jacket hit him full in the face. The sword
clanged on the floor, the hilt landing on his bare toes. He
yelped and stepped back as the door slammed shut with a
thud that shook his coffee cup.

When Grady stepped through the plant doorway, Kirsten
was on him. He took three flat-bladed whacks across his rib
cage before he realized how much the rules had changed.

He set his mouth and parried at his full reach, trying to
adjust. He had never before regarded Kirsten as the enemy.

He stuck his cane far to the left, swinging his sword as
though to slash in on Kirsten's side. She stepped forward to
lunge in after beating back the sword, taking twice the steps
he had.

Instead of waiting for her blade to engage, he lifted his

sword over her head, flipped the cane to directly in front of him, and swung in on her right. She spun around, leaped at his blade, and spun again to counter his return.

This time he flipped the sword upright, bringing it down on her head—turning the blade flat at the last minute, so as not to kill her.

He hadn't expected the blow to land, and it didn't. Kirsten leaped backward with both feet and, catching her balance, charged Grady full-front.

Grady was no longer there; he lifted his cane out of the way just in time. Kirsten shot past him, braked to a stop, and spun to counter Grady's slashing blow to her back. She hit Grady's sword hard enough that his arm stung, but he held on to the hilt as she rushed him. She had defended herself, but it was lousy technique, and Grady could see that he'd made her even angrier.

After ten more minutes of forcing her to leap back, charge forward, spin from side to side, and counter smooth movement with raw muscle, it was over. Kirsten stood, panting and exhausted, unable to raise her arms as Grady stepped quietly forward and grazed her cheek with a flat-of-the-sword tap as gentle as any kiss.

She snapped her head away from him. When she could breathe, she said without looking him in the eye, "You used your reach and my anger. Well done." The last two words were as bitter as an insult.

Grady nodded, too tired and too frustrated to trust his own voice.

Kirsten looked past him. "It's too late for breakfast. Get to work." She left quickly.

Grady followed slowly, exhaustion bothering him more than his limp.

When he got to the forge, his bench was gone. He looked around. "Where's my bench?"

Antony shrugged. Gretchen turned away.

Bernhard looked solemnly at him but gave no answer.

Grady, puzzled, gave up and went to work.

At noon the raised table and bench were gone. There was room at the main table, at least. Grady sat with his knees up beside his ears and ate sparingly; he wasn't hungry.

Everyone talked, but no one addressed him. When he commented on something Antony said, no one responded. After two tries he simply stayed silent.

By late afternoon his back was killing him. He tried working on his knees; if anything, that was worse. He got up gratefully for dinner, until he remembered that no one would talk to him.

After dinner he went to the cooking fireside and waited for his singing lesson with Gretchen. He waited until the hall was empty and the embers barely glowing; then he walked home to bed.

The next morning he felt like an eighty-year-old man who had been severely beaten. There was still no bench, but he was damned if he'd complain about it. He took a smith's hammer, scrap lumber, and a few horseshoe nails. He pounded together a bench. It wobbled, but it was good enough. He spent the morning molding wishing rings in fifty-ring batches; twice, when a batch was ready for testing, Bernhard appeared miraculously, took the test ring away, and nodded on his return.

Lunch was nearly silent, and when Grady returned, his new bench was gone. He hunted up more scrap lumber, made an even worse bench, and carried it with him to the toilet, to dinner, and home that night.

The rest of the week was much the same. Gradually people spoke to him—Pieter first, about assignments. Antony followed, then Gretchen. None of them said more than four or five words.

Whenever Katrina came up to him, Bernhard would whistle and crook a finger, or Gretchen would call her. Once he made a paper airplane out of one of the flying memos, and Katrina whooped while the other memos chased it futilely through the cavern. Kirsten snatched it from the air and frowned. Katrina dropped her head and walked away.

Grady went back to work. There was nothing else to do. His time at the Dwarfworks went on, but only Katrina smiled at him, and one paper airplane, thirty seconds of foolishness, turned out to have been the most pleasant moment in a long and empty week.

TWELVE

GRADY HAD NEVER been so grateful for his return to Rhode Island; normally the countless errands and duties of his week at home were nothing he looked forward to. He was only upset that he carried a silent passenger.

Antony stared out the side window, wishing Grady would go off the road—nothing fatal, just an annoying accident that would be Grady's fault and would cost Grady money. He hated Pieter, who no longer trusted Grady, for asking him to go back to Rhode Island and get maximum load estimates from Susan for the Plimstubb furnace. He hated Kirsten because he felt sorry for her, and she hated that. He hated Grady on general principles.

On the way into Providence, Grady said finally, "I need a favor."

"Bad time to ask."

"I don't have another time. My sister-in-law wants to go dancing. Susan and I are going. It would be a better evening with another guy."

Antony looked at him and said nothing. Grady tried again. "Mary's looking forward to this a lot. She doesn't get out much. We're going to the place she met Kevin."

After a long silence, Grady slapped the steering wheel. "Dammit, I'm not asking you to be nice to me. I'm asking you to be nice to Mary and Susan."

Antony said, "In that case, I accept."

"Thanks." Grady said awkwardly, "You can still stay at the house—"

"The Biltmore sounds fine." Pride was going to be expensive.

"Have a great time." They said nothing the rest of the way in. Antony was terrified when Grady raced a train to the crossing in Providence, and annoyed when he realized that Grady had risked his own life to terrify him.

Coming back into Plimstubb was like putting on an old and loved sweater; everything fit perfectly. His office was just as he had left it, fairly neat (unfiled work in piles) and fairly full (his magazines still in stacks and rows on the bookshelves.

But the IN basket was empty; Warren was keeping all his correspondence.

He found Warren lounging behind his desk, reading the *Wall Street Journal*. The headline, folded over, was more about the drive toward Berlin. Warren laid the paper down casually on top of a folder. "Cavanaugh. Shouldn't you be out on a service call?"

"Soon as Roy fills me in." Grady had made the mistake, exactly once, of asking Roy Burgess, "Where do you want me to go?" Roy, with a loud cackle, had told him. "Did I get any personal mail?"

Warren reached into a drawer and passed it to him. There were Christmas cards from friends and coworkers, and a letter or two from college friends; to Grady's annoyance, all of them had been opened. "Thanks," he said, and Warren's head snapped up at the dryness in Grady's voice.

"I run a tight office," Warren said through set lips. "That means keeping an eye on everything."

Grady glanced around the office. "I see that. Aren't there any sales quotes?"

"What makes you say that?"

He gestured to the table behind Warren. "No prints out, no folders, no letters—"

"No mess." Warren smiled, showing a line of perfect white teeth. "I'm neater than you are; I put them all away." He glanced involuntarily at the file cabinet.

Grady followed his gaze and did a double take; the file cabinet was locked. "Why the tight security? Are we doing more war work?"

Warren sighed exaggeratedly. "You are not doing any sales work. I am, but certainly not war work; the war will end any day. And don't question my filing. If I keep folders locked up, I know where they are at all times."

Grady wanted to leave, but said, "Did a man named Stode talk to you about a second furnace?"

"We corresponded." But Warren looked unsettled; even by mail, Stode was tough to handle. "Actually he wrote you. I wrote back and told him I was handling your workload. He called me and told me—Cavanaugh, did you offend him somehow?"

Grady remembered his last meeting with Stode. "I think he's always like that," he said evasively.

Warren was unconvinced. "All right . . . he told me he needed to order the furnace right away. I told him we were considering taking the order."

"Considering it?" Grady was stunned. "It's a copy of

something we've already done; design time is almost nothing. Plus it's the same customer. Plus it's—"

"Please don't say it's for the war." But Warren's smile was wolfish. "He paid extra for the first furnace. He'll pay double or nothing for this one. A salesman should know when to rush a buyer and when to stall."

Grady, two letters from Kevin in his pocket, thought about telling Warren what he thought of a man who would stall on a contract for the war. Then, remembering Mary and Julie, he swallowed.

"Besides," Warren said, watching him closely, "are you absolutely, positively sure he's with our government?"

"Mostly." Grady saw his opening and took it. "But that's your concern now, isn't it?"

Warren scowled. "Cavanaugh, if you've gotten me involved in something underhanded—"

Grady decided to go for broke. "Maybe you should keep me in charge of it, just in case."

After a frozen moment, Warren forced a laugh. "All right, take it." He unlocked his file cabinet and opened a drawer, rummaging in it.

Grady, behind him, saw the folder labels and sucked in his breath sharply. One folder was Irish—they were neutral, at least. One was Spanish—Spain only pretended to be neutral, and favored Germany. One had an Arabic name on it, and one a name that was Oriental—Grady wasn't sure what. The file cabinet had way too many foreign quotations for wartime.

On an impulse he lifted the carefully folded *Wall Street Journal*. He glanced at the second headline, which was about the marine landing on Iwo Jima; he was grateful that his father was too old for the marines.

The paper was on top of another sales folder for Ireland, with the customer listed only as "SIDHE." The address was in the West. On the sales checklist, under "Export licensing and permission," Warren had scribbled, "not needed."

Grady dropped the paper, peering upside down at the headlines as Warren turned around and pointedly slammed the Stode folder on top of the newspaper. Grady took it quickly. "Thanks." He moved back to his own office and read the correspondence, chuckling, then looked at his desk again, doing a double take.

One of the Dwarfworks' flying memos lay on it. Apparently there was some correspondence Warren couldn't take away.

He unfolded it and read, "Molybdenum fixture for second furnace order. Materials are in; awaiting purchase order to begin fabricating." It was typed on the same machine Grady had used at the Dwarfworks; Antony had signed his full name. There was no attached note. Antony must have written it before riding to Providence with Grady.

Grady wrote on the memo, "Hold fabrication until further notice" and walked to a window with the paper. It flapped south, looking frail in the wind from off the North Atlantic. Grady watched it go, wondering how Antony knew about Stode's second order and why he was so confident of it that he would scout up materials in advance. He closed the window and walked to Engineering.

Susan was gone. Tom Garneaux was studying an article about prizefighters and pontificating about uppercuts to Sonny LeTour, who was on a ladder replacing lightbulbs in Engineering. Sonny looked down, smiling. "You oughta be here more often."

"Tell my boss."

Sonny shrugged, still smiling. "Wish I could. What's new?"

Grady looked around. "Where's Susan?"

"Afternoon off," Tom said. "She's getting a permanent

for some damn reason." He shook his head. "None of the other engineers needed permanents."

Grady chuckled. "Susan and I—and Antony—are taking my sister-in-law out."

"Susan and you?" Sonny looked down at Grady with interest. "Where you going?"

"Rhodes on the Pawtuxet. Dancing and drinks."

Tom Garneaux looked up with interest. "If you see a plug-ugly ex-boxer named Pug Brady, give him my best."

Sonny laughed. "You be careful. Rhodes has caused as much permanent and temporary love as you can get from whiskey, women, and rhythm." He climbed down and moved the ladder under another bulb.

Although Grady trusted Mary completely, he vowed to keep a close eye on her.

For once the car smelled more of perfume than of cigarettes, even with Susan in it. Both Susan and Mary had permanents. Both of them were in heels. Susan looked more like Betty Grable than even Betty Grable did. Mary was wearing more jewelry than Grady had known she owned, bracelets and earrings and a pearl necklace, and she was practically leaning out the passenger window like a dog on a ride. Antony, riding behind her, grinned in spite of himself.

"I'm sorry my mother couldn't sit," Susan was saying. "She loves Julie."

Grady reflected that even threats and blackmail had their limits.

"It's okay, really. I found a girl right in the neighborhood." Mary was barely paying attention. Grady remembered that she had met Kevin at Rhodes, where so many men and women met. "Not for nothing, it's just so good to come back here."

The front entrance was flashy; Grady, used to sales,

thought that the place needed more paint and glamor. The setting, on the river, cried out for elegance; Grady had canoed near here in the summer, and loved the overhanging trees and the way the rear of the dance hall rose straight up like a riverside cliff behind them.

At the cloakroom Grady took their wraps. It would have been easier if Antony had helped him, but he'd rather not ask just now. He tipped fifty cents, feeling extravagant but not wanting to stiff the check girl.

Antony rolled his eyes, but he was trying to take in the surroundings. There was a steady murmur of voices, far louder at this point than the lazy current from the Pawtuxet River.

Almost as they walked in, the fat colored man at the piano grinned. "You're listening to my tribute to the late Mrs. Waller's little boy and his band." He leaned over the keyboard and swung into a flashy intro that became "Honeysuckle Rose."

Susan said in disappointment, "Sometimes they get the big names, like Guy Lombardo or Kay Kyser. It's not our night, I guess."

Grady listened raptly, wishing that Sonny LeTour could have come. Listening with Antony, especially as things stood now, wasn't going to be the same.

"I'll buy drinks if someone will carry them," Grady said. Rhodes served only soft drinks, including the local brand, Warwick Club.

But the bar was three deep in servicemen, mostly navy, buying drinks for girls. He watched enviously as a sailor carried six stacked glasses to a table. Sometimes Grady missed having two free hands.

A barrel-chested man with a broken nose and a cauliflower ear looked their way casually and grinned at Grady, ignoring Antony. "A woman for each arm. What's your after-shave?"

"Bourbon." He looked the man up and down. "Are you Pug Brady?"

The battered man frowned. "My friends call me that. You ain't one of them."

"Sorry. Tom Garneaux called you that; he didn't say your real name."

"Tom Garneaux? You're friends of Black Tom?" They nodded mutely, Antony hesitating only a moment longer than the others.

Susan laughed. "Is that what his friends call him?" She smiled; Grady thought she'd never looked so pretty. "May I call you Mr. Brady?"

"Ah, honey, you can call me Pug." He shook hands all around, like someone joining a fraternity. "Now tell me what you drink. No, sweetheart, I don't mean Coca-Cola." He grabbed the arm of a skinny young waiter, who turned his head to snap at Brady and thought better of it. "That bench over there. Bring them the good stuff, the stuff I sell in the parking lot."

The waiter vanished. Grady was impressed, Antony amused. The waiter materialized instantly with the drinks, but Pug unloaded the tray. "Here you are." He winked. "The good stuff."

"Thanks," Grady said.

"Forget it," he said expansively. "Any friend of Black Tom's. Tell him Pug and Sailor Bill say hello, to him and to that crazy bastard Hammer Houlihan."

He left. Susan poked at her drink thoughtfully. "Drinking from this is an act of faith."

"That's the easy part." Grady tasted his whiskey and nearly choked. He looked across at Susan and Mary, who were sipping their gin with awe.

Even Antony, whiskey glass in hand, sniffed it and looked impressed. This was indeed the good stuff.

Susan chided him, "Antony, you haven't drunk from yours."

"I was brought up not to drink with strangers." He looked at Grady. "Kid, you were not cut out for war." He added grudgingly, "You weren't even cut out for anybody to hate. Listen, Grady—"

But the moment was lost as a well-built young woman, wobbling up to them on heels, nearly fell against Antony. Clearly she'd been out to the parking lot more than once. "Wanna dance?" she said automatically as he steadied her, then focused on him and blurted, "If you wanna, but jeez, you only come up to here on me."

Antony raised his glass. "Well, it's a nice neighborhood, but I think I'll pass." He nodded toward Grady. "Maybe he wants to do the honors."

Grady bristled as she looked dubiously at his cane. "I guess I'm not doing so well," she said vaguely, and tottered off.

Mary said defensively to Antony, "I'll bet you're a great dancer."

Antony smiled at her and said to no one in particular, "Kevin did all right for himself."

Ignoring him, Mary turned to Grady and said, "Will you dance with me?"

Grady felt his cane hung over the chair back but refused to look at it. "Glad to."

The dance was a disaster. Grady, trying to lead, stumbled several times. Mary caught him every time and quickly apologized for being clumsy. They bumped another couple once; the serviceman, an army captain, opened his mouth to say something but saw the cane and turned away. After the song, Grady led Mary back to the chairs.

Susan, sitting patiently with Antony until then, stood as they returned. "I came to dance. Mary, go over to the flag with me." She pointed to the far wall, where women were lined up under a giant American flag, waiting for men to ask them.

Mary half rose, then turned and stared at Grady pleadingly. "You think it'd be all right if I dance? Do you think Kevin would mind, Grady? I'm not gonna leave with anybody."

Antony chuckled. "Do you need his permission?"

Grady sipped at his whiskey, resolving to switch to soft drinks the next drink. It wouldn't do to snap at Antony. "Mary, that's why we came." But he knew she needed to hear it. "I'm sure Kevin won't mind."

Mary was up before he finished, grabbing Susan's hand and pulling her out of her chair and across the hall, to stand with the other women who had come unescorted to Rhodes.

Grady sat beside Antony, trying not to look at him. It's awkward sitting alone with someone who hates you.

Antony sighed. "Nice music."

"Huh? Oh, sure, sure." He hadn't realized he'd been tapping his good foot. "You hear much music?"

"Just the radio. Some movie musicals. You were born after talkies started. I remember when I saw *The Coconuts*. Marx Brothers. I thought Groucho was the funniest thing on legs, but mostly I loved the songs. They were all crummy, but to me they were written by Beethoven's kid brother."

He glanced over at Grady. "Look at Mary. In the Army-Navy game, Army scored first."

Grady, remembering Sonny's joke, looked suspiciously. Mary was in the arms of a cocky first lieutenant who was talking a mile a minute while they danced to "Ain't Misbehavin'." She was laughing politely and nodding, unable to get a word in.

The two of them, dancing carefully at arm's length, reminded Grady forcibly of the ringbearer and flower girl at Kevin's wedding reception. "He'd be closer if he telephoned her," Antony commented.

That was fine with Grady.

After a short consultation, the band ripped into a hot and high-brass version of "The Joint Is Jumpin'." Susan, miraculously partnerless for a moment, spun back toward Grady and Antony, threw her arms wide, and said with a passion that seemed half anger, "Dance with me!"

Grady reached toward her, ready to do his best to jitterbug, and remembered himself sprawled on the cave floor with all the gnomes laughing. He leaned his weight on his bad leg, testing it, and felt the familiar stab of pain and give at the ankle joint. He looked across at Susan, wishing with all his heart that he could be the dancer she dreamed of—

—And, in a flash of joy running ahead of thought, rubbed the ring on his left hand as he wished.

The shock to his ankle made his whole leg twitch. The bone shifted, the muscles tautened. Grady nearly fell.

Susan was suddenly contrite. "Are you okay?"

He pulled her toward him, nearly laughing with the confidence he felt. "Okay? I'm perfect." He spun her into him, bracing her impact with his body as his other arm circled her waist, then let go and spun her back out, gliding easily beyond her to spin her back again. He was Fred Astaire, he was Esther Williams walking on water, he was smoother than polished steel and more fluid than mercury. God, he had missed this.

As Susan twirled into him again, her astonishment turning to delight, he saw over her shoulder and under her outflung hair Antony's face. The dwarf was regarding him sadly, as though Grady had failed some important test. Grady shook his head and concentrated on dancing.

"Sacred Sun," Antony thought with wonder and pity, "you poor mutt." Kirsten, when she found out, would kill him. He considered warning Grady, but shook his head. If Kirsten liked Grady so much, let her find out the truth for herself, no matter what was at stake.

Grady slid past Susan, who looked awkward by comparison, and pulled her close in a shoulder-to-knee embrace that still walked them across the floor. Once he had been athletic and recently he had been lame; tonight he was walking magic.

The last song they danced to, hours later, was slow and sweet; Grady was grateful; the magic was ebbing already. He was Cinderella, and midnight was coming.

The man at the piano sang out, and Grady heard the hoarse tiredness in his voice. The magic was over for the band, too.

But Susan held Grady very tight, and her soprano in his ear had all the energy of a full choir on stage as she sang softly, "I'm flyin' high, but I've got a feelin' I'm fallin' . . ."

Grady's left leg was falling, but he was flying very high.

Antony, a little coldly, insisted on taking a cab to the Biltmore. Grady pushed on him, but at the moment he was too self-absorbed to wonder why it mattered to Antony.

Grady was not by nature devious or scheming, but as he pulled up in front of Mary's house he found himself planning a full-scale campaign for the next stop. "I'll hop out and open Susan's door, walk her up with my cane on my outside arm, get in front of her, and lean on it—she can't shove me aside then—and kiss her good night." He should have felt ridiculous, but he felt like Patton outfoxing Rommel.

And it all went smoothly. He opened the car door, offered his arm, edged in front of her, moved on the step to open the door—

It was ajar.

Grady cautiously moved the door fully open with his cane and brought it up *en garde*, unsure what to expect. The hall was dark; at the end of it, in the kitchen, Rose Rocci said quietly watching them.

Susan said uncertainly, "Ma?" Her mother had lived behind locked doors since Susan's father had left for the war.

Mrs. Rocci said calmly and almost reasonably, "I've been waiting up for you, Susan. Come in."

"Ma!" Susan cried, thoroughly frightened, and Grady was distressed, too; Susan's mother was holding a lit cigarette.

Susan ran to the kitchen, her high heels clicking on the hard wood, and Grady followed as fast as he could, wishing he could keep up and protect her.

But there was no way he could protect her as her eyes went wide and she snatched the telegram out of her mother's hands. Grady moved beside her and read: THE SECRETARY OF WAR HAS ASKED ME TO EXPRESS MY DEEPEST REGRET . . .

THIRTEEN

THE FUNERAL WAS a blur. In the past four years, Grady had attended twelve funerals: two of them for friends from high school, three for college friends, six for the parents or brothers of friends or relatives, and one for his Great-Aunt Kathy, who had died at eighty-six. Grady had been relieved to attend a service that didn't have a flag on the coffin.

This was a service with a flag but no body, just a picture—the picture—of Vince Rocci, tanned and happy beside Sassy Suzie, the plane that was now underwater somewhere just off Iwo Jima. To Grady, the picture only underscored Vince Rocci's absence. The picture was in a brand-new black frame.

Vince Rocci's brother Paulie came down from Waltham to stand with the family; he looked too old to have a brother in the war. Grady had learned, however, that at funerals many people look older than they are.

During the Mass, Grady looked over at Susan and had a sudden, vivid memory of his mother's funeral. He had sat through the Mass surreptitiously stuffing Kevin with chocolates at intervals to keep him from crying. When Kevin was sick later, Grady's Aunt Eileen gave him hell. He hadn't thought of that in years.

The cemetery service for Vince had no grave, just a marker. Otherwise it was like all the other military funerals, except that Grady was watching Susan the entire time. Susan's mother was as solid as granite, an arm around her daughter.

When the bugler played "Taps," Grady looked at him and had a sudden chilling thought: This could have been Kevin. It could have been his father. It could still be.

Afterward, at the lunch in the church basement, there was laughter and gossip; funerals bring people together who don't meet often. Susan's cousins and aunts—there seemed to be dozens of them—all brought covered dishes, including meatballs and cheese in spite of rationing. Grady hadn't eaten this well in Rhode Island since Rose Rocci had cooked for him and for Antony. People, chatting happily, passed bread and bowls up and down the long table. Susan sat at the far end with her jaw set and her face to the wall. Grady sat beside her.

He said once, "I'm glad it didn't rain during the graveside service."

"No grave," she said bitterly. "They call it a cenotaph, a marker without a body."

He nodded. There was nothing to say.

Susan toyed with the plate her mother had made her take and said with no guilt whatsoever, "He spoiled me."

Grady said tactfully, "He must have loved you very much."

She nodded, finishing with her head down again. "And he spoiled me a lot, let's not sugarcoat it. And no one's going to do it anymore, and I'm afraid."

Suddenly Grady understood. "Listen," he said earnestly, "things between you and your mother will mostly stay the same. You'll fight, sometimes you'll laugh—when Mom died, there was a period when we had to find our feet again, when Dad said I was trying to do too much and Kevin said I was trying to boss him around. Finally one day Dad said, 'You don't have to replace your mother. It ain't your job, kid.'"

She didn't smile, but she looked up. He went on, encouraged, "So don't try to replace your father. Your mom's all grown up, with her own house and everything. She'll surprise you."

Now Susan smiled, and there were tears in her eyes. "But you did try to replace your mother a little. That's why you're the way you are, that's why you look after people."

Grady shrugged, embarrassed. "I look after people because people need looking after."

"Don't they, though?" But after a second the affectionate light in Susan's eyes died, and she went back to staring at the faded paint on the basement walls.

When Susan returned to work, Tom Garneaux walked her quietly out to the shop and pointed out her father's hat, hanging in the rafters. For Plimstubb, it was like the Yankees retiring Lou Gehrig's number. Tom hugged her while she wept; then she excused herself and went to the ladies' room. When she came out she was brisk and angry but had no trace of tears about her.

Over the next two days she finished all the current work on her desk. On the third day she requested to work on one of Tom Garneaux's projects and finished that, then took over three replacement parts projects and finished them as well.

Grady called her each night, or tried to. The first night she was volunteering at a blood drive. The second night she was bandage rolling. On the third night he listened to her rant about the headlines on the war in the Pacific—the marines were still fighting on Iwo Jima—and held the receiver numbly while she spat out, ". . . and I hope they kill every one of those ugly, buck-toothed, yellow-skinned bastards!" and hung up before he could say much about why he called.

He stared at the phone. When he first met Susan, she wouldn't have dreamed of speaking of anyone like that. Calling them an idiot, yes. Calling them yellow-skinned bastards, never. The war was like the quenching furnaces at Plimstubb; it put you through something and it hardened you. And it was a wartime project; it made a weapon of you.

He tried not to think about his father, somewhere in the Pacific, building roads and landing strips and writing letters that were censored way too much.

Tensions were running high at the plant, too. Roy Burgess, frustrated at being forced by Warren Hastings to keep Sonny LeTour on when Roy had to lay off so many white workers, rode him harder and harder. Sonny bore it without a single sign that it bothered him, even when Roy gave him the dirtiest maintenance jobs and the heaviest loads and finished with, "Every plant needs at least one nigger."

Finally, one day, Sonny was carrying a box of flowmeters from the loading dock to the stockroom. The glass tubes were calibrated to measure gas flow and were expensive. Garneaux, strolling through the plant, held the shop door for him. Grady, on his way out of the plant to a customer, hurried as best he could to hold the stockroom door.

Someone had left a steel rod on the floor. Sonny's left foot hit it and he flew up in the air, landing hard on the concrete. The box landed beside him with a loud crash.

"Jesus." Roy Burgess appeared from nowhere. "I don't mind your being lazy, Sambo—"

"Sonny."

"Sambo. But I sure as shit mind your being stupid and clumsy. Pick up those shuffling feet when you walk—"

Sonny came up off the floor in one smooth motion, like a twenty-year-old, his face expressionless. Grady didn't even see Sonny's fist.

Neither, apparently, did Roy. He seemed to hang in the air a moment, feet up, before dropping to the concrete. He was limp before he hit.

Tom Garneaux knelt beside him. "He had it coming."

"Doesn't make any difference," Sonny said ruefully. "I'll go clean out my locker."

"Don't be hasty." Garneaux scratched his chin thoughtfully. "There's a way out of this. There's always a way."

Sonny tried to smile. "You always think there's a way, don't you?"

"There usually is," Grady said.

Garneaux nodded. "You're learning. Sonny, if you don't mind excusing us, I don't think you want to see this."

"I'm in enough trouble," he said. He turned in the doorway. "And thanks, even if it doesn't work."

"I should thank you. I've wanted someone to hit him since I got here." Garneaux turned to Grady. "Get a damp cloth."

When Roy came to, he blinked several times. Garneaux said indifferently, "Oh, good. We thought we'd lost you."

Roy said vaguely, "What happened?" and, as his eyes came into focus, "That goddamned, no-good—"

"You slipped."

Roy goggled at him, looking remarkably like one of the bug-eyed aliens on Grady's science fiction magazines.

Garneaux said solicitously, "Don't you remember? You

tried to take the flowmeter box from Sonny, but your foot hit that rod and down you went—"

"Bullshit. The bastard hit me—"

"Face first," Grady said. Roy turned to him. He poked with his cane at the flowmeter box, which tinkled as shards and fragments inside changed position. "You're lucky you don't have a glass jaw."

Roy licked his lips. "You know that's not how it was."

Garneaux nodded, but only said, "I know that two of us will swear that's how it is. Sonny wanted to call a doctor, but I wouldn't let him. Do that and we have to report the breakage."

Roy looked at the box. Grady poked it again. More glass tinkled.

Roy winced. That many flowmeters were worth hundreds of dollars. "You'd hang that on me?"

Grady said sincerely, "We'll try to make sure no one finds out. Right, Tom?"

"Absolutely," Garneaux said firmly. "If I can't sneak in a couple of replacement orders, I've lost my touch. Now stand up."

Roy stood, wobbling a little and looking at them with wonder.

Garneaux raised a finger. "One more thing. Try not to have any more accidents where you hit your head. You might get knocked out again, and God only knows what damage you'd wake up next to. I can't hide the big stuff, Roy. There's a war on, and we can't afford it. Old Man Plimstubb would fire you."

Roy considered foggily. "You're saying I shouldn't—"

"I'm saying think safety first. If you can't lead with your left, don't lead with your mouth. I can't put it any plainer." He patted Roy's shoulder. "Why don't you go get a slug from that bottle you hide in the paint cabinet? You look like you could use it."

Roy gave him a final, horrified look and wandered off toward the paint booth.

Grady said wonderingly, "I never knew about that bottle."

Garneaux frowned. "Drinking at work. That's a bad sign. And it's terrible stuff; I don't see how he can tell it from the paint thinner." He patted Grady's shoulder. "Nice job, kiddo. You're learning."

Grady went out on his service call, not sure what he was learning.

On the fourth day back at work, Susan sat with Tom Blaine in Research and tried to argue him out of his design pessimism until Blaine, shocked at her attitude and the frantic speed she was working at, said he was "more comfortable working alone"—meaning, with his real partner. Susan spent the last hour of work staring straight ahead, not saying anything.

On the fifth day, Grady came to work an hour early, went to the Sales and Research Dead Files—the quotes Plimstubb didn't know how to bid on. He sorted through them, tucked a stack of folders under his arm, and went to Warren Hastings.

Warren was sitting with his feet up, reading a letter and smirking. Without apparent haste he put the letter in a manila folder and dropped the folder in his desk drawer. "Cavanaugh. You're here this week, but I thought you were in service."

"Yes, sir." By now Grady hated the "sir" but didn't know how to stop using it without sounding insolent. "I came by to propose a project."

"There's not enough work for you when you're on half time?" Warren smiled coldly.

"No. I mean yes, there's more than enough, but I'm keeping up." He closed his eyes, concentrating. "I have an idea. . . ."

He had written it down before he came in. Warren reviewed it thoughtfully. "And Rocci's bright enough to do this?" The smile was back. "If she's good, why do I need you?"

"Susan's a genius," Grady said bluntly. "But she's no good for sales. That's where I come in. I'm good for sales."

"We'll see about that." But he was wavering. "Why should I waste time on this?"

"You're not wasting time, you're picking up extra work. And after the war, we'll have new product lines out of all her designs. In the meantime, you can keep going after civilian business."

Warren was trying to find a reason to object. Grady pressed on. "At that point, you'd want to revise her proposals. . . ."

He trailed off, watching. As he expected, the word in Warren's eyes was not "revise" but "steal."

Warren went to the door of the office and looked across Engineering at Susan, who was seated with her head down, sketching frantically, lips moving. Warren smiled almost affectionately. "She is smart, isn't she?"

Grady swallowed an urge to disparage Susan. He didn't want Warren taking too personal an interest in her.

"All right." Warren spun the paper on his desk, moving it to Grady's side. "Sign this."

"What?"

"And date it. I'll keep it on file." He regarded Grady with amusement. "I never do anything without a promise on paper."

Which meant, Grady reflected, that Warren intended to hang Grady if the project went wrong. "Thanks," he said, signing. "I won't forget this." He walked out, the stack of folders still under his arm.

He was shocked; Susan was doodling. He knew she could draw, but had never seen her—well, wasting her time with it. "How's tricks?" he said, and tossed the folders on her desk.

"What are these?"

"Projects we didn't feel able to tackle, and they're still open. Nobody else could, either." He shrugged. "Navy. Army. Air force."

She poked at one, but he was leaning on it and wouldn't let her open it.

"I got Warren's permission to work on them, but they'll need design work, something creative. I mean, look at this."

He opened the top folder, keeping a hand on it. It was facing Susan. She read the description automatically, looked away, read it again, and said thoughtfully, "Glass-to-metal sealing?"

"Radio tubes. Everybody's been working on it—RCA wants it, Sylvania wants it—but the government wants the tube seals tighter." He moved his hand slightly. "And bigger production loads, with greater uniformity at the same time. They want the tubes at the edges of the conveyor belt to come out just as good as the ones in the center."

"We've never built anything like this."

"Neither has anyone else." He kept his hand blocking the rest of the text. "The rest are mostly high-temperature alloys. There's a lot of work with titanium, mostly for aircraft. The government needs a working heat-treating cycle for the metal as much as it needs a vacuum furnace to process it in."

He put a finger on the RFQs and said as sincerely as if he believed it, "Every last one of these is still needed for the war." He added casually, "The tube seals are for radio equipment in the Pacific."

She stared down at them, her lips moving. When she looked up, her eyes were hard but happy. "Get out of my light."

Grady walked away without saying a word, but reflected that for a part-time salesman, he'd just pulled off two sales in twenty minutes. If only he could do that well with Plimstubb's customers.

Frankly, he was afraid to do that well with the new customers, the ones Warren pulled in. The letters and telegrams came in from all over the world: Cairo, Vladivostok, Tibet (and how did a letter get here from Tibet?), and an unpronounceable village that Grady looked up in the battered service atlas with outdated country borders. It turned out to be on a back road in Romania, up in the Transylvanian Alps. The telegrams were coded, which didn't bother Grady a bit, since Plimstubb routinely used commercial codes, as did every firm that wanted cheap telegrams and a little privacy. But these telegrams weren't in any of the codes Plimstubb had used, and that bothered Grady a lot.

And there were other things, like the day that Grady was in the lobby and a sleek black car pulled up. Two men came in, one short, fat, and light brown with angry eyebrows, the other tall, slender, and dark with an amused twinkle in his dark eyes. They looked like an Arabic Abbott and Costello.

In the action stories Grady had read before he turned to science fiction, they would have been called "swarthy" and produced a "wickedly curved scimitar" or a "jeweled but nonetheless deadly dagger" within moments.

Actually they reached into their breast pockets at the same time and produced ivory business card cases, each flipping a card out. The short man's card was white, the tall man's an odd pale green.

The first card said simply "MR. FAHDI" and gave a business address in Cairo.

The second said "MR. FAROUKH" and gave the same address.

There was no telephone number on either card.

"We prefer letters, telegraphs in emergencies," Mr. Fahdi said, examining his ruby. "We are old-fashioned in this."

Grady said, "We're not." He gestured toward the receptionist's area—

And his jaw dropped. Talia, wide awake, was staring at them with the happy yearning of a child seeing Santa Claus.

Mr. Fahdi stepped toward her. "You see us for what we are."

She nodded.

Both men's faces changed, and Mr. Fahdi and Mr. Faroukh bowed very deeply. "Dear lady, now we are so glad we came here. God is great and miraculous."

Warren, bursting into the lobby, broke in, "Was it a difficult voyage?"

They looked at him politely but without comprehension.

Warren tried again. "Was it difficult getting to America?" he said, louder and more slowly than necessary. "Was it dangerous?"

They broke into smiles. Faroukh shrugged. "Dangerous, yes."

Fahdi folded his arms. "Never difficult."

"Good, good." Warren rubbed his hands together. "Come to my office and we'll talk business." He glanced at Grady. "Thank you for greeting them for me." He emphasized the "me." Grady passed him the business cards, which felt oddly warm, and went back to his own work.

An hour later they passed his office, Warren smiling

genially, then edging behind the visitors. He grabbed Grady
by the shoulder and said with a hiss, "Go find out which one
is the boss. They didn't say, and neither do their cards."

Grady followed them as hastily as he could. "Excuse
me . . ." They turned. "I may handle some of your paperwork from here. Which of you should sign for purchases in
the future?"

"In these things I act as Mr. Faroukh's agent," Mr. Fahdi
said flatly.

"He works for you?"

The silence seemed like a chuckle. Mr. Faroukh smiled
down at him and said, "I have in fact done work for him."
He turned. "Though I believe it is your turn to drive."

Mr. Fahdi chuckled. "Rest, my friend. It is my pleasure
to drive."

The two of them took ostentatiously polite good-byes,
with expressions of regret from both of them to Grady. On
the other hand, their affection for Talia Baghrati was the
more sincere for its simplicity. Mr. Fahdi took her hand
through the receptionist's window and kissed it. "Dear lady,
if you should need anything, call me."

Mr. Faroukh said quietly, "You need ask but once." His
dark eyes glowed.

When they left, Talia sighed loudly and splashed herself
with so much perfume that Grady, twenty feet away, found
his eyes watering. He stepped toward her and asked, trying
not to choke, "They said you see them for what they are?"

She was dabbing at her eyes with a handkerchief. "Once
before, when I was a child, I saw one, once." She had the
barest trace of an accent, more than he had heard in her
before. "In the market. He was not in a suit, that one. There
were many young men in suits in Baghdad, pretending to be
like the British, but not him. And maybe he wasn't young.
My mother said to stay away from him.

"But I tugged at his robe, and told him to give me something. He picked me up, and kissed each of my eyes, and he set me down." She laughed while crying. "I've always been angry that he didn't give me something, until now."

Grady mused, "They said you could call them. They don't mean by telephone, do they?" Talia said nothing. Grady said urgently, "What are they?"

But Talia just shook her head, eyes shining. Grady left her alone and went out the front door to give driving directions to the two men. He leaned in the passenger window.

Mr. Fahdi was alone in the car. In the front passenger seat was a black lamp.

Grady reached toward it automatically. Mr. Fahdi shook his head once, and he pulled his hand back quickly.

Warren was waiting in the lobby, holding an envelope. "Well?"

"They're both sort of freelance. Don't accept anything without Mr. Fahdi's signature if you expect to collect." He added, "How did you find them?"

Warren chuckled and tapped the envelope against his shoulder. "Contacts, boy, contacts. The secret of a salesman, and the secret that keeps his job for him." He was in a wonderful mood.

Grady, wishing Susan was there to hear him, said "I thought they were both genial." He pointed to the envelope. "Don't you think you need more records than that from them? There is a war on."

Warren looked down his nose at Grady. "I've heard. I've also heard we're already winning. Why, do you want permission to enlist?"

He walked away chuckling as Grady bit back the first words that came to mind. He needed this job.

• • •

Grady spent the rest of his day in a factory two blocks away, replacing and tracking the conveyor belt on an atmosphere furnace. He had never installed one before, and took more time and care than Roy Burgess would have expected him to.

On the other hand, it was service charged by the hour, the customer didn't mind, and after six hours that involved pulling a wire mesh belt through the furnace, running it back underneath the furnace, splicing the ends together, and tracking its motion slowly to center it on the drive rolls, the belt was running smoothly and perfectly. Grady took his coveralls off and put his tie back on, shaking hands with the plant manager, who was also the owner. "Heat it up to five hundred degrees, let it run for a couple of hours, heat it up to a thousand and do the same, then on up above fourteen hundred. You'll be able to run a full load on it in two days."

Instead of swearing at him about lost production time, the manager said, "Sounds great. Thanks for coming."

"My pleasure, Mr. Wardell."

"Cosmo."

"Okay, Cosmo." He added automatically, "You were lucky that belt was in stock. We sell replacement belts; you should keep one on hand." He glanced at the waiting pallets of assembled but unprocessed valves. "Know what might make more sense? Order a second furnace. You've got the work, and you could swap out parts from one to the other while you placed an order with us. No downtime, and more profit."

"Good idea. I'll call you."

"I'm not in Sales anymore," Grady said.

Cosmo said firmly, "Hell you aren't. I'll call you."

Tom Garneaux looked up from a copy of *The Razor's Edge* as Grady came in. "How's business?"

"Not bad." He told Tom about it. "Now I know ten times more about customers and what they need. If I ever get back to sales, I'll just tear up the tracks selling to our regular customers."

Tom replied gloomily, "If we ever have regular customers again." He jerked his head toward Warren's office. "He's trying to sell to the League of Nations, Fu Manchu, Aladdin, and everybody but the Wicked Witch of the West. Probably he's selling her something, too."

Grady said, "Tom, you haven't asked any questions about my other job."

He winked. "Don't ask me any questions about when I was your age and we'll call it square." He looked grim again. "But you're playing by the rules, I know you are. Him . . ." He jerked his head toward Warren's office again. "Do you think he's cleared any of these clowns with the War Department? If he has, do you think he bothered telling them the truth?"

Grady didn't answer. They both knew he didn't need to.

Before going home, Grady stopped in to tell Warren about the sales lead. Warren was locking up his file cabinet for the night, bent over a file drawer, and talking to himself. Grady smiled to himself and edged closer, ready to startle him—

A second voice answered the first. Either Warren had been watching Edgar Bergen do Charlie McCarthy, or the second voice came from the file drawer.

Grady tiptoed away.

FOURTEEN

THE BED WAS shaking, and someone had hold of Grady's arm. He turned and stared in the dim predawn light and saw no one. He looked down, remembering that he was back at the Dwarfworks, and saw Antony, who looked sullen and something else Grady couldn't catch. Pieter, beside Antony, said, "We need you to drive."

Grady remembered something last night about driving a truck through towns, and he had volunteered. Lately he was glad of any excuse to leave the plant.

But nobody had said anything about starting this early. "Why leave now?" Grady said querulously. "Why not wait till sunrise?"

"The tide," Peter said, and left. Antony stayed barely a second longer to explain. "We need to catch high tide in northern Connecticut."

"In a truck?" Grady muttered. Seconds later he was awake enough to understand; he struggled into his jeans and work boots hastily.

The truck was already loaded and closed up when he arrived. He would have been relieved, but Klaus was standing on the loading dock, waving serpentine arms and gesturing at the tailgate. Pieter, waving Antony and Grady back, went to speak to him. Shadowy gnomes came forward bearing a succession of dark-stained wooden crates and threw them in the back of the truck.

Grady, watching, said fervently under his breath, "Oh, I hate this."

Antony agreed, "It stinks." For a moment they were friends again.

Then Pieter came back. Antony said, "Boss, what—?" and Pieter said curtly, "Let the boy drive the truck and we leave," and the moment was over as though it had never happened.

Grady unstrapped the short-leg blocks from the clutch, gas, and brake pedals and threw the blocks behind the seat. There was plenty of room for one human and three dwarves in the front of the truck.

Grady turned. "Are we headed for a factory?"

"No." Antony's throat was dry. "A ship."

"Then couldn't it have met us at a dock in Manhattan, or on the Hudson River?"

"The receiver never leaves salt water," Pieter said softly. He smiled at Grady. "And I don't think it would be good for him to dock at Manhattan, good for him or for your Manhattan. He remembers it differently."

Grady shut up.

He drove across the Hudson and across the rocky, sparse land toward the coast. No one spoke. At first he thought that Antony was still sulking over Kirsten.

The closer they got to the Connecticut coast, the more subdued Antony and Pieter were. At first Grady assumed he had offended them. Then Grady assumed it was because of their dislike of boats.

Finally he came to a T-intersection; in front of it was a fishing boat up in a cradle. Beyond it he could see only gulls wheeling. He said apologetically, breaking the silence, "I need to know where to go from here."

Pieter stretched up on the seat and pointed. "Head north, up the coast."

He turned, crossing a concrete bridge with slits in the railing like a gun bunker. They were paralleling U.S. 1, the Post Road up the coast, and Grady was wishing he was on it.

Numerous small towns interrupted the road. The houses were squat, one- and two-story affairs with white upright framing at the corners, and post-and-lintel doorways.

The newest were Victorian, with wraparound front porches and widow's walks on top, railings flaked and neglected but intact. There wasn't a single building less than a century old.

Church spires stuck above the towns; a surprising number of buildings in Connecticut were fewer than four stories.

In the cities, the church spires were often red brick with gray shingles, and looked like part of the mills and factories.

Mill buildings were always soot-blackened red brick and usually with a tall square-sided tower rising up them.

The hills around the mill towns were rocky, gray boulders showing clearly between and through the lifeless underbrush.

Vertical obelisks, Cleopatra's Needles probably from shortly after the Civil War, stood on the hills. Below one of them was a bronze equestrian statue with mortars and pyramids of cannonballs at each corner, dedicated to the lasting memory of someone who no longer mattered to anyone at all.

Grady said for something to say, "We're in the middle of nowhere."

"Not yet," Antony said. "Where do you think we are?"

"Close to Mystic?"

Antony snorted. "You could say that."

"I could've said it's close to New London."

Antony considered. "That's true, but it's not as true." He settled back into silence. Grady realized with a stab of homesickness how fast it would be to drive to Providence from here.

The houses, formerly prosperous farmsteads and perhaps roadside inns, were from the eighteenth and early nineteenth centuries; only the telephone poles and the cars parked near them told what era it was.

Farther on, the occasional "saltbox" colonial, two stories in front and one story in back, mixed in with the other houses. Gradually it was as though they had nudged the newer Victorians out, or frightened them away like shabby old men frighten bus passengers.

The last building of any size was a whitewashed church, darkened only slightly with train and factory soot. The front door was boarded shut.

White-and-gray thin tombstones poked out of a slanted cemetery. The stones looked as if they were paper or cardboard, and the wind was blowing.

Grady remembered the white steeple as they left it behind them and realized he hadn't seen a church in a long time. For some reason that made him nervous.

The trees closed in on the roadway as they left the main road.

White birch grew near the water by the winding, slow-running tidal rivers; wild grape vines covered the trees, as though trying to drag them down and drown them. The spaces between the trees grew longer. In one place, Grady saw an acre of junked cars stacked three deep. He wondered how it could possibly have escaped scrap drives and realized that not many people made it out this way.

The last of the trees gave way to salt marshes, broken only by hummocks and by the distant tree line. An abandoned barge lay askew on a mudflat; at low tide it would be completely exposed. Grady had seen marshes like this from the train; at low tide they were a field of grass broken by winding roadways of mud, each with a thin trickle of water in it.

Broad, flat streams snaked through the marshlands. There were small buildings beside them, all dark boards and thatch. Grady thought they might be duck blinds for hunters, or bird blinds for watchers. They were isolated, and their presence made the marsh seem even lonelier.

Square platforms on poles, erected for osprey nests, poked up from the marsh in deserted stretches.

By now the road was little more than two ruts paved with equal parts of gravel and several centuries of oyster shells. Grady drove slowly to keep the truck from bouncing, and because he was half afraid the tires would be sucked down if he missed the gravel.

They crossed three small bridges to get down to the inlet. The last one, a rickety piling-and-beam affair with blown-out tires (fugitives from the rubber drive) hung on the railing to ease wear, shook as they went over. Antony stretched up to stare uneasily at the marsh below. "At least we'll be lighter driving back."

Docks extended to the open water, sometimes stretching fifty or sixty feet over the surrounding grass and mudflats. Several of them were little more than piling and supports, the board surface long gone in storms and floods.

Pieter leaned forward, pointing, and Grady drove down the bumpy ruts to a twisted dock that was nearly black. All the pilings were askew, the boards sagging. Grady shut off the truck and stepped down, looking at the square-sided iron nails holding the dock together. "How long has this been here?" Neither of them answered. "It's like something smugglers would use," Grady said, and was immediately sorry he had.

They unloaded the truck, putting the crates at the end of the dock. Grady looked out at the mist rising from the water, making the marsh grass look ghostly and insubstantial. "Maybe he'll be late." He shivered, wrapping his coat tighter. "Think he'll want to stay for coffee when he gets here?"

"He is never late," Pieter said quietly, "and he never stays."

There was nothing to say to that. Grady watched the mist coiling and uncoiling over the still water.

A few minutes later he shivered again and put his hands in his pockets. "Wow, it's getting cold." It was, and foggier. A breeze from the land had picked up. Antony sat up, and Pieter walked to the end of the crumbling dock.

Grady followed him, testing each blackened board carefully before putting his weight on it.

The fog was now so thick he could barely see the marsh grass on the other side of the inlet. Grady heard, from somewhere over the water, a monotonous and unidentifiable creaking.

The ship, when it appeared out of the fog, startled Grady. It wasn't the bow of a cargo freighter, but the bowsprit of something much older.

There was something under the bowsprit, a time-darkened figurehead. Grady squinted, trying to make it out; it looked like a woman—

The tendrils of mist parted, and Grady turned away, sickened. It might have been a woman, once.

The rest of the ship appeared: gray railing, gray masts like dead trees, gray sails like musty linen billowing as it tacked against the wind. The hull was as blackened as the pier Grady stood on, and it seemed to Grady that, as it cut soundlessly through the inlet, the water recoiled from it. It was sixty feet long, and the mainmast was as tall as a three-story building. Grady wondered how the masts had made it under the telephone poles and realized unhappily that some questions didn't matter.

A single figure stood before the mainmast, a gaunt man with straight hair that was neither blond nor gray. He turned his head to stare at them, and he lifted his hand in greeting. Grady fought the urge to run.

"Vandervecken," Pieter whispered. Grady tried to remember where he had heard the name.

Sad, squat figures moved in the shadows on deck. Grady was relieved to see they were human, and looking again, he was sorry as well.

"Vandervecken's crew," Antony said behind Grady, and Grady remembered the song, from a camp fire years ago:

" 'Till I shipped out on Vandervecken's crew . . .' "

The ship, the *Flying Dutchman*, glided to the pier, and one of the crew tossed a rope down without looking. Grady caught it. The rope was cold and stiff, as though it were nearly frozen. He wrapped it around a piling, glad to let it go.

Two crew members—one a young man dressed out of *H.M.S. Pinafore*, the other more like the deck of the *Potemkin*—slid the gangplank down. Vandervecken stepped quickly onto the dock. He was dressed in dark pants and a dark sweater. He glanced down at the dwarves and smiled without warmth. "So, little men."

Pieter nodded curtly. "Captain."

"You wait here for me, yes?" He still smiled. "I never wait." His accent was thicker than Pieter's. He shifted his feet back and forth as he spoke. He looked down at them. "I got your letter."

A small white paper fluttered off the ship and landed on Grady's shoulder. It huddled against his neck, trembling. He passed it back to Pieter, who shoved it in a pocket protectively.

Vandervecken's feet moved back and forth on the dock. He had not stood still since he had arrived. "Pieter, who is this boy?" He pointed to Grady, and a stray breeze off the water made Grady shiver.

"He works for us. His name is Grady." Pieter added in lieu of a last name, "From Providence." Grady found himself grateful that Pieter had not given his last name.

Vandervecken laughed with no mirth. "I have not been to Providence in a while. They have a good harbor, the Basin. Perhaps you should go with me, boy, and sail there? Perhaps you would like to sail there with me." He called over his shoulder to his crew. "You think he would like to ride? Eh?"

They stared back emptily. None of them spoke or gestured or cast a shadow.

There was a warning nudge in Grady's lower back, but he was already shaking his head. The Basin, a circular pool dredged out for shipping in downtown Providence, had been filled in and paved nearly a century ago.

Vandervecken ignored him; he hadn't expected a volunteer. "You have the metalwork?"

Antony, coming back from the truck, called, "Right here."

He was carrying three wood and iron pulley blocks. The metal on each had been mended, probably heated with a strip of welding material and beaten solid again. The weld had already lost its newness.

Vandervecken took them from Pieter and turned them over, eyeing them critically. "This will do. Thirty dollars off your next shipping price, we said—"

"I remember." Pieter took an envelope from his pocket. "This is our fee." He passed it over, then pulled out a second, grimy envelope. "And this," he said with obvious distaste, "is for the other boxes."

Vandervecken examined the contents of each envelope carefully, putting them away while Grady asked Antony, "What other things?"

Antony pointed with his foot to the stained boxes on the ground near the dock.

Vandervecken read the shipping papers quickly. "These are not signed."

Antony stiffened as Pieter said, "What?"

"I do not take this cargo without someone signing." He passed the papers back to Antony. "There is a note for you."

It was written on dry brown paper in thin, spiderweb handwriting. "Pieter, I would appreciate your signing for this cargo. K."

The right leg of the K was a shadow, the left vertical outstretched pincers, and the upper right bar a curved scorpion tail.

"Klaus's monogram." Antony handed it to Pieter, who crumpled the note with distaste and threw it away. It blew across the sky quickly, as though the air itself were rejecting it. Grady, from the instinct of too many scrap drives, snatched it as it flew by and pocketed it.

Antony said immediately, "Don't sign anything, boss."

Pieter turned to Vandervecken, who folded his arms across his chest. "Without a signature it does not go." He no more looked angry than he had happy. He moved again, and it occurred to Grady that Vandervecken was incapable of standing still for even a few seconds.

Pieter sighed loudly. "I have no choice." He held the shipping manifest against one of the piers and signed awkwardly.

Grady thought he heard a chuckle from one of the boxes. He looked over Pieter's head, reading the ship-to address: Meyer Warehouse, 17 West Promenade Street, Providence, Rhode Island. He blinked; that was a warehouse Plimstubb used.

Vandervecken nodded, handing a copy of the shipping manifest and the payment receipt to Pieter. "Now we can begin." He clapped his hands twice and shouted toward the gangplank. A man in a contemporary uniform from the U.S. Navy brushed past Grady. So, a moment later, did a man in a Confederate naval uniform. A stout, flaxen-haired sailor in breeches strode to the edge of the dock. His face looked like Antony's or Pieter's, except that it was without life or hope.

Vandervecken strode back and forth among his crew. "Load those, quick. Watch how you handle it—drop nothing, you hear?" he shouted without anger.

The last man, barely Grady's age, shuffled to the land end of the dock and stopped. The last box lay six feet beyond him, near the truck.

"Well?" Vandervecken watched, moving from foot to foot.

The young man hesitated. The wind rippled the ribbons on his British Navy cap, which waved gaily in the breeze.

He stared at the captain, and from someone with a soul in his eyes, it would have looked like pleading.

"It is my fault." Pieter hurried to pick up the box, but stopped when Vandervecken shouted, "No!"

Vandervecken walked to the end of the dock and continued, as easily as if they had been conversing cheerfully the moment before, "He is disobedient, that one. I have told him to get the box and he will get it. Go," he said again to the sailor. "Now."

The young man spun around, dashed to the box, lifted it, and stumbled quickly back. He was hardly on land for a second, but it seemed to Grady that the sailor shrank.

He staggered past them, his white hair hanging in his eyes and his hunched back straining as his arthritic hands gripped the crate. His cheeks were sunken in, and a network of wrinkles surrounded his empty, cataract-filmed eyes. The ribbons on his cap hung limp, faded and torn long ago.

The crew stumbled emptily up the gangplank. Grady and the others watched them helplessly, as disturbed by the sailors' fear and despair as by their own failure to save someone, anyone.

Vandervecken clapped his hands together; they made a sharp snap like two boards slapping in a dry winter. "If you have no business more, we will leave." He didn't offer to shake hands, nor did Pieter.

Grady said, "Mr. Vandervecken—"

Antony made a small, sick sound in his throat as, without seeming to move, Vandervecken's arm flashed out and locked on Grady's shoulder. "Captain, boy," he said mildly. "Always you call me Captain."

Grady's muscles tightened and shivered, the cold numbing them instantly, the skin on his knuckles cracking. "Captain, I'm sorry, sir."

Vandervecken nodded. "Captain, yes, that is better." His smile was tight and thin, his eyes light, ice-blue, and if he saw the tears freezing on Grady's eyelashes, he gave no sign. "And you had a question for me. Please, ask."

Grady clenched his jaw as hard as he could to stop his teeth chattering and said shakily, "Who signs for the Rhode Island crates at the other end?"

Vandervecken tightened his grip on Grady's shoulder, and Grady's breath, coming out in short gasps, showed in white puffs. Tears froze on the end of his eyelashes.

Vandervecken's smile thinned out to a line. "To learn that, you would need to ship with me. Does that mean you want to sail with me after all?"

Grady managed to turn his rapidly stiffening neck twice to the right and left. His breath, in agonized gasps, exploded into puffs of white as it neared Vandervecken.

"A shame," Vandervecken said dryly. "I truly am going to Providence, and always I can use more crew. Well, maybe when you are older." Vandervecken brushed at Grady's sleeves, where the mist was freezing solid. Hoarfrost formed where he touched. "But I think maybe you have another question. I can see it in your eyes." He added, "And I will not leave until you ask."

Grady's sinuses ached; his ears burned and reddened with the chill. "What do you do with the money?"

He leaned forward until his face was only inches from Grady's. Grady stood helplessly, locked in place. "I save it," Vandervecken said seriously. "For my retirement."

He laughed, a horrible, loud sound with no joy in it, and spun toward the ship, his long legs flashing back and forth as he strode up the gangplank.

Grady's knees gave. Antony's strong arms caught him under the armpits before his body hit the dock.

Pieter ran back from the truck with packing blankets; he stuffed them around Grady. "Soon we will get you into the warm, and quick."

Grady pulled at the blanket with his barely working fingers. "My shoulder." His chest muscles ached from how hard they had been shivering.

"Frostbite, probably." Antony lifted him under the armpits and bench-pressed him up onto his feet. "We've got something for that. Can you stand?"

"I think so."

The dwarves supported him, and the three of them looked across the marsh. The ship was tacking silently down the stream. The wind had shifted, blowing in off the water. Vandervecken watched them indifferently from the foredeck, then turned to peer impatiently ahead. The wind blew in his face. The mist, dropping its moisture against his cold hair, tracked down his cheeks like the tears he would never cry, and the *Flying Dutchman,* sailing against the wind as always, disappeared into the mist.

Pieter said, "I'm sorry, Grady. We should have warned you." But he was staring after the ship.

Antony said, "What kind of warning would have been enough?"

Grady struggled to smile and failed. "Hey, don't feel bad about me."

"Mmmm?" Pieter, startled, turned his troubled eyes toward Grady. "No, no. I feel bad about what to you just happened, yes. You are young, you will live. But I worry for the other thing." He reached automatically for his pocket, where the receipt for Klaus and the shipping manifest nestled. "And I should, I don't know, something . . . I should never sign for what I do not know. I think maybe it is a bad mistake I have made." He threw the receipt and the manifest on the dashboard; Grady, afraid it would blow out of the truck, pocketed them himself. "Most of all do I wish I had not signed my name."

Antony, chewing a thumbnail, nodded unhappily.

FIFTEEN

T HE WINTER WORE on, and wore at Grady. The news from
Europe was perpetually good, the news from the Pacific
unsettling. Americans had crossed the Rhine, but they were
fighting for Pacific islands a yard at a time. Meanwhile
Plimstubb rattled on, its workers gossiping about the strange
customers Warren brought in and asking Grady hopefully if
there were any word about when he'd be recalled to the
Sales Department.

At the Dwarfworks, unable to get any help from Gretchen,
he worked on his music by himself. Since he had no social
life, he got in a lot of practice, but it didn't replace having
a good teacher.

He could tell that even in the weeks back at Plimstubb he
was smiling less. Roy Burgess pulled him aside and gave
him a fairly obscene and useless lecture on optimism and
customer relations. Talia Baghrati brought him a flaky
honey-and-almond pastry that tasted good even under the
inevitable tang of perfume. Sonny LeTour loaned him a set

of scratchy, obviously well-loved records; unfortunately, they were the blues and did little to raise his spirits.

His mood even spilled over into his choral nights. At a particularly wretched rehearsal, Maestro Mandeville said at one point, "Nicely done, Cavanaugh," and Grady assumed it was pity.

On Sundays Grady would drive even more slowly than necessary back to the Dwarfworks. He arrived in the dark without seeing anyone, and went straight to his cottage.

The sword-fighting lessons continued in the morning, but he and Kirsten barely talked; breakfast was as silent. On his return to the factory floor, only Katrina still greeted him; at odd moments through the day she would run out from behind where she had hidden, laughing and holding her arms out. He would pick her up and swing her around at least once before Gretchen or Antony could call her away, or before Bernhard would whistle to her.

But when the others called, Katrina ran away and Grady was alone again.

Finally one afternoon he finished loading the brazing into the Plimstubb furnace, swept around his area, and waited. When Katrina leaped out at him, he said to her, "Don't go away. Do you want to hear a story?"

She disappeared, but returned with the other children in tow. Grady gestured to his homemade bench and they all sat on it, swinging their heels and listening wide-eyed and open-mouthed as he recited a tale that combined rocket ships (Lester Del Rey), superrobots (Don A. Stuart), killer radio-cabinet robots (Lewis Padgett), the moon (Robert Heinlein), and every other idea he could steal and pack in. The story lasted for twenty minutes and included their chasing each other as robots, stiff-legged, zooming beside each other and orbiting around him as rocket ships, arms swept back for fins, and swimming through the tropical seas of Venus and the canals of Mars. They loved it, and so did he.

As he finished, he noticed that he had attracted quite an adult audience: Gretchen, Bernhard, and a dwarf named Jurgen who worked at the farthest-away forge, all standing with folded arms, watching. Kirsten looked troubled. Only Antony, shaking his head and grinning, seemed to have enjoyed the story.

At dinner that night the adults were colder than usual, and more silent. Grady wondered if taking advantage of the children's company had been a mistake.

But the following day the sun shone brightly and, at noon, the dwarves were all cheerful, talking to each other about how close spring was. Grady listened in silence, not precisely excluded but wishing he could join in. At the end of the meal, before resuming work, the male dwarves raised eyebrows to each other and winked, and they sneaked quietly out the front door. Antony, more hesitantly and with a backward glance at Grady, followed.

Grady, against his better judgment but too curious not to, followed them.

Outside they had assembled a rude table from logs lying near the entrance; Grady saw how the apparently natural logs had been notched to fit together without looking cut and hewn. They were seated on logs at it, drinking from large and full beer steins. On the table were two pitchers of ale, one pitcher still full and foaming.

At the end of the table, upright, was an empty stump, about the height of a chair for Grady.

Grady slid his back leg around it and sat down. Antony, seated at his right, frowned. The others nodded, as though they had been expecting him.

Jurgen grabbed the full pitcher and poured a stein for Grady. "Have some ale."

"Thanks." But Grady looked at the faces around the table and knew the gesture meant little. He pulled the stein over, admiring the smooth head on the ale. He raised it to his lips—

Barely trying to make it look like an accident, Antony bumped the stein, dumping the contents all over Grady.

It had been a long week, and Grady was on his feet in a second, his face beet red with anger. "What the hell's wrong with you? Are you stupid, or clumsy, or both?" They faced each other.

"Nice talk." Antony's face was twisting and working; he was trying to control his own anger. "You picking a fight, kid?"

Grady made no effort at control. "I want to pound you, but I'm not gonna fight somebody half my size."

"That's my worry." Antony added casually, "Or is there another reason you didn't enlist? Lucky thing you broke your ankle, so nobody'd have to know—"

That was it. Grady set his jaw, doubled up his fists, and waded in.

The first punch caught him on the breastbone before he saw Antony's fist move; he rocked back on his heels but did not go down. The second punch, coupled with a leap and a spin, landed on his left kidney. He spun around and pulled his guard up, but not fast enough; on the third punch Antony's fist buried itself in Grady's stomach. Grady doubled over, and Antony went to work on his face.

When he opened his eyes, he was on his back and the sun was low in the west. The air was chilly again, and the disassembled logs of the table lay all around him. Antony was washing his face with a cloth. Antony said with no enthusiasm, "Oh, good, you're awake."

Grady got up on one elbow, grunting with the pain. His

chest felt like a mass of bruises, his stomach was knotted, and his face—he touched it gingerly with his free hand, checking to see if it had any skin left on it. It felt puffy to the fingers, but otherwise all right.

Antony tossed the towel aside. "I just hung around to be sure you'd live. You will." He walked away, but spun around and said with a snarl, still furious, "More than half a century of trying to do right by that woman, who's prettier than apples, and she wants you!"

"Wanted," Grady corrected, but wasn't sure Antony heard him.

He limped slowly and painfully back into the factory. The others saw him come in, then ducked their heads or looked away. He walked to Kirsten's desk and sat down.

"I'll be done in a minute." She was logging orders, the quill pen flying across the ledger and landing in the inkwell as she moved back to the typewriter and filled out invoices. "There. What can I do for you?" she said without looking up.

"I quit."

"No, you don't." She looked him in the eye. "You need the money and we need you. Plus your work is good." She looked back down. "Though we'll have to make some adjustments."

"Are you going to tell me I shouldn't fight?"

She looked him up and down. "Tomorrow morning you'll tell yourself. On the other hand, I'll tell Antony he shouldn't fight."

"Why not? He's good at it." Grady felt his shirt, which was still damp from the ale.

Kirsten saw the motion, leaned forward, and sniffed the shirt. "Oh, my. He knocked that out of your hand, didn't he?"

Grady said nothing. Just now he hated Antony, but felt the dwarf was in deep enough trouble with Kirsten.

She smiled—not enough to look happy, but at least a brief twist. "He won't be punished for that. He kept you from drinking the ale; you should thank him."

"I was just having a drink."

"That would have been your last drink for twenty years." She went on in Grady's stunned silence. "How do you think we've kept safe all these years? You've heard the Rip Van Winkle story; didn't anybody ever teach you not to drink with strangers or with people who don't like you?"

Grady was about to protest that once, not so long ago, they'd all liked him. He remembered why they didn't and bit off his reply. "So I should thank Antony?"

"You could." She went back to her paperwork. "I'm going to discipline him anyway. Saving you or no, he shouldn't have fought you."

Now he couldn't keep still. "He did it for you."

She turned a brighter red than she ever had around the forges. "What happened is none of his business!"

Grady shook his head; the motion hurt. "You're his business."

"His business is here." She gestured around the plant. "The place that keeps him fed, that keeps him alive. The place that makes him happy." She added more honestly, "Made him happy."

"It made me happy, too." Grady stood. "I always thought being in a fairy tale would be wonderful—better than being in a science fiction story. Now if I had three wishes, my first would be that I'd never heard of any of you."

Kirsten looked away and said without anger, "You're not alone. Now I wish I were somewhere else, too, but I have nowhere to go. What mercy would I find in a world full of humans?"

"Beats me," Grady said. "What mercy have I found here?"

There was nothing to say. He went on, "You're not angels, are you? The truth hurts."

Kirsten, stung, said, "The truth hurts only when someone sharpens it." Grady had already turned away.

On his way to dinner, Grady felt something brush against him. He leaned down and patted a walking hearth, thinking how it ought to be funny that the friendliest thing left in his life was a piece of metal. He went to the dinner table and sat in silence with people who hated him, ate a meal he hated, went back to the house he now hated, and lay in bed, wide awake, waiting to get up and go back to the job that had once felt magical.

SIXTEEN

GRADY STAYED IN his own office until noon, taking calls and making calls in the building. At lunchtime he went to Engineering. Tom Garneaux was absorbed in some kind of doodling; Susan, predictably, was working on one of the wartime designs on her own time.

He stood in front of her desk, waiting for her to finish the calculation she was doing. Grady never interrupted a design engineer in, as he said, "midguess."

When she paused, he said, "I need some advice on my manners."

Susan looked at his battered face and said, "First off, never call that nice Joe Louis such a bad name again. How long did you stay in the ring?"

"You should see the other guy."

She passed him a cigarette. "Bad?"

He put it gingerly between his lips. "Not a mark on him."

"Who was it?"

"Antony."

Susan stared at him. "My God, why?"

"Promise not to tell anyone?"

"Who could I tell?" She glanced toward Warren's office. "Yeah, sure, I promise. Trust me."

"Because this would embarrass two friends. Three, if you count me after I've told you."

And he told her the whole story of the party and Kirsten's naked visit to his cottage.

When he finished, Susan frowned. "And Antony pounded you for turning her down?"

"No, it was a lot later. I think he pounded me for the way I turned her down. I guess I didn't say 'no' as well as I should have."

Susan put her fingertips together and stared straight ahead, avoiding his eyes. "No," she said. "No, you did it about as badly as you could have." She looked up. "If I'd come to you naked and you'd made me feel that bad, I'd have killed you."

"I know. And I want to apologize to her, but I feel like I don't know the rules. I'm a stranger there."

"Strange place to be strange."

"Jesus, it's not just strange, it's horrible." Grady burst out with the details of the past few weeks: the pranks, the turned backs, the abuse, the attempt to put him to sleep for twenty years. "Do you know what it's like to work every day knowing that the people hate you, that you can't change that? That you have nowhere to go?"

"I might," Susan said with sudden force. "Do you know how much I want to go through just one week here without hearing 'wop' or 'blow job'?" She shook her head angrily and wiped her eyes.

Grady's ears turned bright red, but he didn't care. "I didn't know, before. Now I understand." He changed the subject quickly. "At least you're getting to work on war projects."

"Not hardly."

"Sure you are. I left the RFQs on your desk."

"And I came up with designs and gave them back to Warren. He's not selling the designs."

"What?"

"He keeps saying, 'the war is ending soon anyway.' He hangs on to the designs, and he's hoping to strike a deal with people like RCA and Sylvania after the war." She waved her arms. "Hasn't he figured out that the first one to do it gets the contracts?"

Grady sagged. "He doesn't need the war. He's got these weird contracts, wherever they came from, and they're better money." He ran a hand through his hair. "We barely knew what was going on with the contracts; now we don't know anything."

Susan tapped a pencil on her desk, faster and faster until it sounded like an angry woodpecker. "Where are they coming from? Scratch that; we've both guessed. The question is, can we prove it, and can we use that to force him back to the jobs for the war?"

"You mean 'blackmail,' don't you?"

"I hope I do, or it won't work." She stood up. "What are you doing for lunch?"

"I brought a sandwich." Grady thought wistfully about having the money to go out for a blue plate special or fish and chips.

"Eat it, wait till Warren's gone, and meet me in his office."

"He locks everything."

"He probably needs to. . . . Tom?"

Tom Garneaux jumped, hastily covering something with his arm. "What can I do for you?"

She walked over quickly. I need a favor—Holy God, Tom, you were working."

The sheet was a neat sketch of a conveyor belt, with a list of tension points labeled around it, a coefficient of friction for the point where the belt hit the drive drum, and a careful, step-by-step series of calculations for tension and loading under heat.

Susan shook her head at it. "This is nice. Do you do this for every furnace?"

Tom, his face scarlet, muttered, "Might as well get it right." He looked as embarrassed as though a nun had caught him selling a reefer. He put the sheets in a folder and dropped the folder behind his considerable library of restaurant and diner menus. "What do you want?"

Susan looked around and said, "I want to look in Warren's files while he's out."

Tom shook his head. "He locks everything."

"That's why I want to learn to pick locks."

Grady inhaled sharply. Tom glanced at him, then beamed at Susan proudly. "That's my girl."

On Susan's insistence, Grady stood watch. Tom took a small packet from his desk drawer (what the hell *didn't* he have in there?) and gazed fondly at the collection of narrow steel pins and angled rods. He talked her quietly through the outer locks; they vanished inside.

Tom stepped back out, passing her the pick case. "Keep 'em. You have to lock everything back in. What are you looking for, anyway?"

Susan gave him a peck on the cheek. "The less you know, the better."

He frowned at her. "Shouldn't kiss me in the office. It doesn't look right." As Susan fumbled for an apology, he added deadpan, "Oh, all right, just one more," and kissed her back. He strode off, whistling.

It was all over in five minutes, which seemed to Grady to take until sunset. Susan came out, flushed with excitement, carrying a battered cardboard box. "It was in a file cabinet. Look at it; I'll bet he's been carrying it home nights."

"Let's take it to my desk." Grady wanted the privacy. "And hurry. Can you carry it?" He knew he couldn't and make any time at all. Susan responded by dashing to his office.

By the time she got there she was panting as well as flushed; she hadn't been excited after all. She slammed the box on Grady's desk and said with a gasp, "This is it. Is Schrödinger's cat alive or dead?"

"Lift the lid and we'll find out." As Susan pulled out a stack of folders, Grady warned, "Get them back in order."

"Does it matter if we get what we're looking for?"

"It does if we don't."

Susan removed the rest more carefully. Grady checked the contents of the top folder, then the next and the next. All the letters were straightforward proposals, counteroffers, and sales correspondence, though some of the letters were from Dublin (neutral), Spain (supposedly neutral, but pro-Nazi), and Baghdad (Grady had no idea). Nothing implicated the gnomes.

He said, "No dice. Let's take this stuff back."

"Wait. What about this?" She reached in the bottom of the box and pulled out an accordion folder.

It was bulky and made of leather or, Grady realized uneasily, some other sort of skin, nubbly and reptilian. The edges were stitched precisely and evenly, but obviously by hand—or, at least, he corrected himself hastily, not by a machine. He undid the string that held the top flap down and peered in, finally growing bold enough to pick the folder up and shake it. Nothing fell out. He pulled it wide open under the light, uncomfortable with how warm the material felt. The folder was completely empty.

He passed it back. "He's probably stashed the paperwork elsewhere."

She frowned. "He wouldn't keep it if it weren't worth something. It's evidence of where he stole his proposals; he'd ditch it in the first trash barrel."

"He might as well have," Grady said glumly. "Not for nothing, it isn't gonna tell us much."

Susan's head snapped up and she stared at Grady. She smiled, and he didn't like that at all. "Don't do it," he said quickly.

"Don't do what?"

"I won't know till you do it, and I don't want to know." He made a grab for the folder.

She pulled it out of reach. "That's why Warren hung on to it. It can tell us more than you think." And before he could react, she tossed it on her desk, smacked her fist down on it, and barked, *"RAUS!"*

She pulled her hand back hastily as the top flap of the folder puckered like an upper lip, hissing as it inhaled, and the whole folder expanded to its fullest width. In the next moment the folder compressed again, and a dry, officious voice said from it, *"Guten Tag."*

"English, please—*bitte,*" Grady said shakily.

After a pause the folder said in a German accent but with flawless diction, "Good day. The following is a list of customers who have requested information on some form of metals processing. Ireland: Connaught. Maeve, no last name, no mailing address, contact through Liam Bailey of Boston. Product, a kind of megaphone for greater sound magnification. Equipment, batch oven. Payment gold, antique. Special note: Test gold by daylight.

"Persia . . ."

The folder spoke for fifteen minutes. At the end, Susan picked it up gingerly and put it in the bottom of the box. She turned defensively to Grady. "Well, that's evidence, isn't it?"

"If you really thought so, you wouldn't have put it back in the box." He rubbed his eyes tiredly, wincing when he pressed on his own bruises. "It's nothing in writing, and it doesn't name Klaus or Warren. We can say where we found it, but it's our word against Warren's—and it's still just a folder."

Susan silently replaced the other folders, then looked up and said, "Then you'll just have to go to the Gnomengesellschaft."

"And do what?" "Die" came to mind.

"You liked adventure serials, didn't you? Sneak around, find proof, and get out."

"In the serials," Grady pointed out, "they always get caught."

"They always escape the next week."

"I don't want to wait a week."

"Exactly," Susan said triumphantly. "So don't get caught."

"I'm not due back there until next week," he said feebly.

"Then they won't expect you, will they? And anyway, you just said you didn't want to wait a week."

Something about the logic of that didn't work, but Grady didn't argue. At least that meant that if Warren discovered they'd been in his files, Grady wouldn't be here.

They repacked the files in order. As Grady closed the lid, he said, "Did you remember to throw Schrödinger's cat back in?"

She looked wide-eyed and—to Grady—incongruously innocent. "I'm not sure." She picked up the box.

Grady looked around his office unhappily. "Do you really think I won't get caught?"

Susan glanced at the box and grinned, but changed her mind and said seriously, "You're very good, and you're very smart. I'm sure you'll be fine."

She left with the box. It irked Grady that Tom Garneaux, at least, had gotten a kiss.

Grady had five minutes to leave before Warren would see him go. Susan walked Grady to his car.

"Susan?" He paused. "One more place for evidence." He reached in his pocket and showed her the papers from the gnome shipment Vandervecken had taken.

"What are you doing with that?"

"Originally I just grabbed it because I didn't want to see paper go to waste. Then when a scrap drive came around, I decided to hang on to it. Now it might be worth something.

"Plimstubb uses that warehouse to store things. The warehouse itemizes and confirms what they have. Roy Burgess has copies of the records." He ignored her frown. "Check to see if you can find who signed for receipt of these boxes; three gets you ten it was Warren."

"You don't ask much, do you?" But she copied the record numbers.

"Would you rather talk to the gnomes? All right, then. If you don't want to talk to Roy alone, ask Sonny LeTour to hang around. Believe it or not, Roy won't cut up rough in front of him anymore."

"I know. Why?"

Grady ignored that. "Get what you can, and if it looks hot, follow me to the Dwarfworks." He pocketed the shipping papers again.

At his car he paused, one hand on the door. "Did you ever read those stories, my dad loves them, of some guy Bertie

Wooster and how these women he knows are always talking him into stealing something?"

Susan smirked. "Stay away from women like that if you can."

Grady had no reply. He got in and shut the door.

Susan tapped on the window; he rolled it down. "And if you get a chance, apologize to Kirsten."

"How?"

"Sincerely. Honestly. Face-to-face." She pointed forward. "Now go, before you lose your nerve or Warren comes back."

Grady left, not looking forward to either task ahead.

SEVENTEEN

IT WAS EASY sneaking into the Gnomengesellschaft. It occurred to Grady that it was also easy sneaking into a lobster pot.

He came into the Dwarfworks by the front entrance and glanced quickly around. Kirsten was not in sight. Antony was in the door of Pieter's office, waving his hands, explaining something. Bernhard, heating a new tray of wishing rings, was frowning worriedly at Katrina and Thom, who were dancing at his feet.

Grady walked to the gnome tunnel. None of the dwarves even looked up. Grady sighed tiredly; even if they saw him, they'd pretend not to.

He edged out of the tunnel into the gnome area, looking around anxiously. The cavern was ideal to hide in; the gnomes had kept the rough-hewn rock of the cave, and the torchlight made for a great deal of shadow. Grady moved from rock pillar to pillar, glancing cautiously ahead before scuttling quietly to the next bit of shelter.

No one was visible. In the corner of the factory, shadows gestured angrily, and claws grew and retracted; some kind of meeting was going on. Evidently the gnomes didn't even make each other happy.

One of them snatched something from another, who growled; they were eating. Grady tried not to think about what they might eat. He looked from side to side, wondering where to start. Somewhere there must be the equivalent of a file cabinet; he wanted to look in it and return as quickly as possible.

In the torchlight Grady passed a number of pit forges, paired with stained anvils and with trays to hold prints and work orders. The work orders were written in a crusty brown ink that Grady was afraid he recognized. He was careful not to touch the prints.

All around him were the products of gnome technology. He saw knife blades with grooves to let the blood run out. He saw what were clearly instruments of torture. He saw a set of bronze implements that looked surgical but had barbed blades. He glanced up and saw a length of chain, twenty feet up, with a wickedly sharp hook dangling from it. All of it made him unhappy, but none of it helped find evidence of a deal between Warren and Klaus.

Finally he was sidling toward the plant offices and around bulk of the living furnace, Garner Stanley Irving. Grady noted with relief that the bellows had been moved away from Irving; perhaps the gnomes were fulfilling their promise to keep him idle.

He moved to Irving's face and paused. A metal framework blocked Grady's way; it was quarter-inch steel, built to withstand loads and stress, and it had a small shelf under the top surface—

It was a frame for a motor. The side pieces of the top

surface had evenly spaced bolt holes; they were drilled for rollers.

It was a powered loading platform, for loading work into a furnace. The end nearest Irving had a series of hooks to hold the platform in place.

Grady whirled this way and that, looking for the inevitable workbench. It sat on wheels to the left, and he was relieved to see that nothing about it implied life or suffering. The wrenches, pliers, and wire cutters hanging from the tool board looked pleasantly normal; the tape measure was calibrated in inches. Even the wiring, piping, and water piping prints looked much like the designs Grady was used to at work.

He blinked. Except for the outline of Irving's body on the print, the designs looked way too much like those he knew.

Runes lined the edges of the print; Grady was afraid to strike them. He understood the designs anyway: an automatic load table, gas-tight ports for inserting thermocouples, electric resistance heating elements that would heat industrial equipment to two thousand degrees Fahrenheit. Atmosphere piping snaked out of the sketched-in body, connected to upright gas cylinders. The prints were held flat with components that looked screamingly normal: gas flowmeters, a proximity switch, a Wheelco temperature controller for a high-temperature furnace.

An additional annotation in the lower left-hand corner said, "Dotted lines indicate wiring for conveyor belt and drive should production increase." Grady looked at Irving, imagining for a horrible fraction of a second a metal belt, heated red-hot, tearing through Irving's body

Irving's soulless eyes stared back at him. Grady dropped his own gaze and looked at the print, hoping to find something reassuring, something normal. The lower right-hand corner of the print had the Plimstubb title block. Grady knew the Plimstubb draftsmen's and the engineer's pencil styles well enough to know that this was someone else's. The draftsman's signature space held the initials "WH."

There was a sheet of foolscap titled "MEMO OF UNDERSTANDING" under the final print. From the cross-outs and insertions it was a first draft. One or two insertions looked to be in Warren's printing, though that was arguable. Grady scanned it hastily, catching the words "previously supplied sample contract," "customer list," "technological upgrade"—whatever "upgrade" meant—and a list of furnace design features available through Plimstubb, though Plimstubb was not named. The memo was unsigned and named neither Warren ("the human manufacturing party" nor Klaus "the contracting officer in charge of the equipment"), but the intent was clear: In exchange for converting Garner Stanley Irving to a high-temperature electric furnace—

Grady shivered involuntarily. The document promised twenty-four-hour operation, seven days a week, year after year. The sales part of him thought numbly that it was just the sort of thing Warren would promise a customer without being able to deliver. The part of him that read science fiction tried to imagine Irving's future, and recoiled from the vision.

"Look," Grady said earnestly, "I'm going to help you. I promise."

The big eyes looked at him emptily.

Grady turned to the living furnace. "Listen: This is wrong. I'm going to stop this. If you understand, blink once for yes."

After a long time, Irving blinked.

"Good," Grady said. He wanted to sound as convincing as he ever had in his life. "We made a deal that said you would—that this wasn't supposed to happen to you anymore. Klaus broke that deal. I think—I know—that I can force him to stop."

Irving stared at him. There was no hope in the big eyes, but he was listening.

"I'm going to leave for a little while, but I'll do everything I can to stop this from happening." He took a deep breath. "If that means you die, is that all right?"

With no hesitation the big eyes blinked once.

"Okay. Try to hang on till I get back." Grady looked around for watchers. He pulled a crescent wrench from the tool rack on the workbench. "Maybe this will make it easier."

He swung the wrench down, backhand, and the proximity switch split in half. He did it again, and the control instrument went from precision calibration to worthless junk. He hit the atmosphere flowmeters, and watched as their rectangular case crackled into something that would never hold any kind of pressure, let alone measure gas flow.

"There," he said with a shuddering breath, "that ought to slow things down." He fumbled around the workbench for any other part that would be crucial to completing the auto-loading project; on impulse he pocketed the memo of understanding. It was unsigned and named no one, but it might point him to more information.

He looked into Irving's eyes and for the first time he felt afraid; in a world where more is better, there will always be someone who chooses to process more through someone else's suffering. "I'll do everything I can," he said. "Believe me."

He touched Garner Stanley Irving, and was more upset that Irving felt vulnerable and human.

Antony saw Grady moving toward Kirsten, looked away in disgust, and did a double take as he realized where Grady had emerged from. Grady ignored him, moving quickly toward Kirsten. Antony swore under his breath and followed.

Grady dragged Kirsten toward Pieter's office as he explained what he had seen and done. Antony listened, his blood chilling; there was no way to hide this.

Grady asked, "Do you think they noticed me?"

"Of course they noticed you," Kirsten said. "The only question is, What will they do?"

Antony said, "We know what they'll do. The only real question is how soon."

Kirsten said, "Then we have to talk to them first. Pieter?" Pieter looked up as she said, "Grady found evidence of a gnome contract violation, he says. He'd better be right; he vandalized their plant."

Pieter looked at Grady and eventually said, "Speak."

Grady told his story again, wondering if there were something else he could have done. "I broke the equipment for Irving. I had to; I didn't want him to suffer—"

"You had to," Pieter rumbled, nodding. "And if you hadn't gone in we might never have known." His face had gone as gray as his beard. "And now what?"

Kirsten folded her arms. "Now we decide what to do."

"No," Pieter said flatly. "I decide. As I did when we had debt, and I made a contract that I thought would maybe help." He stared bleakly ahead at nothing. "So I will do nothing, and the man Irving will suffer, or I break off our business with Klaus, and we all suffer. Which to do?"

Kirsten stared. "I don't even think we have a choice."

Pieter shook his head. "That is why you are not a manager. You have one job. I have all of them, in my hands, right now. I have even more than that in my hands—"

He broke off as something dark and small glided in, a Dwarfworks memo blank fleeing in the air before it. Pieter snatched at the dark thing as it came near the table. He held it up so they could see it.

Pieter turned the note toward them. It was in the familiar spidery handwriting; this note, however, was written in blood:

> To: Pieter Hein, Manager—Nieuw Amsterdam
>   Dwarfworks
> From: Klaus, Project and Contract Oversight—
>   Gnomengesellschaft
>
> Subject: Contract violation
>
> This is to notify you that because of the damage inflicted in our plant by a laborer in your employ, you are now in violation of our original credit and cooperation contract. That document stated that there would be substantial and painful penalties for sabotage or vandalism inflicted on either of our property by the other, unless just cause could be shown.
>   I have forwarded a copy of this communication to my superior, Heinrich.

Klaus's monogram was below the text. Scrawled at the bottom was a less formal postscript: "Now we'll see whether or not your pretty little feet can run for themselves."

"You were right, Kirsten. Now we have no choice." He threw the note on his desk. "You see? Now maybe you see, Antony, what did I tell you?" His hands clenched and unclenched. "You say make it modern, you say nothing will be hurt, I say everything will be. But you listen how well?" He answered his own question. "Not a little bit well."

"Boss," Antony pleaded, "you're not listening now. Klaus has broken his deal—"

Pieter slammed his hand down. "I have listened enough. This time you will listen. This one last time."

Kirsten said carefully, "Perhaps you should wait till you're calm."

"I will never be calm again." He looked at all three of them, his face trembling with anger, and jabbed a finger at Antony. "You, you're fired. And you, Kirsten, because you knew all of this before telling me but you never told me." He turned and said bitterly, "And you, man-child, you mean well but all you have done here is break hearts. You should not have come. Go now."

The young dwarves were silent, stunned. Grady stepped forward. "It's not their fault—"

"Theirs because yours." He repeated, "Go now. All of you."

Kirsten stood still; Antony turned and walked away. Grady followed. After half a minute, Grady looked over his shoulder to see Kirsten following and Pieter, his anger magically gone, watching her sadly.

When Kirsten caught up with them they were at the gate. She swung it closed carefully, automatically checking the seals and placing the camouflage. They waited. Finally she patted the last vine in place and turned around self-consciously. "It's the last time I do it; I wanted it to be right," she said apologetically, and a great weight seemed to leave her. For the first time since Grady had met her, she seemed small. "Where do we go now?"

Grady said immediately, "The diner." He checked his pockets and managed a grin. "My treat. Or Antony's, if we can talk him into it."

The others didn't smile back, but at least they followed him.

Nora had the grace to plop coffee and apple pie with cheddar in front of each of them without comment. She also set a vase with a red carnation in the center of the table and winked at Kirsten, who had the grace to thank her. Grady mumbled around the forkful of pie, "So what do we do now?"

Antony was silently pleased by the "we." "We'd better think. I've never been out of work in my life, not even in the Depression."

Grady thought fleetingly of the wiring worker back at Plimstubb and his boast of working all through the Depression. "Those days are gone. We'll find work. Where else would you go, normally?"

"That 'normally' is kind of a tough word, kid. I'd go to Pennsylvania Dutch country, but they aren't exactly hiring, except for the mines. Anyway, who wants to move? And you"—he turned to Kirsten—"what a comedown this is for you. I'm just so sorry."

A little of the old Kirsten returned. "When we find a job, I'll take it. I've never had trouble with working for a living. And it's not your fault. He's right; I could have stopped you." She added, putting her hand over Antony's, "And I would have, the first time I thought you were wrong."

Despite their troubles, Grady kept his mouth shut and tried desperately to fade into the booth seat for a moment. Kirsten was smiling with tears in her eyes, and Antony was looking at her the way he might have looked at the Statue of Liberty.

When it became clear that they weren't going to leap up and dance like Astaire and Rogers, Grady sipped his coffee and said thoughtfully, "He's got to be nuts to get rid of you. It's even a little nuts getting rid of me."

Antony speared and swallowed a mouthful of pie before answering. "No, kid. The moment he got that memo from

Klaus, he knew what would happen to you if you were captured inside the plant. He wanted you out, and he fired Kirsten and me because—well, because I got you here in the first place."

Kirsten slammed her fist down, and customers four booths away jumped as the silverware rattled. "No. He did it to save you and me, Antony."

Antony shook his head. "You've gotta be wrong. He'd try to save all of us."

"If he could." There were tears in her eyes. "But the moment he read that memo, he thought it was too late. He wanted to save us, save our people. If he fired us both, he'd save a woman and a man, and there was a chance for all of us to go on. That's what he wanted." She glanced at Grady, and she smiled through the tears. "You were an afterthought, to save you from pain. He really liked you, you know."

"Stop talking like he's dead," Antony snapped, but he was distracted. "So he really thought that the two of us—"

"He's always thought we'd marry each other," Kirsten pointed out, "and he was desperate to preserve our people." For a moment her eyes looked far away. "Even though he was a baby, he was there when it happened before. . . . Antony, Grady, you can stay here, but I have to go back."

They said simultaneously "No," and simultaneously shut up.

"I'm going," she said firmly. "Do you think you can stop me?"

Antony spoke first. "You're not going alone."

Kirsten took his hand. "I knew," she said simply. "I always knew. You went to the American war because of integrity, and that's why you'll follow me. It's why I trusted your dreams."

She looked suddenly at Grady. "You don't have to go back with us."

"I do." He looked at them earnestly. "Half my adult life, I've wished some kind of magic would make me whole and I could go to war. I know it's terrible, I know nobody should wish to kill people, but it's what I should have done. Now I have friends caught in a war between good and evil, and they're good and they're fighting evil. I'm going to war," he finished simply, wondering if he sounded like a child excusing staying out too late.

But Kirsten was smiling fondly at him, and Antony was, too. "You know," he said to Grady, "I said a long version of that to Pieter the night I ran away to enlist in the Great War. I wish I could've said it in a few words, like you. I guess if I could, I'd be in sales." He stuck out a hand. "You're all right. I'm sorry I was too jealous to see that."

Grady grabbed his hand and pumped it without wincing at the dwarf's grip.

Kirsten, looking at him, said only, "Welcome to the war."

But before they could leave the parking lot, a truck pulled in, throwing gravel and slewing around before it stopped. For a moment Grady didn't recognize the Plimstubb delivery truck.

Susan leaned out. "Thank God. I was hoping you'd be here."

Sonny, in the driver's seat, waved an arm and bellowed, "Get on board."

They leaped into the back. Grady looked in confusion at the collection of tools, wire, and miscellaneous steel. Then he was hanging on as the truck bumped back to the Dwarfworks main entrance.

He shouted in the window, "What are you doing here?"

Susan bawled back, "I found the shipping receipt." She passed it up to him; he snatched at it before it could blow away. "I got scared of how much trouble you could be in, and I spoke to Sonny."

Sonny said, "And I got the truck. Seems to me you helped me once or twice."

The truck skidded to a stop. Grady climbed out over the tailgate and turned to help Kirsten and Antony, but they had already leaped out, running for the door. Susan and Sonny followed; Sonny was hauling a duffel loaded with something heavy.

They all stood in front of the door, stunned.

The vines were torn down.

Boulders blocked the opening.

A freshly chiseled sign in a medieval style said UNDER NEW MANAGEMENT. The letters had been filled in; the filling was pink.

Kirsten, trembling, touched the "G" and pulled her hand back quickly. A drop of fresh blood ran from the bottom of the letter.

EIGHTEEN

Antony looked at it, and his heart felt cold. "That's like Fraktur. It's a lettering the gnomes use a lot."

Kirsten touched the red dripping from the bottom of the "G." It came off on her finger, but it was drying and darkening already. "We have to go in."

Sonny said quietly, "You know what you're going into, ma'am?"

"Something I've trained for." She rolled a rock back from the hillside and reached in a hole. "Something I've planned for."

She slung a sword on her belt and passed a larger one, the sword he had practiced with, to Grady. "Something I've trained him for, too."

"That's why you mostly knocked on my outside door. You had the swords outside."

"That was nearly always why," Kirsten said crisply. She turned to the others. "Anybody else want one?"

"What I want," Antony said with a weak grin, "is my

army forty-five and ammo. I didn't bring it back from the War."

"Guns," Sonny said. "We shoulda brought guns."

"It was a joke," Antony said. "You shoot a gnome, you get an annoyed gnome with a hole in him. I'll grab a hammer inside; at least that'll hurt them."

Kirsten shrugged at the obvious. "They're easy to wound but very hard to kill."

Antony said glumly, "I'm not sure what grenades would do, but I wouldn't want to set them off underground anyway."

Kirsten passed him a smithy's hammer from the hole. "I knew someone would prefer it."

Susan was thinking. "Where's the main power line for the Dwarfworks?"

"The left wall, a third of the way in." Kirsten gestured. "It drops down from a hole in the ceiling."

"Good." She fumbled in the duffel bag, then closed it. "I brought some things, just in case. Sonny and I will go to the wall."

Kirsten said seriously to Sonny, "Do you hate that she orders you around that way?"

Sonny sighed resignedly, but grinned. "I'd hate to see her change just for me." He stood at the ready, and the five of them looked at each other.

Kirsten said urgently to Grady, "Use your ring now."

Grady stared down at the gold band in confusion. Antony looked away.

Kirsten said eagerly, "Antony didn't tell you? You get one wish. One time when you can make your leg as good as new if you need it. . . ."

She trailed off. Grady was staring at the ring, deeply ashamed.

Kirsten said in horror and disappointment, "Oh, you

didn't." Susan's eyes went wide and she locked eyes with Grady as he raised his head.

Kirsten blinked and said matter-of-factly, "Then we'll do without the ring." She handed him a sword. "Go in at my right; I'll fight with my left. Clear a path to Pieter, then we'll find a second goal."

"You bet." He tested the sword; the chased silver overlay along the blade seemed to flicker with power. "Let's go." He readied his cane and turned to Antony. "Are you—"

He was hefting the smithy's hammer from his tools, swinging it from the shoulder like a baseball bat. He held it just above his shoulder, not resting it; the hammerhead circled like an angry hornet. "Kirsten says when, kiddo. I'm ready."

"Me, too." Susan shouldered the duffel bag of wire, protective gear, and tools. "How about you, Mr. LeTour?"

"'Mr.'?" He smiled at her. "I guess I'm fine, then. You know, I could carry more."

"I'm fine," she said with a return to her usual edge. She lost it as she turned uncertainly to Grady. "At the dance— you used up your ring—?"

"What's the matter, you've never had somebody do something crazy for you?" Grady was looking at the door, at the blood drying in the letters, at the entrance to something unimaginable. "If it makes you feel better, I wish I hadn't now. I liked it okay then, though." He nodded to Kirsten. "I'm ready."

"Ready, Sarge," Antony said. He had his eyes shut tight.

"Yes'm," Sonny said.

Susan licked her lips and nodded, white-faced.

Kirsten smiled meaninglessly to them. "All right, then. One—two—"

There was no "Three." On the beat, she kicked the stone

door against the cavern wall with a smash that sent rock flakes into the air like dust motes, and they charged forward.

Antony opened his eyes, scanning the chaos for Pieter. He saw him, back to the wall and a human-sized broadsword in both hands. Antony shouted, "He's at two o'clock!"

Grady looked but could see nothing but confused masses of shadows. This was why Antony had shut his eyes, to adjust more quickly to indoor light.

Kirsten shouted, "Grady, on my right," and stepped forward.

Grady, blinking and squinting, followed.

In the first few feet he encountered nothing. The floor was covered with spilled work: rings, bracelets, dagger blades, unframed mirrors.

He saw that the workbenches were overturned and on fire. Several of the stalactites were broken, slashed off above the point. The hearths were nowhere in sight; probably they had run off.

He looked up and he saw a moment that made him wish he was still blinded.

Dwarves, the ones he had worked with, were holding weapons, pokers, benches in lieu of shields. He saw Gretchen angrily swinging a broadsword, Bernhard looking terribly concerned as he swung a bloodstained iron bar, Hans with a fire poker catching a blade-shaped claw—

The rest of the cavern snapped into focus.

Beyond the dwarves were the gnomes: distorted, grotesque, their movements alien. They waved limbs shaped into claws, blades, pikes, scalpels. They never stopped shifting and moving, each attack featuring a new weapon. They never stopped smiling, and they never stopped moving forward. The dwarves were wedged into half of the cavern, nearest the door.

Of the gnomes, only Klaus and Heinrich used swords.

Perhaps it was a sign of office, or perhaps they enjoyed the sport of using a weapon instead of their bare claws.

At least the children were nowhere to be seen. Hunt Day had taught them well.

Grady tightened his grip on his sword and shuffled carefully forward.

He first wounded someone by disengaging a blade and slashing down on it to knock it out of the gnome's hand. The blood flowed from the blade and the gnome screamed as he retracted his blade-shaped hand and put it in his mouth like a small child. Grady stood staring, then stabbed him hastily. The gnome screamed again and backed away.

The rest of the way to Pieter was easy for Grady; Kirsten was doing the hard part. Grady swung his sword at anyone who tried to close on them, and occasionally stepped out of the way of stumbling gnomes. He had no time to watch, but Kirsten seemed to be landing two blows for every one he could.

He passed Bernhard, who wore the same worried look he did when heating metal or playing games with children. The heavy iron bar in his hands rang periodically as it struck a gnome and knocked him to the cavern floor.

On the way over to the wall, Sonny had disconnected the transformers from under the Plimstubb furnace and was dragging them toward the power line, taking up slack in the main wire as he went. Susan was talking to him while she struggled with both bags. Antony shouted as a gnome, waving claws like a lobster, leaped over the Plimstubb furnace at them. Grady watched helplessly, too far away.

Sonny swung a crescent wrench into the gnome's head, connecting hard enough to send the gnome flying. Antony hit the gnome back against the wall like a squash player putting away a ball, and the gnome slumped quietly. It was the first one Grady had seen completely taken out of battle.

Kirsten and Grady arrived as Pieter's strength finally failed against two assailants. One waited for the end of a wide swing and kicked the broadsword all the way to the cavern wall; the other, his hand transforming, prepared a barbed spear point for Pieter's throat.

Wishing fervently that he had two whole ankles, Grady dove forward, sliding on his knees, and spun his sword in a wide circle, cutting first behind the knees of the gnome with the spear point, then through the hamstring of the gnome who still had his leg raised for a kick at Pieter.

Pieter hesitated only until Kirsten, legs tucked, rocketed into the second gnome. He was prepared to move when Kirsten regained her feet and said, "Follow me." He followed as closely behind her as he could. Grady, sword at the ready, guarded him.

Grady looked up and shouted, "To Susan and Sonny." Kirsten glanced at him, glanced at them, and began cutting a path to the cavern wall. Pieter, too tired to argue or assist, half dragged himself along as they pushed and cut their way through the gnomes, who were, truth to tell, too happy attacking others to pay attention to a rescue mission.

Susan looked up as Pieter, Kirsten, and Grady arrived.

Kirsten shouted in his ear over the clangs and thuds of battle, "Guard Susan and Sonny while they work." Pieter nodded thankfully, trying to catch his breath.

Grady shouted, "What now?"

Kirsten glanced around quickly and said almost helplessly, "Fight until something changes. Kill or die." Several gnomes turned at the sound of her voice.

"You said they were hard to kill."

She twisted sideways to avoid a spear-shaped arm. "We'll think of something."

Despite Kirsten's best efforts there still seemed to be a lot of gnomes.

Two gnomes, giggling, chanted, *"Ein—zwei . . ."* and dove on Grady from either side. He ducked, sensibly, and sliced the ankle of the one on the left. He heard a scream and quickly stood, slashing the other in the abdomen. One left carrying his foot, the other cradling his intestines, and Grady stared in momentary confusion at the crimson stain on his sword.

After that it was never monotonous, but it was much easier. There was no time to think whether it was dangerous, or whether it was ever going to end.

After twenty minutes, or maybe many hours, Grady realized that the dwarves were going to lose. Nobody was dying, nobody was prevailing, and the gnomes clearly enjoyed all this more than the dwarves did.

Across the cavern, Klaus threw his head back and laughed. He sounded happy and, Grady realized on some dazed level, he sounded at peace.

The laugh was too normal a sound. Katrina ran out from behind a stalactite, giggling. She froze in front of Klaus and stared in confusion.

Klaus smiled and strode toward her on lengthened legs. He raised the broadsword and plunged it toward her.

Bernhard, still looking worried, leaped in front of her. The broadsword knocked his parry aside and plunged through him, but it didn't reach Katrina.

Klaus pulled the sword out and waited. Bernhard, moving jerkily, raised his iron bar, lowered it, turned, and patted Katrina on the head once.

Then he fell.

Kirsten cried aloud and charged forward on the dead run, her sword spinning in her hand like a fan blade. The combatants parted in front of her and closed in behind. Grady moved forward as fast as his cane would let him, but it was too late.

Klaus, broadsword in one hand and the other formed into a blade, moved on Kirsten. She switched from parrying one to the other, her face expressionless; sooner or later she would miss a lunge by the gnome.

A thump hit Grady's back; he turned. Antony, his face contorted with fear and anger, said, "Why didn't you stay with her?"

Grady gestured at Bernhard's body. "She charged in."

"Well, get there!"

Grady looked helplessly at the sea of individual sword-fights. He and his cane stood a better chance of walking across Narragansett Bay.

He said suddenly, "Throw me to her."

Antony did a double take. "Are you crazy?" But he looked across and judged the distance. "Got your cane? Got your sword?"

"Can't do both. Toss the cane after me."

Antony nodded, seized Grady around the waist, lifted him overhead and, grunting, ran forward and tossed him, hard.

Grady sailed over the gnomes; fortunately they were too startled to reach up and slash him. He tucked his knees and tilted his head back, bracing for impact.

Antony's aim had been true; Grady landed feet first in Klaus's back and kicked out hard, ignoring the pain in his ankle. Klaus staggered, dropping Kirsten. Before the gnome could regain his feet, Kirsten had retrieved her sword and was lunging viciously at him, beating his blade aside.

Antony bellowed "Heads up!" Klaus swore as Antony's cane, handle first, sailed through the air and smacked him on the forehead. Grady, limping forward, caught it on the rebound, spun with it, and whacked the head of another gnome.

He saw Susan waving frantically from the cavern wall. She had attached two thick electric cables to the main power line, one above the fuses and one below, with a throw switch between them. Below that, Sonny had the banks of transformers from the Plimstubb furnace.

"Come with me," he said, panting, to Kirsten, and he gestured toward Sonny and Susan. "They're working on something."

Unhesitatingly Kirsten worked her way into the crowd, her progress measured by indignant howls. This time she moved slowly enough so Grady could follow.

"Thanks. Go on back."

Kirsten nodded curtly and dove into the fight. Antony followed her, his hammer swinging ceaselessly.

Susan tossed him a rubber glove, which he tugged on. She give him a rubber apron; he hung it over his neck. The rubber galoshes he slipped on over his shoes.

Lastly, reverently, she handed him a stainless steel rod. Its handle was a mass of hastily wound tape, with a jury-rigged rubber crosspiece. "Sorry it's not better."

"Looks fine." He still had no idea what she was doing.

She untucked his shirt—miraculously and for once it had stayed tucked—and slid one end of a thick electrical cable under it and up his right sleeve. He got the idea and wrapped the frayed ends of the cable onto the rod above the crosspiece; she handed him tape to secure it. He glanced behind him at the rest of the cable, coiled beside Susan. He tracked it back to where Sonny was hastily fastening the ends to the transformer for the furnace. "How much have I got?"

Sonny said, "Cable or juice?"

"Both."

"A hundred and fifty feet of cable. Don't get your feet wound up in it. Or your cane."

He saluted Sonny quickly with the rod, nearly touching his forehead. Susan said quickly, "And for God's sake keep the rod away from your body. You'll have two hundred and eight volts max, ninety-plus amps."

She gestured at the L-pads on the transformers; Sonny had a rubber glove on and was ready to move the current up. "The entire supply for the furnace, if you need it. Think it'll kill them?"

He looked at the fight. "At least it'll scare them. They don't know much about it."

She pointed to the wall. "Plus if you need it—once—I can switch over to the main line. You may not want to do that—"

"Blow the supply?"

"That and heat the rod like a stove. It'll heat up anyway; the resistance is too high." She looked up at him, suddenly concerned. "How will you hold it?"

He didn't reply. "Will I get more than one shot at the full power?"

Her silence was an answer.

This had already taken too long. Grady said, "Put me on the lowest setting you can, and save the big guns for later."

Sonny set the L-pad for the lowest setting. Susan nodded and said, "On the air." She threw the disconnect switch. Grady was relieved that his arm felt no different. He held the point away from his body and, cane in his other hand, moved forward carefully.

A gnome came toward him, brandishing a forearm in the shape of a scythe. Grady parried the blade and felt the vibration as the gnome's muscles spasmed and the weapon lost shape.

The gnome dropped to the floor, stared at his arm

blankly, and backpedaled away from Grady like a crab, terror in his eyes. Grady moved forward to the next gnome.

The next one was touching another; they both fell down, twitching. The other gnomes fell back in confusion, a few at first, then more as the ones in front backed into them. Grady touched any gnome who attacked him, stepping carefully and checking the cable behind him for slack.

The rod began heating up. Thanking God for the tape and the glove, Grady moved forward, stepping from side to side to drive the gnomes back. He spun on his cane as he had with Kirsten, clearing as wide a path as possible and pushing the gnomes toward the tunnel to the Gnomengesellschaft.

He had a close call when Antony leaped beside him to parry a blow aimed for his arm. He twisted sideways, letting Antony take the full blow, and said with a hiss, "Thanks. Don't touch the rod."

Antony, startled, nodded. He was so used to magic that he'd never considered that the rod might hurt an ally. Kirsten, watching, shouted a command, and the dwarves fell back behind Grady, weapons ready to cut stragglers.

Fifteen minutes later, the gnomes were backing into their tunnel—but the tape on the handle was blistering and melting. The glove felt warm. It wasn't meant for this much heat; Grady wished fervently and uselessly for asbestos gloves.

He changed his strategy, disengaging from attacks and moving forward at the same time, trying to look threatening without contact. The gnomes fell back, and only occasionally did he need to touch one with the rod. It cooled marginally.

The dwarves rallied behind him as the gnomes retreated into the tunnel. Grady held the rod high; his arm was getting tired.

Antony stationed himself at the tunnel door and called through cupped hands, "Kid! More juice?"

Grady nodded vigorously.

Inside the Gnomengesellschaft, the gnomes formed a misshapen phalanx on the factory floor. They wheeled to face Grady and stepped forward.

He had no choice; he touched them, one at a time, hoping that their will to fight would give out before his hand did. Grady kept his touches as brief as possible, but it was only a matter of time before he had to drop the rod.

But his attack was working. Grady pressed forward, spinning the rod faster than the gnomes could see, hoping he could dazzle them into falling back.

For a moment it seemed it would work. The phalanx fell back, then fell apart; the last defense of the gnomes seemed to be gone.

Klaus turned to two of his comrades and snapped, "Merger!"

The two gnomes stood side-by-side, leaning on each other.

Grady watched as their bodies ran together, melting and merging. The thing that faced him had four arms and two heads, one of which roared as it threw the body of an unconscious gnome aside.

It was more than eight feet high and looked completely invulnerable.

Grady thrust with the rod. The gnome-thing flinched from the current but kept coming. It extended a claw that looked like a human two-handed broadsword. Grady fell back.

Grady shouted "More juice!" and struck again. In the tunnel, Antony signaled; Sonny turned the L-pad up a connection. This time the gnome-thing, muscles still spasming from the jolt, laughed.

The gnome-thing slashed sideways; Grady ducked. The blow slashed a stalactite off as smoothly as a stone saw. The gnome-thing roared and slashed the fallen tip into fragments.

Grady said mildly to Antony, "I'd like even more, please." He stabbed forward.

He barely kept the rod as the gnome-thing slashed at it; he disengaged quickly as he realized that a full stroke of those claws would have sliced through the steel easily. He pulled back and called over his shoulder, "Anything left?"

"One setting," Sonny said, and moved the L-pad.

The gnome-thing grabbed on to the end of the rod and nearly pulled it out of Grady's hand, current or no current. Grady snatched it away and backed up toward the tunnel for the first time. The gnome-thing gibbered like a gorilla, waving its claws in the air. The assembled gnome troops murmured hopefully.

"Do the big switch," Grady said, panting.

Antony said doubtfully, "Are you sure?"

Sonny poked his head into the hall. He was dragging the transformers with him, giving Grady an extra six feet of wire. Sonny was drenched in sweat from the effort. "Holler, and Susan will pull that other switch. You need that?"

"Get ready." And Grady did the toughest thing he had done in his life, thrusting and slashing forward, beating back the monster that could have sliced him in half with one clear swipe. He moved forward into the hall of the gnomes, twisting this way and that, until even Antony couldn't guess where he was going. Grady's hands felt as though they would char and fall off.

He made a final sweep, a deft move that kept his body covered but traced the point across his adversary's broad chest. The gnome-thing bellowed and attempted to grab the rod, which was already dropping. The claw-arms followed the dropping point down nearly to groin level, leaving the chest unguarded.

Grady pulled back, stabbed for its chest, and shouted, "Now!"

Sonny and Antony shouted in unison, "Now!" Susan threw the improvised fork switch at the main power line.

The spark lit the whole of the gnomes' cavern: the troops of both sides, the human furnace, the piles of misshapen and sinister goods in production, the chain and hook swinging from the ceiling. Grady had a brief, vivid view of it all before the thrashing gnome-thing struck him on the rubber apron and sent him flying backward.

Grady had the sense to drop the rod, which had turned bright red. It hissed against the floor, a cloud of steam between the point and the wet limestone.

The rod dimmed. In the Dwarfworks behind them, the lights went out for good. Susan cringed away from the power conduit, which was a ruin of smoke and sparks.

The gnomes looked at him unbelievingly, then at the now useless sword on the floor. Antony's breath caught in his throat. "Oh, kid, no," he said softly, and for a moment he was more concerned with this one human he had resented than he was with all his race.

Grady sat up, shook his head, and scrabbled for his cane and the rod as he struggled to his feet. The rod was still steaming, but was otherwise lifeless. Ahead of him the two-gnome body lay twitching on the floor, a flicker of flame on his chest, then lay still.

Susan, coming to the tunnel door, said in awe, "You may have blown every light in the Catskills."

Grady nodded, rolling his tongue around his mouth. It tasted like metal, and he was afraid to talk. He stood, facing Klaus next to the corpse.

Klaus stared at him, swallowed visibly, and said with a

roar, "I am not afraid of you!" He leaped forward, broadsword in hand.

"You should be." Grady barely brought the now useless rod up in time. Heavy as it felt, it was barely heavy enough to parry the lunge; Grady could hear his coach shouting at him to use grace and not muscle. He fell back, disengaging quickly and spinning up and over the sword.

Klaus used raw strength to force the heavy sword up, trying desperately to strike the rod from Grady's grasp—

The rod was gone, circling a second time smoothly. The sword flicked upward, and Klaus nearly dropped it.

Grady lunged, praying that his leg would hold under him, and struck upward at the sword with a single, swift beat of the rod.

Klaus's sword spun out of his hand, narrowly missing Heinrich. Inside of a second, Grady had the rod circling in front of the gnome's eyes, like the stinger on an angry hornet. "Susan, go back in and switch to the high setting."

The tunnel between caverns reeked of burning insulation and ozone. Susan said uncertainly, "But the last shot—"

"I know," he said, never taking his eyes off Klaus. "But I still want the high setting." He was smiling, and he had adopted a pose he had seen Errol Flynn take in the *Sea Hawk*. Grady remembered thinking a few seconds ago that he had been doing the toughest thing he would ever do in his life.

"I got you," Sonny said, and flipped the L-pad attached to the now useless transformer. "Don't let any of that rod touch your skin or you'll fly straight to Jesus."

"We've met. I'm not worried." But Grady hoped to God that Klaus still was.

The gnome stared at the rod, at the massive, charred gnome body on the floor, and then, bewildered, at the smoke billowing out of the Dwarfworks. "The high setting."

"For you, nothing but the best." Grady smiled crazily; he was counting on the steaming rod looking even more dangerous this way to someone who didn't understand electricity.

Finally Klaus grunted in disgust and threw his sword aside. "I yield."

In the silence Kirsten said, "Do the rest of you yield, too?"

"Of course," Heinrich said easily. "Since it was Klaus's initiative, it is his surrender. I'd rather assumed you knew that when you answered his challenge."

Grady said, "Not really." The metal taste in his mouth was still strong, and he wanted badly to lie down and rest. "But he was the one challenging me."

Heinrich glanced at the charred two-gnome body on the floor. "Not at first. This day has been—costly."

"I'm sorry about that." Grady meant it.

"Kind of you." But Heinrich sounded dry and disapproving. "But I don't mind healthy competition. Do you mind my asking what happens next?"

Grady had been hoping the gnome would know. One of them should have.

Warren Hastings strode in. His immaculate suit and tie contrasted oddly with the smoking ruins he walked through. "My office has been broken into and my files tampered with. I came to check on you, Cavanaugh." He glanced around at the destruction and carnage and said coldly, "Cavanaugh, I'd better not hear that you've interfered with something else."

Grady was gratified when Kirsten put a blade to Warren's heart and forced him to the wall.

Heinrich, watching, said in puzzlement, "Why is he here?" and shook his head quickly, the top and bottom of his

head wobbling like something in a cartoon. "We have more
pressing problems."

Antony, glancing around at the destruction and carnage
while Grady brandished a useless weapon at the surrendered
gnomes, was inclined to agree.

NINETEEN

T HE TWO SIDES glared at each other. Although the gnomes had yielded, they were still shaped for battle.

The dwarves held swords, axes, and hammers. Grady lowered the useless rod to his side but didn't let it go.

Heinrich, front and center in the band of misshapen gnomes, said almost pleasantly, "Time to begin negotiating."

"Not yet." Pieter was kneeling over the body of Bernhard. Katrina was at the other side of the body, sobbing inconsolably. For the first time since Grady had known him, Bernhard didn't look worried.

Pieter kissed each of Bernhard's eyelids tenderly, smoothed Bernhard's rumpled and torn shirt, and stood. "All right. We bargain. One hour?"

Heinrich glanced around at the wounds on his company. "One hour and no more."

Kirsten said sharply, "Katrina." The dwarf child stood, blinking. "Go and hide again." She added firmly but gently,

"And this time, don't come out until one of us tells you to."

She nodded quickly and scampered off, disappearing into the shadows.

"So," Heinrich said and waited.

Pieter also only said, "So."

"What do you have to offer?"

"It's what you must offer us."

"Then we disagree."

"Yes. We do."

No one said anything for a long time. Grady glanced at his watch; there were forty minutes left.

Antony, a bloodstained anvil hammer in his hand, stood at Grady's left. Grady whispered out of the side of his mouth, "What happens if we can't agree?"

"War."

"Who wins the war?"

"Depends."

Grady looked at the assembly—dwarves in war gear, gnomes transformed into things of claws and armor. "Optimism and confidence," he said, so softly that only Antony appeared to have heard him, and threw the rod aside with a clang as he stepped between the dwarves and the gnomes. "There's a better way."

The participants froze. Klaus said coldly, "Don't tell me there's a better way; I've been disemboweling bipeds since before you were born."

He stood his ground. "By 'better' I mean 'more profitable.' First you get all sides to honor all prior agreements."

Heinrich said indifferently, "It's a little late, and there are no prior agreements."

Grady pointed to Klaus. "He promised to disconnect Garner Stanley Irving. Instead he made plans with us to build a loading system."

"His new loading system is not your concern, and he

should not have promised to disconnect a useful sufferer. In fact, the new system looks quite efficient—wait." His hand shot out and touched Grady's shoulder, ever so lightly. "He made plans with *you*?"

With a great effort, Grady didn't flinch and didn't try to remove the hand. "Not with me. With Warren Hastings."

Klaus said with a snarl, "It's a lie."

"Totally false," Warren agreed.

Grady said, "The design prints for the loader are from Plimstubb."

"They could have been a gift," Heinrich said thoughtfully. "After all, is there any item traded in exchange?"

"Warren's been trying to sell Plimstubb technology to some fairly strange"—he faltered for a word—"customers. Your old customers, I think."

"I found those customers," Warren said coldly. "I did it the way you should have found more of your own." He finished with a twisted smile and a gesture at Grady's cane, "Legwork."

The gnomes chuckled admiringly. Warren was someone they could appreciate.

"There's a talking folder in Warren's office," Susan said. "It recites the list of contacts."

"Does it?" Heinrich withdrew his hand from Grady's shoulder, and Grady knew the gnomes were losing. Heinrich turned to Klaus. "Does it really?"

"I have no idea. If the boy has proof on paper, let him offer some."

Warren, who had begun to look nervous, was more reassured. Klaus edged forward, his eyes hungry with hatred and anger. "And if you have no proof, you should know how I feel about libel."

The gnomes watched eagerly. Antony sighed and moved to defend Grady, whose hand flashed down to his side—

—And pulled some folded papers from his pocket. He stepped toward Heinrich, ignoring Klaus. "This is a note from Klaus to Pieter, asking him to sign a shipping manifesto. This is a copy of the shipping manifesto. This is a warehouse receipt for storage of some boxes, the same size and weight. The receipt is initialed by Warren, to show that he received the boxes."

In the silence, Grady could hear Kirsten and Susan moving up to his right side.

Grady pulled out one more sheet of paper—which was blank. "And this," he said with emphasis, "is a draft of a memo of understanding, referring to a sample contract that Klaus gave to Warren on his first visit here." He added, knowing that Klaus would not be fooled, "Would you like to know who is named in it?"

Warren said suddenly, "I agreed to store the boxes for him without examining the contents."

Heinrich swiveled toward him. "If you are lying—"

He folded his arms. "The boxes are still unopened. Send someone to check them."

"And what about the customer names?"

"The war is on, and we've sent orders to a lot of strange places. Some times I'd ask Klaus about a customer I thought we might have in common, but that's all. If you don't believe me, ask Klaus."

After a long hesitation Klaus said, "I did comment on customers when he asked. I also requested that he store the boxes."

Heinrich frowned. "Why?"

"A private project."

"And the controls for the ever-productive Mr. Irving?"

Warren said, "A gift, as you said."

"Which violates an agreement signed by the Dwarfworks," Antony put it quickly. "The penalty for contract violation—"

Warren said hastily, "I withdraw the gift."

Klaus rumbled, "The loader designs were research, never meant to be put in place. I will return them."

"And that's why I was over there," Grady said to Heinrich. "I work part-time for the Dwarfworks, and I thought there had been a contract violation. By your rules that gave me the right to act, as long as I did no damage without cause." He gestured at the damage in the Dwarfworks. "I'm glad I only damaged Plimstubb's own equipment, which we'll be taking back now. Fortunately, as you pointed out, we operated under your rules. No harm done."

Kirsten said softly to Heinrich, "Can you say the same?" Behind her lay the draped body of Bernhard. "You have violated your own rules. Enforce them."

For a long time no one said anything. Heinrich looked from the paperwork to Warren to Klaus.

Finally he gave a long, rasping sigh. "Mr. Hastings. Klaus. You both are terrible liars. I have no proof of that, however."

Warren relaxed slightly.

Heinrich went on, "But because of your actions, we've violated our agreement with the Dwarfworks, and the burden for that must rest with you." He nodded pleasantly toward Klaus. "It is a management failing."

Klaus paled, a sudden whitening and smoothing of skin that made his face look like a fish belly.

Heinrich's arms, already formidable, extended toward Klaus. "How would you suggest we compensate the dwarves and the humans?"

Grady took a quick breath and plunged in. "Let me suggest, and see if it's not satisfactory."

Once again everyone was staring at him. He went on

reasonably and with seeming confidence, "The Gnomen-gesellschaft buys an electric furnace from Plimmstubb to replace Garner Stanley Irving. That compensates us for the endangering of Susan as a Plimstubb employee and for myself—this time as a part-time Plimstubb employee." One of the gnomes chuckled appreciatively; a look from Heinrich silenced him.

"The gnomes also buy a replacement furnace for the Dwarfworks, which compensates them partially, and the gnomes forgive a portion of the dwarves' long-standing debt. After that"—he glanced sideways at Kirsten's grim face—"the Dwarfworks will need to settle on compensation for the death of Bernhard. Money and punishment, I'd guess, but that's not for me to say."

He folded his arms. "Do it my way and nobody more dies, plus, once you have the furnaces in place, everybody makes a profit. Can you think of anything better?"

This time the silence was thoughtful. Gnomes and dwarves stared at each other.

Kirsten frowned. "If we had more evidence, I'd want Klaus destroyed."

Heinrich bowed. "If we had more evidence, dear lady, I'd do it myself. And Mr. Hastings as well, since the old agreement was under our rules. As it is?"

"As it is," she said heavily, "we will extract blood fee from you, plus the furnace." She looked at Pieter for permission; he nodded. She looked coldly at Warren Hastings, who stared indifferently back. "And we negotiate only with Grady Cavanaugh—assuming that you return him to a full-time position in your Sales Department."

Grady's breath caught in his chest. He hadn't thought to ask.

Susan added, "Specializing in Dwarfworks-related contracts and in contracts for the war."

"But—but . . ." Warren made a last feeble attempt. "He has a part-time job at the Dwarfworks. Who could replace him?"

"I will," Sonny LeTour said calmly. Everyone swung to look at him. "If they'll have me. I can't design furnaces, but I can run them and I can repair them and I'll holler for help back to Grady whenever I need it—"

"And I'd help you," Grady said carefully. "And don't get me wrong, Sonny—I know you can do the job, and this is an amazing place to work. But are you sure you want to come here? It can get awfully lonely being the only one of your kind in a place—"

Sonny's booming laugh startled everyone. As Susan and Grady caught the implication, they both looked uncomfortable.

When Sonny stopped laughing he said politely but with amusement, "It's nice of you to care, and I know you mean well. But I've worked at Plimstubb and lived in Rhode Island, and now I want to leave some."

"Ain't no tellin' where a man like me might go," Grady murmured.

"Mississippi John Hurt."

"Right."

Kirsten interrupted, "So everything is settled, when Mr. Hastings accepts the terms."

"Done," Warren said, with a malevolent glare at Grady.

"And nicely done," Heinrich said thoughtfully. "I do believe they have managed"—he leaned on the word slightly—"to punish you." Warren looked away, his jaw quivering with anger.

"Which reminds me"—Heinrich turned toward Klaus and said with a pretense of delicacy, "In our organization there is a substantial penalty for ineffectual management."

Klaus frowned. "I was effectual. You must admit that."

Heinrich said with mock embarrassment, "I mean that you got caught. You broke our rules and failed to prevail over the rest of us."

The other gnomes leaned forward. To Grady their fangs seemed to grow; perhaps they did. Klaus said hastily, "You have no proof."

"In that case," he said reasonably, "I must assume the lesser of two ills—that you were ineffectual outside the plant. Surely you concede that."

Klaus looked around quickly. The gnomes had moved to all sides of him; Kirsten gestured to the dwarves and the humans, who fell back.

The captive gnome said sullenly, "Granted."

"This incident will go into your permanent record as an employee," Heinrich said with relish. "However, it's a minor infraction, and the punishment will be light, all things considered. I might consider a three-day suspension."

Klaus glanced upward unhappily to the chains and weights bolted to the cavern ceiling. He stretched an arm up and up twenty feet, touching the sharpened hook dangling at the end of a chain, and pulled his arm back as though burned.

"There is also retraining designed to make you more sensitive."

A large gnome, brutal-looking even in this company, chortled and ran a thick finger across a brown-stained rasp. Heinrich continued, "It's very effective."

After an uncomfortable silence, Klaus grunted in disgust. "If it's all the same to you, I'll retain my present status and forgo any change in it for a month."

Heinrich raised an eyebrow. It continued lifting until, for effect, he forced it back onto his face with a thumb. "You must be very confident of yourself."

Gesturing irritably at the chains and the rasp, Klaus snapped, "I have no choice."

"All right." Heinrich pronounced loudly, "Klaus will remain as he presently is for a month. If any of you believes you could do a better job than he, take it up with him before the month is out."

He added a chant in some unknown tongue. Grady felt his hair moving back and forth; the ceiling chain sparked and glowed. The glow descended to Klaus's body, enveloping him; he jerked stiffly back and forth.

Grady whispered to Antony, "What's going on?"

Antony whispered back, "He's being frozen in this form, unable to change shape for a month."

Susan muttered, "Doesn't seem like much of a punishment."

Kirsten rested an arm on Susan's elbow and said quietly, "It isn't, if none of the others bothers him. You've seen how gnomes fight; their whole bodies turn into weapons. And Heinrich has as good as told the rest that they can have Klaus's job if they kill him by the end of the month."

The chant and the glow had ceased. Klaus turned his head, slowly and carefully, like a man with a sprain, to watch Kirsten. "You let me overhear you."

"No." She waved a hand at the group surrounding him. "I let them overhear me."

"Clever," Heinrich purred, "though I promise you I would have said the same. Still, I know you wished to punish him, and instead of disagreeing with your judgment, I concur openly." The gnomes shifted in excited anticipation as he turned to Klaus. "The dwarf has suggested that we promote from within. Do you also accept her suggestion?"

Klaus looked as though he had tasted something bitter. "I accept the suggestion from you—"

"Accept it from her. Unless you wish me to consider something else—"

"I accept." Klaus looked wildly around. "And I will go now."

"Not yet." Grady turned to Heinrich. "The last time we made a contract, we had a contest to see whose rules would govern the business."

"Did you?" Heinrich said with interest. "Oh, yes, the furnace contract, I remember. And you humiliated yourself. Do you wish to try again?"

Grady shook his head. "This time I'm the challenger; it's his turn." He intentionally pointed at Klaus without looking at him. "Since you're in charge of him, I ask you—"

Klaus spat, "These are my negotiations, and you will ask me."

Now Grady looked at Klaus. "I wasn't sure you were still capable."

"I still have my job," he said, snarling. "And I accept."

"We settle by my challenge." He heard and ignored Susan's sharp intake of breath. "Something you've done before—"

"I know the rules, cripple. I beat you with them last time."

"And you accept them?"

"Of course I accept them!" He was annoyed, slavering, beside himself. "And I'll beat you, and you will weep, here, for a long time to come."

"Okay. Just as long as you accept the rules." Grady stepped forward, leaning on his cane. He picked up the cane in one hand and took a deep breath, thinking, *You do this every day; it's just a little farther, that's all.*

And with an easy, one-handed toss, he sent the cane soaring to the ceiling chain.

The cane slung over the sharpened hook, swung dangerously, and, to Grady's immense relief, rocked to a stop. Grady grinned back at Klaus. "Take the cane down."

Two seconds of silence were followed by a chorus of the nastiest laughter Grady had ever heard. Klaus stared upward in bafflement and, furious, leaped. He missed the cane by eight feet. He leaped again and again, reminding Grady of the wolf in Prokofiev's *Peter and the Wolf*; the gnomes' laughter grew.

Finally he stopped, panting and exhausted. The laughter gradually died, and the gnomes shifted from side to side expectantly. A few of them, almost surreptitiously, grew more claws at the ends of their arms.

"Well," Heinrich said pleasantly, "you've made a complete fool of yourself."

Klaus grimaced, afraid for the first time. "I assumed a normal course of negotiations—"

"*Nothing* about this has been normal," Heinrich barked. "Nothing. And all of that which can be laid on you has fallen on you. Know that it is not enough. If I can find more evidence, I will destroy you. And I will look very hard for a way to destroy you."

Klaus bowed his head, defeated. Then he turned slowly toward Grady, and the hatred in the gnome's eyes was stronger than any supernatural glow in the cabin. "Know that what he said, I say to you now."

Susan stepped up alongside Kirsten and Antony, ready to defend him. Grady shivered inwardly, but said without a tremor, "Know this: What you have to say to me now, like it or not, is that this contract will be governed by the laws of the state of Rhode Island."

Klaus nodded slowly, as though his head hurt. "I agree to those terms. That is your right. That is your victory." He gestured toward Heinrich. "Finish the contract with him. I have urgent business elsewhere."

The first of the shape-shifted gnomes, with a hand like a huge scalpel, stepped toward Klaus. Without warning, Klaus threw a handful of rock into the gnome's eyes, bit the wrist of the scalpel-hand, and dashed under the arm of the wailing gnome and down a tunnel.

He was followed by all the gnomes but Heinrich. Some were shouting, some screaming, some baying like a pack of hounds. They all sounded terribly happy.

After the noise of the hunt faded, Kirsten broke the silence. "You should also specify that neither side can harm each other covertly or overtly."

Heinrich nodded. "We would call it a hold-harmless clause." He smiled as though it were a joke. "Your contract holds us to remain harmless as long as it is in force."

Pieter coughed, and they all turned to look. "The rest of this now is money, which is what I do." He stepped forward and put a hand on Grady's shoulder. "Or it is the thing I did here before this young man came. Still, I should finish the contract." He laid down the weapon he held and gestured. "The rest of you go clean up, set things right, find the children. Heinrich and I will discuss." He turned, smiling, to Grady. "You come too, boy. You will deal for Plimstubb now, and for your war, too, I think."

"Yes, sir." He waited for Heinrich and Pieter to leave together, then sagged with a loud sigh. "Wow."

"'Wow' is right," Kirsten said. "You were wonderful."

"Wonderful, hell," Antony said, "he was perfect. I'm telling you, kid—"

But he didn't tell him anything. Susan leaped forward and hugged Grady fiercely, nearly knocking him down. After a moment she let go, eyes shining, and walked away without saying a word.

Kirsten looked at Grady's face. "Now I understand," she

said softly. She shook her head quickly. "Better get in the office."

Grady was still staring after Susan. "What?"

Antony was grinning widely. "Go to the office and dicker, kid, before Heinrich and my boss cut you out of this deal entirely."

He did a double take and checked his watch; there were only five minutes left of the bargaining hour. Kirsten was laughing at him now, and so was Antony, but they both looked fond of him. Grady headed for the office as fast as his cane could carry him.

TWENTY

NEGOTIATIONS WERE OVER in five minutes. Grady, dazed at how quickly things had changed, left Pieter's office to find his friends.

Grady's meeting with Kirsten was brief and embarrassing. She had left the others and gone to the shop floor to evaluate the damage. She could easily have outdistanced him, but wasn't trying; encouraged, he caught up with her near the walking hearths. "Hi."

"Hi." She turned away, trying to coax one of the hearths out from under a rock ledge. "Come on, baby . . . it's okay . . . everything's all right." The hearth stepped out timidly and she stroked it, ignoring the soot on her fingers.

Grady knelt beside her and worked on one of the other hearths. "They'll all get better, right?"

"They're only scared. Being scared isn't fatal."

"Good thing, too," Grady said with feeling. "When's Bernhard's funeral?" He glanced involuntarily back at the body.

It was gone.

"We don't hold funerals. We hide our dead from humans, as we hide everything else." She looked at him bitterly.

"I can't blame you." He took a deep breath; now might be the last chance he had. "I'm sorry I hurt you."

Kirsten, watching him, said nothing.

"You must know you're attractive. Beautiful, I mean." He thought carefully; he'd had little experience in complimenting naked women whom he'd rejected. "You looked very nice—"

"Your ears are turning red."

He gave up. "They do that. Honest, you're beautiful. I just wasn't in love with you." He finished awkwardly but honestly, "And I'm sorry as hell that I hurt you, because you're really wonderful. You're smart, brave, kind"—he remembered a good phrase—"and you're prettier than apples."

She was trying to frown still. "I know who said that. I know my Antony."

"Well, he's an observant guy." The last hearth waddled out from under the ledge; Grady patted it and stood back up. He stared at his hands, not sure where to wipe them and trying not to let the hearths brush against him.

Kirsten started to laugh. "Don't get your nice suit dirty."

He looked down. One trouser leg was charred from Klaus's near miss. The opposite side of the jacket hung gaping and ragged where a scimitar had passed through it. He put his sooty fingers through the hole. "Wow."

Kirsten nodded. "That's right. You almost got a war wound."

He grinned. "Antony hurt me worse." His grin faded. "I hurt you worse, too. I wish I hadn't, but I just didn't know—"

"No. You didn't." Kirsten was frowning, but she looked

pensive, not angry. "And you don't have much time to learn."

Grady assumed that this was a snide reference to his short human life span. At this point he couldn't blame her.

But Kirsten made a decision. "See this?" From her vest pocket she pulled a violet pendant. "Treated amethyst, with a gold hanger."

"Treated how?"

She smiled. "That's right; you've done some of it now. Low-temperature-fired in an oven inscribed with runes, bellows-fed with air from young men and women singing. We can't make it anymore; everyone who knows the song is dead now. My mother said my grandmother had learned it when she was young. Grandmother had said it was very old."

Grady nodded, impressed. "Very old" from dwarves' grandparents meant quite a lot.

Kirsten let it dangle from her finger, crystal point hanging downward. "If you point it at people in love, it shines. I should have used it on you." She pressed it into his palm. "Keep it. I think you'll need it."

"Thanks. I'll keep it hidden, mostly." A thought struck him. "Say, who started all this hiding? And the Hunt Day tradition, and everything?"

"Pieter. Well, the people who raised him." Her forehead puckered thoughtfully. "I've never asked. I know it's nearly as old as he is."

"Then the other dwarves might be doing the same thing—"

"There are no other dwarves."

"How do you know, if they're all so good at hiding?"

Kirsten stared at him, her mouth hanging open.

"For all you know, they're all over the world in little groups, still in hiding."

"How would we find them?"

He opened his palm and showed the pendant, carefully not pointing it at either of them. "Make something like this, something traditional that only your own people would recognize. Sell them through a second party. The others will find you. I could help you set it up—"

Kirsten laughed, and Grady was bucked to hear how affectionate the laughter sounded. "You've changed us enough for a while. But I promise I'll think about it."

She jumped up to kiss him as she had back at Christmas. This time he was ready, and he turned to kiss her as she seemed, once again, to hang lightly in the air beside him.

The humans gathered outside. Grady looked at Sonny LeTour and said in surprise, "You're coming back, too?"

Sonny shrugged. "This isn't my truck. I got to drive it back to Plimstubb, get my car and some things."

"Sure. Listen, anything of mine here that you want to borrow, it's okay."

"Thanks." Sonny looked at Warren Hastings, who was standing apart from them near the car. "Maybe you should let Miss Rocci or Mr. Cavanaugh drive the company car, Mr. Hastings." He sounded polite and respectful.

All the same, Warren flinched. "You can't take it away."

"Now that's absolutely true. I can't. You sure you want to drive it, though?"

He rallied. "Positive." Furious as he was, he held the front passenger door open for Susan.

She said "Thank you," opened the back door, and got in. Grady hopped in front before Warren could close the door.

Sonny, looking concerned, leaned on the passenger window. "What about your own car?"

"You can drive me back for it. I'll ride with Susan."

Warren scowled. "She didn't offer to ride with you."

"One of us should ride with Warren," Susan pointed out.

"Both of us," Grady echoed.

Sonny grinned. "Makes good sense." He continued speaking to Grady, but his eyes were on Warren. "I'll follow you back to Providence," Sonny said softly but firmly. "You need anything, you just wave out the back window. I'll be watching." He walked back to the truck.

Warren viciously ground the ignition. "Of all the damned insolence!"

"You'd think we didn't trust you not to steal the car," Susan agreed.

Warren opened his mouth, shut it, stared at her, and floored the gas, spinning gravel into the headlights of the truck behind him.

Warren said nothing else on the ride back. Susan fell asleep. Grady sat bolt upright, the new contract in an envelope on his lap, one hand on the seal as though he were afraid it might jump away into Warren's hands. Grady hadn't slept in twenty-four hours, but he was damned if he'd take his eyes off Warren.

They arrived at Plimstubb just after four. Warren all but leaped from the car, turned back, and looked disdainfully at Grady as he stepped out to open Susan's door. "Dress better tomorrow, Cavanaugh. It's a normal workday." He stressed "normal" slightly.

Grady nodded. "I'm looking forward to that as much as you are."

His meaning didn't escape Warren, who scowled. "That's the way it'll be, then." Halfway to his car, he spun around. "For tomorrow. But in the future, don't either of you ever make a mistake."

He was gone before Susan had a chance to mutter, "And

we'll be watching you." They walked in, Susan running ahead.

The shop had already gone, and almost everyone had gone home for the day. Grady typed the order acknowledgment sheets, then typed a summary of the work agreement between "Nieuw Amsterdam Metalworks"—he grinned at that—"and Plimstubb Incorporated." He mailed the carbon of the order acknowledgment back to Antony, and left the work agreement and summary on the treasurer's desk for Chester's review tomorrow. Grady walked through the reception area past Talia Baghrati, who smiled at him sleepily and didn't seem to notice that his suit was in tatters.

Engineering was deserted except for Susan and for Tom Garneaux, who was at his desk crouched over something that looked like, and probably was, a restaurant menu.

Susan was at her desk, scribbling frantically and tossing aside one sheet of paper as she started another. He picked up the top sheet without disturbing her. At first it only looked like a series of clumsy rectangles with loops at either end. He looked at the sheet below, a clumsy square with an off-center rectangle coming out of a smaller off-center square, and both drawings snapped into focus. "New furnace design?"

"A mini-CR. Like the one we built for the Dwarfworks, but it'll be a tabletop furnace for small industry. We used to sell to Speidel and Bulova. . . ." She finished the last sheet, a set of BTU estimates, power specs, and frantically scrawled drive calculations, and threw it aside. "And now I'll file it."

"File it?"

"I just didn't want to forget it. There's still a war on." She grabbed a manila folder and stuffed all the papers in it, dropped the folder in her desk drawer, and slammed it shut. "And now I can go home."

Grady checked his watch, startled. It was after five. "Smoke 'em if you got 'em." He lit up her cigarette, then his own. "Busy day."

"I'll say." She continued putting things away, order out of chaos in seconds. "And you didn't even see the second purchase order from Stode yet." She waved a two-page letter at him.

"What?" He grabbed it from her without thinking. "Sorry."

"Don't be; I took it off your desk."

"Don't do that. What if you'd lost it?" But he was elated, not upset; Plimstubb was back in the war. Grady turned to the second page and read the purchase order. "Any major changes?"

"Nothing much. Tighten down the bolts before shipping, that's all; something must have busted loose between here and—well, between here and wherever they put it finally."

"That's it?" The job had been a prototype, for the government as well as for Plimstubb.

"I guess they knew what they wanted the first time. For a customer, that's unusual."

Grady retorted with a grin, "For the government, that's a miracle." He turned back to the letter. "It's all done on the same typewriter."

"Amazing, Holmes. We do that all the time."

"We're not the government." He read the letter:

Dear Mr. Cavanaugh:

Attached to this letter is a purchase order with specifications for a second furnace like the first. Note the differences, which are minimal.

Deliver this furnace within four months of receipt of this letter. Inform Mr. Renfrew as soon as there is a firm shipping date and I will make arrangements.

I am sure that everyone tells you this about his contract, but this one is quite important. Disregard every other in-plant order to complete mine. If you do not have the authority to do this, notify me.

Grady remembered his letter to Stode about the last job, and the telegram from the War Department. He resolved to push the job through in record time, whether Warren would help him or not.

Please provide Renfrew with regular progress reports. I will visit your plant at least once to inspect the equipment.

Sincerely,
Drake Stode, Contracting Officer

Typewritten at the bottom of the letter was a single sentence: "Your efforts on the first job were satisfactory."

Below that was the contract number repeated, and the word "MANHATTAN."

Grady looked at the last line with relief. Tomorrow he could put through a telegram and confirm both the contract number and the project name.

He looked up and Susan was watching him, smiling. She pointed to the last line of the letter. "So we're legit now. Are you happy?"

"Sure. We're back in the war."

"About damn time." She looked behind herself automatically, at the framed picture of her father grinning beside *Sassy Suzie*. She spun back around and resumed sorting papers.

Grady took a deep breath. "Susan?" She grunted, and he went on, "I love you."

Susan's head snapped up and she stared at him, wide-eyed.

"I don't know when it started, or how. I know that the whole time we were fighting the gnomes, I was more scared for you than I was for me."

"But you didn't try to stop me from fighting."

"You can fight for yourself. You just shouldn't have to fight *by* yourself." He hesitated and finished, "And I think you need to fight just now."

"I do." Her fingers moved across the papers aimlessly, and her glance flickered from side to side, trying to avoid Grady's eyes. "I'm sorry. I don't love you yet."

"'Yet?'" She nodded hesitantly, and Grady said, "Then it could happen." She nodded again. "The uncertainty principle?"

"Kind of." Susan, for the first time he'd ever heard from her, giggled nervously; it sounded like music. "I feel like Schrödinger's cat. It makes me jumpy."

"Well, stay jumpy, 'cause I'm gonna open your heart and check on you every once in a while. Didn't you say that an observer can change the event? I can wait and see." Grady thought of Kirsten. "Antony's waited seventy years."

Now she grinned at him. "Don't be that patient." She grabbed her purse and left while he wondered what exactly she meant. He looked after her, thinking that Betty Grable never looked that good in her whole life.

As the door outside swung closed behind Susan, he took out Kirsten's pendant hastily and pointed it toward the last open crack of the door. He thought he saw the faintest purple flicker in it, but it could have been from the sun outside.

Grady pointed the pendant at his own heart and closed his hand quickly, shaking his head and blinking back tears.

As the afterimage faded, someone behind him said, "I should have borrowed a welder's mask."

He turned to see Tom Garneaux, leaning on the neighboring empty desk, watching him. Tom was unembarrassed. "She didn't say yes and she didn't say no. . . ."

"And she didn't tell me to go away." Grady added, mainly to himself, "And I'm not going to."

Tom put an arm around his shoulder. "I told you someday you'd be a great salesman, kid. Start selling. All it takes—"

"I know," Grady said. "Optimism and confidence."

And as he walked back to his own desk, his cane flashing back and forth with the pace he was setting, he realized that now he had both.